Also by Ellis Sharp

Novels

The Dump
Unbelievable Things
Walthamstow Central
Intolerable Tongues
To Wetumpka
Lamees Najim
The Orwell Girl

Short Fiction

The Aleppo Button
Lenin's Trousers
(with Mac Daly) *Engels on Video*
To Wanstonia
Driving My Baby Back Home
Aria Fritta
Quin Again and other stories

Non-Fiction

Sharply Critical

DEAD IRAQIS

SELECTED SHORT STORIES OF ELLIS SHARP

Edited with an Introduction by Macdonald Daly

New Ventures
Seattle
2009

CONTENTS

Introduction

It was the summer of 1991. I had just completed a doctorate
on D. H. Lawrence and Marxist criticism and while my
travels in the byways of Soviet anti-aesthetics seemed
somehow not to have blunted my enthusiasm for the
revolutionary doctrine, I was in thorough emotional revolt
against all narratives modernist and realist. I was thus
somewhat demob-happy and uniquely susceptible to the
seductions of a fiction that combined radical Marxism with
postmodernist aesthetics, had such a paradoxical thing
existed, which I was fairly confident it did not. That was
before I encountered a thin yellow book whose spine jutted
out further than the others on the fiction shelf of a
Glaswegian second-hand bookshop. This jutting-out was a
sure sign of a small press publication done in A5 dimensions,
an ungainly size for a book of fiction, but one at least (like
their cheap duotone covers) that allowed these semi-
professional rarities easily to be detected.

This specimen was called *The Aleppo Button*, was
published by Malice Aforethought Press, and contained
thirteen stories by one Ellis Sharp, in 110 pages.[1] Despite my
usual experience of disappointment with small press
publications (whose professional shortcomings — almost
invariably poorly edited, often amateurishly typeset, usually
containing multitudes of howling linguistic and typographical errors — tend to be matched by writing to which,
at best, one can be only aesthetically indifferent), this one
instantly got me where it mattered: it opened with a tall tale,
which I read in its entirety on the spot, standing there in the
bookshop, in which Joseph Stalin did not die on 5 March
1953, but faked his decease, swam to England, and by 1957
"was a familiar figure on the promenade at Bognor". Indeed,
so popular did Iosif Vissarionovich Dzhugashvili prove with

---

[1] Ellis Sharp, *The Aleppo Button* (London: Malice Aforethought
Press, 1991).

the West Bognor Conservative Association, and so prized was his "personal knowledge of the horrors of Seychellism", that he became the local MP ("the previous MP having disappeared off the pier one foggy evening"), although he did feel obliged to enlarge the list of aliases drawn upon in his Russian period (Koba, Ivanovich, Gayoz Nisharadze, K. Cato, Chizhikov, Vassil, Stalin itself) by changing his name to Julian Iron.

The story (reproduced on pp. 54-61 below) was a hoot — written with great tonal poise, linguistically complex, and confidently taking the imbecile thematic liberties of all great satire — but its idiosyncratic killer touch, for me, was that it seemed to be as well versed as I was in the recondite details of Stalin's insane life and showed a brilliant awareness of the comic potential in much Soviet history, something that any humourful student of the subject soon comes to appreciate. As I have intimated, the author could not have hoped for a more ideal reader: indeed, having bought the book and devoured it later that day at one sitting, I had a peculiar sense, which can surely only happen once or twice in a lifetime, that the book had been written especially for me.

Or perhaps I should say *half the book*. I have in this astringently sifted selection retained four of *The Aleppo Button's* thirteen stories, although I could quite easily, on grounds of quality, have included two or three more, such as "Dead Paraguayans" (a forerunner to the later story which gives the present selection its title) and the manic monologic lecture of "The Aleppo Button" itself. The stories which I disfavour — and for me this will emerge as a general rule in relation to Sharp's fiction, as well as being a principle of selection to which I have largely adhered in putting together this volume — tend to be the shorter squibs in which, although all his typical verbal pyrotechnics are there to be enjoyed, narrative is thin or non-existent, and one has the feeling that his imagination has not been allowed the full obsessive rein it seems to display when in the throes of spinning a yarn. Sharp is generally at his best, despite the seeming aesthetic monstrosity of his consistent and explicit coupling of fiction with dogmatic politics, when he allows himself to do something as traditional as to unfold a story at leisure. He would perhaps eschew my preference for his more "readerly" stories — and I hope that readers of this volume will go back to the original volumes and test that preference for themselves — but, for me, Sharp at his most memorable is not the author of two-page streams of consciousness or brief propagandistic philippics, many instances of which can be found in the five volumes of tales I have here cannibalised. *The Aleppo Button* has several examples of both "writerly" and "readerly" texts, and likewise announces most of the literary techniques and thematic preoccupations Sharp was to pursue throughout the coming decade. The typical Sharp story of the 1990s is usually some kind of blistering critique of mainstream (Conservative, Labour or Liberal) politics, or of fascist or Stalinist barbarism, or a frankly partisan promotion (laced with a seemingly alien wild humour) of either classic Marxist ideology or Leninist-Trotskyite *praxis*. But critique and promotion alike are conducted by means of grotesque Swiftian narration and the deployment of a welter of literary devices as far removed from realism (socialist or otherwise) as could be imagined, all served up in a prose style that glories in the slipperiness, precision and poeticism of the English language.

It is no coincidence to me that the longest story in *The Aleppo Button*, "Dobson's Zone" — which fantastically relates the narrator's intermittent connections with his friend Dobson, who exhibits a ragbag of incommensurable obsessions which he somehow tries to synthesise (namely the Loch Ness monster, the paramilitary career of Che Guevara, and crop circles) — is also my favourite, not least because one passage in it (pp. 16-17 below) explicitly foregrounds what more narrowly conceived political fiction tends to ignore, the necessary magic of words on which the entire enterprise of creative writing, even political fiction, depends:

On our last evening together, drinking whisky, and then more whisky, and then yet more, I have never forgotten how we came (whose idea was it — his or mine? I no longer remember) to open up his Thesaurus at random, selecting quite arbitrarily a single, humble word, and chuckling as our fingers promiscuously roamed back and forth across the pages, up and down, between and below, touching every inch and scrap, every glorious, throbbing vowel and consonant and crackling, pulsating fiery connotation, until at last, drenched in sweat, half-drunk, utterly fatigued by our endeavours, we tumbled into a wordless, innocent and dreamless sleep. Ah, what it is to bathe in language, to cavort there, unashamed, ecstatic, up to the very ceiling of one's mind in beauty and resonance, drifting and gliding amid the harmonic choruses, the plangent chords, hearing the sweet hum of pluralism, soaring across the dazzling ranges of multiplicity, then falling, falling, dizzy, satiated, drained and drowsy, soothed by excess of meaning! (Chess, by contrast, has always struck me as rather a bore.)

When Dobson sets out to "manufacture a mystery" and thus achieve immortality, he does so with a programmatic awareness of *form* rather akin to this love of the workings of language: "for a hoax to be successful and to endure after the perpetrator's death various essential ingredients were required". The "zone" he goes on to describe turns out to be his invention, the inexplicable crop circle. However, it might equally well be a trope for Sharp's fictional *oeuvre*: "It must, in short, provide a Z.C.F.M. — a ZONE for the CON-VERGENCE of FECUND MULTIPLICITY" (p. 30).

Much of this "fecund multiplicity" is to be found in the flights of linguistic fancy into which any Sharp story is at any point liable to soar, sublimely, often without warning. "The Bloating of Nellcock", for example, is a savage satire on the career of Neil Kinnock, then leader of the British Labour Party, who is depicted as a wind-filled Gargantua, a man masquerading as an immense balloon, met in so gas-engorged a condition that the story serves as the fuse which precipitates his imminent momentous explosion. Nellcock's bloatedness is a metaphor for Kinnock's linguistic bombast, which, fittingly enough, is described with a corresponding and carefully crafted fustian:

> At the age of six his future as a deipnosophist seemed certain. Guzzling filched apples, he loved to prattle. Hogging the pie, he invariably piped up and rattled on. Devouring fried eggs and beans, he became voluble, prolix. At puberty he used to perorate under the sheets. One day he became lost in a welter of subordinate clauses and did not return until dusk, panting and red-faced. At sixteen he loved nothing better than to rise to speak, ejaculating in full view of passers-by. How he spouted, shuddering! How he loved to stand on stumps, tuning his rant, oblivious to the pain of the amputees. (p. 44)

We are informed that "'Bloater' is found between 'blitzkrieg', which has one meaning, and 'blob', which has four or five" (pp. 48-9). The narrator, who is writing a book on Nellcock which he has yet to finish, enables himself to do so by following in action the logic of these lexical collocations: he carries out a fatal blitzkrieg on this particular blob by puncturing Nellcock with a harpoon, thus going considerably further in his treatment of his subject than either of Nellcock's previous biographers, who bear in their names ("Dunlop" and "Michelin") their own complicity with his repellent inflatedness. Thus does Sharp make literary our common fantasies of political assassination, a theme to which he returns: a later story, "Nixon's Dog", has the narrator blasting the corrupt American President to smithereens in 1962, long before he can assume office — and the year of the release of *The Manchurian Candidate*, the brainwashed-zombie-assassin movie which Nixon ironically urges the protagonist to see.[2]

The present collection opens with one of the later stories in

---

[2] Ellis Sharp, *Lenin's Trousers* (London: Malice Aforethought Press, 1992), pp. 72-87.

The Aleppo Button, "To the Wormshow". It deserves its priority on account of its first sentence alone, which paradoxically makes it sound like the opening of an epic *Bildungsroman*: "My earliest memory?" But this is just one of the ways in which it succinctly exhibits the typical constituents of a Sharp story. For example, upon paradox there is heaped impossibility: the narrator's earliest memory seems to be of the sensations experienced as an ejaculated spermatozoon — a successful one, as it necessarily turns out. Then there is the literary allusiveness which is penumbrally at work in nearly all of Sharp's writing: the inspiration for this concise five-page monologue is Laurence Sterne's bloated *The Life and Opinions of Tristram Shandy* (1759-67), a text also narrated in the first person which likewise begins (and pretty much remains) temporally concerned with events before the hero's birth, and is discoursing metaphorically about the spermatozoon (or "homunculus") by its second page. Similarly, the narrator of "To the Wormshow" refuses to emerge from the womb until a protracted four-and-three-quarter years after his conception in August 1945 or, in other words, for the entire duration of the post-war British Labour government.[3] But this thematic

---

[3] As ever, there is probably some Marxist sub-text at work, which readers are increasingly unlikely to recognise. In this case, it is Leon Trotsky's immensely funny Darwinian characterisation of the Fabians: "English pigeon-fanciers, by a method of artificial selection, have succeeded in producing a variety by a progressive shortening of the beak. They have even gone so far as to attain a form in which the beak of the new stock is so short that the poor creature is incapable of breaking through the shell of the egg in which it is born. [...] Having been induced to enter the path of analogy with the organic world, which is such a hobby with [Ramsay] MacDonald, we may say that the political skill of the English bourgeoisie consists in shortening the revolutionary beak of the proletariat and thus preventing it from breaking through the shell of the capitalist state." See Leon Trotsky, "Where is Britain Going?" (1925), *Leon Trotsky on Britain* (New York: Monad Press, 1973), pp. 74-5. Sharp actually uses a quotation from this text as the epigraph to the Kinnock satire (p. 43).

politicisation of a literary device is itself taken over, at the end of the story, by a resumption of an intensified voice of satire, in this case the revelation of the young infant's first "actual" memory, served up in prose evoking nausea at and loathing for the world; these are the cadences and semantics of Swift once more. The style returns again and again in Sharp: reading for the first time the later "Dead Iraqis" or "The Henry James Seminar at My Lai" (pp. 109-116 and pp. 229-238 below respectively), one is probably feeling something similar to the appalled amazement of the original readers of Swift's "A Modest Proposal". It is this element of balance or, conversely, dynamism — between the often mistrusted rhetoric of a morally outraged Marxist politics and the more ambivalent and playful deployment of literary language and devices — that seems to me to distinguish Sharp's finer work.

In "Shooting Americans, with Emily", a story in Sharp's second collection, the narrator records the following anachronistic conversation with Karl Marx: "I remarked that whereas a writer's best book is always the first, a singer's best album is always the second. Marx immediately disproved this with references to Malcolm Lowry and Joni Mitchell" (p. 72 below). And it could be disproved by *Lenin's Trousers* itself: Sharp's second is also his best collection. Only because I wished to represent a broad range of Sharp's work across the 1990s have I reluctantly excluded from the present selection "Martina" (a story based entirely on a single typographical error), "Nixon's Dog" (even with its somewhat pat ending), and "Da-Da Vogt" (a furious obsessional monologue put into the mouth of Marx). *Lenin's Trousers* presents (though not exclusively) a number of "alternative histories", or engineered collisions between different ontological worlds, to employ some of the vocabulary then current in discussions of much "postmodernist" fiction.[4] So, in the winter of 1846, Emily Brontë bribed a girl from Haworth to impersonate her while she read a gun

---

[4] See, for example, Brian McHale, *Postmodernist Fiction* (London: Methuen, 1987).

catalogue in a nearby cave. In the summer of the following year, "having made the final revisions to her manuscript", she went to Liverpool, where she "disguised herself as a cabin boy and obtained employment on one of the vessels being used to transport British troops across the Atlantic". She spent the rest of her life engaged in a guerrilla war, sniping at U.S. imperialists in Central America, eventually dying in her lover's arms after a particularly heroic shoot-out. And here is the serious while absurdly comic feature of Sharp's recycling of past cultural icons, lore and booty: unlike a great deal of postmodernist fiction, his intentions are consistently political in nature. What reader of *Wuthering Heights* has speculated, between chapters 9 and 10, that Heathcliff's mysterious disappearing act may be explained in terms of a revolutionary sojourn such as that enjoyed by his creator in "Shooting Americans, with Emily"? But with knowledge of the latter, who could revisit Brontë's novel without considering the possibility?[5]

The technique and its effects recall the superbly violent yoking-together of heterogeneous legends we find, among others, in the earlier collocation of Che Guevara and the Loch Ness monster. Appropriation of revolutionary politics for the purposes of absurd humour is ubiquitous in Sharp, but, rather than the knowing, nudging, trivialising icon-oclasm which is a tic of much postmodernist narrative, the result seems to be exorcism of the earnestness, the deadly

---

[5] Indeed, Heathcliff is missing for the climactic years of the American Revolutionary War and returns in September 1783, the year of its conclusion: "'Have you been for a soldier?'" is one of Nelly Dean's first questions to him. He deliberately neglects to answer it. See Emily Brontë, *Wuthering Heights* (Harmondsworth: Penguin, 1965), p. 133. It has not escaped the present writer's attention that this novel was first published under the pseudonym "Ellis Bell", indicating, perhaps, a further dimension of allusion on our author's part, just as his surname may involve a Sharp nod towards a Swift predecessor.

lack of play, which has ironically come to characterise much subversive politics. These stories don't seek to convert one to revolutionary causes, in the manner of propagandistic prose or socialist realist fiction, but rather draw attention to the failures of imagination, the excesses of solemnity, and the linguistic deadness which has hitherto accompanied almost all previous representations of such politics.[6] Thus "Lenin's Trousers" (pp. 77-108 below) describes at great length how "there is not one Lenin but three Lenins that people write about" — "Saint Lenin", "Lenin the Monster" and "Lenin the Revolutionary Socialist" — only to point out that "whichever of these three Lenins you happen to prefer, it is a fact that none of them showed any interest whatsoever in trousers". But by playing with the possibility of this interest a story (incidentally rooted in truth) gets told of the most unusual kind — and of course it also comically demonstrates, though not without a deep residue of seriousness, the important "materiality" of trousers compared to the negligible "idealism" of the prevalent characterisations of Lenin. *Cherchez l'étoffe*, one might say.

In "The Hay Wain" (pp. 117-47) we encounter the most concentrated and profound of Sharp's transformative appropriations, as well as the most serious in tone. This opens at noon in Manchester on 16 August 1819 with Jack Frake, a once-renowned Shakespearean actor, "hit one day in the street by a cart, bad leg injury, career in decline". Frake gets caught up in the Peterloo Massacre, kicks a soldier, and is spotted doing so by the yeomanry, which means he must run for his life and, wanted for high treason, "set his actor's talents to work" in disguising himself and going underground. "A month later he's in Norwich, three days later at Ipswich", moving from bolthole to bolthole. Close to collapse,

[6] An earlier exception would be Martin Rowson's *Scenes From the Lives of the Great Socialists* (London: Grapheme, 1983), although, as a collection of cartoon drawings, this does little other than restore comedy to Marxism. The medium is not sophisticated enough to prompt any profounder response.

he finds "a white house, deep in mist", and manages to conceal himself for a night in an empty box room at the top of it. "He wakes five hours later to the sound of housemartins chattering outside the window and a dull bronze glow over everything from the noonday sun. Goes to the window. Sees, over on the far bank, a man in his early forties, sat on a folding chair, reading a book. No, not reading a book. Holding a sketch pad and pen. Making two or three strokes, then pausing to look across the river. Looking right at Jack Frake."

It is "almost noon". The house, it turns out, is Willy Lott's Suffolk home; the artist, John Constable. One commentator complains of the famous picture, "exhibited as *Landscape Noon* [it] is now so well known that ... it is ... never looked at, and its 'novel look' is taken for granted".[7] If Sharp's dramatically contrived collocation of English labour history's most notorious slaughter with English bourgeois art's most popular idyll makes us look anew at the latter, it also makes it impossible to see in it what Cormack's ideological purblindness makes out:

Here in the centre is, again, the focal point of the design, which consists of two horizontally opposed diagonals. One leads the eye over to the right to the haymaking, where the white shirts of the haymakers provide rhythmic accents on the horizon. [...] The white smock of the drover nearer at hand is balanced by the light tone of the horizon at mid-left, so that he does not leap out of the picture, but helps the movement into space in the opposite direction. The figures are simply blocked in, and their simple poses also help the timelessness of the scene. Constable, then, to [*sic*] a boundless feeling for nature and twenty years' experience of close observation has created a work which is as pure as he can make it, a memory of his Suffolk home. *The Haywain* owes much of its lasting success to the feeling

[7] Malcolm Cormack, *Constable* (Oxford: Phaidon, 1986), p. 132.

that in this "Idyllium", this image of "rustic life", "the essential passions of the heart speak a plainer and more emphatic language", as Wordsworth justified his own work in a different context, but we should not forget that, equally, even more than in his Hampstead Heath scenes, it also looks back to the high art of the seventeenth century and, in particular, to Rubens [...].[8]

The painting is appropriated here solely in the formal terms which allow it to be abstracted from any determining social context: consequently it is made to signify what is "balanced", "timeless", "boundless", "essential". But if to these qualities the painting "owes much of its lasting success", they are also precisely what cause it to be "never looked at", "taken for granted". For these attributes are so indefinite, so abstract, that they cannot *be* seen.

Nor (if one studies Constable's picture) can Jack Frake, or anything that could be mistaken for him. But no one who reads Sharp's text will look again at *The Haywain* without feeling that he is *there* — without the suspicion, indeed, that he has been *deliberately erased*. One does not *see* anything new *in* the picture: rather, one is made to *confront* it in an entirely different manner. For Frake the scene is anything but "timeless". He is wondering whether to "make a break for it" or "wait for dusk", temporal calculations based on a visual activity ("Frake glances wildly back out of the window") which is the reverse of contemplative. He suddenly hears dogs:

The cattle are gone, the ferryman's gone. The man with his sketchpad has folded up his little stool and is walking away along the riverbank path. He's bent forward, holding up his trousers, the sketchpad half-slipping from beneath his arm as he tries to keep the turn-ups out of the mud. Undisturbed by the sound which rivets Frake's gaze to the yard,

---

[8] Cormack, p. 133.

the ferocious barking, brutes on leashes, brutes with studded collars, straining, slavering excitedly, towing behind them as they burst from around the back of the house half-a-dozen grim, burly constables. As they move towards the doorway below the artist on the far bank disappears from view. Now all Frake can see is the ferryman, back where he was before, punting across a bowed labourer who holds a scythe. (p. 124)

Life-enhancing bucolicism, seen from one bank, becomes death when stared at from the other, for what else can the scythe-bearing labourer, accompanied by his Charon, represent? That Frake's end is meted out to the accompaniment of "the grunts and curses of the heavy constables" amid a knell of "hollow reverberating chimes of a nearby church ringing noon" intensifies the passage's marvellous, terrible resonance. One starts to detect traces of blood in Constable's *Landscape, Noon*.

"The Hay Wain" seems to me one of the most powerful ideological deconstructions to be found in contemporary fiction. One can detect in it a persistent aim of historical materialism, the exposure of the truth, in the words of Walter Benjamin, that "there is no document of civilization which is not at the same time a document of barbarism".[9] *The Haywain* is a "myth" ripe for dismantling, as Roland Barthes takes to pieces bourgeois culture and the western consumerism it serves in *Mythologies*. In "Wine and Milk" Barthes points out that French national euphoria over wine is so habitual that it seems "natural", and the economic basis of its production ("deeply involved in French capitalism, whether it is that of the private distillers or that of the big settlers in Algeria who impose on the Muslims, on the very land of which they have been dispossessed, a crop of which they have no need, while they lack even bread") deliberately and outrageously ignored. Thus to link seemingly innocent everyday pleasures with the barbarities of imperial conquest

[9] Walter Benjamin, *Illuminations* (Glasgow: Fontana, 1973), p. 258.

is, of course, to shatter them: "wine cannot be an unalloyedly blissful substance, except if we wrongfully forget that it is also the product of an expropriation".[10] The "unalloyed blissfulness" which *The Haywain* represents in English culture proves equally brittle when it is invaded by working-class history.

But Sharp knows that there are proletarian myths as well as bourgeois ones. Peterloo (eleven dead) was a mere scrap by comparison with massacres on a modern scale: the vast magnitude of its *impact* on English radicalism routinely gets transferred to the event itself. But in a contemporary Britain in which the labour movement has been in retreat for three decades, such episodes from working-class history have become mythological in a much more damaging sense than this: that is, the nostalgic and romantic celebration of them has come largely to replace radical political action in the present. But there is no such living in the past for Sharp. *The Haywain* does not, he knows, belong simply to the nineteenth century. It is permanently in process, an image in ideological circulation along with those produced today:

> [...] a painting like *Top Gun*, all gloss, myth, fantasy. The judicious placement of flagpole or cart, runway or field, sunset or cloud, labourers or carrier in the Indian Ocean, until the two blur, and now that speck's a MIG fighter, beyond the house lurks a blonde in leather, all sunlight and honey, in which there's no place for agricultural depression, recession, squalor, poverty, the all-night wage slave, the women in the electronics factories of Korea, the tortured of Palestine, the black children with puffy bellies and skull faces and big teardrop eyes, the masses blotted out by the sugar of individual destiny [...] (p. 139)

This is from the second section of "The Hay Wain" (Frake's story occupies only eight of the story's thirty-one pages), the

---

[10] Roland Barthes, *Mythologies* (London: Paladin, 1972), p. 61.

action of which takes place on 31 March 1990, the date of "The Battle of Trafalgar Square" in which 200,000 Poll Tax protesters staged one of the most insurgent demonstrations witnessed in Britain within living memory.[11] Sharp's roller-coaster description of this event is punctuated by "flash-backs" to historical disorders and protests (the Peasants' revolt, the Blanketeers, Peterloo itself), thumbnail philippics aimed at Establishment icons whose statues are met *en route* by the marchers (Richard the Lion Heart, Cromwell, "Sir Winston Twister Dardanelles-Disaster dulled-by-brandy dago-hating [...] Churchill", Earl Haig), and attacks on the media which have replaced Constable in providing reactionary representations of what is to be seen.

At the centre of this physical and textual vortex is Robinson, chased by the police into the National Gallery, who finds himself arrested, in more ways than one, before a familiar painting:

> [...] much bigger than he'd imagined after seeing it all those times on biscuit tins and trays and calendars and hanging on the lounge wall of remote dusty relatives along with the Reader's Digest Condensed Novels and the 22" TV and the hideous china country maids and cherry-cheeked grinning shepherds [...] (p. 137)

He steps towards the canvas to read the gallery description of the painting ("represents a link between the idealism of

---

[11] "The Hay Wain" is clearly indebted to *Poll Tax Riot: 10 Hours That Shook Trafalgar Square* (London: Acab Press, 1990), a virulently anarchistic pamphlet account of this demonstration, and itself a prose specimen worthy of study. There is a brilliantly surreal passage in "The Hay Wain" in which even the inanimate world becomes enlivened by the riot. A wooden chair suddenly appears "suspended in the air, about ten feet from the ground ... tilted, as if about to launch itself into battle. The chair bides its time, enjoying every moment" (p. 132). A photograph on p. 30 of the pamphlet depicts a chair, presumably hurled at the police by a protester, seeming to do just this.

Claude and Poussin, and the future empirical vision of the Impressionists'") and the police assault him, flinging him against the canvas, his blood "spurting in a bright unreal slash across *The Hay Wain* by John Constable R.A." He spends the following moments in a new vision of art — "seeing for the first time a ghost in the murky water" — that mingles with a foreseeing of political corruption (the Coroner's evidence concluding that he perhaps vandalises the painting out of his anarchistic impulses). Thus, as well as putting "real" blood on the picture, does Sharp defuse in advance reactionary readings or critical "inquests" of his text. In the precise image, also, of a violent collision between present and past, and between conventionally different realms of discourse (art and politics in particular), we have the master trope of his fictional method.

While reading *Lenin's Trousers* I was revising an undergraduate course I taught in modern and contemporary English Literature, and I decided to make it the "up-to-the-minute" prescribed text which I usually nominated on the eve of the course.[12] I thought I had better check with the publishers that sufficient copies were available for a large class, and so I wrote to them. My enquiry must have been passed on, because a few days later I got a call from a man with what I considered a rather refined voice, who said, "Hello, I'm Ellis Sharp." If he was surprised that his obscure book had been so instantly acknowledged and prescribed on a Literature course, he didn't sound it. I forget the brittle details of the call (just as I forget most of the detail of the three or four occasions on which we subsequently met) but the contact developed into a full-blown and very memorable correspondence — old style, printed on paper and sent through the post — his side of which occupies a large box file in my possession, another box file being occupied with publications,

---

[12] For the record, I seem to recall that Sharp's book left my students, with one or two enthusiastic exceptions, almost entirely baffled. Nearly all of them avoided writing about it. This was what I expected.

drafts and other literary (and much non-literary) material he forwarded. The correspondence extended over three or four years, on average at least once, sometimes twice a week, until Sharp — on paper a scintillating correspondent — became converted to email and our communications thereafter became briefer and more transactional, for reasons no more likely than the change of medium. It has been a curious friendship, conducted almost entirely through writing.

Its most unexpected consequence, for me, was that I ended up being co-author of Sharp's next book. I believe he had sent me drafts of stories about Nietzsche and Trotsky. Coincidentally, I had a story about Nietzsche tucked away in a drawer and I had recently published a satire involving Trotsky (the latter somewhat inspired, in fact, by the liberation of constraints I witnessed in Sharp's own stories). I sent him both and, as it ended up, we decided each to write two more stories involving hirsute mega-intellectuals, eventually choosing Engels and Freud. The resultant eight stories — each of us being sole author of four — was published as *Engels on Video*, so entitled because the year of publication, 1995, was also the centenary of Engels' death.[13] All of the Sharp stories in the volume seem among his best to me — he was, I think, at the height of his confidence and consistency at this time — and I have represented the book here with his two longest contributions to it, the stories involving Nietzsche and Engels. We felt especially grateful to *The Journal of Nietzsche Studies* for lacerating the book in review: it was about the only periodical to bother.

Many of Sharp's letters to me detailed his ongoing and intensifying political activity, which seemed to oscillate between the *Socialist Worker* newspaper and direct action of an anarchist kind, such as that involved in the anti-roads protests. He was, for example, regularly involved in occupations of land made in the course of a campaign against the M11 link road development near his home in East

---

[13] Mac Daly and Ellis Sharp, *Engels on Video: A Joint Production* (London: Zoilus Press, 1995).

London (the occupied territory became known as "Wanstonia"). I once turned up at his house in my modest Triumph Acclaim and his greeting was a quite curt (although objectively correct) instruction to me to move my car off the kerb. His letters crackled with anti-automobile static. *To Wanstonia*, the collection he published in 1996,[14] occasionally fictionalises these political activities, particularly in the title story, which is an experimental attempt to document (though Sharply) the M11 protest, and in the often hilarious "Scenes from the 39 Day Strike at Thrabb's". The collection on the whole, however, seems to me to lack the élan of Sharp at his best. For example, the stories sometimes repeat old formulae without improvement: the Jane Austen tale, "Spiders", is in some ways a repetition of the earlier, better Emily Brontë story, just as "One Morning Twenty-Nine Carp Were Caught", which identity-switches Lenin and Chekhov, is excelled by "Tinctures, Stains, Relics", a story in *The Aleppo Button* which much more bizarrely swaps the lives of Karl Marx and Charles Fort (of *Fortean Times* fame). "Paper Heart (a story in three albums)" is included here largely to let the "stream-of-consciousness" side of Sharp's fiction be heard; the albums concerned (onto which the possibly autobiographical protagonist's varying fortunes are implicitly projected) are Bob Dylan's relatively obscure *Planet Waves* (1974), the double platinum *Desire* (1976), and the rather poorly received *Hard Rain* (1976). Still, the impressionistic story does not entirely engage me in the way that many other Sharp tales do. But the collection continued to show Sharp capable of virtuoso performances, such as "A Rag", a story which poignantly revisits the scene of Antonioni's cult film *Blow-Up* (1966), and "The Henry James Seminar at My Lai", a text it is not wise to embark upon if one's sensibilities tend towards the comfortable.

In retrospect, I can now see that Sharp was always going off in a different direction from short fiction hereinafter. His

---

[14] Ellis Sharp, *To Wanstonia* (London: Zoilus Press, 1996).

stream-of-consciousness propensities (in contrast with his postmodernist leanings) had always seemed to me incapable of integration with his political obsessions in a satisfactory fictional form until I read *The Dump*, a slab of 50,000 paragraphless words, his first novel, written *à la* Samuel Beckett, a searing, grotesque parody of the Britain of the 1990s.[15] Stream-of-consciousness needs that larger canvas, it would seem. Arguably his finest single work so far, *The Dump* nonetheless competes with *Unbelievable Things*, an exquisite 500-page-plus epic published a mere year later, which blends the English "country house" genre with such incommensurables as science-fiction and, inevitably, the Bolshevik Revolution.[16] In 2007 appeared *Walthamstow Central*, an hilarious novel-length pastiche of cyberpunk plotting and prose.[17]

In the periods between publication of these three novels Sharp produced two further volumes of short fiction.[18] But the swerve of direction is now clear. The texts in both books are very short, sometimes squibbish: narrative mostly yields to lyricism or contrived humour. I have ignored the collection of 2004 entirely, as it yields nothing to compete with the merit of any single text herein, and is rather marred by a nasty tale which glories in the wanton murder of a TV personality (my objection is aesthetic rather than ethical). But among *Driving My Baby Back Home*'s stories of some substance there remain four which, for me, still demonstrate his powers in the short form, though on the wane — or perhaps, more correctly, on the wing. These four texts close this selection. The last words of the final story seem to me, in particular, in their epitaphic summing-up of a major element of Sharp's literary methods, an appropriate point at which to draw the curtain on his achievement in the short story.

[15] Ellis Sharp, *The Dump* (London: Zoilus Press, 1998).
[16] Ellis Sharp, *Unbelievable Things* (London: Zoilus Press, 2000).
[17] Ellis Sharp, *Walthamstow Central* (London: Zoilus Press, 2007).
[18] Ellis Sharp, *Driving My Baby Back Home* (London: Zoilus Press, 1999) and *Aria Fritta* (London: Zoilus Press, 2004).

Introduction

It is very curious to write about an author whose talent is
such that one considers he should have a large audience
when, in fact, the number of those who appreciate his work
is infinitesimally small. Of course Sharp's scalding up-front
politics and the literary demands he makes on his readers
will inevitably alienate him from a mass readership. But it
has been my hope in preparing the present volume that it
will prove to be a lasting introduction to a writer whose
modicum of acknowledgment is long overdue. There is
certainly no contemporary British writer quite like him.

Postscript (2015)

When I edited *Dead Iraqis*, I assumed that Sharp had finished with the short story. It was where he had first made
his unusual mark in the nineties, but by the new century his
energy seemed entirely channelled into novels, short and
long, six of which he has now published. Indeed, I found
nothing in his last book of short stories, *Aria Fritta* (2004),
worthy of inclusion in the selection, and assumed there had
been a definitive end, at that point, to any attempt he might
make to encapsulate his fictional concerns in an abbreviated
compass. Eleven years later, his sixth volume of short stories
proved me wrong.

The Quin of "Quin Again", the novella which occupies the
second half of *Quin Again and other stories*,[19] is the English
experimental novelist Ann Quin, a writer almost as obscure
and unknown as Sharp himself. But at first glance this 78-
page seeming tombstone to Quin appears to put the collection into a state of obvious imbalance, casting a long and
perhaps too substantial shadow over the fourteen much
shorter stories which constitute the first half of the book.
After *To Wanstonia* (1996), Sharp's stories, in gatherings like
Driving My Baby Back Home (1999), became much more

[19] Ellis Sharp, *Quin Again and other stories* (London: Jetstone,
2015).

concise, in the mould of what has sometimes been termed "flash fiction", less prone to extending his particular obsessions into hilarious narratives with surreal, highly bizarre plots. The more lyrical, stream-of-consciousness dimension of his work came to the fore, in which the same riches of language were evident, but the deadly Swiftian irony of his finer earlier stories, not to say to the political satire which had become his trademark, seemed incapable of realisation in a diminished extent of four or five pages per story, often less.

Quin Again on first inspection threatens to be that kind of book until the reader realises that, if the name "Quin" is what unifies its second half, the first is also unified by a single character, who appears in nearly all of the shorter stories, and whose name is Douglas Elijah McMaster. We do not learn this "real" name, however, until "Ridiculous", the third last story of the book. We first meet him under the moniker "Doodles", an appellation which suggests his insignificance, his almost cartoon-like contours, his being a mere creation of the pen, his fictionality. In the first story, ironically called "Finished", we learn of Doodles and Hazel and their erstwhile love, including some gritty details of their pastoral frolics, only to have all the apparent facts of the story denied within two pages. The authorial voice — which we read as that of an older Doodles — commandeers the narrative and explains that the details are false, imaginatively conjured out of his immediate writerly surroundings. He then seems to hear the voice of Hazel herself, travelling down the years, pointing out that he has mixed her up with a different ex-girlfriend (words which he then denies having heard as he peremptorily finishes both with the story and with her, a mere four pages in). Thus is a Gerontion-like narrative consciousness concisely established, in which past memories are elegiacally recalled, but in which memory and imagination cannot firmly be distinguished, and therefore in which the presentation of the realist "facts" of the stories is always subject to internal attack from the narrator's ability to make things up, deny things, or rewrite them differently.

This narrator dominates most of the stories in the collection, and he is the teller of the Quin story too, a presence which binds both halves of the book together. In the second story, "The Writer", a febrile Doodles, high on Valium, goes on a walk which takes him around various points of London. This story too is broken-backed. It could end on its sixth page, but the authorial voice again intrudes with a series of stern correctives, refuting with forensic precision many salient features of the events just described (including the Valium-taking, which might otherwise realistically have been used to explain the discrepancies). He remarks bathetically, in conclusion, "But the route mapped out in this story is entirely accurate." This narrator casts doubt on almost everything, and verisimilitude in these texts is consequently like a small island regularly pounded by the hurricanes and crashing waves of an unpredictable imagination. ("I haven't had any verisimilitude for over two pages," one character complains.)

The turn and endless return to language of experimental fiction can often feel claustrophobic compared to "classic" or realist writing. Some experimental writers really do seem to write as if there is nothing but language and puritanically purge their work of many available affective and narrative elements. The result often reads like the arid production of a skilled machine, as the constant refusal to permit the reader suspension of disbelief gives the text the property of wishing to deny the reader certain time-honoured and dominant aesthetic pleasures. I have always considered Sharp's strength as a writer of fiction to derive from his unerring ability to deploy experimental techniques (in some cases inventing them) while never forgetting that fiction is not primarily read as a manual in post-structuralist linguistics. He used to ensure this, often, by the quite prosaic means of actually telling a story, though never very straightforwardly. Every new narrative was also laced with wit and humour. There were clear political and moral values underpinning (and sometimes overwhelming) his writing too, and these gave the stories their snapping satirical bite.

Quin Again (not sampled in the present reprinted collection for copyright reasons) is the work of an older man: Sharp was in his mid-sixties when it was published. The politics and the humour are never far away, but they recede a little before the unifyingly mordant tone of someone recalling fragments of a life mostly gone, putting half-remembered past joys into a collage with dreams and fantasies and the sense of diminution experienced in the present. As the narrator tells us in one of the stories, the past tense is not only desirable, it is inevitable. (With typical contradictoriness, several of the stories are actually written in the present tense.) There is an undeniably Proustian undertow of sadness and unfulfilled desire, but the writing keeps in check, with its expected vibrancy and verve, any propensities the reader may have for trite emotional indulgence. Sharp's writing is tremendously urbane and erudite in style, and it never attempts to elicit sentiment. In effect, the mordant tone reaches for your bowels rather than your heart strings.

The shorter stories are, however, genuinely overshadowed by "Quin Again", which further distinguishes itself from them by being punctuated, W. G. Sebald-like, with mostly desolating photographs of what appears to be an East Anglian coastal town in winter.[20] (The real Ann Quin drowned herself in the sea off Brighton in 1973.) This long mosaic-like narrative appears to be written (at times at least) by someone claiming to be an old lover of Quin, shocked into renewed consideration of her by news of her death. But the story, which it would be nearly impossible to

---

[20] This visual allusion to Sebald's *The Rings of Saturn* appears to be corrective of its excesses, not imitative of its style: in a novella published in the same year, Sharp has his narrator witheringly condemn Sebald's text as an "arid, bloodless, evasive encyclopaedia of posturing indulgent narcissism" (see Ellis Sharp, *To Wetumpka* [York: Zoilus Press, 2015], p. 42).

summarise, is in no sense really about Quin, nor is it homage. It is at once profoundly serious and somewhat haunting, yet also howlingly funny and screamingly parodic. It contains, for example, a brilliant spoof of John Buchan's *The Thirty-Nine Steps*, as well as a paragraph in which the reader must guess the words that have been deliberately omitted.

While *Quin Again* is technically a collection of short stories, its title story, also its longest by some measure, convinces me anew that Sharp's centre of gravity is now definitively the novella or short novel. No short story of Sharp's is ever likely to lack value, but since the publication of *The Dump* (1998) his investment of his creative gifts has been most rewarding in longer forms. "Quin Again", at a guess, is necessarily gathered with shorter pieces because it could not satisfactorily form a volume on its own. But it makes it clear that Ellis Sharp is less and less likely to paint miniatures.

FROM *THE ALEPPO BUTTON* (1991)

TO THE WORMSHOW

My earliest memory? Shooting through space at immense speed, smacking into sponge and jelly, crawling a short distance in the darkness perhaps, miraculously unhurt. Barely time to get my breath back before suffering the gross, shapeless, slippery embrace of a creature from some far planet with (so I imagine) a different climate, a different gravitational pull... Days, perhaps weeks passed. I was a prisoner. I remember (I think I remember) trying to escape. In parts of Cornwall, among the vast, rainswept granite droppings of long-vanished giants, small openings are sometimes found where rocks have tumbled across each other. It is commonly believed that anyone afflicted by rheumatism or lumbago will be cured if such an opening is entered, and the low, narrow passageway traversed, and the sufferer emerges from the grey, hope-filled fragment of light at the far end. Perhaps I am of Cornish ancestry, or perhaps simply born of a long line of lumbago sufferers — and without question cursed by piles, boils, dry flaking skin, freckles and an hereditary speech impediment — for I remember (I am almost sure I remember) trying to squeeze my way out between the dark, damp, curving walls of my prison.

Later, when I realised there was no escaping simply by my own unaided efforts, I adopted a squatting position. With my fists up against my face, boxer-style, ready to ward off the blows which I feared would rain down upon me when least expected, I thought of St Jerome in his cool lonely cave. I endeavoured to imitate his admirable posture of apparent detached philosophical meditation. Perhaps to avoid showing their faces, my jailors had resorted to sending me my food by means of a tube resembling a piece of old hose pipe. What they passed along it was unimaginative and monotonous — a sort of soupy slop, quite devoid of texture, flavour or primary colours.

Since my release some parts of the ordeal, thankfully, have been blotted from my mind. The lack of fibre in my diet, I suspect, was deliberate, resulting in bodily wastes which were never more than a pale, watery liquid and for which, in retrospect (though my gorge rises at the very thought of it), there was only one medium of disposal.

The small windowless unlit room in which I was kept prisoner seemed to be in close proximity to a mill or factory. There was a persistent, tumultuous THUMP!-THUMP!-THUMP! which went on unceasingly, and which at times was the romantic churn of an old foaming water wheel in some fast deep rural stream bordered by weeping willows, among the branches of which brightly plumaged finches chattered and played, but which more often than not was the dull mechanical thudding of machinery beside a conveyor belt along which armoured car chassis after armoured car chassis slowly moved, attended by a swarm of workers, all wearing goggles.

After some weeks my hearing seemed to sharpen. The THUMP!-THUMP!-THUMP! went on all day and all night — not that I, plunged in utter darkness, was capable of distinguishing them apart — but in time I began to detect other sounds, beyond that rhythmic din. The presence of defective plumbing systems became apparent, making odd rushing noises, squeaks and gurgles, and strange reverberating rattles redolent of a lavatory being flushed on the floor above, or a bath next door clearing its throat, resulting in blockages, trapped pockets of air, palsied shudderings climaxing in sudden liberating explosions, familiar enough I dare say to those luckless enough to occupy low rent multi-occupant properties in dubious neighbourhoods, but which at the time caused me, in my innocence and ignorance, not a little distress.

In prison memoirs you will always find energetic and vigorous personages who, denied their pocket watches and wholly deprived of light, swiftly devise an accurate method of recording the passing of the days and who, though plunged in abyssal gloom, surrounded by mildew and with only a spider for company, are able, when asked the time, confidently to assert that it is a quarter to four in the afternoon, and that the day is the second Tuesday in September. Such prisoners, unbroken by fate, their brains buzzing with chess teasers, old remembered crossword puzzles of astonishing difficulty, and fresh thoughts about metaphysics, language and ideology, invariably learn two foreign languages while in confinement, besides walking six miles a day in a space of two square metres, reconstructing through memory *The Adventures of Don Quixote,* managing two hundred press-ups each day to keep fit and occasionally performing anarchic handstands in order to escape the dangerous enchantments of total symmetry. I was not like that. Much of the time I lay curled up, in a sort of grey half-sleep, bored and apathetic and putting on weight.

It must have been after about six months (although it might have been after only a couple of hours) that I first heard voices. Voices! At first they seemed far away, muffled, indecipherable. In time they grew more distinctive and I was able to tell that they were the voices of a man and a woman. Before long I was able to identify scraps of language. At first the words were dulled and blurred ("MIST-AIR-HAT-LIE" the woman kept saying, incomprehensibly) but soon the words became sharper, crisper, almost audible. I had no idea whether or not these people were my jailors or simply happened to live next door, and at the risk of incurring punishment I began to kick frantically against the wall, hoping to attract attention. Almost at once the woman's voice said, "He's kicking! He wants to be out of there!" So — the woman was part of the conspiracy. As I fell back into the darkness in despair I heard the man's loud laugh. In the days that followed, only too aware of the futility of my actions, I kicked at the wall out of sheer bad temper and spite.

In time I became aware of a third voice. It was a rather brisk, bland, paternalistic voice and it belonged to Dr Lopp. My jailors seemed to be worried about my condition. I was not surprised, I was beginning to worry myself. I had put on so much weight that I could barely move. My head and limbs were pressed tightly against the prison walls. Sometimes I wondered how I managed to breathe in such a cramped, confined space. There were moments of sheer blind panic as I wondered how I could possibly take much more. At such moments Dr Lopp's voice always seemed to intrude, with a banal "Nothing to worry about" or a "Perfectly natural in your condition". Whose condition? What about my condition? I had plenty to worry about. There I was, buried alive like someone in an Edgar Allan Poe story. There was no door in my cell. They would have to smash through a wall to get me out. I might die! I would be lucky to escape with severe bruising and lacerations to face and scalp!

Escape to what? I wondered afterwards. The wormshow? Theatrical, cruel and implausible events organised upon the curving surface of a large globe hurtling through space, vulnerable to collisions, explosions, innumerable disasters both natural and man-made, a world squeezed beneath capitalism and state capitalism, crawling with hungry worms beneath every foundation stone and bed of roses and green well-tended lawn. *El gusano amaestrado con possibilidades infinitas!*

After 46 weeks even Dr Lopp became a little anxious. After a year he decided the matter was best hushed up and dealt with in a private nursing home. I remember being transported here and there, poked and prodded, cruelly jolted, woken up without warning, and being generally treated without any consideration whatsoever. Once or twice I was even taken, bundled up in my sleeping bag, blindfolded, into a cinema where I was obliged to listen to the soundtrack of *Madness of the Heart* and *The Astonished Heart* and *The Small Back Room*. Probably, possibly, surely not, and yet perhaps as a result of this shocking experience it finally happened. Earth tremors occurred, initially mild, then severe. A massive force took hold of me, crushing me, squeezing me, forcing me towards a distant watery light. Huge spades of wood were jammed against the sides of my head and turned slowly, causing me excruciating pain. With a final massive explosion of blood and slime I was brought out into a bare, unattractive room smelling of raw meat and disinfectant, where a masked giant bore down upon me with a pair of scissors and a determined look in its eyes.

And that is the story of how I was conceived at sixteen minutes past eight on a sunny August morning in 1945 and remained in my mother's womb until my birth at one minute past midnight on April 1st 1950. When I look back over that strange, dark phase of my life, I can only assume that my mother's body, intoxicated by what it had learned, through osmosis, from her mind (she was a great fan of Trotsky and Victor Serge) was spontaneously attempting, out of kindly charity and in defiance of all biological orthodoxy, to delay for as long as possible my entry into that golden age of Labour government when, under that great leader MIST-AIR-HAT-LIE, food and clothing were rationed and workers had to get by on a weekly ration of thirteen ounces of meat, one-and-a-half ounces of cheese, six ounces of butter and margarine, one ounce of cooking fat, eight ounces of sugar, two pints of milk, and a solitary egg, when striking dockers, gas workers, miners and lorry drivers were denounced, spied upon and prosecuted, when, on eighteen different occasions, the government sent troops across picket lines to take over strikers' jobs, when, for the first time in British history, compulsory military service in peacetime was introduced, when conscripts were sent off to fight and die in Korea, when the goodwill of South Africa was actively sought and cultivated in exchange for gold and uranium, and when, in total secrecy, an atomic weapons programme was introduced.

I will shortly be fifty years old. I am almost completely bald and live in Croydon. I am an accountant. I have neither wife nor children. I wear glasses with anti-glare coated lenses, for safe vision with no irritating reflections. I adore watching old black and white films starring Kathleen Byron. I enjoy listening to Wagner and reading the works of Darwin. I vote Labour, always with the same deep misgivings. My life has been entirely lacking in excitement or incident apart from the time I attached a PAVEMENTS ARE FOR PED-ESTRIANS sticker to the windscreen of a scarlet Ford Sierra illegally parked on the footway of Walker's Way, Penge, and my seven years as a Maoist guerrilla in Peru.

My earliest memory? My earliest memory is of lying sprawled upon my parents' lawn, tangled in the straps of my reins, wailing with fear and disgust at the slow approach of an earthworm, its dimensions hideously bloated by infantile perspective, extreme emotion and, later, by the awesome optical illusions created amid the muddy, backward surge of passing time.

Dobson's Zone

"Matters of war are more subject than most to continual change."
Miguel de Cervantes Saavedra, *The Adventures of Don Quixote*

One measures a circle, beginning anywhere.

Charles Fort, *Lo!*

1

Dressed in combat gear, merging with the landscape, high up on the hillside, crouching, tense, expectant, waiting...

Who now remembers Che Guevara?

There was a time when it seemed as if every college student in the Western hemisphere had the same large scarlet poster taped to the wall above the bed. Che's young, handsome face, framed by black curls, the famous black beret with the red star badge... The Doors and the Stones and the Incredible String Band poured from the speakers, a stick of incense trailed a thin blue sweet sickly trickle of smoke across the room, there were late nights and extraordinary mornings, endless coffees, and endless talk of Marx and Mao and Marcuse, revolution, poetry, giant newts, plesiosaurs, the death of the novel, and music, music, music. And all the while comrade Che was with us, paying no attention to the distracting activities taking place on the bed or on the floor, looking out across the room through a pale screen of fumes, seeing some distance beyond the window the plump mauve-complexioned Dean of Students (who was soon to be extinguished at a stroke, aged fifty-three, by an out-of-the-blue hammer-blow coronary), crossing the empty walkway in the rain, his *Daily Telegraph* tucked under his arm, muttering to himself, a worried, anxious look upon his face...

Giant newts? Plesiosaurs? Yes, plesiosaurs. And giant newts. In the 1960s everything seemed possible. Even the likelihood of a living herd of plesiosaurs (or possibly a lonely giant newt) paddling to and fro in a rather narrow lake beside a main road in one of the most densely populated nations in the world...

On June 12th 1967, high up in the hills of Bolivia, Che and his group of guerrillas, knowing nothing of plesiosaurs or giant newts, set out on a long march to the Grande river. It was a grey, overcast day, and by late afternoon the weather had worsened. A strong south wind brought a night of cold and rain. The next day, June 13th, the going was hard and the group marched on for only an hour, to the next watering place. They had just enough food for five days.

At Loch Ness the morning of June 13th 1967 dawned bright and clear, and the loch was as flat and calm as a mirror. The group leader at the headquarters of the Loch Ness Phenomenon Investigation Bureau looked out of his caravan window and saw that conditions were perfect. Whether or not plesiosaurs prefer warm weather and are drawn to the surface with the salmon, or whether they are simply easier to see in those conditions, was a conundrum unendingly and enthusiastically debated at the local bar at the end of a long, tiring monster watch. The group leader was committed to the second theory, although, as all investigators ought to, he retained a half-open mind and was perfectly willing to be persuaded of the other man's point of view, provided that the facts were there.

The team was roused, and the watchers, binoculars always at the ready, set off in their green Bedford vans to their surveillance posts at selected lay-byes along the north shore of the loch. There the powerful 35mm motion-film cameras would be taken out and set up on tripods on top of the vans, and the watcher or watchers would unfold aluminium garden chairs, sit down, tune their transistor radios to the Light Programme, and, dressed in combat gear, merging with the landscape, tense, expectant, waiting, begin the long day's gaze...

At that time of the year volunteers were scarce (numbers would rise substantially in July and August) and each observation point had only a single watcher. It was a risky procedure, for if a plesiosaur erupted out of the dark waters while the observer was off the platform brewing tea valuable seconds would be lost in hurrying back to the camera, getting the lens in focus and on target and pressing the correct button. It would be no use the observer swearing that the object had been unmistakeably a huge, living creature, at least forty-eight feet long, with two dark brown humps, the suggestion of powerful flippers and a bearing and demeanour unquestionably identical to that of the supposedly extinct marine dinosaur portrayed in the Natural History Museum postcard which was pinned to the wall in the crew's mess — not if all that the witness could back up his astonishing assertions with was some rather grey, scratchy film of what looked like nothing more than a windrow or at best a boat's wake. No. What was required was stark, unambiguous motion film of a gigantic unknown animal, proving beyond all doubt that the so-called "Loch Ness monster" was not hatched from human folly or the requirements of a tourist area suffering from economic recession and the closing-down of the local railway and steamer routes but something very wet and very real. "The right man in the right place at the right time" — that was the slogan that ran through each observer's mind when the sheep woke the crew, baa-ing stupidly or urinating loudly against the caravan walls in the doubt-nurturing emptiness of the night.

At 11.40am G.M.T., at the very same moment that troops of the Bolivian army were searching for Che Guevara, the observer stationed at the camera point opposite the tiny village of Dores saw an unidentified object cutting across the surface of Loch Ness, leaving behind it a vivid wake. He began filming. Almost at once a second object appeared in the viewfinder, on a parallel course. It was the tourist boat, *Scot II*. Instantly the first object appeared to accelerate and crash-dive.

When Dobson first arrived at Loch Ness the following week he found the atmosphere at Bureau H.Q. still electric with excitement. Word was the beast was in the can! That would make the sceptics choke on their laughter!

Having made a careful study of the subject prior to travelling north, Dobson was an upholder of Gould's by then unpopular giant newt theory. Even at the age of nineteen Dobson was a fanatical book collector, and he had snapped up the original June 1934 edition of Lieutenant Commander Gould's now classic *The Loch Ness Monster and Others* for two shillings and ten pence in a long gone second hand bookshop in South Street, Chichester. Like most other people in those days Dobson had heard of the famous monster, without ever thinking very much about it. Gould's book proved to be a shattering experience, for it demonstrated almost beyond any shadow of doubt that Loch Ness contained at least one gigantic unknown animal. Witnesses had seen as many as eight humps on the creature, and it seemed to be anything from forty to sixty feet long.

The sentence which, more than anything, sent a shiver along Dobson's spine, was this one: "A vastly enlarged, long-necked, marine form of the newt is the hypothesis which, however improbable it may appear, I should personally be inclined to favour, and I am glad to note that it has recently been endorsed by Mr. Malcolm Burr, D.Sc., in *The Nineteenth Century*." Even the sceptic is likely to be stopped in his or her tracks by a statement like that. Smiles, smirks and other facial antagonisms may well find themselves ebbing involuntarily, helpless before the powerful recognition that the statement was not only not made lightly but emanated from a Lieutenant Commander in H.M. Royal Navy (Retd.), a man who had knocked about in some pretty odd corners in his time, a man who was nobody's fool, and who was, moreover, backed up by a Doctor of Science. And while Dobson had never come across *The Nineteenth Century*, it sounded like a reputable, balanced publication, in an altogether different league to, say, *Punch* or that new magazine called *Private Eye,* which you couldn't get in any of the newsagents but only from the man with the eyepatch and the rather grubby raincoat who stood all day in the shadows of the railway bridge by Portsmouth Central, his interesting little collection of foreign magazines and fringe publications spread out on the pavement before him.

2

Even in those days Dobson was a striking figure. Aged nineteen, he looked nothing like Che Guevara, except perhaps for his unusual height, which he perversely exaggerated by wearing elasticated boots with massive Cuban heels. His hair was silvery-grey, he favoured yellow corduroy waistcoats and out-of-fashion collars held in place by a gold pin, and he stuttered. Dobson also had the unusual habit, injurious to his frail grasp on good health, of carrying an enormous rucksack of books around with him wherever he went — even if it was just a few yards down the road to post a letter. Dobson did not like to talk about this, but it seems that ever since reading about the mysterious and devastating explosion, equal to a thirty megaton bomb, which occurred as a result of an unknown projectile from space hitting the Yenisei forest in a remote region of Siberia at 7.16am local time on 30 June 1908, he had lived in mortal terror of being caught out by a similar event and of having nothing to read. At the age of twelve Dobson apparently constructed a home-made computer considerably in advance of its time solely for the purpose of working out the statistical probability of his being within a one hundred metre range of a good bookshop or library in the event of the abrupt extinction by powerful explosion of that intricate accumulation of wires, tubes, drains, sound stages, prisons, armaments factories, dockyards, museums, germ warfare establishments, arterial highways, exhaust pipe repair workshops, galleries of American expressionist art and sundry other artefacts popularly called Western Civilisation. The odds were not good. Hence the khaki rucksack.

Although I was not able to see more than a fraction of the

books in his sack that bright morning in late June 1967, I did manage to spot his yellow-jacketed Gould, a copy of the Corgi paperback edition of *Lolita* bearing an encomium from the DAILY EXPRESS ("writing of tremendous vitality and variety of mood and texture. Everything is here, cruelty, learning, robust humour, pathos, romanticism, true affection"), a couple of books — *Maquis* and *Horned Pigeon* — about the 1939-45 war, the *Selected Poems* of T. S. Eliot, the first Penguin paperback edition of *Under the Volcano,* a Heinemann Educational edition of *Gulliver's Travels* carrying the heartwarming information, "A number of passages which might be considered offensive have been omitted from this edition", the first December 1965 edition of the Signet Classic text of William Shakespeare's *The Comedy of Errors,* with extracts from Shakespearean criticism, including Hazlitt's observation that "This comedy is taken very much from the *Menaechmi* of Plautus, and is not an improvement on it. Shakespear (*sic*) appears to have bestowed no great pains on it...", what, if I was not very much mistaken, was the Norwegian translation of *Jude the Obscure,* the Pelican edition of I. A. Richmond's *Roman Britain,* an abridged edition of Frazer's *The Golden Bough,* a volume of the love poems of Ovid, translated into English, a large, battered one-volume Oxford English Dictionary, a Webster's, a Nuttall's Standard Dictionary of the English Language, a brand new hardback Roget's Thesaurus, the 7/6 Fontana paperback of *Doctor Zhivago,* with a full colour photograph of Julie Christie on the back cover, a novel which, according to *Time* magazine, showed that not even Communism could destroy a people's hopes and humanity, and lastly the four-shillings-and-sixpenny Penguin anthology *The New Poetry,* with Jackson Pollock's "Convergence" spread across the front cover, spine and back, reproduced by permission of the Albright-Knox Art Gallery, Buffalo, New York. The froth on the surface of Dobson's vast pool made my own holiday reading — a *Selected Poems of Thomas Hardy* and a copy of *Titus Groan* — seem faintly risible.

Dobson's Zone

For six mornings Dobson rose at dawn and I drove him to one of the camera points along the loch. After his first day at the loch he abandoned the idea of a solitary giant newt and was converted to plesiosaurs. He watched with extreme concentration and enthusiasm, in a state of tense expectation, his bulging sack of books at his feet and his forefinger never far from the ON button of the Newman Sinclair. Birds which neither Dobson nor I knew the names of crossed the sky, or crouched on twigs, defecating and making implausible noises.

We became friends, united perhaps not only by our love of books, our indifference to foliage, strange grasses, butterflies and animals, but also by our silences. I have never much enjoyed talking, believing it to be, like television, a dangerously slick, fallacious method of communication (apart from the not insubstantial medical dangers inherent in excessive lip fatigue and abuse of the jaw muscles). Talking is for politicians and those who deal in second hand cars, life insurance and double glazing. Lovers get by with passionate glances, caresses and the transmission via maids and loyal valets of billets-doux, babies find screaming a perfectly adequate method of ordering a meal or a drink, drunks manage to survive with the aid of a mumble, a vomit and the occasional hearty belch, and those of us not ashamed to call ourselves intellectuals live out our lives amid the pleasures of solitude, assisted only by the printed page and, at most, pencil, typewriter or ballpoint pen, and the occasional exchange of a card or teasing cryptogram.

If Dobson had lived longer I feel sure he would have become as keenly interested as yours truly in British Sign Language. As it was he got by with nods and winks and, when absolutely unavoidable, the occasional stuttered word. I well remember how one morning a line in Hardy's poem "The Convergence of the Twain: Lines on the loss of the *Titanic*" struck me as peculiarly apposite to our interest in sub-surface matters, and I quickly scribbled down on a piece of paper, "The sea-worm crawls — grotesque, slimed, dumb, indifferent", and then handed it to Dobson. He glanced briefly at it then indicated that he wished to borrow my pencil. I passed it over and watched with muddily beating heart as Dobson annotated my message. He wrote fast, very fast. I gazed, dazzled, as at the centre of a silent universe the sharp point of graphite looped and zig-zagged across the white papery void in a blur of speed which in retrospect strikes me as very reminiscent of a twenty-four pin dot-matrix printer set in the Draft mode. Then he passed the scrap of paper back to me.

Greedily I devoured the riches he had laid before me: "Sinking of the T trivial compared to Tunguska. But give me sea-worms any day to people. Strange how both disasters begin with a T. Convergence an interesting word. Bears various meanings apart from collision course, including confluence, assembly, focalization, coming to a point, tangential and vanishing point. The opposite of divergence — contradiction, going apart, divarication, parting of the ways, crossroads, ramification."

On our last evening together, drinking whisky, and then more whisky, and then yet more, I have never forgotten how we came (whose idea was it — his or mine? I no longer remember) to open up his Thesaurus at random, selecting quite arbitrarily a single, humble word, and chuckling as our fingers promiscuously roamed back and forth across the pages, up and down, between and below, touching every inch and scrap, every glorious, throbbing vowel and consonant and crackling, pulsating fiery connotation, until at last, drenched in sweat, half-drunk, utterly fatigued by our endeavours, we tumbled into a wordless, innocent and dreamless sleep. Ah, what it is to bathe in language, to cavort there, unashamed, ecstatic, up to the very ceiling of one's mind in beauty and resonance, drifting and gliding amid the harmonic choruses, the plangent chords, hearing the sweet hum of pluralism, soaring across the dazzling ranges of multiplicity, then falling, falling, dizzy, satiated, drained and drowsy, soothed by excess of meaning! (Chess, by contrast, has always struck me as rather a bore.)

Our last evening... and then divergence, divarication, the parting of the ways. Next day, instead of rising at dawn to watch the loch, we departed with our headaches and our luggage to Inverness railway station. In my mind I can still see Dobson, sweating with effort as he hauled his bulging sack along platform 3, and groaning mysteriously as he boarded the Lowestoft train. He had failed to catch a glimpse of the monster, yet his faith (despite that groan) seemed undimmed and in its prime.

3

Some days later I received an envelope postmarked Great Yarmouth. It contained a short letter from Dobson, dated July 6th. This, of course, was the very day that Che and his men left Barchelon and headed for Pena Colorada. While I sat in the shade of a weeping willow, sipping lime and lager and watching the sun slip away behind my parents' privet hedge, Che was getting closer to the Alto de Palermo. I went indoors and watched television. At ten I went upstairs, brushed my teeth, and went to bed. I re-read Dobson's letter and then put out the light. I fell asleep. Little did I realise then that, while I slept barely above sea level in my parent's quiet Bognor villa, Che and his men were descending from 1,600 metres, heading for the nearest grocery store.

Is Pollock's "Convergence" structured or is it merely a random splattering of paint? Is there balance there, and pattern, secret symmetries of colour, lurking surprises, strange discoveries, teasing testimonies to brilliant brush-strokes? Or is it just a mess, a mockery, a confidence trick of the trade?

I expect somewhere there is a book that gives the answer. I wish now that I had looked Dobson in the eyes and bluntly put these questions to him. At the time, knowing his distaste for the spoken word, I kept my silence. and now I am doomed

17

until I die to wander a bleak Dobson-less terrain, a wilderness of infinite bewilderments and moss-coated regrets.

It was Dobson who told me what occurred after Che's visit to the grocery store. The plan was to seize a vehicle coming from Sumaipata, drive to the chemist's shop there, raid the hospital, purchase some tins and sweets, and then return.

In the event no vehicles came from Sumaipata. Instead six of Che's men stopped a lorry that was coming from Santa Cruz. No sooner had the lorry been halted than the plan began to go wrong. Another lorry drove up. They waited, tense, silent, for the lorry to go by. The lorry slowed down and the driver stopped to offer help. Che's men seized the driver. But the driver was not alone. A fierce argument broke out between the revolutionaries and a woman who had been travelling on the lorry with her daughter. The woman, quite understandably, had no wish to see her daughter leave the relative safety of the lorry's cabin for the unknown dangers of a Bolivian road at night, especially when the notion had emanated from a group of ruffians with names like Coco and el Chino. How was she to know that these men were revolutionaries, motivated by a well-intentioned desire to transform Bolivia from a corrupt puppet state governed by yankee imperialism into a socialist society free from squalor and exploitation?

At this point a third lorry came along the road. The driver quite naturally stopped to see what was going on. By now the road was completely blocked. Almost at once a fourth lorry arrived on the scene.

Is Pollock's "Convergence" about the chaotic unravelling of plans and structures? Does it offer a droll comment on the nature of loose endings in the post-modernist era? Am I fooling myself when, in the top left hand corner of the painting, I see a partial representation of the course of the rivers Piojera and Angostura, balancing, in the lower right hand corner, what looks very much like the route of the railway line just north of Boyuibe? Dobson would have known — and now it is too late, too late, too late.

4

In his letter (which, surprisingly, made no mention of Loch Ness or the monster) Dobson explained that he had been offered a place studying English at the University of East Anglia. He gave me the address of his flat on the Unthank Road in Norwich and said he hoped I would keep in touch. I wrote back at once giving him the news about my place at Portsmouth Polytechnic, where I was to embark on a Cultural Studies course.

To my surprise I saw very little of Dobson over the next ten years. I had expected him to make the journey up to Loch Ness the following summer, but my letter suggesting we monster-hunt together went unanswered. While my enthusiasm was just as great the next year, and for several years afterwards, Dobson, astonishingly, seemed to have lost all interest in the subject. I was at first bitterly disappointed that I would not be seeing him again, and later I was hurt that he did not answer my letters. It was not until the first anniversary of Che's death, long after the cameras had been unscrewed from their sturdy wooden tripods and put away for the winter, that I received a reply which explained his remarkable indifference to the Loch Ness monster. Dobson had become a revolutionary socialist!

Life, he explained in a letter which I will never forgive myself for mislaying, was too short to waste in pursuit of empty chimaeras. (Dobson was still evidently fond of words and dictionaries.) Apart from the fact that anyone who hoped to take life seriously was required to read — where available in translation — the collected works of Marx, Engels, Luxemburg, Lenin, Trotsky and Mao (which in 1968 stood at four hundred and seventy-eight volumes, with many volumes still outstanding), there were innumerable urgent matters to attend to, including attendance at picket lines, demonstrations and union meetings, as well as paper sales, the pasting-up of posters at night, weekly meetings, study sessions and the annual summer camp. If there was any time left over it had to be spent on brushing up his Norwegian and learning French, German, Spanish and Italian. If, between the hours of 2am and 5am he had time to spare, then he allowed himself to relax with a good book — *Joseph and his Brothers,* say, or *Á la recherche du temps perdu.* The letter concluded with an invitation to meet him in Trafalgar Square the following Saturday at noon.

Was it Dobson's idea of a joke that he omitted to inform me that a quarter of a million other people would be there? Probably not, probably he was simply tired and had completely overlooked the fact that I had no idea which of the fringe Trotskyist groups he would be associating with in that turbulent sea of red flags and shimmering banners. Gazing down from the low wall in front of the National Gallery I found the scene momentarily reminiscent of that tortuous canvas by Pollock. Blobs of black, swirls of scarlet, a curling trail of yellow... For a while I wandered among the crowd, looking for a tall figure dragging a sack of books. I was dimly aware of booming, indecipherable speeches washing across the square, mutilated by gusts of wind. A... MERRY... CAN... PEARLY... CHASM!... VENOM!... WHIRR!... HOOT! HOOT! HOOT! pockets of the vast crowd seemed to be shouting. I pressed on through the throng. No sign of Dobson. Then, suddenly, the crowd thickened, pressed more tightly together, and I realised I was trapped. Next moment we were off, surging like a great river through central London. I remember a flag being burned, fists raised in the air, chanting, a line of policemen lunging at us with raised truncheons and contempt and hatred in their eyes... While others bravely fought back, I pulled out my copy of *The Great Orm of Loch Ness,* held it over my head, crawled between the legs of a constable and scuttled like an escaped lobster up the nearest side street.

Dobson wrote three days later to say that he regretted he had not been able to attend the demonstration as he had had to go into hospital for an operation. He envied me my good luck in having been there and promised to get in touch when he was fully recovered. I wondered if his illness — unidentified — had anything to do with the weight of his sack.

As it turned out, I did not see Dobson until December. He telephoned, inviting me up to Norwich for the weekend. That was the first shock: Dobson had become a keen talker. His stutter had vanished, and as we walked from the railway station to the bus stop I was astonished by the fluency of his discourse. The second shock was the absence of Dobson's book-crammed rucksack. He no longer limped or gasped as he moved, but trod the cracked asphalt surface briskly, bombarding me with statistics, quotations, angry information and argument.

Unemployment had reached half a million and was rising — the highest for twenty-seven years! The Labour government had abolished free school meals for the fourth and subsequent children of large families, simply to save a miserable £4 million! In London thousands of tenants of the G.L.C. had marched against a 7/6d rent rise to County Hall. In Londonderry the police had brutally attacked civil rights marchers! Meanwhile the wars of imperialism — Vietnam! Biafra! — went on and on.

In truth, Dobson was in danger of becoming a bit of a bore. I could read all about that sort of thing in *The Guardian*. It had nothing to do with me. I had no desire to reproduce myself once, let alone four times. Large families invariably signified Catholic parents, in the grip of absurd superstitions. If they chose to spurn pill, coil or sheath, that was their affair. Admittedly the 7/6d rent rise sounded a bit stiff, but somehow I did not think that if the rise was abandoned the tenants would rush off and spend the money on a

Pasternak novel. It would doubtless be frittered away on beer and cigarettes and broken-down second hand cars. In any case, I reflected, exasperated, there were other, more important things in life — for example, the identity of the Loch Ness monster.

"There's a new theory," I said. "A chap called Ted Holiday reckons Nessie — he calls the beast an orm, by the way — is nothing less than a unique evolved form of giant marine worm. He's written a book proving it. Apparently over in the States they've recently discovered a new fossil, *Tullimonstrum gregarium.* Admittedly the largest known fossil is only fourteen inches long, but Holiday reckons it looks just like Nessie. You've got to admit it's a pretty fascinating idea."

"The sea-worm crawls — grotesque, slimed, dumb, indifferent, eh?" said Dobson sardonically, athletically springing aboard a cream-coloured double-decker which waited for us, silent and empty, by some railings.

At first I had no idea what he meant, and then I remembered.

"As a matter of fact, old sport, we know quite a bit about the sinking of the *Titanic.* Your Thomas Hardy puts the whole thing down to a mysterious convergence of ice and ship organised by a couple of pseudo-mystical entities called 'The Immanent Will' and 'the Spinner of the Years'. The fact is, there was nothing mysterious about its sinking. It sank because of commercial greed in the pursuit of the Blue Riband. The ship was travelling too fast and too far north. It sank with heavy losses because third class lifeboats were left out to boost profits. The figures speak for themselves. Sixty-three per cent of first class passengers were saved, while seventy-five per cent of those travelling third class were drowned. The *Titanic* was a floating symbol of capitalism. They might have just as well called it *The Herald of Free Enterprise* or something like that. And when Hardy drivels on about 'No mortal eye' being able to foresee what was going to happen, he's talking as much garbage as your man Holiday. The Loch Ness monster can't possibly be a giant evolved marine worm because there's no such bloody thing! What's more, no one's ever filmed the back of a gigantic unknown animal at Loch Ness, all they've ever filmed is an out-of-focus boat a long way in the distance while in a state of extreme stress. Read their books, for God's sake! Half these people are going through a mid-life crisis! They don't want to go on being aeronautical engineers and living in a bloody semi-detached in Reading. They want adventure! They want to hunt dragons! Who can blame them? Capitalist society exploits us, alienates us, twists and deforms us! It creates false needs! And if the need to look for extinct marine dinosaurs in a bloody lake in Scotland isn't a false need then I don't bloody know what is!"

6

We passed a cinema showing *Wuthering Heights* and a Green Shield Stamp shop. I gazed hotly out at a bird crouched on a wire and a man walking by in a blue raincoat. It was starting to rain.

To get to Dobson's flat it was necessary to walk along a side street off the Unthank Road, and plunge down an alley deep in long grass and a trail of domestic refuse. Up the alley was a gate, through the gate was a scruffy backyard containing two metal dustbins and a jungle of weeds. A track of crushed thistles led to some wooden steps, at the top of which was a black door, the panels of which someone had once begun painting green. Dobson shared the flat with two or three others, none of whom appeared that long wet weekend. Whether they were elsewhere, or simply in a horizontal stupor in their rooms, I never knew. Dobson gave the front door a vigorous kick, and it creaked open.

Inside lay dust, darkness and the most astonishing collection of empty bottles I have ever seen. The furniture seemed to consist largely of wardrobes, upon the tops of which were stacked brown suitcases, hat boxes and numerous old biscuit tins. The vague memory of a film in which Albert Finney plays the part of a homicidal maniac who keeps a severed head in a hat box on top of a wardrobe surged briefly in my mind, then rapidly ebbed.

Dobson's room contained an enormous pine double bed with a salmon-pink cover, a boarded-up fireplace, a Bush gramophone with one of the new "stereo" speaker attachments, and a rickety chest of drawers. Half a dozen chocolate-brown cushions were scattered around a faded rug and about thirty LPs were stacked against the far wall. Above the bed a poster of Che Guevara was attached to the wallpaper by golden drawing pins. It was the first time I had ever seen what was to become one of the biggest selling posters of the next five years. On a small bedside table lay an open Green Shield Stamp book, half filled. By the bedside lamp a cutting from a magazine had been sellotaped to the wall, and I went over to see what it said. As I closed the door behind me the doorknob came away in my hand. Dobson seemed unsurprised by this. Taking it from my hand he pressed it back into the hole in the door. Then he went off to make coffee. The cutting said:

WANTED

ONE HAROLD WILSON
FOR THE FOLLOWING CRIMES:

Gun running to Lagos; terrorizing and black-mailing British workers and students; colluding with racists Smith, Vorster, Callaghan, Nixon.

Height: none. Nationality: Sicilian.
Distinguishing features: smug expression and a sanctimonious whine.

Dobson returned with two thick china mugs and handed me the purple one with ARSENIC printed on the side.

Without a word he went over to the record player and for several hours we listened to Simon and Garfunkel, the Doors, Leonard Cohen, the Rolling Stones, Deep Purple, Fairport Convention, the Incredible String Band, Donovan, Bob Dylan, Van Morrison, Tom Paxton and The Velvet Underground.

When the music stopped Dobson pointed at the record player and said in a low voice, "It was the Which? Best Buy, you know." He added with a smile: "If you are capable of trembling with indignation every time that an injustice is committed in the world then we are comrades."

I was not at all sure that I was, but he told me Che's story anyway. When he had finished he went over to the chest of drawers, pulled out a pamphlet and gave it to me. "You can keep it," he said The pamphlet repeated much of what he had just told me. It ended in a flurry of exclamations.

Guerrilla warfare in Bolivia is not dead! It has only just begun! Che's dream will be attained through armed struggle, which is the only dignified, honest, glorious, and irreversible method which will motivate the people! No other form of struggle is purer. Guerrilla warfare is the most effective and correct method of armed struggle! Guerrilla warfare in Bolivia is not dead, it has only just begun! Bolivia will again resound to the cry of VICTORY OR DEATH!

"Thanks."

7

I did not see Dobson again for ten years. In 1973 I made my last visit to Loch Ness. By now the Investigation Bureau had closed down and I camped in some woods on the south shore. Dressed in combat gear, merging with the landscape, high up on the hillside, crouching, tense, expectant, waiting... My vigil was in vain. It seemed the monster or monsters had outwitted everyone, including me. In 1974 I met and married Matilda. Matilda adored dancing and abhorred Scotland. I loved to waltz with her. She had an Australian accent (although born in Berlin she had been brought up in Darwin). Matilda and I embarked on an epic, whirlwind tour of half-empty dancehalls in seedy seaside resorts. I learned to thrill to the music of the Palm Court Orchestra and the sight of salt-blighted tropical plants languishing in pots. Matilda wore polka-dot dresses with yellow spots (ideal for someone like her, who lived off soft-boiled eggs and who, although she did not know it then, had Parkinson's Disease). She was thrillingly, throbbingly alive. We were young and in love. We laughed at each other's jokes, we kissed and caressed and caroused, we danced the night away and drank champagne at dawn. We loved as no one has ever loved. The following year, amid rage, tears and much broken chinaware, unable to stand each other's presence for a moment longer, we divorced. If I mention Matilda at all it is simply to show that during most of the nineteen-seventies I became preoccupied by other matters, to the almost total exclusion of plesiosaurs possessed of Scottish nationality.

I say almost. My old interest in the subject flared up again when, in the autumn of 1975, it became known that an astonishing sequence of extraordinary underwater colour photographs had been taken at Loch Ness by a team of American scientists earlier that year. When they were published they created a sensation. One showed an animal with a rough, red-brown skin and two appendages — obviously flippers — estimated at thirty to forty feet long. A second showed the underbelly of the monster with what were evidently parasites hanging from it and a dark patch which was described with gentlemanly delicacy as "possibly the creatures anal fold". A third, the most sensational of all, bluntly identified by one expert as "the most remarkable animal photograph ever taken", showed the monster's head, in stark close-up, from a range of only eight feet. Its mouth was open and inside was what appeared to be teeth; two horns protruded from the head, and the face was divided by a bony ridge. It was hideous, unnerving, amazing, stunning

— and every feature of the face precisely matched the contours of the fossilized remains of a plesiosaur!

If I had not met and fallen in love with Martha Saxby I would probably have rushed off back to Loch Ness and spent another fruitless fortnight scanning its dark and enigmatic surface. But Martha made it clear she had no truck with plesiosaurs. She was a member of the Militant Tendency and if I wished to go on sharing her affections there would be no time for nonsense like that. She enrolled me in her local Labour Party branch and let me in on the great plan. Having de-selected the local MP (a rather slippery character named Eric Eel) and replaced him with a Militant, the Parliamentary Labour Party would in time be transformed, would nationalise the top one hundred companies, and would bring the capitalist system to heel, inspiring the devotion and enthusiasm of the broad mass of toilers whose minds were at present temporarily drugged by tabloid newspapers, sport and television.

What happened in the course of the next six years would make a novel in itself, although I do not think I shall ever write it. I quickly tired of the Labour Party and all its tendencies and instead devoted my spare time to the lives of the Brontës. Martha fell out with her comrades over their attitude to feminist tapestry, abandoned the revolution, became bored with weaving, and started a subscription to *Flying Saucer Review,* thereafter spending long hours of the night in our back garden with an astronomical telescope and a gleam in her eyes. There, crouched between two dustbins, she displayed the same gritty commitment and devotion to the cause as once went into standing outside the local post office clutching a thick pile of unsold copies *of Militant.* In November 1978 she left me, and ran off with Dennis, a ley-line enthusiast from Dorking.

Glumly, I went away to review the wreckage of my life. Taking nothing with me but six packets of Kendal Mint Cake, a life of Emily Brontë and three Leonard Cohen albums, I rented a house in Glastonbury for a fortnight.

Each morning I climbed the famous Tor and gazed out at the misty distances, my life a Martha-less blank, my mind a film theatre showing continuous performances of The Life and Times of Martha.

On my last morning as I panted up the steep slope to the summit I saw that there was a solitary figure already there. It was, of course, Dobson. We recognised each other at once, although I am not sure how we managed it.

"What! Are you here?" he muttered in a rather distracted way. He looked terrible. His eyes were sunken, his hair white and thinning. There was a long, white scar under his chin, as if he had successfully fought off an assault by a maddened Fundamentalist wielding a scimitar. He was wearing sensible corduroy trousers and a navy blue duffel coat.

"Still looking for plesiosaurs?" he said, with a sardonic smile. I flushed and grunted something about the slow accumulation of the evidence.

"Still trying to overthrow capitalism?" I added, rather feebly.

Dobson ignored this. "Looking back," he said in a low voice, "I am struck by the curious similarities between the activities of the Loch Ness Phenomenon Investigation Bureau and Che Guevara's little army. The attempt to prove the existence of a large unknown animal, the attempt to overthrow the regime in Bolivia by guerrilla warfare... Both missions involved young, long-haired men dressed in combat gear, with a romantic, sixties, everything-is-possible attitude... and both missions were, of course, doomed to failure. Take a look at what Che wrote in his "Analysis of the Month" for June 1967 — that very month, my dear friend, that you and I first met! *The almost total lack of contacts continues... The morale of the guerrilla stays firm and the will to fight increases.* There are curious parallels, are there not? Failure heaped upon failure, and the refusal to see that the whole enterprise was doomed from the very beginning. The quickening of morale and commitment in such a context has an oddly religious ring to it... and then the notion that all one needs is the right publicity... *if it can be proclaimed widely, it will be a great factor in enlightening people.* Rupert Gould or Che Guevara? And these illusions are in the end dangerous, for they breed cynicism, despair, apathy... What has happened to the glorious mood of the 1960s now, eh, my friend? It has fizzled away into a lot of nonsense. Lyotard and Baudrillard, post-Fordism, the world made safe for Nietzsche and NATO. In effect the assimilation of the young radicals into capitalism accompanied by despair, helplessness..."

"So what are *you* doing nowadays?" I enquired, to change the subject.

"As a matter of fact, I am searching for immortality," he replied.

"Ah," I said, uncertain of how to respond. I wondered if Dobson had joined one of those sects run by Rolls-Royce-owning charlatans with long hair and massive beards.

"By means of a zone. Or, if you like, a joke."

8

I did not understand, and said so. Dobson put a finger to his lips and said: "Later." Then, in silence, he led me down the Tor to the field where his gypsy caravan was parked. His horse Engels was tethered nearby, cropping the grass and occasionally swishing his tail. We went inside and Dobson poured two glasses of whisky, which he proceeded to drink. Then he poured two more, and a third for me. He explained briefly that since we had last met he had been married twice, had seven children who lived with their mothers in Crete and Doncaster, and had purchased the caravan from a film company which was closing down. It was, in fact, the caravan used in the making of Powell and Pressburger's wonderful *A Canterbury Tale*, and although he would rather have had the Mini from *The Satanic Rites of Dracula*, it was all he could afford.

"Now about the joke." A glow came into Dobson's eyes as he began to explain that if a man wanted his name to endure after his death, and if he had neither the talent to paint, nor to compose a symphony, nor to write a major world novel, nor to overthrow a state in the name of the people, nor the strength to erect in interesting patterns standing stones weighing forty tons each, then he ought to manufacture a mystery. But for a hoax to be successful and to endure after the perpetrator's death various essential ingredients were required.

"It must be entirely novel, yet with hints of an ancestry. It must be baffling yet plausible. Once visible it must be constructed so as to encourage the mystery-mongers and occult-property-speculators to heap up a vast tower of rickety theories. It must entice the imagination and encourage a throng of competing, mutually exclusive explanations. It must be stupidly simple to invent yet give birth to generations of commentary. It must be a labyrinth which entices the seeker-after-truth to enter, and then imprisons her in a wilderness of perplexing and half-possible speculations. It must, in short, provide a Z.C.F.M. — a ZONE for the CONVERGENCE of FECUND MULTIPLICITY. The productions of such a zone will range from the crudest scepticism to a sixteen-volumed explanation replete with photographs, sketches and innumerable eyewitness statements. It must..." But here Dobson gave a strange groan, and fell silent. A prominent blue vein which ran from his left temple into his bleached hair began suddenly to mimic the flutterings of a cabbage white which had appeared at the window. "My joke," he eventually managed to whisper, "began last year."

Towards midnight Dobson told me what he had done. In the second week of January 1977, after Cordelia had taken the children, the Cortina and the credit cards, and left for Doncaster, he had eight nights in a row experienced a recurring dream. He was standing on a hillside looking down at a circus when, suddenly, a tremendous storm broke overhead. Thunder thundered, lightning crawled across the sky, torrential rain crashed down and a fierce wind began to tug impatiently at the straining ropes of the big top. Spectators and performers burst out of the exits and ran off into the night, as the circus tent broke loose, whirled away into the sky and vanished. At once the storm ended, the night ebbed and the noonday sun burned down on the empty arena. Gazing down at the circle of yellow sawdust, Dobson felt a sudden powerful sense of well-being. He turned, and there beside him sat Che Guevara, handsome, smiling, alive, with a semi-automatic machine pistol tucked inside his trousers. He held out a Polaroid photograph. "This is it, amigo," said Che. "No one could argue with *this*." He passed it across. There in the picture was the Loch Ness monster, in full profile, with a yeti seated on its hump. The yeti (female, full-breasted and with a demure smile) was holding on to reins attached to the monster's neck. In the background could be seen Urquhart Castle. Above the castle's ruined tower hovered a silver flying saucer about the size of a double-decker bus. From one of the windows of the saucer stared the face of Harold Wilson. He looked worried about something. Judging by the position of the dark shadows on the blue water beneath the castle walls the photograph had been taken at about two-fifteen in the afternoon on a Tuesday in July.

"A stupid and meaningless dream," Dobson added, "but it gave me an idea. Have you ever heard of the mystery of the devil's footprints?"

Apparently one winter's morning in the nineteenth century people living along the Cornish coast woke up to find large, mysterious prints in the snow. They began by the estuary at Fowey and went in the direction of Lostwithiel. Not only were the prints unlike those of any known animal or bird but they ran in a straight line, over hedges, walls and rooftops, for fifty-seven miles, before abruptly terminating in the middle of a forty-acre field. There seemed to be no natural explanation. That it was a hoax seemed impossible. It was a genuine and never-repeated mystery. Known as the mystery of the devil's footprints, it had lingered on over the years in books devoted to such arcane matters.

"Now, amigo," said Dobson, parodying his dream-Che, "take a look at this."

He handed me four black and white photographs. They each showed fields under snow in rural landscapes devoid of people or buildings. In each field could be seen a dark circle where the snow had either melted or been crushed. The remaining area of each field was unblemished and footprint-free.

"You will have noticed that each photograph bears a number on the back. The first was taken near the village of Dumble on February 8th. The second shows Tanner's Bottom six days later. Number three shows a field below Warminster Hill, March 14th. The last one was taken from half-way up Glastonbury Tor on April 1st. Oh, and there's also this."

He handed me a cutting from the *Shaftesbury Advertiser*, April 10th 1978.

CIRCLE BAFFLES FARMER. Farmer Derek Archer says he is baffled by a twenty-foot-wide circle of melted snow which appeared in a field of barley on his farm last week. "I've been farming here for forty years," he told our reporter, "and I've never seen anything like it." Police said they had received no reports of helicopters in the area, and as no damage had been done they would not be taking the matter any further.

"The joke," said Dobson quietly, "has begun. Would you like another whisky?"

"But how — Do you mean to say that *you* — ?"

Dobson raised his forefinger, tapped the side of his nose and winked. "Not now," he said. "Some other time." He took the photographs and the press cutting and slipped them into a foolscap envelope.

The next day Dobson still refused to discuss the matter and I returned to Leytonstone not a little irritated by his teasing silence. As happens in all the best narratives, my work (which involves chiming hammers and sixteen-millimetre projection — I will not baffle you with the complex details) took me back to Glastonbury a few months later, and I decided to look up my old friend. This was easily accomplished, for he was once again seated by the Tor's summit, and as I approached from below that cold late May morning I had a clear view of the greyish fluff interlaced with strands of scarlet cotton which clung to the inside of his turn-ups. Dobson looked old and ill. When I asked what the matter was he said simply, "No snow."

We descended to the Syringe and Quoit, where we swiftly drank ourselves into a stupor. "It's all gone wrong," Dobson muttered. The mild winter had ruined everything. He had completely overlooked the rapid depletion of the ozone layer with the ensuing global warming — a process which seemed likely only to be accelerated by the newly elected Conservative government, deeply committed as it was to the internal combustion engine and major reductions in the factory inspectorate.

We parted with a brief handshake by the statue of King Arthur. "You must understand that my commitment to the overthrow of capitalism is unwavering," Dobson said. "The future seems to me to be full of possibilities greater than any we have glimpsed throughout the past..."

Two nights later he phoned me up. It was half-past-two in the morning. Dobson sounded drunk. "I've cracked it!" he shrieked. "I've got it all worked out. It's perfect. A minor modification! Instead of midwinter it's midsummer madness! Why I never thought of it before I'll never know!"

"I have no idea what you are talking about," I muttered angrily. "Don't you know what time it is?"

"I'm talking about my joke! My immortality! My zone!"

"Not now, Dobson."

"I won't tell you what it is. I'll send you something. I want you to promise not to open it for nine years."

"For God's sake — ".

"Promise!"
"Okay, I promise. Anything to get back to — ".
The line went dead.

9

A week later a large brown recorded delivery envelope
arrived from Dobson. Inside was a slightly smaller large
brown envelope marked NOT TO BE OPENED UNTIL
JUNE 1987. I slipped it into an empty file at the back of the
bottom drawer of my filing cabinet and promptly forgot all
about it.

I heard nothing more from Dobson and my work took me
north, not west. In 1980 I met Norah and we set up house
together. I did not return to Glastonbury until four years
later. It had been a fabulous summer and the sky was azure,
my cheeks lobster pink and the hosepipe ban still in force as
I drove west through a parched landscape of fields recently
devastated by yellow combine harvesters. I drove into
Glastonbury, left my car at the Camelot car park, and made
my way to the Syringe and Quoit. I think I half expected to
find Dobson inside, bowed over a crumpled paperback, three
empty glasses on the table, the half-congealed froth in each
glass slipping and slithering in fits and starts down the
plastic sides, constructing strange white galaxies inhabited
by complex life forms (my mind — my scrupulous, dazzling
mind — instantly conjured a sketch for a nine-hundred page
sci-fi saga about a vast, dying empire in the far corners of the
universe which learned that the riddle of its destiny lay on
planet earth, and which despatched a hero through time to
unravel everything, a hero who, once upon the earth, promptly forgot all about bis mission and instead became an
abstract impressionist painter, calling_himself "Pollock", and
whose muddy and miraculous canvases endeavoured to
capture the blurred, spectacular, colourful view from the
time-capsule moments before acceleration tumbled him into

34

oblivion, whereupon the empire sent a second hero, who discovered the horrifying truth, that the empire was simply the fading froth in Dobson's third glass, and who, even as he saw the shocking truth, was too late to prevent the barmaid scooping away the relevant glass and obliterating ten million complex endeavours with a wanton burst of tap water). But Dobson was not there. Dobson was not there for the simple reason that the Syringe and Quoit was not there. It had been demolished to make way for the Avalon Centre, an indoor neon-lit emporium through which the visitor might wander, along an aisle lined with potted plastic spider plants, lost for choice amid Guinevere's Grill, Lancelot's Leathergoods, Merlin's Menswear and King Arthur's Kitchen. I turned on my heel, found it an intoxicating experience, turned three or four more times, was cautioned by a security man, and fled to the Tor. I was in luck. The Tor had not yet been levelled in order to construct a bypass or a car park, and I hurried up the steep, familiar slope. In the field below I could see white blobs which formed plausible representations of rabbits, evidently frightened by something. In the next field two white horses galloped towards a distant gate. It was a still, silent morning, and no birds sang. I continued along the narrow path, Humming "Jerusalem" to keep my spirits up. I did not seriously believe I would find Dobson there at the summit, fluff still clinging to the inside of his trousers, so you can imagine my surprise when I saw his familiar, Dobsonish profile stencilled against the blue sky. I say *you can imagine my surprise* and retract it at once. How can you possibly hope to imagine even a shred of my rich, complex, inner life? Besides, my unimaginable surprise gave birth to a yet more untransmittable wealth of emotion when Dobson turned, and I saw that it was not him at all but a bearded man with a pair of X7 binoculars around his neck and a chart of the zodiac held in his right hand. Beyond him, just over the brow of the hill, stood a party of Japanese, a couple from Texas, and a second bearded man. I asked number one beard if I might borrow bis binoculars for a moment, and scanned the countryside below.

The sedge had withered in the pond by the A361. The sky over Dumble had the rose colour of Stalin's acne. Smoke was rising from numerous fields, as farmers carried out the old country tradition of incinerating the stubble. Soon the air was thick with the oily stench of blazing gasoline and scorched earth. I kept the field of vision moving in a slow circle, like the long, opening shot of Roeg's *Far From the Madding Crowd*, and soon spotted Dobson's unmistakeable figure. He was walking along a country lane, keeping close to the hedge, holding an orange Sainsbury's carrier bag in his hand.

The car was a dark saloon. Whether or not the driver was an abstract expressionist or a carpenter will never be known. In the last months of his turbulent life Jackson Pollock drove like a maniac, but anyone with experience of our roads knows that the building trade produces just as many crazed, stupidly dangerous drivers as romantic art. The car was a squat, dark bullet on a collision course with Dobson. As I explained to the police, I can tell at a glance the difference between an elasmosaur, a plesiosaur and a giant newt, but to me Fords and Peugeots and BMWs are all just cars. It was a car, a black car, and it was going far too fast. The concept of pedestrian use of the highway was clearly alien to the driver (as it is to so many drivers). Dobson couldn't see what was coming. The convergence of fast car approaching the bend on the wrong side of the road and innocent pedestrian, the inevitability of the collision, was visible to no one but myself, 292 feet above sea level, looking down on everything like God.

It happened very quickly. Dobson might have been an Evenki nomad, strolling through the Yenisei forest at 7.17am on 30 June 1908. He was tossed up over the bonnet, bounced along the roof of the car, and then fell, at speed, head first, on to the shimmering asphalt. I tried to focus on the car's number plate but the lens was a misty blur and my hands shook uncontrollably. A thick, acrid cloud of smoke swept unexpectedly across the scene, blotting it out. There was a sudden, astonishing, unexpected lightning flash, a dramatic clap of thunder, and then the rain began bucketing down. I thrust the binoculars back at their owner and began running down the Tor.

10

On 7 July 1967 a man who lived in a sugarcane field sold Che and his band a pig. The man seemed friendly. Che wrote, "I wanted to extract some of his teeth, but he preferred not to have it done." Where is that man today? Where are his old, rotten teeth? Where is the man with the eyepatch who sold fringe publications under the railway bridge in Portsmouth? What happened to the man in the blue raincoat, hurrying through the Norwich rain? On 7 October 1967 an old woman goat herder blundered into the hiding place of Che and his depleted comrades, and was taken prisoner. Three of the guerrillas went to the woman's home, where she had one crippled and one dwarf daughter. She was given 50 pesos and told to tell no one that she had seen them. Then the seventeen comrades set off by moonlight along the canyon, leaving many tracks. On the radio they heard that the army had the guerrillas encircled by 250 troops between the Acero and Oro rivers. *The news seems to be a red herring*, wrote Che. Those were the final words in his diary. The next day Che and his men were discovered hiding in a narrow ravine, and surrounded by a large body of soldiers. Che was wounded and captured. He was taken to the nearby village of Higueras. After twenty-four hours of captivity he was machine-gunned from the waist down. He did not die. Later he was shot with a pistol.

Dobson was luckier. He died instantaneously of multiple injuries. I did not attend the funeral. I had no wish to meet obscure aunts and uncles who lived on different planets, and who had never hunted plesiosaurs or plotted the overthrow of capitalism.

I returned to Kidderminster, and Norah. There I found a note waiting for me in the bedroom of the empty house. "Remember Dicky, who mended the lawnmower and who was interested in royal ghosts? We are in love. I am leaving you. Do not try to find us. Farewell — Norah."

I gazed at the note in stupefaction. What on earth made Norah think I could possibly want to pursue her? I was over the moon. I let loose a loud whoop — then, out of respect for Dobson, I chased the whoop around the room, silenced it and put it back in its cage.

And so the years go by. Norah never came back to me and I never heard from her again. Eric Eel, of course, is now the Opposition's Front Bench spokesman on the environment (and the part-time director of a company specialising in the disposal of nuclear waste).

I live alone, childless yet happy. My hearing has virtually gone, my vision has grown dim. Though almost totally immobilised, I have taken out life membership of the Pedestrians Association. It is, I think, what Dobson would have wanted.

And now it is time to look back, to sum up, to put a frame around the chaos. What is there left to say?

Once, I remember, Dobson described an amusing episode involving a visit made to the University of East Anglia by the distinguished thinker, writer and politician Roy (now Lord) Jenkins. This was during the time of the Nigerian civil war, when Jenkins was a senior member of the Wilson government. As Jenkins began to speak a device resembling a gigantic clock was wheeled on to the stage behind him. Perplexed, aware that one or two people in the audience were beginning to titter, Jenkins mopped his brow and glanced back to see what was going on. All he could see was a board with numbers on. But as he spoke the numbers began to change. A young man in the audience stood up, shook his fist at Jenkins and screamed, "MURDERER!"

"As I was saying—".

But more and more of the audience were getting up, more and more students were shaking their fists and shouting. "Murderer!" "War criminal!" "Child murderer!"

The board was a score board. As Jenkins spoke the score board calculated how many Biafrans had died during each minute of his speech, as a direct consequence of government policies which Jenkins supported. As the dead rose in a metaphorical heap behind the politician's portly figure, Jenkins's face (which even then was a hideous mix of mottled mauve and blackcurrant blotches) became even more discoloured. The meeting broke up in disorder.

The scoreboard was Dobson's idea. I think it was probably the most brilliant moment of his life — surpassing even his zone.

Dobson's zone?

There is no such thing, of course. It is impossible to prove. Feel free to dismiss it. It is merely one more "explanation" amid a score or more. Perhaps the phenomenon is, as Cory ingeniously asserts, the consequence of excessive watering of crops using an old-fashioned circular irrigation machine, or perhaps Meaden is right (although I do not think so), and it can simply be put down to an as-yet-unknown-to-science axisymmetric body of ionized gas known as plasma with usually (but not always) a vertical axis of rotation.

All I ask is that you consider the facts.

By 1980 the Loch Ness Monster had finally expired. The film of a wake shot in 1967 turned out to be the only success in a ten-year surveillance — and that probably showed only an otter. The full colour underwater photographs turned out not to be of plesiosaurs but the rotting remains of trees lying on the bed of the loch. The monster's hideous head was dragged to the surface and found to be an old tree stump. There was not a scrap of evidence left which would have convinced anyone other than someone with severe learning difficulties, or an American science professor. The Loch Ness Monster is dead! Long live crop circles!

Crop circles?

Strange circles of flattened wheat!

They began to appear in the Wiltshire area in 1980. They re-appeared in 1981 and 1982. At first there were only a handful, later they multiplied like rabbits. More than one thousand cases have now been recorded, and hundreds photographed. They range from the size of tractor tyres to that of roundabouts on the Al. They have spread across twenty-six counties. They have crossed the border into Wales (but, strangely, not Scotland). They have begun to be seen in the United States, France, Italy... They no longer appear exclusively in wheat but in barley, oats, rye, sugarbeet, maize, and tobacco. Now they are no longer simply circles or double circles or big, planetary circles attended by small moons. Now they have developed rectangular arms, astonishingly reminiscent of Spanish windmills...

It was only the other day that I remembered the foolscap envelope. The contents were, I regret to say, something of a disappointment. I have no idea what Dobson thought he was playing at by sending me a child's inflatable ring, a tiny bag of sand, half a dozen stalks of straw and photocopies of Kafka's "The Giant Mole" and Borges' "The Circular Ruins". It was, I suppose, his idea of surrealist humour. It must have been a similar impulse which caused him to leave me in his will a small blue plastic model of a plesiosaur and (bafflingly) a pair of stilts.

It is late and I am tired. Little remains to say. Sometimes I take down from the shelf my world atlas and look at the map of Bolivia. It is a cat, ears pricked, alert, watching something. It is the face of a man with ragged hair who has been taken into custody, and the purple-brown mountain ranges of the south west are the ugly bruises on his cheek and chin... It is the obscure, throbbing heart of a continent gasping for breath, with an American boot pressed to its throat.

I cannot recall reading anything about Bolivia in the newspapers for a long, long time.

Che and his extraordinary example are constantly growing

in strength throughout the world. His ideas, his portrait and his name are banners in the struggle against injustice by the oppressed and exploited and they arouse passionate enthusiasm in students and intellectuals everywhere.

Not any more, Fidel. Nowadays, wading through rivers and crawling through undergrowth with an M2 is not regarded as the way to go about things. No one advocates rural guerrillaism as the most attractive route to socialism in the modern epoch. Nowadays, if you drop by at someone's house for coffee and a chat about the best anti-imperialist strategy, chances are national liberation through guerrilla struggle won't even be mentioned. The reason is, of course, that it long ago became evident to anyone with a scrap of intelligence that the development of a powerful working-class movement based in the factories and the formation of independent working-class organisation culminating in the seizure of power by the proletariat supported by the mass of toilers and organised into Soviets is vastly preferable to guerrillaism or Castro's Cuba, with its complete lack of any of the fundamental organs of proletarian power.

It is late, and I am old, old and tired. You will by now have noticed the scar beneath my chin... Since my throat operation I can scarcely speak. I am bruised, I bear the marks of old, painful injuries. I live, like my dear Uncle Toby, amid the memory of old campaigns... I will never return to Loch Ness, never again wheeze my way up Glastonbury Tor. If I was a much younger man I expect I would hurry to the nearest crop circle and walk around inside it, taking photographs and jotting down important measurements. I would thrash out with my comrades the correct strategy for solving the mystery. We would stride briskly to the summit of a Wiltshire hill with our X7 binoculars, and crouch there, in combat gear, merging with the landscape, tense, expectant, waiting...

Memory, sweet memory.

I will always remember that last evening at Loch Ness, when Dobson and I opened up the Thesaurus. The word —

the marvellous word! — we hit upon, quite by accident, was DELUSION. Delusion is unfactual, unhistorical, wide of the truth, devoid of it, unsound, implausible, fantastical, ill-informed, coinage of the brain, crinkum-crankum, falsehood, flight of fancy, jiggery-pokery, wangle, swiz, red herring, hoax, bluff, spoof, leg-pull, diversion, hocus-pocus, insidious, collusive, bogus, sophisticated, not natural, work of fiction, extravaganza, vagary, whimsy, rhapsody, imaginative exercise...

I have never forgotten, never really understood, Dobson's sigh and the strange wink he gave me as he finally closed the book.

The Bloating of Nellcock

towards me did run
A thing more strange than on Nile's slime the sun
E'er bred...

John Donne, *Satire 4*

...episodes of this sort, which at first sight seem to be amusing and
indecent curiosities...

Leon Trotsky, *Kuda Idet Angliya?*

1

His childhood. He was born — But let's skip the strange
intercourse of sweating, watchful toad with crafty weasel,
the enigmatic alchemies of yellowish amphibian's froth and
glaucous faeces, the peculiar movements of something out
there, beginning to wriggle, quickening into life upon a mud
bank, made sulphurous by the sun, chilled by the moon, the
original, the one and only Nellcock.

Let us simply say that he was not the first homunculus to
emerge out of the vast seaweed-strewn wastes of the Nurrud
estuary in Dyfed. Just as you would go to Wiltshire to see a
crop circle or to Inverness-shire to encounter a plesiosaur, so,
picnicking innocently by the Nurrud one bright April
morning long ago, you would not have been especially
surprised to see Nellcock's tiny figure coming ashore. Even
then, though mystified at what had happened, understanding nothing of his situation, he still managed to dilate
and contract at will, and repeatedly, the small oblong
aperture situated at the top of his windpipe. And so, still
trying out the tones of his voice — one moment a warm,
whirring Nurrud brogue, the next a piping Welsh whine, now
the poignant twang of public reminiscence, then a matey
drawl — his little toes made their first poignant contact with
dry land, that realm where destiny waited. The next instant
his tiny, fiery red eyes sighted a tub abandoned at the
roadside. Although it was an old tub, and rather dirty,

instinct made him sprint towards it. He began (it was an historic moment) to thump it.

At the age of six his future as a deipnosophist seemed certain. Guzzling filched apples, he loved to prattle. Hogging the pie, he invariably piped up and rattled on. Devouring fried eggs and beans, he became voluble, prolix. At puberty he used to perorate under the sheets. One day he became lost in a welter of subordinate clauses and did not return until dusk, panting and red-faced. At sixteen he loved nothing better than to rise to speak, ejaculating in full view of passers-by. How he spouted, shuddering! How he loved to stand on stumps, tuning his rant, oblivious to the pain of the amputees.

Not everyone was sure about Nellcock. A wise old woman prophesied that he would be prone to venery by reason of wind. She did not live to see whether her prophecy would come true. The following day, en route to an appointment at the optician's, she was on the top deck of the Swansea bus, puffing on her pipe and chuckling over Lenin's treatment of the renegade Kautsky in her Chinese edition of *Imperialism, the Highest Stage of Capitalism*, when a wheel came off. Her name was Hattie. The bus plunged into a gorge, killing fifteen. Nellcock heard the grown-ups discussing the disaster next day. He shrugged. He was more interested in his magic egg. Many years later, a famous figure, he became adept at feigning shock and sorrow at news of earthquakes, train crashes, bomb outrages, deranged meteorites manipulated by left-wing agitators, unruly prickles lobbed by Irish louts, drunken Italian rabbits, and foul-mouthed militant thistles, all of which secretly delighted him, facilitating, as they did, the opportunity for public use of his larynx. Only for exploding gas mains did he truly grieve.

The magic egg had been a gift from Hattie, given the day before she boarded the doomed omnibus. Although she did not find Nellcock an attractive child, she was prepared to give him the benefit of the doubt — provided, of course, that he gave no evidence of being a social-chauvinist or sought to deny the possibility of national liberation wars in the imperialist epoch. Nellcock rewarded her with warbled denials, an ingratiating smile, and some hollow words of thanks.

2

His appearance. He emerged from the deiparous estuary mud with bedded hair standing on end, beetroot-cheeked, hooped in flab, this paunch big with a spare pair of lungs. His locomotive powers were much the same as an ordinary person's, except for that powerful muscular tug to the right, which as a young man he corrected in the traditional manner of all Welsh homunculi by feigning an extravagant lean to the left. This posture served him well until it was no longer important.

What did Nellcock really consist of, apart from empty words and wind? This question has never been authoritatively answered. As the only person to witness his birth (I was on a nearby hilltop with a pair of X7 binoculars and a butterfly net, maintaining a lonely vigil for strange phenomena) let me place on record, for the very first time, the facts. Nellcock consisted of skin, fat, flesh, veins, arteries, ligaments, glands, genitals, humours and articulations. He was an invertebrate but not an inebriate. His brain was about the size of a centipede's, and like the centipede he was capable of adopting many different positions in order to escape from difficult situations. His meseraic veins became obstructed when he was forty, as a consequence of which the passage of the chilus to the liver was corrupted, and turned into rumbling and wind. His head was exactly the shape of a child's building block, but bigger. The shape of his head determined the following two behavioural traits: (i) when faced by a line chalked on the ground he would always halt and prostrate himself; (ii) when afflicted by toothache he avoided dentists and sought a cure in the incantations of a witch whose charges were very reasonable.

There was a sly, vindictive expression on his face the day he removed the wheelnuts from the floor of the garage, when Quelch's back was turned. Quelch was the mechanic at the bus depot. He was distantly related to Hattie, who only the year before had given young Nellcock a conjuring set. MERLIN'S BOX OF WONDERS contained three plastic cups, four small fluffy balls, a pack of marked cards for observing with the aid of "Merlin's magic spectacles" (which were plastic and pink) and a white wand. They inspired in the boy a lifelong interest in sleight-of-hand, deception, circumvention, meretriciousness, guile, insubstantiality, cozenage, pettifoggery, wiles, ruses, feints, dodges, diversions, legerdemain, ventriloquism, tokenism, simulacra, mummery and imposture, together with an appetite for audiences, whom he loved to dupe, gull, manipulate, bamboozle, string along, cajole, lull, soothe, flatter, inveigle and shanghai in a shameless, barefaced manner crammed with false pleas, evasions, concoctions, and make-believe.

"Strange," thought Quelch. "What on earth has happened to those wheelnuts?"

He groped beneath the Cardiff coach, something he loathed. In his heart of hearts Quelch did not wish to go through life dressed in filthy overalls, with grease on his cheeks and oil-stains on his socks. Each morning as he opened up his box of spanners, he remembered what Nietzsche once said: "A philosopher is a man who never ceases to experience, see, hear, suspect, hope, and dream extraordinary things..." Quelch was sick of gaskets and pistons and big-ends. He was sick of Wales. When the time was right he planned to leave for Uruguay. There he would make a clearing in the primeval forest, build himself a cabin, grow lettuce, and really get to grips with epistemology, astrophysics and constitutional theory.

In the pungent darkness his fingers vainly raked the coarse sticky surface of the depot floor.

"That you, Quelch?" said a voice.

"Yes," said Quelch, cracking his head on the exhaust pipe. Quelch paused to wonder whether or not the dull, metallic, reverberating sound in his ears was that of the exhaust pipe vibrating or an intriguing aural illusion stemming, perhaps, from a mild concussion.

"It's me, Squibb," said Eck. Eck was a sallow hulk who liked kidding. He had many missing teeth and was especially interested in mountaineering, boxing, developments in Marxist theory and candy floss. "I saw your ankles and thought I recognised the stains. Have you seen Nellcock? I have something for him."

"He was in here earlier. He said he was looking for you. He'd heard of your interest in carburettors."

"That wasn't why I wanted to see him. Hattie told me she'd lent him her copy *of Imperialism, the Highest Stage of Capitalism*. Apparently he wanted it for a vanishing trick. He's a clever lad and no mistake. Hattie says he dresses up in a socialist agitator's red cloak and a working-class cloth cap, throws her book over his left shoulder, waves his wand, takes two steps to the right, and — hey presto! The cloak and the cap have disappeared and in its place you see a moderate's yellow waistcoat, a realist's dark tie and a pragmatist's navy-blue blazer."

"I've seen it done before. Lots of times."

"Ah, well. The lad still has a long way to go. Anyway, the problem is I'm supposed to be giving a talk tonight at the Institute. Next week someone's coming to talk about the Aleppo Button, and I need to put up a good show. I was thinking it was high time I gave the lads a popular outline of imperialism touching on finance capital, the export of capital and the division of the world among capitalist combines. I need to bone up on the way in which the export of capital abroad becomes a means for encouraging the export of commodities. I'm a bit rusty in that quarter."

"Sorry, can't help you there. I'm looking for some wheelnuts."

Quelch wriggled out. "Eck! But I thought — ".
Eck grinned and departed.
"The Swansea bus! It's gone! And the wheelnuts aren't on the nearside front wheel!"
Quelch threw down his spanner and at once ran to his lodgings in the next village. He raced upstairs to his room and began hurriedly thumbing through Parmenides and Heraclitus for tips on what to do next.

3

His biography. This is not the first, far from it. Soon after Nellcock attained high office the first one appeared, by Dunlop. Then there was a shoddy paperback by Gland, a substantial tome by Croup, and a two volume study by Michelin. Hagiographies, all. Can you believe that not one of them mentions Hattie, or the wheelnuts? Not one of these writers has managed to spot the witty, unmistakeable allusion to Nellcock ("the bloat king") in *Hamlet,* III, iv, 183.

Mine is not yet completed. It will end, next Saturday, with the puncturing of Nellcock, his expiry, and the sound emitted as he diminishes, a sound which I fully expect to resemble a garrulous gasp, followed by a piggy squeal, and then an indecent squirt, a whoosh, and finally a plangent whinge, in E flat.

4

His favourite food. The bloater, naturally. What precisely is a bloater? This is the sort of question Quelch adored. "There are two kinds of knowledge," he'd say, clenching his monkey-wrench and throbbing. "There is KNOWLEDGE OF FACT and there is KNOWLEDGE OF THE CONSEQUENCE OF ONE AFFIRMATION TO ANOTHER." The bloater illus-trates this better than pylons or castanets. "Bloater" is found between "blitzkrieg", which has one meaning, and "blob", which has four or five.

"Blitzkrieg" is a barren, one-dimensional word, redolent of caterpillar tracks, and boots, and helmets passing through holes in hedges. "Blob", by contrast, is not fascist but fecund and fun-filled. There is a movie called *The Blob,* which perhaps you too have seen, a long long time ago. Perhaps, when Nellcock has been dealt with, we can run off to Cromer, and live under assumed names in one of those little bungalows along the fast crumbling cliff, and grow old together, chuckling over the faded, unreal, possibly unreliable memory of the blob cornered in the supermarket aisle, if it is truly possible to corner a blob, which in real life, outside the needs of a Hollywood story line, I doubt. "Blob" means "a blot" or "a round drop" or "a nought" or "a spot of colour" or "a drop of liquid" or "a small roundish mass" or "an alien life form sometimes found in North American desert communities". Between blitzkrieg and blob lies the bloater, a humble herring dried with smoke. Nellcock (and here I must point out that, though my options are open, I personally favour delaceration) ate his first bloater on the day he was elected to Parliament. He sank his slightly decayed teeth into the butter-sodden tangy tingling texture. Later, occupying high office, he habitually gorged himself on bloater paste sandwiches while travelling to and fro in a shiny black limousine. His adoration of the bloater became a part of his public image, like his ginger freckles, his interest in throat pastilles, his profound rapport with dogs, nurses, jelly babies and shrimps, and his fine taste in classical music. But not even his closest aides ever thought to ask if all that butter was good for him.

5

His assassination. When did I first decide to exterminate Nellcock? Was it the wet November night I stayed home and watched *The Manchurian Candidate* on television? Was it the hot afternoon I crushed six wasps with a rolled-up copy of *The Times Literary Supplement*? In my childhood I remember watching Tim next door tear open a penny banger and empty the powder upon a chrysalis, then toss on a lighted match and screech with pleasure (Tim is now Under Secretary of State for Employment). Was it then that I first came to be interested in pest control? Or was it the unexpected ending of *The Parallax View* which gave me the idea? I am not sure.

6

His bloating. It began slowly, then accelerated. To bloat is to cause to swell. It is to puff up. It is to make vain. Fast speaking is a consequence of abundance of wind, the inescapable consequence of bloating. To bloat is to grow turgid, to dilate. Nellcock took on a slippery marine air. He spoke rapidly, with a pronounced delacrymation. Soon he would have no further use for limousines or sofas. He was evolving back to the salt sea. He was becoming soft and bald and glistening. I decided that a lightweight one-man harpoon would be just the ticket. Fortunately I am an extraordinarily tall person, so there was no problem concealing it under my trench coat. I read in the newspapers that Nellcock had been invited back to Dyfed to unveil the Kautsky memorial at three o'clock. After harpooning Nellcock I planned to sink to my knees, discard my coat, rub myself in vanishing cream and crawl among the confusion of ankles, chanting in a Glaswegian accent, "Kautsky's theoretical critique of imperialism has nothing in common with Marxism and serves only as a preamble to peace and unity with the opportunists and social-chauvinists, precisely for the reason that it evades and obscures the very profound and fundamental contradictions of imperialism!" I was confident such a strategy would deflect suspicion, but just in case it failed and I had to resort to brute force I packed eight copies of *Moby-Dick,* a novel which I have always found invaluable in brawls, riots and civil wars. As things turned out Nellcock travelled to Dyfed by aerostat, with fifty-seven supporters. Just before his ascent he gave a short speech to an assembly of baggage handlers, reporters and pug-owners in which he called for greater state investment in the bloater industry. "Let me say one thing," said Nellcock. "Let me say unequivocally, and unilaterally, and unrelentingly, and unambiguously, and unendingly, that there is, and was, and will be, and should be, and must be — ".

Only after the wicker gate had been shut and the aerostat had faded from sight was it discovered that the batteries in everyone's equipment had gone flat. Since none of the reporters present had actually listened to more than Nellcock's first thirty-one words (which they had heard on innumerable previous occasions) his last public speech cannot confidently be reconstructed, although a pug-owner named Dolly swore she had woken up and heard something about the need for greater state investment in bloaters.

If it had not been for the scarlet bloater on the aerostat's side I do not think I would have made the connection as I sheltered on the dry side of the bus-disaster cross on the bleak rainswept hillside. Blobs of rain clung to the crumbling names engraved on the base of the monument and suddenly there it was, looming out of the clouds. A huge fish was painted along the ribs of the vast craft. Almost by instinct, hoping against hope that it was not a red herring, I raised the harpoon and fired. There was a soft explosion, followed by a tremendous hiss. The aerostat shuddered, and shot off erratically back in the direction of Japan. The basket tilted abruptly, and a plump, unmistakeable figure toppled out.

Nellcock drifted gently downwards, as if in slow motion. The absence of bone structure, the size of his brain and the wind resistance created by his massive girth all helped to put a brake on his descent. He did not fall vertically, but in a slow, deliberate trajectory to the right. As he fell, he gabbled.

A stream of inaudible subordinate clauses fluttered from his rear. For a moment a gap opened up in the storm and the sun came out, and there, three hundred miles distant, I saw the noble architecture of the House of Lords. Nellcock saw it too, and began to flap his arms vigorously, as if hoping to make it that far.

Perhaps the harpoon had caught him a glancing blow and pierced his skin. All I know is that suddenly Nellcock seemed to get smaller and smaller and was no longer drifting but falling at great speed. By an uncanny coincidence he landed in the Nurrud estuary, at the exact spot from which he had emerged forty-nine years earlier. At the point of impact there was a sudden eruption of muck, followed by the foul stench of putrefaction and liberated gases. Nellcock was never seen again. The aerostat and the fifty-seven supporters made an emergency landing in a wheat field outside Cardiff (leaving a ball of crushed wheat which three weeks later was hailed as the first Welsh crop circle). The government held a trained Irish seagull with a sharp beak responsible. Holding my nose, I made my way down the hillside and hurled the harpoon into a deep dark pool beneath a massive waterfall. Then I hurried home to complete the final page of my book.

7

His magic egg. For many years it was on display in the Museum of Class Traitors outside Bawdy (parking, buffet facilities, no pugs or bulldogs please). By this time the egg had taken on the appearance of a small withered object the size of a rat dropping. Beside it in the glass cage were the instructions, translated from the Mandarin by the Dutch importer:

(i) Put the little creature into water, see what kind of strange creature it will become? After one hour it will swell out and grow thirty to fifty times in a single day.

(ii) It grew in size after one day but see! Ho prester! It

shrinks to its original size gradually when you take it from water. If you want to play again just put it back to water and it will swell out as before.

(iii) Do not put into your mouth, though it is not harmful to bodies. Do not transport by aerostat. Keep it carefully please!

The egg was lost, along with everything else, in the great Dyfed earthquake. By that time Eck had long since left for the Cordilleras, where he suffered greatly from toothache. Quelch took up skin-diving but stayed well away from waterfalls. Then he developed a strange aversion to water and became a familiar figure along the beaches of St Bride's Bay, shaking his fist at the sea and abusing Heidegger. The local Job Centre, hearing that he wished to live and work amid sand, loaned him a child's spade and sent him to Morar. The rain drove him away. Quelch is now in Egypt, helping to repair the Sphinx. The end.

The Story of Julian Iron

People remember Stalin in different ways. Dissident Soviet bibliophiles used to whisper that his fingers were unexpectedly buttery, and that books returned after a comradely loan would be found to contain page after page stained with blurred grease prints. Then there are the lurid tales put out by historians and journalists (few if any of whom had ever met the man) portraying him as a devious, dubious, paranoid, blood-drenched tyrant. It is true that one or two revolutionary groups have attempted to set things straight by publishing instructive pamphlets attesting to Stalin's astonishing intellect and his keen interest in Marxism, linguistics, calculus, underwater archaeology, chess, palindromic verse, nutrition, ballooning, and biology, but on the whole the picture remains a negative one.

The problem, it seems to me, is that everyone remembers Stalin's Russian period and completely overlooks his later years in England. Consider, for instance, the windswept seaside resort of Bognor Regis. Nowadays if you were to hop out in front of passers-by in the high street and shout "Joseph Stalin!" they would probably mutter, "Communist monster!" or edge nervously away, blank expressions on their plump, flushed faces, as if you were mad. Only one or two would remember that he was once the local M.P., regarded in his time as a first rate constituency worker, whose passionate concern about the erosion of the esplanade did not in any way detract from his interest in local canals, his encouragement of the West Wittering Poet's Circle or his determination to get a better deal for pig farmers.

Stalin has only himself to blame for the uneven contours of his reputation. Fatigued and bored by the strains of high office, it was entirely his own decision to disappear. And what better way of disappearing than to convince the world that you are dead? When I read the story of how poor Lavrenty Beria stood beside the fresh corpse, shouted, "What a marvellous day! We are free!" — and then first one, and then the other eye opened — When I go back and look one more time at the communique of the Central Committee ("Comrade Stalin has suffered a cerebral haemorrhage affecting vital areas of the brain") — When I read the medical bulletin — *pulse rate of 108/116 a minute, irregular; the heart is enlarged to a moderate degree* — I seem to see Joseph, devilish fictionalist that he was, crouched in the fading shadows, chuckling quietly to himself. The waxy appearance of the corpse was widely noted.

He needed an accomplice. What a typical master stroke to get chubby, merry-eyed Nikita Kruschev not only to arrange his crossing of the border but also to denounce him at the Twentieth Party Congress. Brilliant! Any lingering doubts which the Soviet people may have had about the reality of their leader's death were finally extinguished. The result is that even today almost everyone in the USSR firmly believes that Stalin died in Moscow in March 1953.

Here in England there is less excuse for such illusions. In 1957 Stalin was a familiar figure on the promenade at Bognor. His portly profile was often to be seen as he took a brisk afternoon stroll past Butlins holiday camp (its high wire fences stirring who knows what memories of the land he had abandoned). It was not long before he became a popular figure around the town, even something of a "character". Mature ladies in deckchairs, their plump bottoms subjecting the pink and vanilla striped canvas to extraordinary tensions, would spot him in the distance and beckon him impatiently to their sides. Then, sure of a sympathetic response, they would release furious complaints about litter and tourists. Upon sighting Stalin, dogs would likewise experience a strange helplessness in the rear of their bodies and would enthusiastically seek to attract his attention, wagging their tails dementedly. Small boys would run whooping to beg boiled sweets and sherbet lemons, and if you gazed into the misty, rosy distance you would be sure to see fishermen, beaming as they scraped their herring and nodding their old wise grizzled heads in greeting. Stalin was like that: he brought out a comradely feeling of warmth and affection in everyone who met him.

There is even the story of the ladybird which flew from a hedge and landed on Stalin's shoulder. At first the little creature simply wandered the slopes of grey corduroy, bemused by its almost mystical sense of well-being. Then, gazing up at that great chin in the sky, it realized where it was. Holding up its first two legs the ladybird used the now obsolete Paget-Gorman sign language system to communicate to Stalin its delight at encountering him — after which it repeated the message in morse, deftly manoeuvring a blade of grass across the black spots on its shell. Stalin — it was typical of the man — returned the greetings, firstly by Paget-Gorman, then by tapping on his teeth.

My father was one of the first people to become friendly with the lonely Russian exile. When he first arrived in Bognor Stalin did not go out much. He remained behind a closed door, prone to gloom. In those days he was living in a bedsitter above the Chinese laundry opposite Woolworths. His supply of black market sterling was almost exhausted, and in winter he was reduced to a battered one-bar electric fire for warmth. Stalin set out to improve his English and each day his vocabulary and intellect did battle with the crossword puzzle in the *Daily Express* and two or three pages of *My Early Life* by Winston Churchill.

When, at last, the Russian shyly emerged from his solitude, it was this latter habit which first drew him to my father's attention. Three days in a row my father, strolling home from his solicitor's office near the pier, had observed the shabbily dressed gentleman with the thick moustache immersed in that interesting book. On the fourth day my father could contain himself no longer. He stepped briskly across to the seafront bench where Stalin sat with his back to the wind and squeezed the stranger's plump hand. Though momentarily shocked by the spongy softness of the Russian's flesh, nothing impeded his blurt of blue enthusiasm. "A remarkable story, sir! Remarkable!" Stalin, perplexed by my father's gasps of delight, then gratified, then slightly baffled by the sky-blue mist forming between them, blushed and mumbled something deep, incomprehensible and profound. Then he allowed himself to be persuaded back to our house for a warming glass of port.

"This is Jane," said my father, indicating my sister, who in those days was a flat chested rectangle topped with a porridge-grey face. Jane smiled politely through her silver brace and went back to her magazine.

My father's face darkened. "And that," he added, glancing at the shadowy corner where I squatted, prodding a spider, "is Midge."

Stalin beamed down at me through the cobwebs from a great height. "Hello, Midge," he said. His face seemed to be veiled behind a grey, wiry mesh. He bent down and gave me a sudden, unasked for hug. The pressure of Stalin's embrace sent three or four pockets of stale gas spurting at an implausible velocity from the prison of my body. These abrupt and unexpected explosions caused our guest to jump back, trembling. Old war memories, I suppose. While my father stood crimson faced, frozen, mute, Stalin regained his composure. For seventy-five seconds (I was timing him with my Mickey Mouse stopwatch) the great Russian chewed thoughtfully on a length of cobweb, then spat it out with a scowl. Stalin's cheeks and chin, I saw, were red and pitted with pockmarks. I burst into tears and he at once dissolved into a shimmer of strawberry blotches and raspberry smears.

"He's not used to strangers," my father gruffly explained, glaring at me as he hurried Stalin out of the room.

In truth, my father was ashamed of me. At that time I was only seven years old and my abnormality was not immediately obvious. Not that it had escaped my class at school — hence the nickname. I think my father felt that it was unnatural for the Secretary of the West Bognor Conservative Association to have a midget for his only son. It reflected badly on his virility. It smacked of anarchistic traits roaming wildly through his genes.

I will say this for Stalin. My diminutive stature (I am only just three feet tall) did not bother him at all. In fact I think he rather liked small people. As our friendship blossomed he never once mentioned our first, unfortunate encounter. Indeed, he seemed to have a special regard for little Midge. How well we hit it off! I loved to hear from his own lips the story of his great journey to England; of how he hid in forests and lived off berries; of the birds which he strangled with his own hands. "Develop superhuman qualities, Midge," he used to confide, "and they will always see you through."

Saying this he used to recall how, despite having both arms incapacitated by mildew, he was not deterred from jumping from a liner's white hatch into a black ocean. Aligning the stars against the tip of his nose, he found his way from the Baltic to the North Sea, which (to counteract the threat of *ennui*) he swam on his back, mastering imaginary chess conundrums and using the third and fourth toes of each foot to propel himself at a steady four knots until he reached Lowestoft.

Stalin soon became a regular visitor to our house. He brought me tanks (which were always losing their turrets and their caterpillar tracks) or dumpy little men holding flame throwers. While I smashed the Third Reich and the international Trotskyist conspiracy, the adults talked politics in the room above. Stalin had broken the news of his real identity to my father quite early on. At first my father had been a little perturbed by the unexpected revelation but he soon recognised that the Russian would be quite a catch for the Conservative Party. As J.S. shrewdly pointed out, he himself had personal knowledge of the horrors of Seychellism which ought surely to be brought to the attention of the voters of West Sussex.

I regret to say that not everyone in the West Bognor Conservative Association welcomed the newcomer. It was not so much the natural healthy-minded Conservative mistrust of foreigners, it was more the question of Stalin's past.

At the meeting called at the Conservative Club to discuss the question of whether or not to admit Stalin to Party membership my father strode on to the stage, raised his powerful arms and quelled the mutterings. In those days, before his unhappy collision with the lunar module, he was an impressive figure — six foot six of muscle and scar tissue, with blazing blue eyes and bright black hair. His teeth were as white as the cuttlefish which littered Bognor beach at low tide, his moustache conjured memories of the Battle of Britain, and his nostrils were pear shaped and manly. He spoke in a clipped, metallic voice, like the red weighing machine at the end of the pier.

He quietly explained to the assembly that it was preposterous to believe that one man alone could possibly be responsible for the deaths of seventy million or twenty million or however many million it was supposed to be.

Besides, he cried, Conservatives had always prided themselves on their tolerance — not like the other parties. Could not bygones be bygones? Was it not water under the bridge? My father pointed to J.S., sitting quietly at the back of the room, completely absorbed in a copy of *The Gathering Storm.* "Does he *look* like a mass murderer?" he thundered. All the middle-aged women present shook their heads. "My friends," he continued, "we Conservatives are not, like Seychellists, swayed by empty emotion and sentimentality, are we?" (More shaking of heads and cries of "No!" and "Certainly not!") "My friends, we Conservatives pride ourselves — do we not? — on our realism." (Cries of "Yes!" and "He's right!") "Above all else we know that life is cruel, that some are born to succeed, others to fail. Let me remind you that Sir Winston Churchill himself always had a tremendous respect and admiration for our friend sitting back there. He helped us out in Spain, in Greece, in all *kinds* of places. He has played his part in ridding the world of the scarlet fever of Bolshevism. I might add that our friend is not one of those namby-pamby softies who believes in sparing the rod or the noose. He believes in punishing the criminal — not in featherbedding him!" (Applause.) "What is more he has many interesting new ideas regarding the development and expansion of our prison service. My friends, I call on Joseph Stalin to say a few words here to you tonight."

There was warm, friendly applause as Stalin, nervously stroking his damp moustache, put down the book and made his way to the front of the room. He began with a few well received remarks about England, its invigorating climate, its proud traditions, Shakespeare, potted jam, kettles, the Brontës, thatch, the Mau-Mau menace, Westminster Abbey, the need to protect the interests of the manufacturers of china egg cups with legs on, dog excreta on the esplanade, the unacceptable colour of the pier weighing machine, potted jam, Shakespeare, and the inestimable virtues of the royal family. He compared this to the black nightmare of Seychellism — the long queues outside deserted bakeries, the form-filling and bureaucracy, the seizure of the widow's mite, the bad weather, and the stifling of all free enterprise and personal initiative. He warned against easy answers, the shallow emotive appeals of Seychellists to the redistribution of wealth and other chimaeras. He concluded, his voice trembling, by calling for more soldiers, policemen and prison officers to help put the Great back into Britain again.

The applause was loud and long. Within three years he was the town's Member of Parliament (the previous M.P. having disappeared off the pier one foggy evening). Soon afterwards he married my sister, who by then was no longer a rectangle but a figure eight, with swellings. Now he was no longer "Mr Stalin" but simply "Joe". Before long he had changed his name to Iron. Julian Iron. It was thought best. Central Office had sent advisers down. He was being groomed. He visited television studios, took elocution lessons.

The following year Julian and Jane moved to an even safer seat in Buckinghamshire. Dumble is one of the smaller rural constituencies, with many quaint cottages and haystacks. People there have redcurrant-coloured cheeks and watery brains. I have only been there once, but I retain an impression of tractors, bigotry, muddy boots, Range Rovers, greed, shotguns and boundless stupidity.

The Story of Julian Iron

I blame my deformity for the subsequent estrangement. My sister, I know, never liked me. Besides, it was easy to understand how I would be only an embarrassment at their dinner parties and garden parties and campaign breakfasts. Nowadays Julian is something of an elder statesman, silvery-haired, with twinkling eyes, a wouldn't-hurt-a-fly lovable old gentleman, whereas I am still only three feet tall and prone to wind. Julian attends banquets and constituency dinners and talks loudly and authoritatively about Africans, canals, Europe, and missiles, whereas I live alone and dine on pilchards and bread. My only interests in life are moths, earthworms and astro-archaeology. I have no hobbies. My life of insignificance at this shabby, windswept, seaside hostel is, I suppose, the very reverse of Joe's brilliant career. Only the other day I saw him on television, looking a little fatter and a little older but sounding just the same as when I knew him.

He occupies, as you may be aware, an important position in the present administration.

FROM *LENIN'S TROUSERS* (1992)

SHOOTING AMERICANS, WITH EMILY

We used to lie in the undergrowth, shooting Americans. Emily seemed to like that more than anything. More even than music or sex. She was a surprisingly good shot.

Those were grand days when I used to go out shooting Americans with Emily. Just grand. I first met Emily in the bar of a hotel in Realejo. It was dark in there. In a corner, on a raised platform, a pianist with greasy hair was playing "I Wish I Was in New Orleans" real slow. Behind the bar, illuminated by a candle in a bottle, was a print of Crunlop's famous aerostat engraving and a shelf on which the proprietor had lined up his collection of bone china plesiosaurs and toby jug bigots. Emily was dressed in black and almost invisible. Getting closer I could smell the whisky. She was picking her nose with the index finger of her left hand. The index finger of her right hand was slowly moving across a grid of figures on a timetable. She was staring at the timetable and frowning. "Can I be of assistance, ma'am?" She recognised my accent at once. Me hers. I wondered what a girl from the West Riding was doing so far from home.

Her family, she explained, pulling something from her sack under the table and chomping on it. Yes, she would have another whisky. A dribble of mango ran down her chin. Her family. They drove her to it. Sister Charlie a real bitch, sister Anne a pious worm. Her brother (who could blame him?) a drunk. Her father nowt but a whinging hypochondriac, obsessed about bad air and the menace of infection. Christ, what a bunch! Luckily three of them were short-sighted. As for the fourth, Branny, he was in a perpetual stupor. Branny would not have blinked had an elephant borne down upon him in a white lace dress, bellowing that its name was Queen Victoria.

In the winter of 1846 Emily bribed a girl from the village to impersonate her. They tried it for a week while Emily sheltered in a cave, reading a revolvers catalogue. The village girl was thin and pasty. She dressed in drab black clothes and was of a moody disposition. Nobody noticed the difference. Emily drew up a contract stipulating that the girl should impersonate her for a period of not less than two years. In the summer of 1847, having made the final revisions to her manuscript, Emily headed for Liverpool. There she disguised herself as a cabin boy and obtained employment on one of the vessels being used to transport British troops across the Atlantic.

That was the version I liked best. There were many others. Panning for gold, harvest moons, a torrid romance with a short story writer in Newport News. A fling with a Bronx banjo manufacturer. Great cities, perfumed bedrooms, mornings with icicles dripping from gutters. Stallions, rivers, paddle steamers, grizzled sea captains, an ivory toothbrush. A device for removing hairs from the ear. A surgeon specialising in tumours of the gut. Emily was a great fibber. She blamed it on her Yorkshire upbringing and the heat.

British troops across the Atlantic? At the beginning of 1848, British troops occupied Nicaragua's only Atlantic port, San Juan del Norte. The port was to be the terminus for a proposed canal. The British troops expelled the Nicaraguan authorities. England now controlled the Atlantic terminus of the proposed canal.

At the end of March 1848 Elijah Hise was appointed U.S. charge d'affaires for Central America. His instructions from Secretary Buchanan spoke of the importance of cultivating friendly relations with the states of Central America. The political turmoil of the region was deplored. Hise was advised to enlighten the indigenous population of the shining example represented by the U.S.A., where all political controversies are decided at the ballot box. Hise was enthusiastic about his mission. He had a dream. His dream was to see slavery introduced into Central America.

I'm only trying to explain. When I say we used to enjoy shooting Americans I should explain. We didn't just shoot any Americans, only the ones that *deserved* shooting. Of course what I didn't know then was just how many Americans deserve shooting. You meet them, you think, what amiable open-hearted folk. The men genial, the women bubbly and bright. Sweetly perfumed, even. With healthy, shining skin. Moreover genial, good with a flow of words. A little pig-ignorant of their nation's foreign policy, perhaps, maybe a smidgeon dumb concerning the sources of the pillaged wealth that makes America great, a trifle paranoid, a little arrogant and self-centred but nevertheless a warm friendly people. Then next thing they go do something which shows what they deserve, and with a weary sigh (because although shooting Americans can be good fun it also tiring and tremendously time-consuming) you make for the carved oak chest where the rifles are stored.

Emily was no fanatic. She was capable of looking ahead to the time when shooting Americans would no longer be necessary. "One day," she whispered, bleeding copiously from a wound in her breast, "we will be free of these Americans. We will put away our rifles and settle down together in a ten-room villa with many books, two cats and a grand view of a tranquil brown river..."

The thing that really bugged Emily was what the Americans on the river did. 1848 was the year Gordon's Passenger Line of New York opened their fast route to San Francisco. First there was a boat trip down the east coast of the United States to the port of San Juan del Norte. There the passengers transferred to large canoes for the long trip up the San Juan River to Lake Nicaragua. They then sailed to Granada, 120 miles across the lake. From there they went by horse (of if you were a second- class passenger, by mule) to the Pacific port of Realejo. From Realejo it was a short trip by boat to San Francisco.

What the Americans on the river did was this. As the canoes glided up the San Juan River, the Americans opened their stout valises and their leather cases and their carpetbags and took out their revolvers, their pistols and their rifles. Then they opened fire on the Indians who lived along the lush, fertile shore of the great river. For 122 miles the American passengers had tremendous sport, blazing away at large breasted half-naked women washing clothes, blasting down angry muscular young men waving spears, plugging white haired village elders holding up magical wooden carvings, blowing away dark skinned gesticulating boys, pumping lead into plump perplexed babies, licking their wet American lips at the hilarious, glorious sight of jets of blood spurting from Indian backs and Indian bottoms and Indian breasts, of hands blown clean away, of legs smashed and broken, of bodies writhing, falling, dancing, of heads exploding like rotten turnips, and roaring with loud, hearty American laughter at the sound of shrieks, screams, agonized cries, wailings, death rattles, gasps, chokings and weeping, sailing on into the distance eating ham sandwiches and drinking beer and saying "Boy oh boy!" and "Hey man!" and "How about that!" and "Did you see the one I blasted up the ass?" and all the other things that Americans say when they are having one hell of a good time.

After her fourth whisky Emily confided that she thought it would be a good idea if we broke into the Realejo gun shop and headed east to do something about it. And so we did. Long after all this happened I paid a mainstream painter to execute a handsome oil entitled "Shooting Americans, with Emily". This was in London, of course. I kneeled on a sofa and aimed a broom handle at The Monument through the window of my apartment. I was trying to remember the colour of the river at noon. Emily the painter did from a faded snap. I asked him to come up with a *sometimes a woman knows what she must do* expression, which he managed superbly. The painter's name was George Arnold Wilkinson and mostly he specialised in Scottish glens at sunset. I had to pay him extra for a midday painting. He wanted to include a stag and some jovial hunters, but I wouldn't let him. We compromised by letting him portray the Americans not in a humdrum canoe but in a paddle steamer. The paddle steamer he copied from a book about paddle steamers. If memory serves it was entitled *The Glory of the Paddle Steamer.*

Shooting Americans, with Emily

I was so pleased with the painting that I decided to commission Wilkinson to paint another one, entitled "Hunted". I knew he would find the title enticing and that when he learned that it did not include a stag or a line of jovial huntsmen he would grow querulous and expensive but that was a risk I would have to take. I had in mind a vast canvas, a good thirty feet long and fifteen high, with myself and Emily Brontë in the far left upper corner, ascending a Nicaraguan hillside pursued by U.S. marines, a dribble of blue ants the far side of a far-distant sunset-drenched canyon located at the far right.

Unfortunately my letter came back marked "Addressee Dead". Wilkinson had contracted typhus from his close friend Potato Jones. He left an unfinished oil of "The Hunt by Urquhart Castle" and debts amounting to eleven thousand guineas.

The U.S. marines hunted us for four months before they finally caught up with us.

I can still see Emily sitting down on that moss-covered tree trunk in the nameless valley where they surrounded us. She puts the rifle down. Leaning forward a little, she vigorously scratches her rump.

In those weeks, towards the end, she suffered greatly, heroically, from constipation and wind. The U.S. marines had laxatives, and we had none. For days on end her only expression was a grimace. She pressed her few remaining teeth together tightly, sending shivers through her gums. She dug deep until she bled, for the comfort of a different pain. How she suffered! A single turbulent rush was enough to send an entire flock of hummingbirds rushing in a blind thrashing panic to Honduras. Her matutinal eruptions panicked even the most hardened of vultures. I waited, rarely disappointed, for her gloriously sustained expulsions to rip and bubble through the soporific noonday jungle like the scrape and squeal of a thousand saws. I watched, entranced, sniffing the air keenly as, swathed in sulphur, she descended the mountain slopes like an early morning mist.

Emily, Emily.

Since I was a muck-smeared lad of three I have always been fond of grubby girls who reek, and no one stank more pungently than little Emily. Her breath smelled excitingly of putrefying grass. Her body was washed by a tide of foul, lifeless crabs. Rotting lilies drooped from her dank, thrilling scalp. Aphids had dripped upon her back, impudent birds had voided their wastes across her shoulders. The jungle brought us together. Its steaming dankness and hot earth fertilised the firm dry ground of comradeship with billowing desire. I have never forgotten that first morning when I seized Emily Brontë, crushed her against my chest, smothered her in kisses and stripped away her rags. It was like passing through a rainbow of deep, shimmering odours. Beneath her daiquiri-splattered chemise lay soiled, complicated undergarments stained lemon-yellow at the crotch. When at last I laid her gently on the grass and licked her naked body I was astonished at her saltiness. She was crusted with the deposits of all the tears of all the men who had kneeled there before me, weeping helplessly. My tongue grew frenzied and numb as it wormed and burrowed and ploughed its way through the tidemarks and the dirt. Beneath the salt surface of her unwashed contours lay the rich, damp, fertile, dark chocolate dirt of Nicaragua, which after a good hour of licking gave way to the sharp, peppery, dusty dirt of Mexico. More impetuous licks brought me to a hot strange unidentifiable dirt which whispered of cotton fields and banjos and wild moonlit nights. Then there was a dry, stale unpleasant dirt, as if my naughty, dirty waif had lain in doorways in Chicago or amid dark alleys in the Bronx. There were traces of other brief, filthy adventures, mere specks and smears, until at last I reached the moment when, aged twenty-five, my darling had first renounced hygiene. It was marked by a delicious, final, admirable layer of no-nonsense Yorkshire dirt, its creamy stench redolent of insanitary drainage systems and dead sheep.

Up until this moment if I had had to sum up Emily Brontë in a single word it would have been *grimy*. But now that word would no longer do. She lay there naked and pale as cream cheese. Her breasts had been sketched in a hurry and left incomplete; the skin of her belly sagged between the stark frame of her rib cage. Calculation shone through the slits of my alligator's eyes; goatishly I lifted up her papery, insubstantial body and flipped her over on to her red, bony knees.

She glared at me but said nothing. I sensed in her a steely commitment to the propriety of the missionary position, the consequence perhaps of a narrow, backward religious upbringing. I tore off my clothes and crouched behind her, the chill breeze at my rear fanning my lust. My hippopotamus bulk, my elephantine limbs, my hairy body fell upon her waif's thin form. I was earth and water, gross, heavy, sweating; she was fire and air, elusive, temporary, ungraspable. We came together with a sudden soft squelch. My stony lust met her moist acceptance; my throbbing desire sparked and jetted against her motionlessness; my gasps and grunts and bellowed ardour soared above her open-eyed silence. At the height of my passion she glanced back disapprovingly. She remained mute throughout.

Sex with Emily Brontë was always like that. While I was inquisitive, athletic, feverish, she remained cool and detached, often occupying the time by picking shreds of pineapple from between her teeth. Now I began to understand about the thick crust of salt which had formerly coated her skin.

Ping! went the bullets. The repercussions multiplied along the valley walls. Emily sniped eight marines before they finally got her. She held them off until dusk, enabling me to slip away under cover of darkness. I hid out in the mountains for a year, living off roots and berries. Then I returned to England, disguised as a philosopher.

In London I became friends with a delightful German émigré named Karl Marx. "Stay off drugs," he cautioned.

"Get a grip on yourself. Do something useful. Join the International Working Men's Association." We drank a few beers and discussed that bastard Vogt.

I offered Marx a spoonful of opium but he waved me away. "Can't you see I'm busy?"

I asked whether it was his opinion that the 26 Commissars of Baku were beheaded or shot, observing that while there seemed to be no doubt as to the fact of their execution and to the fact that the atrocity was carried out by British troops there did seem to be some doubt about the manner of their murder. Marx irritably pointed out to me the irrelevance of the question. "What matters is to study in depth the policy of British imperialism in the Caspian region at the beginning of the civil war."

I promised that I would.

I played him some Victor Jara tapes. I introduced him to *Various Positions*. Marx nodded approvingly. "That's good," he said. I remarked that whereas a writer's best book is always the first, a singer's best album is always the second. Marx immediately disproved this with references to Malcolm Lowry and Joni Mitchell. Marx confided that he preferred jazz. He seemed a little down in the dumps but hauled out his borrowed copy of Barton's *Observations on the Circumstances which Influence the Condition of the Labouring Classes of Society* and read a few pages. It was not long before anger had driven off the blue devils.

Oh! Just, subtle and mighty opium! Eloquent opium that summonest to the chancery of dreams. My addiction, I regret to say, put an end to our friendship.

Now it is almost the end of the century and I am slowly, gloriously, sluggishly-squalidly, going out of my crumbling serpentine mind. The trumpeters play bright in the street, a guitarist plucks at the overhead wires. A crumpled cherub thumbs his grubby lute and I — I have a greater compass both of mirth and melancholy than another. A circus clown bangs a broken drum in the yard, an actor in black tosses a human skull from palm to palm. Wreathed writhing emerald leaves swarm and copulate along the sill. Mustard and lilac butterflies skip and multiply only inches before my eyes, a glockenspiel vibrates painfully in the derelict villa. The dust tickles the emerald leaves' lush, sweating erogenous zones. Leathery lizards scamper across the stained walls, hide behind dark paintings of sodden England. I am waterlogged and clumsy, at the mercy of the moon. It stares as I roll with the tides. Leathery lizards skip across the bathroom sink and vanish in a flash of light that hardens into foil. Soot in my throat as the sun turns the raging gladioli into fire and the bougainvillea explode.

We live, Emily Brontë and I, in a ramshackle ten-room villa at the edge of a cliff. Tens of thousands of books are lined up on shelves, or lie in heaps, or are piled in towers by the bedside. Our bedroom is large and empty apart from the big double bed. Our bedroom is large and shining. The walls are the colour of custard. In the mornings we watch the steam rising from the jungle and hear the shrieks of the frantic, copulating monkeys. In the morning Emily writes, in the afternoons she potters about the garden wearing a Panama hat and holding a watering can. The monkey-puzzle tree is in good health, the bougainvillea is in blossom. The hedges are rich with white roses and the mountains are higher than the Alps. Our two cats, Flossie and Gradgrind, chase butterflies or paw at rivers of ants or bring us gifts of mutilated mice. Money seeps in through the walls, enabling us to make periodic trips to Buenos Aires for new books and cushions.

Emily had her first orgasm last year and since then things have gone swimmingly. She is no longer papery and motionless but animated and flushed. Explosions of pleasure erupt from her throat and multiply among the canyons. She shrieks and gasps and I am in sudden torment, sudden terror. She strokes the sweat from my brow, she speaks tenderly to me, but her words are no sooner spoken than they become that most dreadful of all things, the past. Her words fall away like the inflamed leaves of autumn. Her words are gold, then a dangerous cardiac purple; a moment later, a forlorn shrivelled yellow. The clarity of her love for me turns murky inside a minute. Her smile is streaked with rigor mortis. Her body no longer tastes of dirt and salt but of ash and marble. She gets up from the bed and leaves the room and the bed becomes a raft, swept at sea. I am alone with my addictions, my appetites. I am spooning opium, I am feeding my habits. I am drifting in gorgeous interspace like a stunned gull. And Emily? She has gone to other occupations — peeling potatoes, cutting the grass, picking her nose, finishing her novel, lying down alone to die. She is gone from the room forever, and I am what I always was, a slippery hairy fellow, a sort of eel which has evolved into a monkey, tormented by time and tapping at a keyboard.

Nonsense! (he cried, with a hearty smile, slapping backs, robust as ever).

Emily has just come into the room. She is wearing a Mona Lisa smile. She says she has news for me. She smiles shyly, tenderly. She is going to have a baby. My baby. Our baby. A baby! A wibbly-wobbly-glubbly-wubbly-dribbly-drubbly baby! A baby that will cry and sob and shriek and whimper and leak and gush and stink and laugh and smile and gurgle and wake us up, night after night after night after night! A radiant prospect! I grin like a clown, I whoop like a lout! I embrace her, press my gross hairy hands across the rumour of her bulge.

HOOOOOT! Sudden, unexpected. Hoot of something in the distance, noise of an engine. The sunlight evaporates, dense dark cloud slides across the sky. Between rapture and rupture is a single slurred vowel, the grunt of someone shot. We step out on to the balcony. An enormous paddle steamer moves round the bend and comes towards our house. It is packed with laughing Americans. They whoop at the sight of the Indian families washing their clothes at the river's edge. Some of them start taking potshots. An Indian woman is thrown back onto the ground, a purple gash in her dark breasts. A child's head explodes. The Indians begin to flee, run to the cover of the trees. The laughter and whoops of the Americans ring across the valley. Two more Indians fall, shot in the back. A baby abandoned at the water's edge begins screaming until its head bursts like a paper bag.

I look at Emily and she looks at me. I know what she's thinking. It's easy not to get involved when you're white and on the side with the best weapons and the most killers. Don't get involved and nothing's going to happen. Think of the baby. Misery or bliss, contentment or death. Emily doesn't spend more than a moment or so thinking about what her response should be. She looks at me and nods. Death; misery. *Hurry.* I unlock the old oak chest and take out the rifles.

From rapture to rupture is a single slurred vowel, a bullet's sludgy impact. Emily Brontë lines up a plump American in her sights, a triple-chinned man with baggy twills and a yellow plaid waistcoat, a gross overweight bigot soundly in need of a good puncturing. She is smiling a grim smile, her eyes hard with the knowledge of the injustice of things. Her face is thin and pinched; her body feels like marble. She looks so old, she's coughing. She tightens her brawny Yorkshire finger on the trigger. Stretched out on the black sofa, she shiveringly perceives that between rapture and rupture lies that little linkage, a child's streak of ink, black ink, and a child she'll never know. The deck of the paddle steamer is slippery with blood, the Americans are shrieking, indignant. The paddle steamer is turning, leaving a huge wake. Washington will hear of this. Events like this cannot be tolerated. *Send for the marines.*

Emily is very weak, now. She opens her eyes once, smiles, closes them again. Her pulse is the merest flicker. Bullets continue to ping and crash in the deserted rooms of the villa. I put Emily over my shoulder and slip out the back. I head for the mountains. We'll find a cave, a cool cave. It's so hot, so hot. On through the wreathed writhing emerald, the trumpeters playing brightly, the glockenspiel ringing. Leathery lizards skip past and vanish, gladioli burn fiercely, butterflies everywhere. Orchids, eucalyptus, Elijah Hise, vultures.

Exhausted, I lie Emily Brontë gently on the ground. She is limp, unconscious. I feel in my pocket for the cartridges. The sunlight magnifies and clarifies everything. The United States seeks to cultivate friendly relations with the states of Central America (a circus clown bangs a broken drum nearby). The political turmoil of the region is deplored (scarlet and indigo butterflies skip and multiply only inches from my eyes). In the United States all political controversies are decided at the ballot box (we have our rifles, our cartridges; when the Americans come we shall be ready for them).

LENIN'S TROUSERS

Our story begins — But perhaps it is best to begin with the trousers. Trousers, in concealing legs, reveal much about the wearer. The lack of interest in Lenin's trousers on the part of historians and journalists is curious. Examine a man's trousers and you begin to touch his inmost being. Consider the case of the novelist, Thomas Hardy. At the height of his fame Hardy refused absolutely to let go of his trousers. As the nineteenth century moved towards the twentieth royalties poured down upon him as copiously as Dorset rain. His wife fretted and badgered him unceasingly. In vain. Though he could have had a brand new pair every day of the year, Hardy continued wearing the same trousers for twenty years.

Two conclusions follow. Either Hardy was pathologically mean (a common fault in the super-rich) or he despaired of ever again finding a pair as comfortable as the ones he was wearing. Of the two possibilities, and for personal reasons, I favour the latter.

Let me make a confession: I have legs of an unusual shape. Slender at the shin, thickening at the thigh, my legs have never yet found a pair of trousers that fit with the precision and the comfort that sets the soul at rest. Worse, the whole process of purchasing a new pair of trousers is one that almost physically sickens me. I stride towards the brightly lit menswear in a state of acute anxiety. Nauseous and nervous, I paw at the racks and try to remember if I am a 32" waist or a 34" waist. Am I short in the leg or long in the leg? What if I am a 33" waist with short-long legs? The low hum of muzak blanks out my mind, an ingratiating eager-to-please assistant bobs at my shoulder, chattering, making recommendations, urging me towards the changing room. Once inside, the torments continue. I am panting, in the middle of struggling to force on the new pair of trousers, when the curtain tweaks back. It is the smirking assistant, anxious to know if everything is fine — as if everything could possibly be fine in a world ravaged by disease, starvation, grotesque inequalities, homelessness, poverty, torture and repression. "Fine," I whisper, my face scarlet, my armpits dripping, my arms straining to drag on those accursed trousers in that cramped floodlit cubicle which multiplies my humiliation in the floor-to-ceiling mirrors.

I know one thing: if ever I find the ideal pair of trousers you can be sure that I shall hang on to them, through thick and thin, through war and revolution, through fame or obscurity or whatever else the future may hold in store. This, I am convinced, was also Hardy's position.

If Hardy had heard about what happened to John Reed his tenacious grip on those trousers would surely have doubled in intensity. After publishing his classic account of the Bolshevik revolution, *Ten Days That Shook the World* (1919), freelance journalist Reed returned to Russia. In the summer of 1920 the thirty-two year old Reed went on a five-day train trip to a conference in Baku. Everywhere the railway stations had been destroyed by the Whites; everywhere the sidings were full of the half-burnt wrecks of coaches. After Petrovsk the track ran alongside the shore of the Caspian Sea, and whenever the train made an extended stop Reed rushed off for a swim. Once, in his haste to get dressed again, Reed tore his trousers. A fellow comrade described this as "a tragic event, since of course he didn't have any others with him".

Ten days after his return from Baku, Reed fell ill. His clothes were in rags, his trousers still torn. His temperature shot up; he felt dizzy. Headaches pushed and blundered behind his temple. Because of the imperialist blockade of Russia no medical supplies were available. There followed a stroke, paralysis, death. Typhus, the doctors had said. Typhus? Most probably typhus. Almost certainly typhus. But it is a curious coincidence, is it not, that from the moment Reed tore his trousers his life went into a spectacular decline? Not only did Reed suffer the anguish of a torn pair of trousers: back in Moscow he was unable to obtain a new pair. Is it an exaggeration to say that when a man tears his trousers he tears something irreplaceable, deep inside himself?

To be sure, yes.

No.

That is —

As far as Lenin's trousers are concerned... The documentation concerning Lenin is mountainous; the data relating to his trousers of vexingly microscopic dimensions. I have always believed that to understand any man or woman of historical significance, whether they are novelists, metaphysicians, politicians, critics, philosophers, sociologists, military strategists or revolutionary socialists, it is necessary to read not only *everything* they ever wrote — books, articles, letters, memoranda — but also all the books in their library. It maddens me when I encounter lecturers on Sterne who know nothing of the letter to Dodsley sent (most probably) in October 1759, let alone prattling economists grossly ignorant of the tables attached by Marx to his letter of July 6, 1863. Even among those who call themselves Marxists it is common to come up against those who look blank when you mention Boxhorn, say, or John Forbes Watson, let alone Tuckett, Vanderlint and Urquhart.

In the case of Lenin these difficulties are exacerbated by the sheer volume of his writings as well as by the size of his library. Lenin's energy was prodigious, both as a writer and a reader. His *Collected Works* amounts to some 47 volumes. He may have owned only a handful of pairs of trousers in his lifetime, his shirts may have been grey and unfashionable, his wardrobe generally risible: not so his bookshelves. Lenin owned 10,000 books in 20 languages. His addiction to books (often the dreariest books imaginable, books stuffed full of statistics, books by Hegel, books crammed with trade figures, Herbert's *System of Synthetic Philosophy,* books bursting with obscure data on wages, profits and interest, books about supply and its relation to demand, not to mention *Nerves,* a book discussing the nervous system, its intricate mechanism, and the strange phenomena of energy and fatigue, together with some practical reflections) was not unique. Trotsky was similarly addicted, a journalist who visited him at his home sardonically observing, "In all corridors and passages there were piles of books, and once again books — the nourishment of revolutionaries, as ox blood used to be the nourishment of the Spartans."

The awesome total of books owned and written by Lenin is, however, dwarfed by the fantastic quantity of books which have been published *about* Lenin. Tap in that solitary pseudonym to a library mainframe and watch it trigger a flashing, massive avalanche of titles. *Vladimir Ilyich Lenin, Biografiia; Lenin: Building the Party; Lenin: All Power to the Soviets; Lenin: The Revolution Besieged; Lenin's Government; Lenin: The Man, the Theorist, the Leader; Lenin and the Bolsheviks; Lenin Lives!; Lenin and Philosophy; Lenin's Last Struggle; Leninism Under Lenin; Lenin's Moscow; The Life and Death of Lenin; From Lenin to Stalin; A Film Trilogy About Lenin* ... not to mention *Lenin* by Conquest and *Lenin* by Gorky and *Lenin* by Lukács and *Lenin* by Pospelov and *Lenin* by Shub and ...

One or two of these authors had the advantage of knowing Lenin; one or two have taken the trouble to learn Russian and read all the way through the *Collected Works*. I am certain not a single one of them has read those 10,000 books which Lenin drew on to formulate his thoughts. Sifting through the books about Lenin it quickly becomes apparent that there is not one Lenin but three Lenins that people write about.

Firstly, there is Saint Lenin, born into a progressive family; an instinctive Marxist and revolutionary who at the age of thirteen understood profoundly the need to build a revolutionary party; who grew up, never breaking wind or picking his nose like other boys; who redeemed mankind, aided by his faithful comrade-in-arms Joseph Stalin, a comrade who (as is proved by many inspiring oil paintings) always stood deferentially yet commandingly beside Lenin at moments of danger or when great decisions needed to be made, often indicating with his pipe the correct course of action, which Lenin, not having perceived it himself, agreed to at once with a smile and a profound wise nod; who, on the rare occasions that he frowned, frowned at the activities of Lev Davidovich Trotsky, a rabid and bitter enemy of Leninism who was admitted to membership of the Bolshevik Party in 1917 but who did not accept Bolshevism and who continued his lifelong activities as a splitter, waging a hidden and open struggle against Leninism and the Party's policy and constantly opposing the Party's general line and its programme of building socialism in the USSR; Saint Lenin, whose body, smoothed and plumped by beeswax and mortician's fluid, was laid beneath a glass sarcophagus in a massive mausoleum of porphyry and granite; Saint Lenin, whose mummified body, over the years, has, as one might expect of a saint, turned from that of a wrinkled, old, grey, tired man with discoloured hands into a much younger, healthier, sprightlier figure, with rosy hands and a splendid complexion, looking for all the world as if he has just popped into his coffin for a nap on a drowsy summer afternoon; Saint Lenin of the innumerable paintings and the folk art; Saint Lenin of the busts and monumental reliefs and the painted papier-mâché boxes; Saint Lenin of the hand-embroidered banners and bone china dinner plates; Saint Lenin of the pedestals, reaching out for something, clutching his cap in the wind, gazing intently at something, or cupping his bearded chin just like Shakespeare, deep in the deepest of thought.

Saint Lenin had a twin and his name was Joseph; so, too, has the second Lenin. The second Lenin's twin is also named Joseph; they are, moreover, identical twins. If Joseph was a terror, why, so too was Vladimir. Indeed, responsibility for Joseph's misdemeanours must be firmly pinned on Vladdy, who set a very bad example and should have known better. I cannot think of a pithier summary of this particular Lenin than that coined by Professor Alfred Meyer, for whom Lenin's career expressed a "deep-seated hostility towards everything that exists". This hostility can clearly be seen in the many Soviet statues of Lenin: Lenin grimly leaning forwards to crush a passing butterfly in his fist; Lenin scowling at the fierce wind which obliges him to hold on tight to his cap; Lenin reaching up to yank with brutal, unnecessary force at a just-out-of-reach lavatory chain of the sort nowadays only seen in the homes of the very poor or the very rich. I speak, in short, of Lenin the Monster, Lenin of the fanatical will, Lenin the heartless, ruthless conspirator, Lenin the cynic, beguiling, crafty, collusive, pitiless, insidious; Lenin the schemer, the nullifidian, the tergiversator, Lenin the ascetic, cold and hard as stone, hard as nails, hard boiled, heartless, icily detached, inhuman, whose cold laugh would have sent shivers down your spine, Lenin the splitter and scoffer, obsessive, crushing complexity with his dogma, his precepts and principles, his system, his tenets and articles, his rubric and catechism; Lenin the ideologist, the Marxist, Lenin of the closed mind, doctrinaire, foul inventor of Democratic Centralism, authoritarian, unshakable, totalitarian from the tips of his toes to the brutal blunt bald cranium; Lenin the man whose frightful example demonstrates the folly of socialist ideals, and how preposterous and unrealistic notions of equality, control of the means of production and other chimeras lead with inevitable logic to coils of barbed wire, mass graves, walls, jackboots, guards, watchtowers, empty bakeries, guard dogs, economic chaos, low living standards, bad weather, and the persecution of poets; Lenin, a man at the mercy of dark impulses of destruction, terrible as Lucifer, chilling as Dracula, a man to make you tremble and give you sleepless nights. Lenin, whose face, in death, looked restful and untroubled, until some days had passed, when the skin began to shrink and twist, contorting the features of his face so that, as one scholar sombrely notes, "he looked angry and sullen, tormented by guilt" — as well he might!

Lastly, dwarfed, overshadowed, sandwiched between the first two Lenins is a third Lenin, a homeless Lenin, a short

stocky figure with a big head set down on his shoulders, bald
and bulging; a Lenin who disappeared in the dead of winter,
a Lenin scattered across the continents, a man who, if you
had met him, you would never have realised was a leader;
Lenin whom Mrs Zelda Coates remembered getting down on
to his knees at her sister's house and hooting and shrieking
with the children; Lenin the incomparably great revolutionary figure of the twentieth century; Lenin who wrote of
the way in which, after their deaths, attempts are made to
turn revolutionary leaders "into harmless saints, canonising
them, as it were, while at the same time emasculating and
vulgarising the real essence of their revolutionary theories
and blunting their revolutionary edge"; Lenin, whose widow
urged that there should be no memorials, no naming of
palaces after him, no vast commemorations in his honour: "to
all these things he attached so little importance in his life";
Lenin with a hole in his shoe; Lenin whose *Collected Letters*
has never been published; Lenin of the shabby cap; Lenin
("Without you the sun would set forever on my life and the
world would be a cold and empty place...") of Kollontai's
stupefyingly banal novella; Lenin who seemed colourless,
uncompromising and detached; Lenin who was sometimes
wrong, who made mistakes; Lenin without picturesque
idiosyncrasies; Lenin who had the power of explaining
profound ideas in simple terms; Lenin who was irritable,
depressed, shy, good humoured, exasperating, exasperated,
human, brilliant; Lenin who combined with shrewdness the
greatest intellectual audacity; Lenin whose voice may yet be
heard in the importance and noise of tomorrow.

Whichever of these three Lenins you happen to prefer, it is
a fact that none of them showed any interest whatsoever in
trousers. Lenin the Saint was in a dimension far removed
from anything so vulgar and common as trousers.For Lenin
the Monster trousers were, at best, simply something he
wiped his blood-drenched hands upon; he was far too busy
designing concentration camps to worry about fashion. Lenin
the Revolutionary Socialist, if he thought about trousers at

all, would not have thought of how he looked in them but of their manufacture, of power looms and mills and worsted, of machinery and factories, of Factory Acts and legislation and inspectors, of wages and the extraction of surplus value, of rates of profit, of imports and exports, unpicking those tattered trousers until they had revealed the oily and bloody nakedness of capitalism and war.

Did Lenin know of trews and breeks and galligaskins and of the historical development of trousers; did Lenin, with his insights into the future of capitalism, envisage future trends? In a turbulent era of mass graves and imploded empires, in a world of cords and flannels, did Lenin ever consider the possibility of drainpipes and bell-bottoms and Levi's?

I think not. There is simply no sign that Lenin ever took the slightest interest in clothes at all, let alone in his trousers. He showed none of the keen dress sense of his comrade Stalin, for example. Can you believe that when Lenin died the undertaker was actually tactless enough to dress the corpse in Lenin's dark double-breasted suit? You might well ask, what on earth is the point of being a revolutionary if you don't *look* like a revolutionary? Luckily Stalin was soon on hand to give a flourish of style to the proceedings, insisting that the corpse change its clothes at once. And so it was that Lenin was displayed in his open coffin wearing a nifty semi-military khaki jacket, which, as I'm sure you'll agree, shows that whatever else may be said against Joseph Stalin, he knew a thing or two about PR.

Now about those trousers. There is no evidence that Lenin favoured a particular pair. He was not obsessive; he was not like Thomas Hardy. During the long periods of exile Lenin may well have hung on to his trousers for four or five years, but never for twenty, and only because of poverty. There was no vanity in the man. He would never have dreamed of deliberately wearing shabby clothes as a pose. When things looked up Lenin was perfectly willing to buy a new pair. Given that these matters are not in dispute, why, then, did the British Government, in 1918, spend 1,200,000 roubles on a plot to obtain Lenin's trousers? This was what vexed my Uncle George.

Our story begins (ah, how I have always, always, wanted to tell a story which begins with *Our story begins*) (my second dearest wish is to write one which ends with *But that is another story*) with a sheet of paper. To be more precise, a sun-yellowed foolscap sheet which had originally mellowed on some portly, important person's desk, in London, many years ago. Rubber stamped, signature scrawled, approval given, the sheet had been passed to Accounts, filed away, forgotten. Forgotten until that cold November day in 1957 when Maureen Hopper, owner of three grey hairs, the same age as the dying John Reed, whose trembling hand gave advance warning of the disease which was shortly to incapacitate her, collided in the basement corridor with Uncle George, spilling her three o'clock tea over his brown leather shoe and scalding a small area of his right foot, causing him to gasp with pain, let go of the file in his hand and fall on to his left knee, in the conventional posture of an enraptured lover about to make a proposal of marriage, which for a few incandescent moments Miss Hopper believed to be the case, her heart thudding, loneliness, her taste for cheap paperbound romances and the excess of wax in her ears conspiring to misinterpret my uncle's groans as the sighs of a long hidden passion, a pleasing fantasy terminated only by the rising pitch of my uncle's excruciating sufferings and the strange sight of her suitor peeling off his sock and staring at a red-raw area of skin.

"Grog!" my uncle, sprawled now on the mud brown linoleum, seemed to be repeating, sometimes in German, which encouraged Maureen Hopper to become aware of the mishap which had occurred and sent her rushing off for bandages and a jug of water, leaving my uncle stranded in a solitude during which he at last perceived the trifling slip of paper which had fallen from the fat dusty file he'd been carrying along that long, cold, dark, narrow corridor in the basement of the great grey building on Whitehall — a slip of paper upon which was written *Lenin's trousers* and a sum of roubles which made his eyes swell with amazement.

Plump, pink, bland, rubbery, deferential, lacking strong feelings about anything much, and with a passionate interest in filing systems, my uncle was the perfect civil servant. His employment as a clerk had begun in 1937 at the age of eighteen. In those days, before he purchased Gordon, he was pale, slim, hard-working, quiet, polite and trustworthy. He always wore a poppy for Remembrance Day. He saw no reason to conceal his admiration for the Royal Family, whatever their ups and downs. On major royal birthdays he drank a half pint of stout to celebrate. He did not smoke; he never overindulged. He believed a woman should know her place and ought never to expose her armpits — not even to her husband. His superiors found him to be an admirable little fellow and, now twenty years later, Uncle George was on the verge of promotion from Clerical Officer Grade Four to Administrative Officer Grade Seventeen, the thought of which made him dizzy with excitement, especially on those occasions when he panted after Gordon through the well trampled undergrowth of Epping Forest. My uncle lived in a bachelor's one-bedroom maisonette in Walthamstow and Gordon was his goose, which he kept behind chicken wire in the eastern half of his west-facing garden. Gordon was a wild, ill-tempered goose and he was always escaping; both he and my uncle were a familiar sight in the quiet suburban streets of Upper Walthamstow in the early nineteen-fifties, Gordon screeching and hissing hideously and darting after terrified cats and dogs, or skipping gaily towards the Forest, with my uncle (clutching a broom handle, a leash and a butterfly net) in anguished pursuit.

The slip of paper lying on the floor beside his scalded foot perplexed and disturbed him. A glance told my uncle that the sheet of paper did not belong with the neatly bound file entitled War Office Lead Pencil Expenditure 1926-28 but somewhere else. Evidently no one had missed it, which was perhaps not surprising, as the sheet was dated 1918. Hearing the slap of heels getting closer, and mesmerised by the incredible words *Lenin's trousers*, my uncle impulsively and furtively slipped the receipt into his pocket, a few seconds before Maureen loomed through the swing doors and handed him a refreshing glass of lime juice. He gulped down the lime juice, experienced agonizing pains in his stomach and was rushed to hospital, where, after an excruciating medical examination and a drugged sleep, a psychiatrist talked amiably to him, asked him to tick some boxes (he was delighted: there was nothing George liked more than putting ticks on important pieces of paper) and went away and wrote a report about my uncle's reduced vigour and suicidal inclinations — a report which obliterated at once my uncle's prospect of promotion, and led him to curse Maureen Hopper's absent-mindedness, which had caused her to confuse her bottle of lime juice cordial with an adjacent green bottle containing a fluid which, when used regularly, prevented chalky limescale deposits forming under the rim of lavatory bowls and other important household surfaces.

Embittered and angry, my uncle said nothing about the intriguing receipt for Lenin's trousers. He was a changed man with a dull ache in his stomach and a burning sensation in his throat. He cursed Maureen Hopper for her clumsiness and her idiotic error. He cursed the fatuous psychiatrist for his ridiculous report. He cursed the Civil Service for requiring psychiatric reports on all staff who needed their stomachs pumping. He cursed his pet goose, Gordon, for escaping into Epping Forest again. He cursed the weather on the day he went back to work.

My uncle's formerly affable superiors now regarded him with sombre suspicion and spoke to him coldly. They did not want to have anything to do with a man who might well cause a future delay on the Northern Line by hurling himself under a train. Consumed by fury at their ingratitude, my uncle devoted the next few months to a private quest to find out more about the mystery he had stumbled upon. He had always understood (upbringing, school, newspapers) that Lenin was a Monster, a Menace and a Madman. My uncle chuckled at the unseemly thought that perhaps in some as yet obscure but sensational way he could be revenged upon his superiors by causing them *embarrassment*. There is nothing the Civil Service fears more than embarrassment and *bad publicity*. My uncle wheezed; he chuckled; he drank two pints of stout in ten minutes and felt light-headed and very happy.

His secret work prospered. He discovered that approval for the attempt to obtain Lenin's trousers had been given at the very highest levels, that the trousers had not been obtained in 1918, and that the matter had evidently been dropped. There was clear evidence — numbers of files which turned out not to exist or which had been missing for fifteen years, brittle crisp-shaped fragments of paper still clinging to filing rods — that most of the material had been removed and destroyed. HMG, having failed to obtain Lenin's trousers, did not want anyone else to know what it had been up to. My uncle could understand that. HMG wouldn't want the French or the Americans to succeed where it had failed.

What was it about Lenin's trousers that made them so valuable? This was what my uncle couldn't understand. Were priceless jewels stolen from the Tsar hidden in the turn-ups? Was a top-secret chemical formula sewn into the inside left pocket? Had the Bolsheviks secreted their plan for world domination somewhere inside the legs? He had borrowed a biography from the local lending library and looked at the photographs. Lenin's trousers looked just like everyone else's at that period in history. Uncle George peered for hours through a magnifying glass but was unable to discern any suspicious bulges, not even when he turned the book upside down. Why had the British Government wanted to obtain such a cheap, common object for such an incredible sum? The only way to find out was to go to Russia, obtain the trousers and subject them to a thorough examination.

Lenin's Trousers

After spending some time puzzling over the word "patronymic", my uncle succeeded in filling out his visa application form and, in July 1958, having decided that this time Gordon would have to survive in the forest as best he could, he caught the 8.09am from Victoria. Belgium, the two Germanys and Poland slid by his window. In the second Germany the ticket collector had a sub-machine gun and a snarling Alsatian dog, in Poland the parallel rail line had buckled and a gleaming locomotive lay on its side, as if Lawrence of Arabia had recently passed that way. Warsaw was a dark blur resembling the area around Clapham Junction, Brest was cold and pale and an officious dwarf in a postman's uniform jabbered at him hysterically and threw out his arms when he tried to take a photograph of the sun rising above the shunting yard. The gauge of the track changed at the border; the Soviet train was unexpectedly large and spacious, and an elderly woman dressed in black brought him many glasses of steaming amber tea, shaking her head with a puzzled look when he looked in his pocket dictionary and tried to say the Russian word for milk.

Moscow was dark and dismal, the streets wide and unexpectedly quiet, his hotel vast, cold and glum. The food was appalling. His Intourist guide, a rather grim grey sexless girl called Sasha who occasionally exploded with gobbets of Shelley or lengthy quotations from *Hard Times,* insisted that first he visit the Exhibition of Economic Achievement. This turned out to be in a park, where distortions of Tchaikovsky boomed from poor quality speakers hidden in trees and small boys hailed him as "mistair yank" and badgered him ceaselessly for chewing gum. He trudged through the Great Hall of Tractors, watched a scratchy hour-long documentary on hydro-electric power and wandered gloomily around a House of Folk Art devoted to scenes from the Great October Socialist Revolution. It was, he reflected, even worse than the Festival of Britain. At the end of it Sasha thrust at him a small clay tablet portraying the Winter Palace and angrily told him of the British Government's refusal to allow the USSR a licence to import Cliff Richard's records.

It rained.

Sasha took my uncle to Red Square and showed a card to the guards which permitted them to go to the front of the gargantuan queue of people waiting to enter Lenin's mausoleum. My uncle said their evident devotion and enthusiasm reminded him of those peculiar people who line up in the rain for Wimbledon tickets or who jostle greedily outside Harrods at the beginning of January. Seeing my uncle's officially sanctioned queue-jumping, the people at the front began to shout and shake their fists. Although my uncle did not know more than a few words of Russian he understood very well the suggestions that they were making. Sasha looked grim and hustled him towards the mausoleum entrance.

Inside it was cool and dark except for the blazing lights which shone down on the mortal remains of Vladimir Ilyich Lenin. Jackbooted guards stood at attention, clutching machine guns and scowling. My uncle blinked in the sudden darkness, perceiving a stiff waxwork effigy arranged on a kind of dais, decorated with red velvet trimming of the sort you saw in Indian restaurants. Suddenly, tears swimming in his eyes, oppressed by the viciousness of time, the dead load of the years, the grey lined face that surprised him in the shaving mirror every morning, he remembered a long-ago visit to Santa's grotto at Selfridges when he was six. My Uncle would have liked to linger and step over to take a closer look at the corpse, but Sasha took hold of his arm and pulled him firmly towards the exit. His lasting impression was of a shining yellow forehead resting on a pillow like a priceless jewel, and then he was outside again in the cold Moscow air, and it was starting to rain.

It occurred to my uncle that, though it was commonly acknowledged that Lenin had been laid to rest in trousers, the display in the mausoleum had been so arranged as to keep those trousers out of sight. Was this by accident or design? Had the trousers been removed long ago for safe keeping? It hardly seemed to matter. Whether the trousers were in the mausoleum or buried away in a safe deep inside the Kremlin, they were out of his reach. Fortunately from his researches he knew that there was one other pair of Lenin's trousers in existence...

It rained.

Sasha took him to an exhibition of Soviet Space Achievement and he enlarged his knowledge of boosters.

It rained.

Sasha took him to an enormous department store and bought him an ice cream, which turned out to be excellent.

It took him a week to recover from food poisoning, after which he travelled north to Leningrad, to an equally grisly hotel. It was not until three more days had elapsed that he was at last taken to 52 Lenin Street to visit the V. I. Lenin Memorial Museum. The Museum was situated in the apartment where Lenin had lived for four important months in 1917. Here Uncle George was obliged to leave his shoes with an attendant and put on a pair of felt overshoes. Then he was permitted to enter, Sasha at his side, animatedly pointing out the two iron bedsteads slept in by Lenin and Lenin's wife, Lenin's brother-in-law's desk at which Lenin used to work, Lenin's favourite armchair and Lenin's brother-in-law's dining room table, at which Lenin sometimes ate and around which Lenin sometimes held meetings. Sasha seemed genuinely thrilled by her proximity to these objects, despite having encountered them on eight hundred and thirty-seven previous occasions. My Uncle George was thrilled too. On Lenin's bedstead lay (as if Lenin had just popped out to the bathroom to brush his teeth and would be back at any moment in his red flannel pyjamas) Lenin's jacket and (my uncle's heart went berserk) Lenin's trousers.

Lenin's trousers! As in all the photographs they looked perfectly ordinary. But how to get near the trousers, let alone steal them? A rope shielded the bedsteads, and probably there were hidden alarms and invisible rays. A uniformed attendant stood in the corner, staring suspiciously. Another attendant loitered in the doorway. Sasha herself was a devout Young Communist composed entirely of granite and State purity. It all seemed hopeless. Rain crackled on the windowpane and my uncle's momentary elation began to ebb.

Back at the Aurora Hotel, my uncle sank into a cubicle in the dimly lit bar and ordered a vodka. "Vodka is not made from potatoes," said Ivan with a smile, sliding onto the cushioned bench opposite. "Vodka is a diminutive of our word for water. In Bulgaria they say it drives away boils."

Ivan had engaging blue eyes and a frank, friendly manner. He explained he was an electrician. He loathed the regime. He dreamed of a new life in Bognor Regis, about which he had read in books. "It must be wonderful to live in Bognor. The fishermen's nets flapping in the breeze. The play of sunlight on the sea. The bowling green, the well stocked shops, the greengrocer's where you can buy bananas and pineapples."

"I've never been there myself," said my uncle, adding: "Your English is very good."

Ivan insisted on buying a bottle of vodka, and before the level had sunk to the top of the label my uncle had begun to tell Ivan all about his secret mission. He told him about working in Whitehall and about Maureen Hopper and her stupidity; about the receipt for one million two hundred thousand roubles; about the psychiatrist; about Lenin's bedstead; about his fears for Gordon, all alone in Epping Forest. He did not perhaps quite manage to tell these things to Ivan in a strict chronological order, and he felt that there were perhaps important episodes in his narrative which he had intended to include but had inadvertently omitted, but Ivan, nodding and beaming and stroking a moustache which had surely not been there earlier in the evening, seemed to understand.

My uncle had no memory of leaving the hotel with Ivan but

he did dimly recall arriving at a house where someone took his coat and where Ivan ushered him into a large room with mirrored walls and an enormous bed and a delightful young woman who said her name was Olga and who, rather to his surprise, took off her clothes and then began to remove his, beginning an exciting dream which seemed to go faster and faster and faster until he was hurled out of it, and found himself lying in bed at The Aurora once again, the walls of the room, and also the entire contents of the room, spinning slowly around the throbbing axis of his forehead, while in the street below a team of workmen vigorously dug up the road with sixteen pneumatic drills.

Ivan had, thankfully, disappeared; my uncle did not see him again. Nor, equally thankfully, Olga. Indeed, he felt an enormous sense of relief when he left Leningrad and continued his itinerary. The rest of his trip — Moscow again, then Kiev — passed uneventfully. In leaving Leningrad he was of course leaving behind Lenin's trousers, but my uncle convinced himself that his mission had simply been *to reconnoitre* and that he would return at a future date, perhaps with others, and pull off the seemingly impossible. After all, the British government had given up in 1918 and four decades had passed by; it hardly mattered if he left the matter to the following year, or even later still.

At Brest, Sasha gravely shook his hand and presented him with a book about Great Soviet Leaders; my uncle groped among his vests and handed over his one remaining bar of Cadbury's Fruit and Nut. Sasha brightened at the sight of chocolate, then looked glum again. She shook her head and tried to explain with a bogus bright smile that Soviet Fruit and Nut bars of a quality far surpassing those produced in the capitalist west were due in Moscow shortly, delayed merely by snow on the track at Glib. Regretfully she had to decline his gift. Then, clicking her heels, she was gone.

My uncle sat in the vast deserted waiting room at Brest, remembering the events of the previous three weeks. Blurred impossible memories of Olga throbbed in his mind, bringing colour to his cheeks. He thought suddenly of Gordon (poor, forlorn, screeching Gordon) and wondered how he was getting on in Epping Forest. Suddenly a hand tapped him on the shoulder and he started guiltily. He had the crazy notion it was Olga's husband, armed with a pistol, but to his relief and surprise it turned out to be Ivan.

Ivan was no longer dressed in an electrician's smock but in a smart blue suit. He was carrying a small brown case. With a slow, immense wink he opened the case and took out something wrapped in paper. My uncle claimed afterwards that he knew what the present would be, even before Ivan invited him to unwrap it. It was, of course, a pair of dark trousers — Lenin's trousers.

But how — ?

Ivan explained. As a state electrician he worked all over Leningrad. When the rewiring job came up at the Lenin Memorial Museum (they were installing a new lighting system, the better to illuminate the furniture) Ivan remembered his dear friend George. With a gift here and a gift there he had managed to wangle himself a place on the team. It was easy enough to steal Lenin's trousers and substitute another pair: it was simply a question of waiting for the right moment. The right moment had come, the task had been swiftly accomplished and no one had noticed the substitution.

My uncle found himself trembling with joy and terror. How many years would a foreigner caught at the frontier with Lenin's trousers get? Ivan did not share his anxiety. "Easy-peasy-lemon-squeezy," he said. "Simply put Lenin's trousers in your case and pretend they are your spare pair. No one is going to look twice at a pair of trousers."

Sound advice: no one did.

"But how can I ever — ?"

Ivan gave my uncle a hug. "Send me an enlarged colour photograph of Bognor beach. I may never get to Bognor in this life but at least I can dream."

Sobbing manly tears they hugged and parted and waved

goodbye, Ivan so consumed with emotion (my uncle recalled) that he actually seemed to be laughing as he walked out of the station and into the large black chauffeur-driven limousine that whisked him away to his next rewiring task. Communist Russia may be evil and grey, my uncle reflected as the train pulled out of the station, but at least their workers do not have to hang around for hours at bus stops.

It took three days to return to England by train. Trembling with excitement and anticipation, like a child on Christmas Eve, my uncle did not dare to examine the trousers until he was back home again in Walthamstow. Before doing so, however, he was obliged to make a fuss of Gordon, who much to his surprise was sitting behind the chicken wire as good as gold, smeared with blood and evidently genuinely delighted to see him again. A glance at the putrefying carcases and bones which littered the garden showed that Gordon had survived by feasting on the neighbourhood cats and dogs. "Good old Gordon!" said my uncle, beaming with approval (he had never liked cats or dogs) and giving Gordon a bowl of brandy as a reward for his loyalty and initiative. Then he went inside to look at Lenin's trousers.

At first he laid them out on his bed and gazed at them as a bridegroom might at his bride. He licked his lips and ran the tips of his fingers along the seams. It may have been his imagination but it was as if he felt a tiny crackle of electricity, making him gasp.

The trousers were in surprisingly good condition. On the other hand, you had to remember that in those days they made things to last. Quite probably they were pre-revolutionary trousers. That would explain their hardly-worn-once look. Dared he?

He dared.

Slipping off his own trousers (which were horribly crumpled after three days spent on trains), my uncle tried them on. No good: they were too long in the leg. The toes of his pink slippers protruded from beneath the floppy turnups like tongues. My uncle sank his hands into the pockets and found that they were empty. He was disappointed. It was exactly what he had expected, nevertheless he was disappointed. He had been counting on Communist carelessness; he had hoped beyond hope that something — something more than just a handkerchief containing brittle samples of Lenin's mucus — would have been overlooked. A notebook, say, containing Bolshevik plans to kidnap a member of the royal family, or to blow up the Eiffel Tower. Something worth one million two hundred thousand roubles.

But there was nothing. There was nothing when he took off the trousers, held them upside down and gave them a good shake; there was nothing when he ran an iron over them to see if there was anything lumpy hidden in the lining; there was nothing when he ferreted around in the turn-ups with a small screwdriver and a toothbrush. When he held the trousers for four hours before a fire no hidden messages materialised on the seat of Lenin's trousers, or on the legs, or even around the flies. The buttons of Lenin's flies were not made of rubies or gold but were ordinary common or garden buttons. He examined every inch of those trousers with his magnifying glass: nothing. He turned them inside out and scrutinised the lining mercilessly: nothing.

My uncle became melancholy. He lost interest in bacon and eggs and pork chops and lamb cutlets and all the other highlights of his old life. Now he ate little more than buttered toast. He began to drink milk and rum and swear at his neighbours. Returning to work, he encountered Clara Hooper in the corridor and set off a fire extinguisher all over her, for which he was sacked. He neglected Gordon, who ran off to Epping Forest and did not come back (crushed by a speeding articulated lorry on the A11). By the time the first blackmail demand arrived, accompanied by a cautionary 5" x 7" print of Olga sprawled open-legged on the bed with my uncle crouched goatishly over her, it was far too late for him to begin a new career as a Soviet spy.

He started wearing a cap like Lenin's and a jacket and waistcoat like Lenin's. He put on Lenin's trousers and began to make speeches in front of the bathroom mirror. "Comrade Bolsheviks!" he shouted. "Today Russia, tomorrow the world!" Imaginary crowds cheered and applauded; imaginary hands lifted him on to the top of imaginary tanks. He spoke from balconies and stages, he took off his cap and waved it in the direction of the future. He leaned over the sink and was sick.

Cocaine is used in medicine to relieve pain; small doses of cocaine have been given to allay vomiting; it has been said to cure sea sickness. Cocaine may be used to soothe pain in the eye due to the presence of a foreign body. In moderate doses the bodily and mental powers are greatly increased; a feeling of happiness and excitement is obtained; all sense of bodily or mental fatigue is abolished. Vomiting, in pain, with severe eye strain resulting from the presence of a foreign body's trousers, it was only natural that my uncle be prescribed cocaine by his local physician, Dr Ende, a slovenly incompetent whose diet had inflated him like an aerostat.

Bored with Walthamstow, my uncle found a flat in Bayswater, where he spent many happy years in a curtained room listening to Pink Floyd albums and surviving on an inheritance which had arrived out of the Dickensian blue in the conventional nick of time. Lenin's trousers he wrapped up in a supermarket carrier bag and passed on to his mother, a withered little woman named Patience. Patience lived in Tottenham and was very good at canasta, a card game of Uruguayan origin. She must promise, he said, always to look after the package for him. She promised, and there it remained, on top of the wardrobe in her bedroom, next to the box of old postcards, along with a journal in which uncle George set down in code everything that had happened leading up to his possession of Lenin's immensely valuable yet curiously worthless trousers.

Grandma's ninetieth birthday was a splendid affair, with hordes of friends and relatives (just about everyone, in fact, except for uncle George, who maintained a brooding and obscure existence in his Bayswater flat). Grandma had been born on 5th November and her birthdays had always gone with a bang. This one was no exception. My cousin Charles busied himself with the bonfire, the guy and the fireworks; my cousin Eugene volunteered for the drinks and the potatoes. Distracted by the chance discovery of my uncle's journal and the teasing enigma of his code, I avoided volunteering for any tasks. Shutting myself away in the outside lavatory, I began to crack open the long-ago tale of uncle George and Lenin's trousers. For what seemed like hours people kept turning the knob and banging on the door, while I called out "occupied!" or "busy!" in a variety of voices and ingenious accents.

The end of the journal was maddening. Actually to get hold of Lenin's trousers and still not solve the mystery! I felt certain my uncle had overlooked something — something very, very simple. What happened next is, of course, monstrously predictable. Opening that lavatory door I stepped outside into the night. Ignoring the cheers of the crowd as the bonfire was lit, I ran off to seek out Grandma, who was sitting in the parlour playing cards with some ancient white-haired friends. But of course the trousers were not there, and yes, my cousin Charles had taken them for the guy, and yes it was too late, too late, too late.

Or was it?

I ran like a madman down the garden, barging people out of the way. I ignored the intense heat and reached out to seize hold of the guy, whose heart was on fire but whose trousers — Lenin's trousers — were only smouldering. Even as I wrenched them off the guy's straw and paper body the trousers erupted in flame. I let go with a yell of pain. The trousers went WHOOSH! and turned into a black crumbling two-legged ghost. A white, unburnt, angelic fragment soared towards me. I snatched it out of the air, and saw that it was the label. Holding the smouldering fragment gingerly between thumb and forefinger I glanced at the words printed there, words which — I screwed up my eyes, looked again at the label, was forced to let go as flame returned to the charred cloth and gulped it up in a single yellow blaze that burnt the tips of my fingers.

I staggered back from the intense heat. I could have sworn that the label on Lenin's trousers read MADE IN — No! Impossible! Unbelievable, ridiculous! My heart began to pump with emotion. A thick slew of smoke billowed into my face, choking me. A few dark flecks of fibre rose on a hot current of air, then tumbled back into the heart of the fire. The bonfire blazed with renewed intensity and I retreated up the garden. Tripping over a pile of potatoes, I narrowly avoided being hit by a wailing mis-launched rocket. Spurting cone-shaped fireworks produced a purple and silver daytime through which I wandered, dazed, aware that one or two people were glancing in my direction and grinning.

The bathroom mirror reflected a middle-aged clown with florid, sooty cheeks and a grimy nose. A piece of charred paper had lodged in the clown's receding hair. When I took hold of the paper it crumbled to powder, obliging me to comb and comb until my scalp was sore and tingling. My striped shirt was ruined, my suede shoes smeared and scorched. It was not until the next morning that I became aware of the hole in my anorak caused by a malicious child's sparkler, and the burn mark on the left leg of my expensive green corduroy trousers.

I limped away into the night, sick at heart.

There really was a receipt. My uncle was not deluded in that, only in all the other things. Had he been a little better informed about events in Russia after the Bolshevik revolution he would not have needed to abandon one wild goose chase (Gordon) for another (Lenin's trousers). Had he read *Ten Days That Shook the World* he would not only have begun to understand what really happened in Russia all those years ago but he would also have learned that on the first day of the socialist revolution Lenin appeared at the Smolny "dressed in shabby clothes, his trousers much too long for him".

The Bolshevik revolution came as a considerable shock to

everyone. It just goes to show what can happen when a disciplined revolutionary party dedicated to Marxist ideas begins influencing masses of discontented workers and coming up with inflammatory slogans about peace and bread. Once working people start believing they can run their own lives and do without landlords, bosses, newspaper magnates, nobles, princes, kings, emperors or tsars — once working people start understanding dangerous notions like surplus value — once people stop caring about smartness and whether or not their trousers are too long in the leg — once workers start realising that the existing structures of government and the army and the police and the judiciary exist to serve the interests of capitalists — once such things happen a fire is lit which, if not extinguished, can spread.

Enter Sidney Reilly.

In Reilly's opinion Bolshevism was "the greatest danger that has ever threatened civilisation".

Reilly called the Bolsheviks "the Bolos".

Reilly, born 1874, was the only son of a wealthy landowner and contractor. He had two sisters. One, Elena, committed suicide when she was eighteen. His eldest sister, Marie, was terrified of mice and married a doctor. A photograph of Reilly at sixteen shows a scowling youth with psychopath's eyes and thick sensuous lips. A photograph of Reilly taken in 1918 shows a twinkly-eyed lounge lizard with a Mephistophelean moustache and beard. Reilly grew up to become a rich, reactionary charmer. He was a prodigious liar and fantasist. He could never look a camera in the eye. In the handful of photographs which survive Reilly is looking sideways, to his left. The left is where Reilly feels threatened. Women adored him. He possessed eleven passports. He was a talented linguist. He was a bigamist. According to one version of his life Reilly was an expert at "poisoning, stabbing, shooting and throttling". As a slippery, nasty, murderous extreme right-wing thug Reilly was quite naturally regarded as first rate material by M11c (as the British secret service called itself in those days).

Reilly, originally born in Russian Poland, was sent to Moscow by M11c in May 1918. At first Bolshevik Russia was a relatively peaceful place. The Bolsheviks ended Russian participation in the Great War and began to put their socialist programme into practice. In January 1918 someone tried to shoot Lenin, but missed. By May of that year the British diplomatic representative in Moscow, Robert Bruce Lockhart, was conspiring to overthrow the Bolos. He supplied the Foreign Office with a plan whereby on the night of an Allied invasion all the Bolshevik leaders would be murdered, allowing the formation of a new government "which will be in reality a military dictatorship". In fact by that date British troops were already in Russia. On 6 March a division of marines commanded by Major General Frederick Poole landed at the Arctic port of Murmansk. By July there were eighteen anti-Bolshevik governments in what remained of the old Tsarist empire. That same month Lockhart and the French Consul General in Moscow handed over ten million roubles to finance espionage and sabotage by the White anti-Bolshevik National Centre group in Moscow. On 2 August Poole landed at Archangel and seized the town, aided by a detachment of Royal Marines, a French battalion and fifty American sailors. The anti-Bolshevik plots ramified, financed by the governments of Britain, France and the United States. Explosives were stored in the flat of the French government representative. By the summer British, French, American and Japanese troops had landed in Russia in support of the White counter-revolutionary armies. At the end of August, with Moscow and other Russian cities on the verge of starvation, Allied agents blew up food trains at Voronezh station. The British government had previously supplied £1million for the purpose of sabotaging the Russian Baltic fleet: Reilly had a better idea, which was to spend the money on overthrowing the Bolshevik leadership.

Reilly dreamed of the capture of Lenin and the seizure of his trousers. He handed over those 1,200,000 roubles to a man who he believed could bring such an event about. What my uncle never understood was that it was not the trousers that were important but Lenin's legs and underpants. Reilly planned to parade a trouserless Lenin through the streets of Moscow and turn him into a laughing-stock.

The plots thickened. On 30 August a leading Bolshevik, Uritsky, was assassinated in Petrograd, and Lenin was shot and seriously wounded in Moscow. What Reilly didn't know was that the Bolsheviks knew all about his conspiracy to capture Lenin and his trousers. There were mass arrests. Lockhart was imprisoned.

Reilly went into hiding. He spent several nights in a brothel, hiding in the room of a girl in the last stage of syphilis. The girl laughed, said her name began with a "C" and Reilly had to guess. Clarissa? No. Claudia? Niet. Cecilia? Clara? Celeste? No. The girl stank. Her chest was yellow as butter, her cheeks the colour of porridge. Her mouth was foul and oozy.

Syphilis occurs in three stages. A month after contracting the infection a small, hard, painless sore appears. A slight colourless discharge leaks from the sore. The glands in the region of the sore enlarge. The sore goes away, leaving a small blemish on the skin. This happens after two or three months have elapsed.

The girl looked to be about ninety. She had sunken eyes. She shook. She had a squint.

Christine!

No.

After three months the germs have been transported in the blood to all parts of the body. The germs are shaped like a corkscrew. How many spirals? From ten to twenty-five. The germs get down to business: severe headaches, fever, pains in joints and bones, severe anaemia, a dreadful rash all over the body. The germs invade the heart. They drill their way merrily through the walls of the blood vessels. They get into the nervous system.

Cynthia?

No.

If left untreated, the secondary stage appears to clear up and there is a period of freedom from symptoms which may last from two to twenty years. In the third and final stage (Claudine? No) tumour-like masses proliferate disgustingly. Your nose rots. Ulcers and sores as big as oranges erupt across your skin and in your liver and bones and in your mouth and all over your tongue. Cancer of the tongue is common. Your brain and spinal column fill up with pus and putrefaction. You get dizzy. You look awful. You're literally falling apart.

C chuckles, hideously. Wanna fook me, mistair?

Niet.

Guess. You god to guess.

Cecilia.

You had that one.

Hmm.

Her rippled thighs liberally plastered with chancres, excrescent formations reminiscent of fungus, glittery discharges. A tendency to omit words or syllables.

I've got it. Cathy!

Wrong again, Reilly.

The girl shrieked with laughter. She was obviously suffering from general paralysis of the insane. Halted and stumbled over long words. Slurred speech. Said twice parts of words. I give up, Reilly said. He was bored and frightened and disgusted. He hadn't had an erection since he'd entered the room. It was the way he could see the tops of her upper teeth through the hole where her nose used to be. Unforgettable.

"I tell you. My name is — my name is — ". (Hysterical shrieks, general stench, watery oozings, leakages of blood.) "My name is — ". A gobbet of something resembling phlegm smacked against his lapel.

"Cap-eat-all-ism!"

A bad joke! And his lapel smelling like a rotten egg! Reilly screamed and ran from the room. False papers took him to

Petrograd. He escaped on a Dutch freighter, feeling itchy. Back in England (the rash was nothing; everybody gets rashes) he was awarded a Military Cross for bravely, if unsuccessfully, attempting to detach Lenin from his trousers.

To cut a long story short (which is the best cut of all), Reilly spent the rest of his life conspiring against the Bolsheviks. To finance the anti-Communist crusade he invented "Humagsolan", a miracle medicine which cured headaches, spots, cancer, constipation and syphilis. Especially syphilis.

"Humagsolan" flopped. Undeterred, Reilly devised a plan whereby (once the wretched Communists had been disposed of) a British banking combine could take over the entire Russian economy. The Central Bank would also run an intelligence network and control the Russian press. The monarchy, naturally, would be restored to the throne. Unfortunately things did not quite turn out that way and, somehow or other, bafflingly and infuriatingly, that tiny handful of Bolshevik madmen succeeded in routing the innumerable armies and the combined efforts of Britain, France, Japan, the USA, and the Whites.

Reilly did not give up so easily. The Bolos might have won the civil war, but that didn't mean their troubles were over. There was encouraging evidence that radishes were thriving under the new regime. Reilly liked the sound of radishes very much. Radishes were Lenin's term. Lenin meant people who were red outside, white within. Under the influence of the radishes the signs were that Bolshevik rule was changing. There was also encouraging evidence that the opposition in Russia might yet act to overthrow the Bolsheviks, a notion which also appealed to Reilly's dear friend Winston Churchill. All that was required was a definite plan of action. If proof of such a plan could be obtained an approach would be made to Henry Ford. "Once his interest is gained, the question of money can be considered solved," Reilly enthusiastically noted. If not, Russian museums could be burgled and their art treasures sold in the West.

On 25 September 1925 Reilly crossed the border into Russia to meet the political council of "The Trust", the organisation which was to overthrow the Bolsheviks. Unfortunately for Reilly "The Trust" was run by the Soviet security service, and was designed to flush out counter-revolutionary conspirators. On this occasion Reilly's false passport did not save him. Removing Reilly's trousers, his captors discovered him to be wearing expensive underpants bearing his initials...

I limped away into the night. Two teenage girls by a bus shelter pointed a finger at me, whispered something and hooted with laughter. I wandered on through empty streets, past illuminated shop windows filled with cheap jewellery, sofas, TVs and videos. Once I slipped on some leaves and some people in a passing car wound down their windows and shrieked something. Soon afterwards I slipped on a piece of discarded fruit, which I observed without smiling was a banana skin. I reflected how I had never found clowns or slapstick amusing. My sides refuse to split with uncontrollable laughter at the sight of people having buckets of blue paint poured over them or having their trousers removed. The very word "gag" makes me gag; I abhor drollery, I loathe waggery, I detest jocosity. Practical jokes make me wince; comic virtuosity is not my cup of tea. You can keep your caprices, your fun, your jests, your clowning. Tomfoolery and buffoonery bores me, funny business makes me scowl. Comic turns make me puke; farce sends me to sleep; custard pie humour makes me yawn until my jaw aches. Life is too short for a laugh a minute; knockabout comedy doesn't knock me out but sends me fleeing. I hope I make my position clear. Give me back my trousers, and a pox on your japes, wisecracks, badinage and leg-pulls.

I remembered the fate of Bim-Bom, the famous Russian clown. When the Cheka arrived in Moscow in 1918 it is said that some of its members were not amused by Bim-Bom's jokes about the Bolshevik government. Some Chekists entered the circus ring to arrest Bim-Bom, much to the laughter of the audience, who thought it was all part of the act. Bim-Bom fled, and the Chekists opened fire. The joke was over: panic and pandemonium.

Historians tell this tale to show what humourless authoritarians the Bolsheviks were. The same historians tell us the story of the plot to remove Lenin's trousers as if it was one of the jolliest japes imaginable. And if it had been successful, and after Lenin had been marched trouserless through the streets of Moscow, what then? Having seen him humiliated in public, the imperialist powers, their prime ministers and their presidents and their generals and their police chiefs and their secret agents all chuckling amiably, would doubtless have made the troublesome fellow go all the way back to Geneva by his original circuitous route and, their troops and moustachio'd policemen guffawing broadly, would have seen the wretch off at the Finland Station to catch the next draughty, cold, uncomfortable third class connection to Geneva.

I think not.

As I walked homeward under a twinkling sky still streaked by rockets and amid a silence punctuated by the distant boom of explosives, I understood that it was not Lenin's trousers they were all after but his life, his voice, his perceptions. It would not have been many minutes after the removal of his trousers before they would have begun the beatings, the torture, the mutilations, the cutting-out of the eyes, the tearing out of his tongue, the crushing and breaking of Lenin's hands, the obliteration of his dangerous brain. There would have been laughter, but it would not have been the pleasant Senior Common Room laughter of the historians.

I must have had a little too much to drink that night, for next thing I found myself standing on top of a red pillar box shouting, "Remember the execution of the 26 Commissars of Baku! Never underestimate the ruthlessness of the British ruling class!" The police were called and I ran off up an alley and crawled into a cardboard box.

"It's a coon," said the first PC, shining his torch on me. This I indignantly denied, assuring him that owing to a sequence of small misadventures I was simply a trifle grimy. Putting on a scouse accent I passed myself off as a homeless northerner seeking to make good in opportunity Britain. I denied having anything to do with the shouting of offensive slogans from a pillar box.

The two young moustachio'd officers held a short conversation during which they decided I was in too filthy a state for them to want to arrest me under the 1824 Vagrancy Act. To relieve the tensions of their stressful and often tedious occupation they therefore relieved themselves upon me, gave me a sound kicking in the ribs and a brisk truncheoning of shoulders and arms and concluded their fun by making a number of colourful threats as to what they would do to me if they ever found me in their manor again. With a squeal of tyres they vanished into the night.

The next day, showered, shaved and changed, and having decided never again to attend a fireworks party or to over-indulge in alcohol, and vowing also always to cross over the road if a pillar box loomed on my side, I strode off to the reference section of the local library to enquire where I might find a revolutionary socialist party in the Leninist tradition.

The rest is history.

I have always wanted to tell a story which begins as this one begins, and now it is done, it is finished with. It is time to draw the curtains and put out the light, time to take off my clothes and put on my pyjamas, time to hang up my trousers (taking special care to see that they are not creased) and to get into bed.

Pyjamas, did I say? Pyjamas remind me of what had completely crossed my mind. I refer to the other pair of trousers in the case. My uncle, wandering off down dark labyrinths of his own devising, never learned about these other trousers, which were worth at least 600,000 roubles. You see, it was not simply Lenin's trousers that the British

Government were after but also Trotsky's. Get rid of Lenin and Trotsky and the whole wretched Bolshevik show could be wrapped up once and for all (who knows, perhaps they were right). But as we know, it was not Lenin and Trotsky who lost their trousers, but Sidney Reilly.

It occurs to me that this last sentence is misleading. Some years later Trotsky did lose his trousers, or rather his pyjama bottoms. At the time he was lodging in the House of the Soviets in Granovsky Street, Moscow. On January 17, 1928, early in the morning, the G.P.U. came to take Trotsky away. Trotsky locked himself in his bedroom. The G.P.U. smashed down the door. Dressed in his pyjamas, Trotsky refused to put on his clothes. A G.P.U. man seized Trotsky's pyjama trousers. Another G.P.U. man lifted first one leg, and then the other. His slippers were removed, then his pyjamas. Keeping a tight grip on Trotsky's limbs the G.P.U. men held the great revolutionary out for their colleagues, who were holding Trotsky's clothes.

Soon Trotsky's trousers were forced on to him; his shirt was buttoned; he was dressed.

Some plots involve the forcible removal of trousers; others involve the forcible putting-on of trousers. Some plots fail, others succeed. Sidney Reilly was shot in the Lenin Hills on November 3, 1925. My uncle George died of cocaine poisoning at 25 Powis Square at 9.58 pm on July 12, 1969. As for Trotsky, he was dragged to an empty railway carriage in a lonely Moscow shunting yard. The carriage was taken to a deserted station 50 kilometres from Moscow. There it was linked up to a train travelling all the way to Pishpeck-Frunze. It took a week to get to Alma Ata, across the snowdrifts and the mountains. For three weeks he stayed at an inn on Gogol Street. From there —

But that is another story.

DEAD IRAQIS

In a society like ours there are bound to be disagreements about this and that. It is only natural. But although we may disagree on many things, I think we can all agree on one thing. The nice thing about dead Iraqis is *they don't smell.*

Some years ago, as you may remember, dead Iraqis were turning up all over the place. At the time there were various theories about why this was happening but thankfully all that is behind us now and we can set aside our differences and get on with the business in hand.

Let me say something else about dead Iraqis. They are not nearly so much of a nuisance as dead Paraguayans. Dead Paraguayans are cumbersome, frequently blood-splattered and almost always attract flies. They smell disgusting. Dead Iraqis, on the other hand, are lightweight, portable and, on the whole, easy to manage. At most they give off a light powdery odour, not at all unpleasant, redolent of potting compost in a rose-bordered rural shed.

Of course, I am not pretending that there aren't sometimes difficulties. For example, you can (with much smoke, gasoline and difficulty) burn dead Paraguayans, whereas dead Iraqis are already so scorched and charred there simply isn't any more you can do in that quarter, no matter how great your resolve or your store of boxes of matches and jerrycans of flammable liquid.

It was a bright May morning when my wife Giacinta first came across Iraqi remains in the house. There must have been three or four dead Iraqis involved (it is always hard to be precise where dead Iraqis are concerned, because of the intermingling). They were scattered across the kitchen floor when she went down to make the breakfast. After the trouble we'd previously had with dead Sudanese she said it came as a pleasant surprise to find that all she needed to do was vacuum them away with her portable electronic Dust Devourer (it recharges itself at night and is a real money saver). The handful of coal black specks left smeared on the linoleum she wiped off in a jiffy with a few drops of lemon scented liquid multi-surface cleaner specially formulated to cut through greasy dirt, grime and human remains with the minimum of fuss.

Then there was the time my son Jason came home late one night and found half a dozen dead Iraqis in his room. Not at all perturbed, he called up his friends and invited them round. Soon Mike, Jake, Jute, Ike, Jock, Pete, Jack, Packer, Dibs and Luke were sitting around, drinking beers and poking at the Iraqi remains with my daughter Dune's knitting needles. Dune didn't know, of course. She was in Glasgow attending a conference on Dutch elm disease. After taking turns to taste the ashy remains on the tips of their tongues the boys decided dead Iraqi was best described as "gamey", "smoky" and "piquant". They popped half a cupful in the coffee grinder, then sprinkled the powder on eleven steaming hot bowls of tomato soup. "Hey, Jason, this is brill!" "Not half."

All through the night they played loud music by Iron Maiden and discussed setting up a rock group called The Argonauts. Until dawn they argued about who should learn to play guitar, who should sing, and who should drum, then they all went home to sleep.

Three days later Dune came home. She told us many remarkable things about fungus infections affecting elms. Then she went upstairs and began screaming.

There was a dead Iraqi on her bed!

I say a dead Iraqi, in fact it might have just been the burned remains of a piece of paper blown in through the window from somebody's bonfire. Some dead Iraqis are so insubstantial they are barely identifiable for what they really are. We didn't waste time pondering the matter. Out came our trusty "Dust Devourer" and the mess was quickly disposed of.

There was one occasion I don't think I shall ever forget. It happened one February. I woke up, pulled back the bedroom curtains and discovered a quite astonishing heap of dead Iraqis in our front garden. There were so many that some of them had spilled over the top of the hedge and onto the pavement.

I rang the Town Hall and asked for the Dead Iraqi Disposal Officer. At first the number seemed permanently engaged, and then when I did finally get through I was told by a rather surly woman that Mr Claggart, the Dead Iraqi Disposal Officer, was away on holiday. His assistant, Ms Winter, was off sick. In the end they put me through to Mrs Fish, who wasn't at all helpful. She told me she normally only dealt with dead Peruvians. She wanted to know how many dead Iraqis we had in our garden.

At that point I am sorry to say I became petulant. How was I supposed to know how many dead Iraqis were in my garden? You know how it is with dead Iraqis — they are almost always papery and fused together. It is like someone emptying two hundred packets of crisps in your garden and asking you how many individual crisps there are. There might have been a thousand dead Iraqis, there might have been ten thousand. I told Mrs Fish it was quite ridiculous expecting me to give her a number. Mrs Fish said it was no use me adopting that attitude. She said she had a form to fill in and it was bad enough her having to cross out "Peruvians" and substitute "Iraqis" without additional complications. She said if she didn't fill in one of the boxes then nothing would be done. The boxes started with "Under Ten Dead Peruvians" and went up to "Over Twenty Thousand Dead Peruvians".

I imagined Mrs Fish to be a large buxom woman with hair the colour of dirty straw, who spent a fortnight every summer in a caravan in Cornwall, although as I discovered later she was the spitting image of Marie in *The 120 Days of Sodom,* having almost no hair left, a nose which stood askew, dull rheumy eyes and a mouthful of teeth yellow as sulphur, as well as a buttock devoured by an abscess. She suffered from amblyopia and spent every summer working with clowns and Belgian acrobats in a circus in Dorking. Her husband, Mr Fish, who had formerly worked in the Chief

Executive's Department, had left her when she refused to start wearing wigs and had gone to live in Tunisia, where he was slowly learning off by heart the *Collected Poems of W.B. Yeats*.

"Alright. Say five thousand!" I snapped, although as I hope I have made clear I was not at all confident of the accuracy of this figure. I suppose it was because I am a bit of a stickler for facts and truth that I snapped, and needless to say, having snapped, I became completely paralysed and lay on the floor in two broken pieces, gasping for breath and unable to move, while the shrunken voice of my imagined blonde kept saying, "Hello, are you still there?" for some time, until she at last put the phone down and subjected me to the unending whine of disconnection until that joyous moment when my wife returned from the shops, saw at once what had happened, shrieked, dropped her dozen fresh eggs from Sunny View Farm and ran for the superglue and the string.

They stitched me back together in casualty and my wife drove me home in our Peugeot 605 SVE 24 with its peace-of-mind inducing ultrasonic alarm and optional extra security key pad. I relaxed in the electrically adjustable leather seat, ran my fingers over the Californian walnut double sealed door which had shut with such a deep, satisfying soundproofed thud. I felt the cares of life slip away even though we hadn't even left the hospital car park! I basked in the warmth from my heated seat, wallowed in the warm sunlight and the silent mastery of the electronic climate control system, gazed up at the electronic sunroof, admired what *Autocar and Motor* had authoritatively described as "the comprehensive and clear instrument panel" and took comfort from the knowledge that Peugeot's engineers had built in an automatic electronic ride control which would keep our journey smooth by constantly adjusting the settings of the shock absorbers between hard and soft, based on information received from sensors around the car (each of the shocks, incidentally, contains a tiny electric motor that carries out these adjustments in just a hundred-and-fifty thousandths of a second). It felt good to be in a car which, having spent seven hundred hours in a wind tunnel, had the best drag coefficient in its class. Just for good measure Peugeot had added three silencers to the exhaust and double sealing for any pipes or wires passing from the engine to the cabin.

They'd even mounted the engine on its own hydraulically dampened suspension system!

I was grateful to Peugeot for helping me take my mind off our little front garden difficulty. As I'm sure you'll appreciate, I wasn't going out of my way to be awkward with the Town Hall. A couple of hundred dead Iraqis, say, is no problem for anyone. Because of their crisp, mixed-together papery texture even the elderly and infirm can shovel up dead Iraqis in that sort of quantity. Two hundred dead Iraqis will fit quite nicely into a single black rubbish sack (I know, I've done it). But frankly no one should be expected to deal on their own with five thousand dead Iraqis. For that you definitely need a skip or a light truck. I am sure everyone will agree with me when I say that five thousand dead Iraqis is a problem for the Council, not for the individual. This, surely, is what the Community Charge is all about.

Besides, as I have said, some of the dead Iraqis had spilled on to the pavement. A householder surely cannot be expected to be held responsible for the actions of the wind!

Just at that moment my wife, who had been overtaking a petrol tanker, found herself driving at speed towards a heavy goods vehicle coming right at us. She braked hard but it was too late, and there was a hideous wrenching tearing smashing noise as the juggernaut sent our Peugeot careering off the road and down an embankment.

I regret to say that Giacinta was rather badly decapitated in the accident. I didn't come out of it too well either. I had to spend six months in our local hospital, until it was closed in the latest round of sad but necessary cuts. When the hospital closed one of the consultants was kind enough to put me out into the car park. He even gave me one of his old plastic macs to shelter under.

By this time I had lost my job, but at least my son stood by me. Jason sent a registered letter from Hawaii, where he was working as a chartered accountant. The envelope contained a silver coin and enabled me to pay an enterprising urchin to transport me home from the hospital in his wheelbarrow. Dune, I am sorry to say, had long since severed all connections with her family and had become a revolutionary socialist. She always was a rather shapeless, restless girl. She left on a windy Wednesday, after spray painting REMEMBER THE 26 COMMISSARS OF BAKU across her bedroom wall, as well as on the wall of the local barracks. At present she is living in Croydon and (so I am told) has developed a special interest in Rosa Luxemburg's *Accumulation of Capital.* I last heard from her in October. "Imperialism," she wrote on the back of a postcard of the bones of a Tyrannosaurus, "stabilises capitalism over a long period but threatens to bury humanity under its ruins."

As the boy trundled me up the street in his wheelbarrow three of my stitches burst, and I began to drip blobs of bright red blood. But this was nothing to what I experienced when we finally reached the gate to number 13. I couldn't believe it. I was livid. I bellowed with rage, making the lad with the wheelbarrow jump so much he let go, tipping me out onto the ground.

The dead Iraqis were still in my front garden! The Council had done nothing, nothing at all! I gave the boy his silver tenpenny piece and ran indoors, bandages flapping, leaving behind me a trail of small shreds of flesh. Hungry starlings and sparrows swooped down excitedly; gulls squealed in the sky and wondered whether to join in the feast.

I telephoned the Town Hall and demanded an explanation.

In a tired voice the same surly woman explained what had happened. All the Dead Foreigner Disposal departments had been closed in the last round of cuts. Mr Claggart had obtained new employment as a home practitioner in Babinski's Reflex. Ms Winter, driven mad by autophony, had thrown herself off the Post Office Tower. She did not know what had happened to Mrs Fish.

Many years later I learned from another source that Mrs Fish had gone off to work as a lion tamer with the Lithuanian State Circus, until a mishap off the coast of Newfoundland led to her being swallowed by a whale.

As for the dead Iraqis... In the weeks that followed ceaseless rain reduced many of them to a dark, pulpy sludge, some of which I used to bed down my roses. The rest of the sludge my second wife Lorna placed in a bucket and stirred in butter and sugar. Then she baked the mixture in the oven for thirty minutes at gas Mark 4. The vicar said it tasted delicious and could she do some more for the church fête?

Those dead Iraqis who remained brittle and did not turn into sludge finally vanished from our front garden in various ways. The neighbourhood dogs found many of them reminiscent of bones (or perhaps there actually were traces of bone at the heart of those charred fragments) and helped themselves with a merry wag of their tails. The crispy papery sort were (from a householder's point of view) the best, as they simply blew away on the wind, or crumbled in a matter of days to a fine powder. Jason took a small packet with him back to Hawaii, "as a reminder of home". Of the rest, Lorna mixed an awful lot of them with water, in order not to disappoint the vicar. The five or six hundred or so that remained gradually vanished into the soil, or became hidden by our fine display of privet, violets and primroses. Soon, I am sure, we will all have more or less completely forgotten about that strange time when dead Iraqis seemed to be everywhere. Perhaps, for keen gardeners like myself, a certain darkness in the topsoil will remain, or perhaps a few black specks, stubbornly clinging to the underside of fresh green leaves. But probably not, probably all traces will wash away and vanish utterly. If we do remember them at all (and I cannot see it happening very often, what with inclement weather and then the ensuing fine sunny hot spells as well as the call of garden front and back not to mention the many small time-consuming domestic chores and also not forgetting the broad and varied choice of television that is available nowadays) it will be in small, inconsequential ways — the peppery taste of a bowl of tomato soup, say, or the sight of a dog waving its tail, or even the faint distant reassuring rumble of the refuse lorry as it enters our street, its stout rubber-gloved crew whistling cheerfully as they pick up the heaped black bulging sacks of rubbish and toss them, one after the other, again and again and again, into the dirty grinding jaws of the ceaselessly turning crusher at the back.

10.30am-4.45pm, 3 March 1991

THE HAY WAIN

1

One of those days when everything is pretty as a picture. Noon. The sun is shining, the sky's a blank blue. Just a trace of clouds, motionless, to the south. For some reason (not sure what) everyone has stopped. Everything's at a standstill. An old diseased-looking oak nearby, trunk puckered by boils, branches; leaves motionless.

Frake, wedged deep in the crowd, sees a high, lone swift pinned against the blue. Immobile. Frake wonders again why they have stopped. Frake, Jack Frake. A thin, wiry man of about thirty. Intense blue eyes and the white trace of a scar beneath his chin. Born in Birmingham, made his mark as an actor in Liverpool, his Hamlet astonishing. Hit one day in the street by a cart, bad leg injury, career in decline. Reduced to an attendant in *Antony and Cleopatra,* a harsh sluggish messenger, a servant, a limping Knight in Lear's train. Scene shifter in *Romeo and Juliet,* wheezy lugger of logs in *The Tempest.* Then out. Drifted the city, wrote comic songs, the occasional *jeux d'esprit.* Got by. Drifted south, drifted east. In a blue-lapelled coat a little the worse for wear. Pale waistcoat with two or three grey stains, kerseys, mud-splashed topped boots. And now they're off again, time to put your best foot forward, Jack Frake, and limp on into History.

At the front two rows of six youths, each holding a branch of laurel, followed by the men of several districts in fives. The band, playing on whistles and flutes, a drummer boy, a whiskery grinning toothless old man scraping jauntily his ancient violin. And then the colours, some of silk, gold on a green background: PARLIAMENTS ANNUAL, gold letters on a blue background; LIBERTY AND FRATERNITY, on a tall pole (further indicating the inspiration and influence of the French Revolution); a liberty cap, made out of crimson velvet, braided with the word LIBERTAS and with a sprig of laurel pinned to it. Followed by the remainder of the men of the districts, in fives, from such places as Birch and Bowlee and Back-o'-th'-Brow, Hopwood and Heabers and Blackley, Wood-street, Heywood, Little Park. All labouring men, dressed in a white Sunday's shirt, with a neck cloth, and behind them a column of women and children, who dance to the music of the band, sing popular songs, make merry, and alongside the procession thousands of sympathisers, stragglers, well-wishers, including Frake, Jack Frake, in his stained waistcoat and muddy boots.

At Newtown the Irish weavers pour out of their huts and cheer, some dancing, some weeping, gazing at the great green banner, emblem of home, and the band strikes up "Saint Patrick's Day in the Morning". And so they come to the outskirts of Manchester, passing through the gully of a road below St Michael's, along Blackley Street and Miller's Lane, down Swan Street and Oldham Street, cheered by the townspeople, and in the footsteps of other processions from other parts, the Lees and Saddleworth Union marching with a black flag, on it in white capitals EQUAL REPRESENT-ATION OR DEATH, beneath it LOVE with two hands joined, and a heart, and on to Piccadilly, down Mosley Street, along the left side of St Peter's Church and into Peter Street, to a wide unbuilt space ahead of them occupied by an immense crowd, which cheers and applauds the arrival of yet more demonstrators. And as Frake stands there, amid the crowd, more and more marchers turn up, feeder columns, successive parties arriving, the multitude swelling, swelling astonishingly. No one there's ever seen anything like it, and they stand there, waiting, hearts thumping, talking, laughing, waiting, someone playing on a flute, someone dancing a jig, a man in the crowd saying something (can't hear what) to cheers and applause from those around him, waiting for the speaker, waiting for justice, equality, an end to things as they are and the start of things as they might be. And time goes by with a bright jaunty tick and a crisp merry tock, thirty minutes go by, and there's music, distant music. Music, distant shouts, cheering. It is the arrival of the speaker. Mr Hunt is here! Orator Hunt and his party, approaching from Deansgate, preceded by a band, people waving flags. How many there — eighty thousand? A hundred thousand? Cheering, shouting, clapping, hurrahing. And now here comes the barouche, with a woman in the driving seat. Inside the carriage: Mr Hunt (standing, smiling), Mr Johnson, Mr Moorhouse, Mr Carlile, Mr John Knight, and Mr Saxton, a sub-editor on the *Manchester Observer*. And now a single eighty-thousand-throated shout of welcome, dying away as Hunt mounts the hustings. And now the music ceases as Hunt steps forward, removes his white hat, and addresses the crowd.

Has scarcely begun before Jack Frake hears noises off, and a strange murmur back over by the church. Frake on tiptoe catches a glimpse of cavalry in blue and white uniforms, approaching slowly, swords in hand. "The soldiers are here," someone says. "We must go and see what this means."

Says someone else: "Oh, they are only come to be ready if there should be any disturbance in the meeting." Words hardly out when the cavalry raise their sabres, slacken reins, strike their spurs into their steeds and charge the crowd. "Stand fast!" someone shouts, a cry taken up by others: "Stand fast!" "Stand fast!" "Stand fast!" The cavalry begin to sabre people in the crowd. Swords slash down at hands and arms and heads and faces and shoulders and breasts, slicing through skin and muscle and veins and flesh and skull and bones. Shrieks and screams and cries and groans of agony terror shock anger fear anxiety. "For shame!" "For shame!" and then "Break! Break! They are killing them in front and they cannot get away!" and there's a general cry of "Break!" "Break!" Hunt and his companions disappear off the hustings, and now the Manchester yeomanry join in the attack, frenziedly destroying flags and flag staves, banners, wreathes, then turning to stab and hack at anyone in range, girls, young women, old women, boys, lads, children, who scream for mercy as the swords flash down and split open bodies with a sharp spurting hissing spray of blood. A massacre: the Manchester yeomanry aided and abetted by the 15th Hussars, the Cheshire yeomanry, soldiers of the 88th foot with fixed bayonets at the lower corner of Dickinson Street, four pieces of horse artillery at Deansgate and two hundred special constables. The man holding the green banner staggers as the staff is cut in his hand, next his shoulder is split in two by a saber slash from a member of the Manchester yeomanry. A young woman, her face all bloody, her bonnet hanging by the string, staggers away covered in big purple-brown bruises. A horse sends its forefeet into the head of the big drum and rolls sideways. Frake, frozen, rage in his heart, a quarter inch of air between his soles and the grass. Frake frozen, a lean fiction unharmed by the swish of a sabre passing through his wrist. Frake coming to life, twisting, ducking, running. Frake dodges as the puffy-faced laughing shining-eyed yeomanry ride by, and seizes a broken stave. Jabs it hard in the rump of a galloping mare, which rears, upending its rider. Paunchy red-faced man with silver hair and bulging eyes. Frake darts forward and kicks the man hard in the crotch, sees him curl up in agony, choking and gurgling. An action witnessed by two of the yeomanry, who come at him with their sabres.

And now Frake's running for his life, dodging behind the wreckage of the hustings, jumping over broken and bloody banners, swerving past screaming bleeding figures, running towards the nearest house, swerving away when he sees the special constables by the door, darting towards a dark narrow muddy alleyway and hurling himself down it, hearing the thud-thud-thud of the cantering horses behind, leaving behind a sunlit deserted space littered with a crushed-flat, muddied, bloodied cap of liberty, and numerous other trampled caps, broken bonnets and crumpled hats, bloodied shawls, scores of shoes, scraps of torn bloodstained clothing, a dead body here and there, a mound of corpses over in the direction of the church, another heap by the new houses with the closed curtains and blinds, and nearby a man of about forty flat on his back and still alive, hands pressed upon a great bubbling gash across his stomach, not far from a lifeless girl with staring glassy eyes, flies flickering here and there in the sultry motionless air as the yeomanry dismount, wiping their sabres in the grass, easing their horses' girths, adjusting their accoutrements, a sunlit space where the only sound to be heard is the low murmur of the dying, the occasional snorting and pawing of restless horses, and the excited buzzing of flies. Frake runs like a madman into King Street and on into Market Street, not slackening his pace until he reaches High Street. Here he brushes back his dishevelled hair, unpins the sprig of laurel from his lapel and walks on in a slow, casual manner, as far as the hill at Collyhurst. Here, hiding in some trees, he narrowly escapes capture by a group of the Manchester yeomanry, who are combing the suburbs to capture stragglers, and who are looking in particular for Jack Frake, whose description has been circulated, whose name is not yet known.

At a nearby cottage he buys old clothing and returns to the clump of trees to set his actor's talents to work. Half an hour later a tall, pale, feeble old man with a handkerchief tied over his mouth and dressed in an old fashioned long-waisted surtout with broad metal buttons hobbles with his stick slowly back to Manchester. There, everything seems to be in a state of confusion: the streets patrolled by troops, police and special constables, the shops closed and silent, the warehouses shut up and padlocked, the Exchange deserted, the artillery on alert, and thousands of pikemen reported to be converging on the city from Oldham and Middleton and elsewhere. And next day, among the other notices, a charge concocted by the yeomanry in revenge for their colleague's badly bruised scrotum, WANTED FOR HIGH TREASON, JACK FRAKE, sometime ACTOR of LIVERPOOL. It's time for Frake to be on the road and he heads east. A month later he's in Norwich, three days later at Ipswich. A tavern keeper at Trimley St Mary reports him as a suspicious personage, and the constabulary come for him at nightfall. Three of them, big sullen heavy men with paunches. THUMP-THUMP-THUMP on his door at nine. "Open the door!" No answer. "We'll not say it again!" No answer. They kick the door down and rush in, truncheons held high. Too late. Frake's gone. He's half a mile away, running, by dawn a far black blob shrinking into the far grey misty fields. The constables depart. They'll be back tomorrow with the dogs. It's their country. They'll flush him out. As Frake well knows, the tension in his throat tightening, a hammer thudding pain behind his temple, things — poverty, hunger, fear, illness, the cold, age, the forces of the State — closing in on him, while dark birds pass overhead in silent flocks, and unseen creatures scurry and slither in the dark under-growth, Frake kneeling to claw at the hard soil, unearthing a turnip, squatting in the dew-soaked grass and gnawing at the tough white flesh, feeling sick and sick at heart and hideously alone, out-cast, a poor solitary wretch, a stranger in a mist-covered land of fences, ditches, far farms and barking dogs, shivering and sobbing in the chill dawn, under a blank colourless sky, then getting slowly to his feet, groaning at the aches and spasms of fire in his bad leg, going on across ditch and narrow stream, by hedgerow and winding path, across fields and water meadows, until, close to collapse, he sees the house.

A white house, deep in mist. Tall redbrick chimneys and a red slate roof. Filling out with colour as a blood-orange sun rises from the far flat horizon like an eye, the lurid unreal eye of a man who has been beaten, a man coming to in an empty space, raising his head, looking at the world with the one eye that opens, the other bruised and tightly closed, seeing a dreamy tranquil valley of romantic mists and motionless objects, a tree, a cloud, a ditch, a fence. And now it's an aerostat, a dreamer's device, a wild experiment rising across the sluggish villages, wiping away the dullness, putting a golden sheen on dirty cottage walls and stagnant ponds, heading for the stars, losing itself in the sky, becoming what it always was, the familiar sun, shining down on Frake as he crawls on hands and knees through the undergrowth, making his way round to the back of the house, the mist all gone now, discovering to his surprise there's a river there, cattle up to their knees, and in the distance a ferryman punting someone across the water, and a strange dull thumping which matches the tired beat of his heart. Sees an open door and crawls inside. Cool and dark in there. Cool and dark as the — Quick! Someone's coming. A maid. Bustles past, clanking some tin jugs. Didn't see him, crouched behind that high-backed chair. He slips through the deserted parlour, snatching a bread roll and an apple from the big table cluttered with tongs, saucers, spoons, cheeses, pans, a bowl of fruit, knives, and hurries breathless up a narrow twisty stairwell. Upstairs there's a short corridor, on one side a neat bare whitewashed bedroom, on the other a dark box room full of dusty old furniture, abandoned packing cases, a small table covered with boxes of apples wrapped in paper, miscellaneous junk draped with cobwebs barely visible in the opaque grey light leaking in from the tiny grubby window. Frake shuts the door behind him, makes a space on the floor, and lies down. Devours the roll and apple, throws the core under a nearby chest of drawers, then pulls a length of old frayed carpet over himself and goes to sleep. He wakes five hours later to the sound of housemartins chattering outside the window and a dull bronze glow over everything from the noonday sun. Goes to the window. Sees, over on the far bank, a man in his early forties, sat on a folding chair, reading a book. No, not reading a book. Holding a sketch pad and pen. Making two or three strokes, then pausing to look across the river. Looking right at Jack Frake. He seems to be drawing the big white house Frake's hiding in. A comfortable looking well-off sort of man. Distracted, suddenly, by a figure approaching along the riverbank, calling out to him. An officer of the law, carrying a truncheon. Asking him something. The man with the sketch pad shakes his head. Asking him something else. The man says something, can't hear what. Points in the other direction. The officer walks away. The man with the sketch pad fidgets with his neckscarf, brushes some imaginary crumbs from his blue expensive jacket. Waves away a wasp, continues sketching. Apparently drawing the big white house Frake's hiding in. Frake wonders what to do next. Stay in the house, in hiding? Doesn't look like anyone ever uses the boxroom. Or make a break for it? Too dangerous, in broad daylight. Almost noon, blue sky, bright sun, a few clouds. Scrap of pale windblown moon. Best to wait for dusk, keep to the hedgerows and the dark. Then, out of the blue, he hears the dogs. Frake glances wildly back out of the window. The cattle are gone, the ferryman's gone. The man with his sketch pad has folded up his little stool and is walking away along the riverbank path. He's bent forward, holding up his trousers, the sketch pad half-slipping from beneath his arm as he tries to keep the turn-ups out of the mud. Undisturbed by the sound which rivets Frake's gaze to the yard, the ferocious barking, brutes on leashes, brutes with studded collars, straining, slavering excitedly, towing behind them as they burst from around the back of the house half a dozen grim, burly constables. As they move towards the doorway below the artist on the far bank disappears from view. Now all Frake can see is the ferryman, back where he was before, punting across a bowed labourer who holds a scythe. The river is grey and empty and empty and grey there's still that strange dull thumping in the distance, merged with the hollow reverberating chimes of a nearby church ringing noon, chime after chime and the strange dull thumping, the batterings of heart and pulse, the unbearable close howling of maddened animals, chimes, the grunts and curses of the heavy constables.

2

Noon, and one of those days when everything is pretty as a picture. Sun shining, sky a blank blue. Just a trace of clouds, motionless, to the north. For some reason everyone has stopped. The people in wheelchairs wait patiently, the dancers pause. Everything's at a standstill. Time to look around. Robinson, wedged deep in the crowd, sees a high, lone swift pinned against the blue. Immobile. To one side a glassy tower, some trees undisturbed by any breeze. On the other the river. And nothing's happening, nothing at all. Why? And in the emptiness, the waiting, Frake's born. In Robinson's imagination. Frake. Jack Frake, let's call him that. Dressed in the clothes of a hundred-and-seventy years ago. And what would that be? A Tolstoy smock? No sooner born than ebbed away. A thing of scraps and patches, a paper creature. Paper Jack. The banners sway and they move off and Jack Frake fades. Along the embankment, passing the Rodin. Now they're coming to the Palace of Westminster, soon they'll be turning left up Whitehall to the square. The chanting's beginning now, NO POLL TAX! NO POLL TAX!

An old story, a long story. *Lords of manor as wel men of Holy Church as other make complaint that the villeins on their estates affirm them to be quit and utterly discharged of all manner of serfage due as well of their body as of their tenures and will not suffer any distress or other injustice to be made upon them and gather themselves together in great routs and agree by such confederacy that everyone shal aid other to resist the lords with strong hand and much other harm they do in sundry manner to the great damage of their said lords and evil example to others to begin such riots so that if due remedy be not the rather provided upon the same rebels greater mischief which God and BBC and ITN News forbid may thereof spring through the realm.*

And now we arrive at Old Palace Yard, now we come to the first of the statues and monuments to England's proud and noble history. First, children, there's war criminal, anti-Semite, mass murderer and religious bigot, Richard-the-raddled-with-clap-Lion-Heart, raising his sword above the Japanese cars in the House of Lords car park. A little further on, Oliver Cromwell, genocidal butcher of Irish folk and bloody liquidator of the Levellers. Across the road, hunched on his pedestal in Parliament Square, the gross, blister-faced figure of Sir Winston Twister Dardanelles-Disaster dulled-by-brandy dago-hating Edythe-Baker-in-the-hay-rolling Churchill ("*Edythe was hated by the Churchill family. But she was a great comfort to Winston*"), fan of Franco and Stalin, applauder of Mussolini's "victorious struggle against the bestial appetites and passions of Leninism", hater of Trotsky and Gandhi, acrobatic leaper from anti-Semitism to fanatical Zionism, admirer of that "indomitable champion" Adolf Hitler (*Evening Standard*, September 17, 1937), his language at times curiously like Hitler's, describing Soviet Russia as *poisoned, infected, plague-bearing* ... and referring to *swarms of typhus-bearing vermin* ... *political doctrines which destroy the health and even the soul of nations* (1929). A helicopter chattering overhead, and men on the high buildings, dark figures with zoom lenses, video cameras, telescopic sights, binoculars.

And of this opinion was a foolish priest in the county of Kent called John Ball who would say thus: What have we deserved that we should be kept thus enslaved? What reasons can they give to show that they are greater lords than we, save by making us toil and labour so that they can spend? They are clothed in velvet and soft leather furred with ermine while we wear coarse cloth; they have their wines, spices and good bread while we have the drawings of the chaff, and drink water. They have handsome houses and manors, and we the pain and travail, the rain and wind, in the fields. And it is from our labour that they get the means to maintain their estates. Thus John Ball said on Sundays when the people issued out of the churches in the villages, for which many of the common people loved him, and such as intended no good said how he told the truth. And so they would murmur to each other in the fields and in the roadways, as they came together, affirming the truth that John Ball spoke.

Drums and tins banging, chanting, NO POLL TAX! Up

Whitehall to the Cenotaph, lump of concrete TO OUR GLORIOUS DEAD, beyond it the shrunken figure of Sir Walter Raleigh, the political prisoner, the man who first brought lung cancer to England (*Go tell the court and Thatcher...*). Not forgetting bloody Haig, Earl Haig, half-witted, inept, blood-drenched Haig, emerging on his horse from the top of an escalator, still dreaming of forcing a gap in the Hun's lines and sending the cavalry on to the gates of Berlin... The paranoid imperial gates and high wrought iron fence unlawfully placed across the entrance to Downing Street, in a style curiously reminiscent of the Romanov dynasty...

Jakke Trueman doth you to understand that falseness and guile have reigned too long and truth hath been set under a lock and falseness reigneth in every flock. No man may come to truth but he sing si dedero. *Speak, spend and speed, quoth Jon of Bathon, and therefore sin fareth as wilde floode, true love is away, that was so, and clergy for wealth worche hem woe. God do bote, for now is time. So these unhappy men of London began to rebel and assembled together. And the commons of Kent came to Rochester and there met a great number of the commons of Essex and those who came from Maidstone took their way with the rest of the commons through the countryside. And there they made chief over them Wat Teghler of Maidstone, to maintain them and be their councillor.*

Everywhere the rows of mounted police, ominously still and waiting, waiting, waiting; the police crammed into the side-street military-green coaches, hunched over their *Suns* and *Stars*; the police lined up and watching with overtime eyes, dead eyes, hostile eyes. *PO-LICE. COP-LIE.* A push, a shove. Sudden shrieks; turbulence. What's going on? What's that? A small sit-down. At the entrance to Downing Street. A baton charge — Some sort of trouble and — Everyone running this way and that, chaos. Enter the short-shield cowboys. A wave of grim constables, truncheons arcing, battering, a responding rain of cans, the sticks off banners. A flag from the

Cenotaph is burned, the crowds swaying, shifting, lines of police move across both ends of Whitehall, trapping the marchers, diverting the others. Mounted police pour out of a side street half-way down Whitehall and charge at the marchers. Smashing glass. A woman sobbing on the kerb, uncontrolled, sobbing helplessly, another woman reaches down, comforts her. *If we look back to the riots and tumults, which at various times have happened in England, we shall find, that they did not proceed from the want of a government, but that government was itself the generating cause* (Tom Paine). The mounted police ride at the crowd, driving people back, back to where the skips are in the M.O.D. yard. The Union Jack is hauled down from the M.O.D. building, torn to shreds, cheers. Masonry is removed from the skip, broken into pieces, the windows of the M.O.D. building start to tinkle and smash. Chaos, confusion, shrieks, cries, sirens, yells, NO POLL TAX!

Frake, Jack Frake. And behind that white house where he hides? The parasites. Namely: 2,880 persons comprising the Royal Family, the Lords Spiritual and Temporal, the Great Officers of State, and all above the rank of Baronet, with their families, closely followed by 234,305 Baronets, Knights, Country Gentlemen and others having large incomes, supported ideologically by the toadies, the arselickers, the opportunists and creeps, to wit: 61,000 Dignified Clergy, Persons holding considerable employments in the State, elevated situations in the Law, eminent Practitioners in Physic, considerable Merchants and a rabble of Manufacturers upon a large scale, and Bankers of the first order, with their families. After which the Thatcherites of the era, the proto-fascists, the only-too-happy-to-assist-in-the-running-of nuclear power stations, guided missile systems, concentration camps, you name it, namely: Respectable Clergymen, Practitioners in Law and Physic, Teachers of Youth of the superior order, respectable Freeholders, Ship Owners, Merchants and Manufacturers of the second class, Warehousemen and Respectable Shopkeepers, Respectable

Builders, scum like that, with their families, some 1,168,250 personages, give or take the odd sudden unexpected death from swilling too much port and the roast beef of old England. All bearing down like a ton of bricks on 1,279,923 menial servants, 8,792,800 Artisans, Agricultural Labourers, Working Mechanics and others who subsist by their labour in various employments, with their families, and underneath them, down there under the scowl of the fat, red-cheeked magistrates, out there in the fields, resisting the currents of the age, the Paupers and their families, Vagrants, Gypsies, Rogues, Vagabonds and idle and disorderly persons, supported by criminal delinquency, some 1,828,170 shocking and disgraceful persons. Not overlooking, of course, the forces of the State, an entity best perceived through the cool lucidity of Lenin's mind, remembering V.I.'s pungent, timely and unsurpassed definition of the State as a power which arose from society but places itself above it and alienates itself more and more from it and whose power consists *of special bodies of armed men having prisons, etc.* (ah, the big etcetera!), *at their command* which at this moment in time, children, amounted to the officers and non-commissioned officers of the Army, Navy and Marines, some 931,000 men, ready to order their subordinates to shoot, stab and imprison anyone who dared to upset the apple cart or the hay wain. Or to put it another way, to beat, maim, imprison or kill anyone who dared get in the way of the 47,437 families who comprised the British royalty, nobility and gentry, and whose income, though themselves being utterly unproductive, amounted to £58,923,590 per annum, at a time when the pound was worth a hell of a sight more than it is today. A time, children (1816-1822), of severe economic distress and hardship (you know who to) following the end of the war with France, e.g. end of 1816 a mass meeting at Spa Fields in London turned into a riot, the following month an attempt made on the life of the Prince Regent.

Trafalgar Square in chaos, hand-to-hand fighting outside St Martin's in the Fields, blue boiler suits in V-shaped wedges throwing themselves at the crowd, blue boiler suits crouched behind circular polycarbonate short shields 514mm in diameter, blue boiler suits hitting out with their truncheons, grabbing individuals at random, retreating. *It is considered an advantage to have the word "POLICE" on each shield as this may have an inhibiting effect on rioters.* Sticks and rocks raining down on the white South African Embassy, thick black smoke pluming upward, some Portakabins on Grand Buildings ablaze, NO POLL TAX! Bolts, fire extinguishers, rubbish, rains down on the boiler suits.

Therefore the king returned towards London as fast as he could, and came to the Tower at the hour of Tierce. And before the hour of Vespers the commons of Kent came, to the number of 60,000 (a figure disputed by the Metropolitan Police, who say that barely 8,000 troublemakers were involved), to Southwark, where was the Marshalsea. And they broke and threw down all the houses in the Marshalsea and took out of prison all the prisoners who were imprisoned for debt or felony and they levelled to the ground a fine house belonging to John Imworth, then Marshal of the Marshalsea of the King's Bench and warden of the prisoners of the said place and all the dwellings of the jurors and questmongers belonging to the Marshalsea during that night. At the same time the commons of Essex came to Lambeth near London, a manor of the Archbishop of Canterbury, and entered into the buildings and destroyed many of the goods of the said Archbishop and burnt all the books of register and rules of remembrances belonging to the Chancellor, which they found there. And the commons of Southwark rose with them. And at this time the commons took their way through the middle of London and did no harm or damage till they came to Fleet Street, where the men of Kent broke open the prisons of the Fleet, and turned out all the prisoners, and let them go whither they would.

The window of the Army Careers shop is smashed, fragments of Jack Frake reflect from splintered glassy fragments. Someone hurls a rock at the Midland Bank, some people are pushing a crash barrier through a window in the Embassy. A police line forms across St Martin's Lane, preventing people from leaving the Square. Covent Garden, the West End. A TransAm car turned upside down like a beetle, amid tipped-over dustbins. Windows of the Hippodrome smashed. A showroom of expensive cars trashed, a stamp shop window broken, stamps pouring out into the street, escaping like butterflies... A barricade of burning sports cars. Cecil Gees stripped bare, clothes strewn along the gutter, sunglasses, porcelain ducks... Stragglers arrested, manacled so tightly hands turn blue, hurled into vans, eee-aaaaw, eee-aaaaw, away, gone.

Of a sudden four white police vans come speeding down the Strand and someone is hit, a body flies through the air and lands in a heap on the side of the road. A woman, furious, bangs angrily on the driver's window, spits on it, drags her hands through her hair. Two vans reverse away at high speed, two vans are surrounded, metal barriers are being pushed under the wheels, a torrent of bricks slam down on the mesh-protected windows, snatch squads come running to the rescue, blue helmets, round shields, truncheons slamming down on anyone not in uniform... Mounted police gallop in front of the Embassy, a woman is knocked to the ground and falls under the horses, astonishingly she's not killed. Mounted police charge a crowd of onlookers standing at the entrance to the Mall. Chaos, confusion, windows breaking along The Haymarket, Regent Street, Portland Place, Cambridge Circus, Charing Cross Road, Covent Garden. St Martin's Lane, Long Acre, Tottenham Court Road, Oxford Street... A strange assembly of — Flash cars catch fire, sirens, fire tenders, hoses, police running here and there, Alice in Wonderland smoothing her long hair, screaming NO POLL TAX! NO POLL TAX! A burnt out Porsche.

And then they went to the Temple, to destroy the tenants of the said Temple, and they cast the houses to the ground and threw off all the tiles. They went into the Temple church and took all the books and rolls and remembrances, that lay in the cupboards in the Temple, which belonged to the lawyers, and they carried them into the highway and burnt them there. And even the most aged and infirm of the lawyers scrambled off, with the agility of rats or evil spirits. And then they went toward the Savoy, and set fire to divers houses of divers unpopular persons on the Western side: and at last they came to the Savoy, and broke open the gates, and entered into the place and came to the wardrobe. And they took all the torches they could find, and lighted them, and burnt all the sheets and coverlets and beds and headboards of great worth, for their whole value was estimated at 1000 marks. And all the napery and other things that they could discover they carried to the hall and set on fire with their torches. And they burnt the hall, and the chambers, and all the buildings within the gates of the said palace or manor.

And in the Square, outside the National Gallery, a chair appears. A four-legged wooden chair with a back formed out of a single semi-circle of wood. The chair, tipped back, is suspended in the air, about ten feet from the ground. A dozen horsemen are grouped nearby, heads turned, staring through their visors at the chair. The chair has flown here from Borley Rectory, flown here at immense speed to linger amid the confusion. The spirit of carnival surges down the wide streets, the Lords of Misrule are cackling and shrieking, the World's Turned Upside Down: the Metropolitan Police are perplexed, enraged, terrified. The chair is tilted, as if about to launch itself into battle. The chair bides its time, enjoying every moment. Soon the chair will fly away; soon it will all be over, soon this will be yesterday's news, a tiny footnote in history. The historians will get to work with their Tipp-Ex and the chair will vanish as if it had never existed. Take a long look at the chair: appreciate the symmetries. No painter is on hand to register the Gallery's Hiroshima dome, the blackness of the chair's frame against the grey colonnade, the circle of bright light on the seat of the chair, the dark inhuman blobs of the helmeted heads of the mounted police. No surrealist is present to celebrate the strange conjunction of domestic chair and dark horsemen, dream-like dome and set of traffic lights. End the freeze-frame: let it roll on, let the chair go hurtling towards the horsemen and crash against the flanks of a horse. The snatch squads jerk into animated motion and grope their way towards the onlookers, rubbish showers down on the bodies of armed men, Robinson swerves and sprints along the edges of the crowd, aware of the snatch squad doggedly in pursuit.

1819 Peterloo. In the words of George Carter, M.A., *Outlines of English History: Facts, Dates, Events, People*, late Headmaster of New College School, Oxford, "in the terrible charge of the soldiers several persons were crushed to death attempting to apprehend a popular agitator known as Orator Hunt". A lie, a distortion worthy of BBC and ITN News.

1819 Peterloo. An event preceded by Memorable Events.

1812 The first steam vessel, the *Comet,* plied on the Clyde.

1813 Westminster Bridge was first lighted with gas.

29 July 1818, James Norris, J.P., to Viscount Sidmouth: "I am very sorry to inform your Lordship that from all I can learn, Messrs Drummond, Bagguley, Ogden, Knight, and in short, all the men who disturbed the public peace last year, have been most active for several months past in disseminating amongst the lower orders at meetings convened for the purpose in the different lesser towns in the neighbourhood the most poisonous and alarming sentiments with respect to government of the country, and have continually inculcated the idea of a general rising, and I am disposed to think that this idea gains ground and that in consequence the working classes have become not only more pertinaceous but more insolent in their demands and demeanour..."

Respectable Manchester was frightened when the Blanketeers met, and laughed them to scorn when they were dispersed. No wonder at the laughter! What could be more absurd? And yet, when we call to mind the THING then on the throne; the THING that gave £180 for an evening coat, and incurred enormous debts, while his people were perishing; the THING that drank and lied and whored — when we think that the THING was a monarch, on which side does the absurdity really lie?

Swann's Way. Joseph Swann, a radical hatter from Macclesfield, up before the bench for selling illegal, unstamped radical newspapers:

BENCH: What have you to say in your defence?

DEFENDANT: Well sir, I have been out of employment for some time; neither can I obtain work; my family are all starving. I sell the newspapers for another reason, the weightiest of all; I sell them for the good of my fellow countrymen; to let them see how they are misrepresented in Parliament. I wish to let the people know how they are humbugged.

BENCH; Hold your tongue a moment.

DEFENDANT: I shall not! for I wish every man to read those publications.

BENCH: You are very insolent, therefore you are committed to three months' imprisonment in Knutsford House of Correction, to hard labour.

DEFENDANT: I've nothing to thank you for; and whenever I come out I'll hawk them again. And mind you, the first that I hawk shall be to your house.

Swann hustled out, out of the court, out of history, out of human memory, almost, but not quite, not quite...

Chaos, screams, sirens, crashings, NO POLL TAX! NO POLL TAX! Trafalgar Square. Police on horseback charging the crowd like Cossacks, odd flashes of Eisenstein flickering in Robinson's mind. Robinson retreats, finds himself in a throng, looks up at the noble statue of King George IV, royally dressed in a rich white crust of pigeon shit, in the corner of Trafalgar Square. Rocks, bottles, scaffolding poles fly down on the far side, a shower of placards, sticks, *the rabble and dregs of the people, and the devil's agents on earth*

The Hay Wain

— *the agitators* (John Constable, R.A.).

MEMO: *Find out more about Constable and Sir Robert Peel.*

St Peter's Field was obliterated from existence (as even now, children, they are physically destroying the field of Naseby). St Peter's Field was obliterated from existence, yes. The bourgeoisie tore up the grass, bricked over the bloodstains, built the Manchester Free Trade Hall there. "Unctuous Free Traders" Marx called them; 1846 "the introduction of the free trade millennium". Free Trade! *Free trade has exhausted its resources: even Manchester doubts this its* quondam *economic gospel,* laconically observed Engels in the Preface to the first English edition of *Capital,* 5th November (!) 1886. Free trade, which as Marx caustically noted meant trade with adulterated goods (6 kinds of adulteration of sugar, 9 of olive oil, 10 of butter, 12 of salt, 19 of milk, 20 of bread, 28 of chocolate, 32 of coffee etc.). The bourgeoisie built the Free Trade Hall, years later a grudging plaque. THE SITE OF ST PETER'S FIELD WHERE HENRY HUNT, RADICAL ORATOR, ADDRESSED AN ASSEMBLY OF ABOUT 60,000 PEOPLE. THEIR SUBSEQUENT DISPERSAL BY THE MILITARY IS REMEMBERED AS "PETERLOO". Beautifully vague, hey? Nothing about the eleven murdered demonstrators, or the four hundred slashed and mutilated by sabres.

In the nineteenth century Ford Madox Brown was commissioned to paint a series of murals on the history of Manchester: he was forbidden to include Peterloo.

Crushed caps on the road, police caps, a red wreath, score upon score of discarded NO POLL TAX placards. The ashen, burnt-out Portakabins, smouldering... And over there, the National Gallery. You'll be safe there, Robinson. Culture will protect you. All those paintings will cushion you from what's happening outside. Robinson runs up the steps, one-two-three-four-five-six-seven-eight-nine-ten-eleven-twelve steps, pushes past the tourists, pushes through the revolving door, the pursuing police reflected in the glass like in an old jittery silent movie, his breath coming slowly, gulping like he was drowning, into the hallway. Ahead: two flights of steps, which he takes three at a time, then a tiled floor, COMPASSION beneath his feet, DEFIANCE, a fat man in a tin hat looking like Winston Churchill (it *is* Winston Churchill!), and on, into the shop, pushing his way up the central aisle, pushing past people buying art books and cards and the German language guide to the Gallery, and behind him the snatch squad, six of them, heads down, moving like rugby players.

And later, at Smithfield, the king sent the Mayor of London, William Walworth, to ask the common people to send their leader to him, whereupon Wat Tyler came forward and took King Richard by the hand and shook him warmly by the arm and said: "Brother, be of good comfort and joyful, for you shall have, in the fortnight that is to come, praise from the commons even more than you have had yet, and we shall be good companions." And the king asked what the common people wanted, and Tyler explained that there should be equality among all people save only the king and that the goods of Holy Church should be divided among the people of the parish and that there should be only one bishop in England and only one prelate and all the lands and tenements now held by them should be confiscated and divided among the commons and that there should be no more villeins in England, and no serfdom or villeinage, but that all men should be free and of one condition. To this the king gave an easy answer and said that he should have all that he could fairly grant. And then Tyler was attacked by Walworth, who slashed him with a cutlass, and one of the king's household, who sneaked up behind him and ran a sword through his body three times, and the king rode out to the commons, commanding that they should all come to him at Clerkenwell Fields.

Ahead: some sort of exhibition, two mute uniformed attendants with fish mouths, staring at him, and staring beyond him, about to say something, wondering whether to intervene, as Robinson rushes past them and darts off to the left, into a side gallery, in his mind the dim memory of a North Entrance and a possible way out. Ahead: Titian's *The Death of Actaean,* though, turning left past it, all Robinson is aware of is a woman in dark, ripped clothes with an exposed breast and some sort of disturbance in the background, a red pain moving through his lungs as the yellow splash of Van Gogh's Sunflowers blazes by and slips from view, and directly ahead of him the washed-out blue of Seurat's Bathers, reminding him of the long time ago when he visited the Gallery with Martina and they stood before it with crackling pounding hearts in the high noon of their love, at the height of summer, that incandescent summer of the drought, which ended when she went back to her own planet, and he walked all the way to The Flask, saying much as now "Heugh, Heugh, Heugh" like an old winded broken horse, and just as he got to the cinema in Golder's Green where later he went alone to see *The Omen* the first few pattering drops of rain, metallic, a little unreal, like he was walking through the last lines of *The Waste Land* or some such, a poem which seemed to hang over them as they trudged here and there from airport to station, from hotel to hotel, from bed to bed, from park to park, exploring the green spaces, travelling to and fro on the Circle Line, the Northern Line, drifting through the City, into the Whispering Gallery, into St Magnus Martyr, a needle-sharp remote silvery memory quit at the sudden sight of a da Vinci, and there in the corner, hemmed in by an El Greco and a Rembrandt, much bigger than he'd imagined after seeing it all those times on biscuit tins and trays and calendars and hanging on the lounge wall of remote dusty relatives along with the Reader's Digest Condensed Novels and the 22" TV and the hideous china country maids and cherry-cheeked grinning shepherds, *The Hay Wain* by John Constable, R.A.

And while King Richard was soft-soaping the crowd (whose heads at this juncture in History were alas stuffed with oppressive iron rubbish about the divinity of kings),

Walworth, the Mayor of London, sped back to the City and commanded those who were in charge of the twenty-four wards to make proclamation round their wards, that every man should arm himself as quickly as he could and come to the king in St John's Fields. And when the king had reached the open fields he made the commons array themselves on the west side. And presently the aldermen came to him in a body, bringing with them their wardens, and the wards arrayed in bands (remember what Lenin said about the State, children), a fine company of well armed folks in great strength. And they enveloped the commons like sheep within a pen, a technique used by the forces of the British ruling class on numerous occasions since, e.g. Peterloo, Red Lion Square, Southall, Orgreave, Wapping, or for that matter Whitehall on March 31st 1990. *But this time it isn't working, the crowd's not running, it's all gone haywire.*

HAY, *n.* grass cut and dried for fodder. HAYWIRE (colloq.) tangled, in disorder, distracted [f. use of hay-baling wire in makeshift repairs]. WAIN, *n.* wane, a wagon; a carriage for the transport of goods on wheels.

The Hay Wain by John Constable, R.A., enormous after all those flat lustreless reproductions. Begins at knee height, rises up a couple of metres high, three wide, within a heavy fussy cumbersome Victorian gilded frame. *Suffolk was in many respects the most highly organised of English farming areas and* — And in 1822 Constable wrote: "My brother is uncomfortable about the state of things in Suffolk. They are as bad as Ireland — *never a night without seeing fires near or at a distance.*" The farm labourers setting fire to the HAYRICKS and HAYSTACKS and — The room's a dead end, no galleries off it, nowhere else to run, you're trapped. Stand there, Robinson. Don't panic. The room's deserted, the attendant's seat is empty. Don't panic. Pretend to be just another tourist taking a keen interest in our cultural heritage, ignore the tramp-tramp-tramp of your heart, which might be the nearing ominous clatter and thump of heavy police boots. Robinson glances at the green rope supported by a row of brass poles on circular stands which keep the art lover a discreet distance from the rugged surface of each masterpiece, preventing accidental scratchings and scrapings of the unique surface. Robinson steps across to glance at the white card pinned to the wall — *"The Hay Wain, therefore, represents a link between the idealism of Claude and Poussin, and the future empirical vision of the Impressionists"* — then moves to the left to stand, time spinning dizzily, before the very heart of the great canvas. *Tramp-tramp-tramp* goes the army marching past outside, Goodbye Leicester Square, and now he notices what he has never noticed before on biscuit tins or calendars or plastic trays or on the wall of his aunt's flat in Bradford, those tiny figures bending in the field beyond —

And after Walworth had set the wardens of the City on their way to the king, he returned with a company of lances to Smithfield, to finish off with his thugs the wounded Wat Tyler. But Tyler was not there. And it was told him that he had been carried by some of the commons to the hospital for poor folks by St Bartholomew's, and was put to bed in the chamber of the master of the hospital. And Walworth went thither and found him, and in the best traditions of the Israeli Gestapo occupation forces had the wounded man carried out to the middle of Smithfield, in presence of his fellows, and there beheaded. And thus ended Wat Tyler's wretched life, a man you'll never find pictured on British commemorative stamps.

The Hay Wain by John Constable, R.A. Dog, fisherman. Red vase in the window of the house. Tranquillity. A painting like *Top Gun,* all gloss, myth, fantasy. The judicious placement of flagpole or cart, runway or field, sunset or cloud, labourers or carrier in the Indian Ocean, until the two blur, and now that speck's a MIG fighter, behind the house lurks a blonde in leather, all sunlight and honey, in which there's no place for agricultural depression, recession, squalor, poverty, the all-night wage slave, the women in the electronics factories of Korea, the tortured of Palestine, the black children with puffy bellies and skull faces and big teardrop eyes, the masses blotted out by the sugar of individual destiny...

Then Walworth had Wat Tyler's head set on a pole and borne before him to King Richard, who thanked Walworth greatly for what he had done. And when the king saw the head he was, like the man in *Bring Me the Head of Alfredo Garcia*, delighted, and he had it brought near him to abash the commons. And when the commons saw that their chieftain was dead in such a manner, they fell to the ground for mercy for their misdeeds, poignantly demonstrating the dangers of personality cults and the underlying need for an organised revolutionary party ready and willing to meet a murderous ruling class on its own terms. *Then the king ordered Walworth to put a helmet on his head because of what was to happen, and the Mayor asked for what reason he was to do so, and the king told him that he was much obliged to him, and that for this he was to receive the order of knighthood. And Walworth made a great show of modesty saying that he was but a merchant and already fully occupied by trade and profiteering and exploitation of the masses, but finally the king made him put on the helmet, and took a sword in both his hands and dubbed him knight with great good will. And the king gave Sir William Walworth £100 in land, for him and his heirs. And in due course a great road was named after him, which is there to this day (Walworth Road, London SE17), and because Walworth sums up everything which it stands for — the market economy, double-dealing, toadying to the royal family, betrayal of working-class interests, opposition to anti-poll-tax campaigns, slavish obedience to the law, and unstinting support for the violence of the ruling class — the Labour Party has based its headquarters there, children, at number one hundred and fifty.*

Clatter of heavy boots and they're there, in the room, the snatch squad, grunting like hogs, and one cries, "That's him, Sarge!" and they come at him, six of them, truncheons drawn, rage on their faces, the same faces that you saw at Cable Street, the same faces Orwell saw at Olympia, the same faces you saw at Red Lion Square and Southall and Lewisham, the same faces you saw attacking the crowd outside Grunwicks, the same faces you saw at Orgreave, constable country, faces that don't alter when Robinson folds his arms and says quietly, "There's no need for — ", a sentence, a life sentence, a foolish sentence coming from someone who has heard of the 26 Commissars of Baku and who ought to know better, a sentence that goes unfinished as the first truncheon smashes him on the left shoulder, sending a wave of pain through his body, a sentence that never will be finished as blow after blow rains down on him, the faces unchanging, the faces that hate these red bastard troublemakers, the faces that don't half have a larf as on the morning of the demo they're told that the loony left are going to be out in force and the day promises to be a tasty one, right tasty, the twisted, sweating faces that bob behind a shower of blows, a shower of blows that send Robinson spinning, that drive him down, that knock him to his knees, a shower that doesn't stop, a shower battering his shoulders, thumping his ribs, winding him, bruising his thighs, bruising his back, toppling him over that green rope, and the Sergeant's thump to his temple, the thump that sends a spurt of splintered bone and blood showering over the officers' overalls and over their blue helmets and spurting in a bright unreal slash across *The Hay Wain* by John Constable, R.A., closely followed by the soft hollow slippery brown noise of Robinson's body slumping against the painting, Robinson's split head smearing down the canvas, obliterating the two men and the wagon in a crude ketchup splash.

And afterwards, of course, came the bloody repression of the masses. The king sent out his messengers into divers parts to capture the malefactors and put them to death. And many were taken and hanged at London, and many gallows were set up around the City of London, and in other cities and boroughs of the south country. And some the king granted pardon, on condition that they should never rise again, under pain of losing life or members, and that each should get his charter of pardon, and pay the king as fee for his Seal twenty shillings, to make the blood-drenched little creep even richer than he already was. And after the end of the rising, a deputation from the people of Essex appealed to the King for justice and freedom and the relief of the poor. But the King repudiated his Seal, saying: Oh miserable men, hateful both to land and sea, unworthy even to live, you ask to be put on an equality with your lords! Serfs you were and serfs you are; you shall remain in bondage, not such as you have hitherto been subject to, but incomparably viler. For so long as we live and rule by God's grace over this kingdom we shall use our sense, our strength and our property so to teach you, that your slavery may be an example to posterity, and that those who live now and hereafter, who may be like you, may always have before their eyes and as it were in a glass, your misery and reasons for cursing you, and the fear of doing things like those which you have done.

Blood dripping from the gilded frame, puddle of slippery blood on the shining polished floor, and now Robinson is dying, dying unexpectedly on a Saturday afternoon in London, and his head flops and dying he has a sudden vision of the system in which he's enmeshed, in which they're all enmeshed, struggling muddily, half-blinded by blood and television and the dense laminated pages of the history books and —

And John Ball among the fifteen hundred people from various counties executed for their part in the rising. John Ball arrested at Coventry, taken to St Albans, and there, in the great tradition of English civilisation, hanged, drawn and quartered.

Robinson gazing up at "The Hay Wain", seeing for the first time a ghost in the murky water, seeing the small dark cracks like a falling net across that oh-so-innocent Suffolk sky, seeing what looks like a patch of rhubarb in the bottom left corner, seeing the red vase wobble like the amoeba under the microscope twenty years ago at school, the red vase now a red blob swelling, a drifting red balloon, a scarlet salty tongue and a thick sludgy voice calling, calling. *Christ, Sarge, you've killed the bastard*, the Sergeant undoing the straps of his helmet, taking off his black leather gloves, wiping his hands on his overalls, mopping his face, says *Fucking shut up, Briggs. Keep fucking calm. He was resisting arrest, right? Right mates?* (Right, Sarge.) *He was struggling violently, right? We used minimum force, right?* (Right, Sarge.) *Don't piss yourself and we'll see this thing through together, right mates?* (Right, Sarge.) *Everyone'll be on our side, remember that. The Commissioner. The Federation. The papers. And if it fucking comes down to it, the Coroner. Now fucking go and call for an ambulance.* (Right, Sarge.)

And there were numerous others, whose names mean nothing nowadays, men like John Shirle, of the county of Nottingham, who was taken *because it was found that he was a vagabond in divers counties the whole time of the disturbance, insurrection and tumult, carrying lies and worthless talk from district to district, whereby the peace of the lord the King could be speedily broken and the people disquieted and disturbed; and among other dangerous words, to wit, he said in a tavern in Bridge Street, Cambridge, where many were assembled to listen to his news and worthless talk: That the stewards of the lord the King, the justices and many other ministers of the King were more worthy to be drawn and hanged, and to suffer other lawful pains and torments than John Ball, chaplain. For he said that he was condemned to death falsely, unjustly and for envy, by the said ministers with the King's assent, because he was a true and good man, prophesying things useful to the commons of the realm and telling of wrongs and oppressions done to the people by the King and the ministers aforesaid. Which sayings redound to the prejudice of the crown of the lord the King. Therefore by the discretion of the said assigns he was hanged.*

Christ, Sarge, the picture's messed! Don't fucking panic! It's not fucking important! But Sarge, it's famous! It must be worth a packet! My sodding sister-in-law has it on the wall over her telly! Red, spreading. Reminds Robinson of the start of Roeg's *Don't Look Now,* the slow dreadful ooze, the sinister music, the prickling sense of doom and then — The deep, rich colours ebb. The room expands. Immense and grey as a mausoleum, and cold, cold as a mausoleum, and Robinson, dying, sees stone and bones and structures, things stripped bare, a vision (he drunkenly felt) a little like (don't be bloody ridiculous) Marx's, that cold pauper's winter of 1857, the winter of the seven workbooks, *Grundrisse der Kritik der Politischen Ökonomie,* "the antithesis to political economy — namely socialism and communism — finds its theoretical pre-supposition in the works of classical economy itself". Sketch of a sketch for six massive studies of CAPITAL, LANDED PROPERTY, WAGE LABOUR, THE STATE, INTERNATIONAL TRADE, THE WORLD MARKET, the skin of things stripped away, burrowing into value, money, credit, capital in general, sorting through capitalism's gubbish, *dissolution of communal property without* [Here the manuscript breaks off], vampire capitalism feeding on blood and young bodies, a dead thing, a husk, something like the personnel manager in *Martian Time-Slip,* or shall we say a hideous machine, a machine that has taken over, like — like that vast slow block-like unstoppable probe in *Star Trek IV: The Voyage Home,* bringing destruction to the planet, but not to be stopped by a couple of whales, surging over Stalin, getting him (state capitalism!) to do its bloody bidding, until no further use, then Gorbachev-Yeltsin-whoever, unending, yet not, finally, unstoppable, the final choice socialism or barbarism, the Culture or utter emptiness, choked canals, broken machines, mass graves, camps, a landscape of desolation, a Martian landscape of death in which, as the day wanes, wraith-like, Robinson glimpsed the Home Secretary, whose name he could not remember, a yellow eyed, sallow-pink, plump, shifty, curiously flaccid man, looking as if even *he* didn't quite believe the tide of half truths and oily insincere regrets oozing from his slug lips, and contriving to blame the Labour Party for the disgraceful scenes in Whitehall, which made Hatmadder very cross indeed, so that his seventeen chins wobbled uncontrollably, and denials slipped from those sherry-flushed wool-padded cheeks, Blabberhat was he called? Whatever he was called (and the names were crumbling, now; the buildings were beginning to crack and collapse; *Earthquake* was replaying inside Robinson's head) he wanted listeners to know that the Labour Party utterly condemned the violence and backed the police two hundred percent, Tweedledee adding *I hope there have been a substantial number of arrests, I hope the people responsible for the violence will be convicted and awarded very severe sentences,* a message reiterated by Nellcock himself on the next day's news, Tweedledum Nellcock, statesmanlike, grave, full of gubbish and gas, not to mention the Commissioner's spokesman and the oily-tongued man from the Police Federation. The police investigation of the police the usual monstrous farrago of corruption and lies, moustaches shaved off, beards grown. The inquest held in the dark cramped rotting dilapidated Coroner's Court before the Coroner, Dr Arnold Rupert Adolf Tory-Bigot, who would refuse to call a jury until forced to do so by a successful legal appeal, the jury then being selected from an appropriately white upper-middle-class *Times* and *Telegraph* area of London, the jurors not chosen at random but selected by the Coroner's Officer who is — Catch 22! — a policeman, and whose directions to the jury would be biased, rambling, repetitious, confusing and confused, and who would put it to the jury that Robinson had perhaps *deliberately* cracked his head against the painting, the fracture being caused not (as everyone had assumed) by a police truncheon at all but by *the frame of the painting,* Robinson's motive possibly being a wanton and who knows even *anarchistic* desire both to discredit the police *and* to besmirch the one real masterpiece of English art. Robinson foresees it all, his eyes rolling, his eyes wandering about, his tongue stuck up, extremely dazed, unable to speak now, vague, confused, the Suffolk mist closing in, rubbing his head, the pain getting more severe, laid on the stretcher and rushed out of that place, the ambulance siren wailing, the surgical registrar running down the corridor, Robinson's pulse dropping rapidly, Robinson thrashing about, Robinson's left pupil dilated and unreactive, unconscious now, slipping from the grip of the police, running with Frake out of that white house, plunging with Frake into the brown calm river, holding his breath for half an hour just to fool 'em, surfacing underneath the hay wagon, hearing the thick Suffolk accents of the men on the wagon, hearing they've caught Frake, hearing the dogs, the bellows of the thick-necked red-faced bushy-moustachio'd constables, sinking back under the surface, sinking into the mud, worming his way into the mud, holding his breath spectacularly, watching from the back of the crowd as Frake is hanged by the neck until dead, deep now in the cold cold mud, respiration slowing alarmingly, bubbles and froth, blurry and frosty and smeary and salty and dizzy, taken straight to the operating theatre with symptoms indicating rapidly developing brain pressure, a large extra-dural haematoma on the left side caused by a blow which has fractured the skull, his condition deteriorating during the operation, dying at midnight precisely, buried in a grave which no one now visits, his sister dead in a car crash in Africa, his parents dead of grief, his friends drifted off into other lives, and Robinson (he sees it all, dying he sees everything) remembered now only in passing after other riots, other deaths, in revolutionary newspapers.

Reader, the police were completely exonerated. Sergeant Bull has just been promoted to Detective Inspector. The Coroner's jury's verdict was Death by Misadventure. And as everyone agrees, the restorers did an absolutely first class job on the painting, with not a trace of bone fragment or blood left visible. Our art critics are unanimous in their verdict that, since its restoration, "The Hay Wain" has an altogether startling new freshness and clarity. This assessment, together with the unfortunate Robinson episode (now thankfully behind us) has made "The Hay Wain" even more of a crowd-puller than before. Indeed, as someone remarked only the other day in *The Times,* though a cruel and ghastly accident, the Robinson incident was, taking the longer view, and from the perspective of art and aesthetics (not to mention Constable's reputation), the best thing that could possibly have happened.

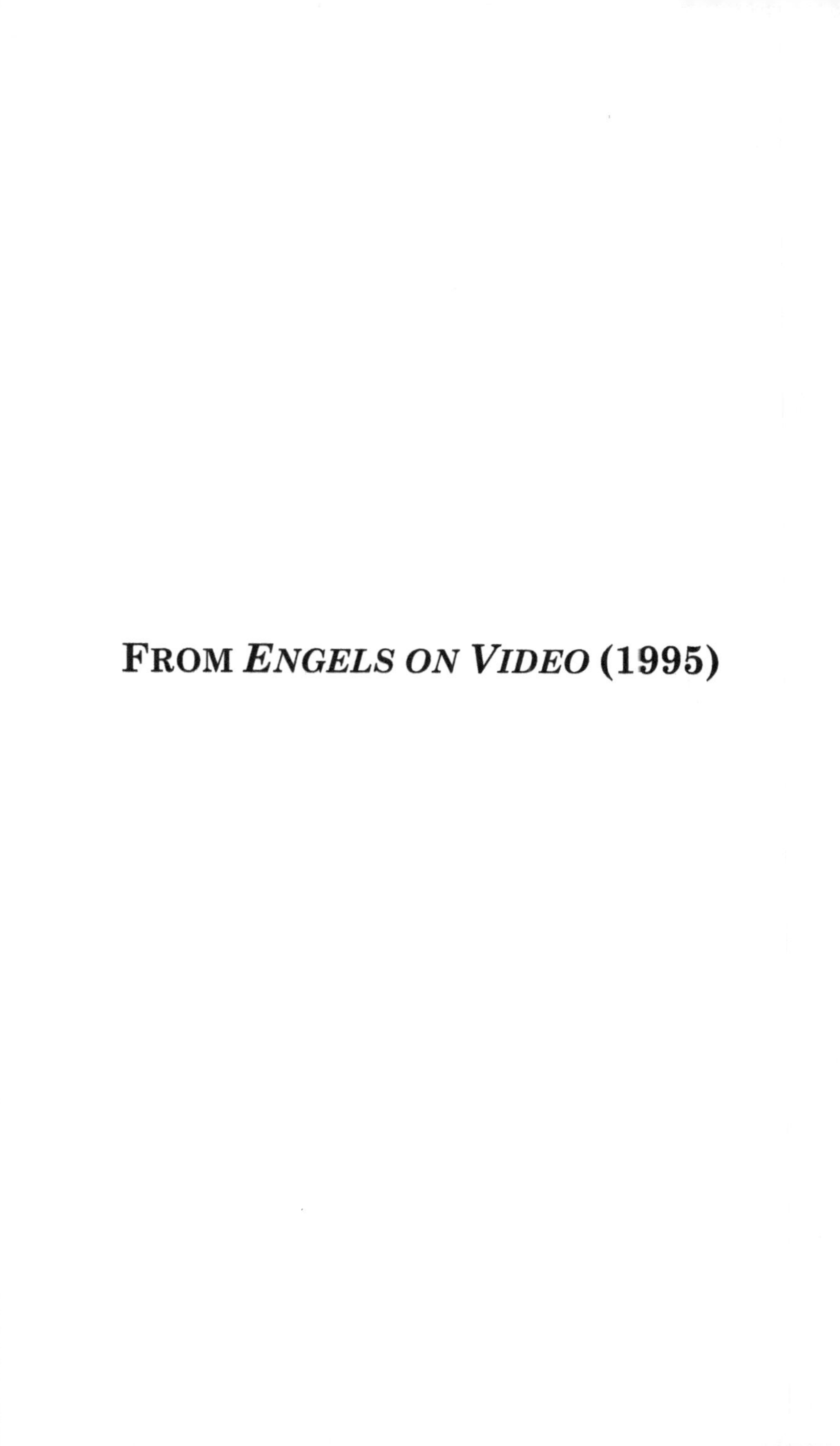

FROM *ENGELS ON VIDEO* (1995)

An Interview with Nietzsche's Moustache

1: *They arrived at Nietzsche's moustache much later than planned*

They arrived at Nietzsche's moustache much later than planned. This was because of a number of unexpected hold ups (a hold up, a landslip of decayed mayors, a dangerous precedent, some disturbing statistics, a demonstration against Dostoyevsky's poetics, a second hold up, a second demonstration [this one against Dostoyevsky's politics], a cascade of toads across Carshalton, a shower of worms on Ilkley Moor, an Act of God, an Act of Parliament, an indecent act, an act of folly, an acclaimed actor, a protest march by redundant cosmologists, a deranged telephone caller with no axes to grind, a third hold up, an unknown creature five metres long — Bulb said eight — which both agreed was somewhat reminiscent of a diplodocus and which had straddled the narrow highland road with a lamb in its mouth then plunged off into the peat-black loch with a massive splash which left ripples pulsing across the mirrored surface for a good hour, a bad hour involving wheelnuts and a foot pump, a fallen tree blasted by lightning caused by a bad-tempered drunken Viking god committing vandalism with a sledgehammer somewhere above cloud level, a smash and grab, snippets of information wantonly discarded by a realist novelist, a memorial procession for the 26 Commissars of Baku, a lorry which had shed its load of Conservative Party slogans [flimsy royal blue sheets twisting and dancing in the gusts and rising up into the sky so that if you looked up the entire firmament seem to shine with PROFITS BEFORE PEOPLE! and GREED BEFORE NEED!], a kiss-and-tell saleswoman pursued by royal photographers and two eminent professors of venereology, a bouncy castle, a bolt from the blue, a burst sewer, plus paramedics attending to a cabinet minister whose penis had been inadvertently severed by a whore with lockjaw).

The colossal philosopher loomed above them.

"I hear he's a super man," Bulb remarked, as they parked by the NO SMOKING sign.

She climbed out of the car. "What a gorgeous sunset," she said with a tiny cry of pleasure which almost required an exclamation mark.

She was twenty-six and had grown up in Felixstowe. She was used to seeing bloody Conservatives. The snows were early that year.

Bulb pointed.

"Reminds me of the sky in *La Pointe de la Galère*. By Henri Edmond Cross. Do you remember the day we went to see it? It was the day you taught me that 'subingression' meant 'a hidden entrance'. The day you first told me you loved me. I have never forgotten how lights BURNED RED in the cottages and SLEEPY VOICES could be heard beyond the gates, and the LOUD SINGING of skylarks and the SOUGHING of the WIND."

Bodrum shook his HEAD.

"Pity. If you did I think you, too, would be surprised by the way the luminous, layered gingery tints of Nietzsche's moustache strongly call to mind Cross's painting."

Bodrum grunted. He was concentrating on the task in hand. "Pass me that mattock and the wrenching iron."

"Sure thing."

A moist breeze. Ropes. Effort.

An hour went by, dragging a sheet of dusk behind it. Just when Bulb was beginning to get very tired of sitting beside him, and of having nothing to do —

"Got it!"

The subingression — located at last!

The difficult first paragraph was way behind them now and they began to relax. Looking back, they could see evening's shadows lengthening over the heap of decayed mayors. The Conservative slogans had been picked up by a portly little man — at first Bulb mistook him for the bouncy castle — who looked very pleased with himself as he painted red roses on them; he seemed dimly familiar, but no matter how hard she tried she couldn't remember his name. The bouncy castle was not far away. It was being deflated by clowns and put in the back of a decrepit truck.

They went on, and the first paragraph vanished from sight.

"Look! The rumours aren't true!"

"I never believed that they were."

Soon they were moving through dense undergrowth. At times they could hear behind them what sounded like the metallic rasping of a scythe. Bodrum explained it was probably only caused by rust but Bulb wasn't convinced. Nietzsche's moustache was surprisingly foliaceous; fetid, even, in parts. Thick bushes alive with muffled, indistinct murmurs were entwined with mute bindweed. The ground was not as malacodermous as they had anticipated; on the contrary it had a cratered, musty-dusty lunar roughness. The lunar analogy was underscored by a faint aroma of cheese, not at all unpleasant (and not one of your bland village post office cheeses either, but a classy one such as emmenthal or gruyère, the very thing for knocking up a bubbly delicious Fondue de Berne, say), not to mention the torn, rain-soaked H. G. Wells paperback lying beside the path, puffed up by wetness, reminding Bodrum of his great discovery that any paperback immersed in a bucket of water doubles its bulk within twenty-four hours, a boon in his student days when his bookshelf supported but four anorexic volumes: Ellis Sharp's *A Haunted House*, Jim Thompson's *The Future of an Illusion*, Virginia Woolf's *A Hell of a Woman* and Sigmund Freud's *The Aleppo Button*.

Bodrum slashed energetically with his machete.

Slash! Slash! Slash!

2: *At first he felt as jaunty and buoyant as Fats Wallers' "The Minor Drag"*

At first he felt as jaunty and buoyant as Fats Wallers' "The

Minor Drag", recorded three months before publication of *Our Exagmination round his Factification for Incamination of Work in Progress,* with Fats on piano, Eddie Condon on banjo, Charles Gaines playing trumpet, Charlie Irvis trombone, and Arville Harris clarinet, alto and tenor saxophone.

Bodrum sweated copiously. He could feel BLISTERS beginning to form on his PALM and FINGERS and wondered why *machete* had displaced *matchet* in everyday speech. The Fats feeling ebbed. He felt a pang of melancholy, thinking of the dictionaries of the future and of how *matchbox* and *matchless* would, one day, conforming precisely to recumbent fold theory, close up the gap and snap together with a sharp metallic click and *matchet* would vanish as if it had never existed, like the Euston Arch or St Peter's Field, Manchester, or the old chestnut tree smashed down on Tuesday 7th December 1993 at George Green, Wanstead, something which would no doubt give ideas to *maceration* and *machiavellian,* two of the vilest words in the language, a perfect pair for Parliament or the Regional Crime Squad, one soft and smooth and affable, the other a sharp-eyed crafty brute, so that between them, if *machete* wasn't careful, it would be breaking down and admitting everything, and would be led before the jury cowed and sullen, and be seen to be guilty as soon as you clapped eyes on it, a brown-skinned word if ever there was one, a foreign troublemaker coming over here to consort with decent Anglo-Saxon verbs and put native nouns out of work, and sending *axe* and *cutlass* into a dreadful panic, so much so that, to be blunt, they completely lost their edge with their wives, not to mention all the anxiety and heavy drinking and lack of sleep, so that the verdict would not be in doubt, especially with the Prime Minister and the Prince of Wales both making lots of speeches about the population's perfectly natural fear of being swamped by alien expressions (not least all the trouble caused by hoity-toity intellectuals with rhombicosido-decahedrons, airy-fairy architects with elliptical paraboloids,

university lecturers irresponsibly promoting lexical ex-
hibitionism and metalepsis, and, last but not least, Marxist
troublemakers clouding the minds of decent young people
with talk of commodity fetishism, the valorisation of capital,
reification, revisionism and that most revolting of all words,
which, as the P.M. pointed out at a very well received speech
given at the Lord Mayor's Banquet, he could not bring
himself to utter in front of civilised people, but which it was
high time to recapture for *the circular motion of a body on its
axis* and to get rid of that other sense, which he had no
intention of mentioning and which the only sense that
mattered — *common sense* — PROLONGED APPLAUSE —
abhorred), so that it seemed likely that not only would
machete be disposed of but *macaroni* and *macaroon* would be
eliminated too, making BODRUM realise how important it
was, once the interview was completed, to get back to Little
Gidding and lay in sufficient stocks of all three from the local
hypermarket.

"Wait for me!" Bulb shouted, scrambling along the trail of
felled and tangled hairs. "I don't want to get lost."

Bodrum paused, sat down on a stump, mopped his brow
and examined his crop of blisters.

"Melancholy again?" she enquired tenderly, catching him
up.

Bodrum nodded. "A touch of flatuous melancholy, I think.
That which the Arabs call myrachial. Diocles supposed the
ground of this sort of melancholy to proceed from
inflammation of the pylorus, though other experts assign the
mesenterium distempered by heat or the stopping of
haemorrhoids, the inevitable consequence of bad diet, care,
griefs, discontents or some sudden commotion or perturbation of the mind. Randolotius drank the decoction of
wormwood and was freed, but unfortunately I left ours
behind in the medicine cabinet. Not to worry. I'll hum the
Phrygian cadence from the slow movement of Bach's fourth
Brandenburg concerto. That always perks me up."

He began HUMMING. After a little while he picked up the

machete and continued hacking a path through the dense hair.

"Are you *sure* Nietzsche won't mind?" asked Bulb, a little anxiously. And what if Nietzsche ITCHED? Overgrown fingernails RAMPAGED in her mind, thrashing about, engaging in wild, orgiastic bouts of SCRATCHING. What if there was a forest fire? What if nineteenth-century moustaches fell from fashion? They might find themselves suddenly smothered in choking scented foam, with a razor coming at them like the plane in *North by Northwest*! And that wasn't all that was bothering her. Bodrum's quick swinging motions reminded her of that long ago drizzly day Dick Bodzon had baled his punt on Coniston, kneeling on the thwart and shifting every minute or two to get his weight on the other knee, all the while maintaining a steady scooping, oblivious to the drops of sweat which clung to his spectacles, dim already with the light, feathery rain, until, finally, the *Georg Friedrich Wilhelm Hegel* was as dry as he could get it without a sponge and he had worked the bottomboards back into place and stood on them, wondering whether to hoist sail, and had seen the sun come out over the coppice, where the going was every bit as tough as inside Nietzsche's moustache, and without another word (for Dick had never been much of a one for words) had clipped the halliard to the strop on the yard, hoisted away and, as the red sail went up, was suddenly drenched with the water that had collected in its folds.

"Fuck, shit and piss!" Dick had cried, and somehow she had not been at all surprised when Dick had gone off to the University of Nottingham to write a doctoral thesis on "Blood Knowledge in The Later Novels of D. H. Lawrence", the glittering academic career which had then seemed to lie ahead of him tragically terminated by streptococcal septicaemia, caught from a splinter of infected wood on a lavatory seat vacated only thirty seconds earlier by a young woman who, having aborted her foetus and flushed it away, was naturally anxious not to be late for the term's first lecture on

An Interview with Nietzsche's Moustache

Mrs Gaskell, none of which Dick could possibly have foreseen on that grey, wet day he had stood watching water trickling from his trousers and along the boom, and who had then irritably given up, lowered the sail and bundled it loosely along the gaff. Dick had got nowhere with her, unlike Ben, whose name was greasy with intimacy and who, just six weeks later on the river at Richmond, had slipped his oily fingers into the elastic of her pants, yanking them down in the narrow canoe and, while she lay under Ben Bulben, who was big as the rumours had said, her knees raised and something wet and hard sticking into her bottom, had loudly grunted and gasped above her in the manly, energetic style he'd acquired from the movies of Richard Gere.

"Nietzsche won't mind a bit," said Bodrum, a little tersely. He glanced at the MAP. They pushed on in the amber twilight, passing the carcass of a singular looking land animal with four very short legs, the feet armed with long claws of a brilliant scarlet and resembling coral in substance and the body covered with a straight silky hair, perfectly white.

"What's that?" cried Bulb, pointing at something ahead of them. It looked like a stagnant pond.

It *was* a stagnant pond.

It was an attractive emerald green rimmed with a mauve froth. Bulb couldn't help thinking of Rothko but decided to keep mum.

Picking up a stick Bodrum prodded the pond's thick scum. It had a treacly quality. Bodrum half-expected the stick to fly from his hand, devoured by the jaws of a terrifying monster. But nothing happened. He threw the stick away and, kneeling, dipped a finger in.

Relief flooded his face. "It's okay," he said, his voice still a little trembly. "It's only soup. Pea soup, by the taste. I was forgetting that we should have expected this. Remember what that mountain guide in Zem am Ziller told us? *Nietzsche is a very messy eater.* Well, he would be, when you think about it, wouldn't he? A moustache this size."

"Awesome ... The grandeur of it. I'm reminded of — I'm reminded of — ". But she couldn't at that moment remember what Nietzsche's moustache reminded her of. It was something immense, she knew that. Something she had seen in the Nile valley? The lush jungles of Peru? Dusty Rome? A sun-sodden Greek island? It was no use. Her mind was a warehouse of gigantic memories but each one was draped in cold blue plastic sheeting.

Bodrum held out a palmful of cold soup. "Try some."

"Not in a million years!" (Like Chekhov, Bulb was fond of grand statements.)

They skirted the pond and walked on. The minutes passed.

"Look! The rumours *were* true!"

"How disgusting. Of course I can't say I'm surprised."

Big hairs loomed all around them, tall, strong, indifferent in the immense solidity of their life, which endures for ages, to that short and fleeting life of the two intruding bipeds who crept among their shadows in search of an interview.

Once Bulb thought she heard a white rabbit but an hour later she decided she'd been mistaken.

"Watch out!" Bodrum shouted. He seized Bulb roughly by the arm and dragged her clear.

"Crumbs," he explained, pointing. "Deadly as quicksand. Once in..." He dragged a finger across his throat and winked. "Remember what Alphonse said? You know, that old codger we met in Chamonix?"

Remember Alphonse? How could she forget him! A grizzled, elderly man, dressed all in pink, with an ultramarine cravat around his neck and so miserably lean that he looked as if he had not got an ounce of flesh on his bones. His face was as sharp as a machete, and the skin of it was as yellow and dry and withered as an octogenarian's scrotum. His eyes, of a metallic grey, had a very disconcerting trick, when they encountered your eyes, of looking at you as if you might conceivably own, and be willing to lend, a copy of Rockenbach's *De cometis tractates novus methodicus*, published in Wittenberg in 1602, whose author, knowledgeable in Greek, mathematics, philosophy and law, wrote his book using old sources which he did not name, asserting that in the time of King Typhon of Egypt a comet appeared, fiery, of irregular circular form, with a wrapped head, in the shape of a globe, and of terrible aspect, clearly the same comet mentioned by Lydus, Servius (who quotes Avienus), Hephaestion and Junctinus, who depicted it as an immense globe (*globus immodicus*) of fire, also as a sickle, a short-handled semicircular-bladed implement used for lopping and trimming which, combined with an instrument for driving nails etc., with a hard solid head at right angles to the handle, appeared on the national flag of the U.S.S.R., symbolising a peasant and a worker.

Forget Alphonse? — impossible! He might have been a progressive parson or a gay police sergeant on holiday or an astronomer with a fondness for stuffing peaches down his stockings or an alcoholic loss adjuster or a fat potter from Potto or a noxious aromatherapist or a qualified wind-surfer — or anything else you like, except what he really was. But though she remembered Alphonse as if it was only yesterday, she couldn't for the life of her remember a thing he'd said!

She shook her head and heard a slight jangle of jewellery. Her old shrapnel wound was playing tricks again. She shivered and adjusted her bra fastening.

From the innocent looking drift of crumbs she averted her gaze. The drift was only four or five metres wide and looked innocuous as a split bag of sand. But Nietzsche's fondness for toast was no JOKE. The crumbs were hard and sharp as uncut diamonds. One careless step and the next thing you knew you'd be up to your waist, sinking slowly, while ten thousand tiny fragments of razor-sharp bread raked your skin to shreds. Suffocation, in such circumstances, was a blessed relief.

"Wait for me!" she SOBBED, as Bodrum HURRIED ON ahead of her, still SLASHING ENERGETICALLY with THE MACHETE.

3: *"This is horrible!" yelped Bulb*

"This is horrible!" yelped Bulb, of a sudden, gripping Bodrum so hard that he gasped. Her face was pale as oatmeal.

"Ssssssss!" she hissed, the memory of snake scenes in Indiana Jones movies merging effortlessly with that of the afternoon she and Potato Jones (no relation) had paid twenty francs to enter a marquee on the quayside at Paimpol (a port associated with the novelist Pierre Loti, a friend of Proust, though exactly what the association was she'd forgotten, her recollection of the town's Rue Pierre Loti wrapped in an obscuring sea-blue summer haze which had yet to reach as far as the page on which Henry James had copied a paragraph of Loti's, passing it on to Edmund Gosse and urging him to read it aloud, remarking "perhaps you will find in it something of the same strange eloquence and rhythm as I do: which is what literature gives when it is most exquisite and which constitutes its sovereign value and its resistance to devouring time"), in order to see the reptile exhibition, which, apart from one or two catatonic lizards and bored-looking frogs, had largely turned out to feature rows of glass fish-tanks capped with unnervingly flimsy-looking chicken wire, each tank containing knots of black, writhing, angry-sounding snakes except for the one at the end, where an immense solitary python — or was it a boa? — eyed them malignly, swaying and pumping itself up with a fury of atomic intensity. *"Look!"*

Ahead of them a row of strange, distorted figures stretched into the distance, writhing helplessly amid iron coils of hair.

Bodrum pulled her back. "Don't go near them!" he cried. He glanced at the map, and said in a whisper, "The Avenue of Grotesques. We've strayed from our path. We need to turn sharp left."

"But — ".

"Best not to look at them, poor wretches."

"But who *are* they?"

Bodrum sighed. He pulled out his telescope. Bulb saw his hand tremble.

"Not a pretty sight. They're all feeble-minded and in the grip of terrible contradictions. Just look at those knots they're twisted into! There's no hope at all, I'm afraid. Once one of those loops has got them, that's it. The ones who aren't suffering from xerophthalmia are sure to have pernicious anaemia or degeneration of the spine. Many suffer from all three." Bodrum adjusted the telescope. "The ones nearest to us are a very average bunch. I can make out a Canadian Progressive Conservative. Next to her there's a Mexican — a member of the Institutionalised Revolutionary Party. Then an American disciple of the Austrian fictionist, Sigmoid Fraud. Then a Frenchman — a follower of Baudrillard." He gazed in fascination at the crows pecking at the spicy sawdust spilling from perforated skulls. "Poor wretches."

He passed Bulb the telescope. She shuddered, and handed it quickly back. The bodies along the Avenue were twisted into almost unimaginable contortions. Most were bent forward like hunchbacks, and the heads of many had grown forward, pushing through the stomach and emerging from the back. Their spines were broken or bent or completely circular. Wrists sprouted from kneecaps. Octopus eyes stared dully from swollen buttocks. Anuses were the size of mouths, and mumbled long strings of gibberish. Bodrum slowly scanned the Avenue until a spasm shock his arm. With a yelp of horror he dropped the telescope.

"What is it?"

"Are you sure you really want to know?"

Grimly, Bulb nodded.

"A Trades Union Congress General Secretary. From England. The worst case of *Bureaucraticus bursitis* I've ever seen. The fellow has become almost completely transformed into a sort of fish. Covered in whale blubber — but not a whale. More like a sea slug. Slimy and slit-eyed and smells like an eel. He's saying something. Listen." It was true. A gigantic pig-coloured anus opened and closed to an irregular rhythm. Sometimes it released a low, grumbling fart, sometimes it abruptly erupted with a spurt of greyish muck, but most of the time a low, monotonous babble hummed from it, clearly audible across the forest clearing. *Noddercolonoffpod, noddercolonoffpod, noddercolonoffpod*, was it saying?

Bodrum remembered. Years ago, now, it seemed. Even then the man had seemed so grossly fat and so unable to speak words capable of forming a simple coherent sentence as to resemble a flabby alien experiencing difficulties as, tentatively, in fits and starts, it dipped its appendages experimentally into the language.

Remembering, Bodrum suddenly realised what the creature was trying to say. A look of unspeakable pain was on its face, and re-focusing the telescope he saw that one of the iron bars had cut so deep into the flab that the creature had been almost split in two. Small dark birds were feasting on the dull brown scabs or sipping from the dribbles of sperm-grey slime. But instead of crying "Help!" or "Please release me!" the slug continued to mutter its old refrain, *Need a cooling-off period, need a cooling-off period, need a cooling-off period.*

Bodrum sighed. Zoologists had long ago proved that since the creature had never experienced a temperature higher than ten below zero, the very last thing it required was cooling down. But despite the best efforts of science, nothing had changed. The miserable wretch had continued crawling around on its stomach, bellowing that it was on fire, that there was nothing that could be done, that the mountain could never be climbed, that everyone should go home. When prodded with a stick it licked toes, slithered after scraps of faecal matter, and sporadically burst into shrill song. Somehow Bodrum was not really surprised to learn that the creature had found itself hopelessly enmeshed in Nietzsche's moustache.

"Let's go," said Bulb. "I can't bear it here. The smell ... I feel like I'm going to puke."

An Interview with Nietzsche's Moustache

Bodrum slipped the telescope into his pocket and hurried
her away.

4: *Bulb looked at her watch*

Bulb looked at her watch and saw that it had stopped. She
shivered. "I'm cold," she said. "I want to go back."
  "Back where?"
  "To the car."
  "But we're almost there! Besides, it will be night soon.
There'll just be time to set up the tent, ask the moustache
one or two questions, and have some supper."
  "I hate it here. It's nothing like what I imagined.'
  "But gentlemen in England now abed will be livid they
weren't here. It's the adventure of a lifetime! Just imagine
how impressed people at parties will be when you nod and
smile and say, *yes, I have travelled throughout the entire
extent of Nietzsche's moustache, I have taken my meals in
each of its corners, my pride, my torment, my joy.*"
  Bulb pouted.
  "It's just one vast mass of hair. It's boring."
  "What on earth did you expect? Sandy beaches?"
  "I don't know. But something more than just hair. It's...
oppressive. If I've learned anything from Nietzsche's
moustache it's the tremendous fact of our isolation, of the
loneliness impenetrable and transparent, elusive and
everlasting, of the indestructible loneliness that surrounds,
envelops, clothes every human soul from the cradle to the
grave, and, perhaps, beyond."
  "I know the feeling but you must realise it's not the
moustache's fault. It's just a *mood*. A rainy day can have the
same effect. You get the blues. You experience droopiness,
enervation, dejection, spleen and world-weariness. Then
before you know it, you're humming a Phrygian cadence or
there's another translation of *Der Prozess* or a new Pet Shop
Boys album and reality takes on a different coloration —

indanthrene blues mingling with cadmium yellows, sending the burnt umber and the greys packing. Fancy a chocolate biscuit? You know how important this interview is to me. It's something I've wanted to do all my life. Don't you understand? The onus is on me."

"The what?"

"The onus."

Bulb gave him a strange look. "The *what?*"

"The onus," he muttered. His voice had trailed away, lost confidence in itself, become a parched broken whisper, a thin grey spectre without a compass, struggling across a vast waterless plain entirely lacking in elderly dromedaries with the eyes of conundrum-chewing philosophers or cheerful Arabs with silver thermoses of chilled water and potted meats and stocks of antiseptic ointment and fly spray, or even mountains, let alone those comforting mock-Victorian signs you found in town centres, exquisite curly ironwork redolent of an era when gunboats patrolled scorching coastlines and lumpy continents and ragged islands around the globe were soaked in blood-red, signs bearing the legend THIS WAY TO HERITAGE CENTRE or TO PUBLIC LAVATORY. He felt his body temperature drop, as someone brusquely pushed him inside a refrigeration unit. Cadavers rolled past him in a blur, swathes of meat coated in lard, ribs. He was having one of his attacks again.

"The *onus?*' Bulb was saying, still giving him that strange look, as if he had said something altogether different, something disgusting, and he knew what was happening, the limitations of her vocabulary were undermining his faith in language, causing one of his attacks, when individual words seemed to lose all meaning, even a simple everyday word like *milk,* say, *or jug,* or *mangonize,* words which if said often enough became lumps of sound, lumps it seemed both ridiculous and unseemly to offer anyone else, and about as meaningful as prodding a pillar box with a gurnet, so that the word *onus* began to breed with obscene speed, and every tube and wire of his being to ring with an echoing *onus-onus-*

onus, and the soft patter of scurrying feet, corkscrew snouts drilling feverishly through his mind, causing bridges to shudder and collapse and tall buildings to develop ominous crack patterns at street level, while he sent in an ace division of meaning to try and save the situation, doing his very best, his arms reaching out and grabbing hold of a suitably thick, solid hair, the sweat pouring down him, swaying, while connecting a flow of sparks to his vocal cords and managing to croak, "You know, *onus,* meaning *burden.* As in *onus probandi,* the burden of proof."

Bulb stared at him blankly. She seemed frightened of him. He'd always adored her resemblance to the beautiful blonde Nazi in *Indiana Jones and the Last Crusade* but now she was starting to resemble Shelley Duvall in *The Shining.*

Bodrum could feel the veins standing out on his brow. Clenching his fists he muttered, "Comes between *ontology* and *onychia,* for Christ's sake! Same page as *ontogenesis, oofy* and *opera-bouffe.* Have you forgotten last July in Valtos already? We walked along the deserted bay, entranced by dead jellyfish, watching the swooping oystercatchers. We picnicked on windswept cliffs, eating tuna sandwiches and chewy roasted nut bars containing hydrogenated vegetable oil, glucose and glycerol and lecithin. We made love by the camp fire and on the warm sand of empty coves and among the waving ferns. The song we lewdly-laughingly played every day was "(When You) Squeeze Me", the one Fats Waller recorded on August 10th, 1939, just ten days before Joyce wrote to Frank Budgen from the Hotel Schweizerhof, Berne, enclosing the *Daily Herald's* one sentence review of *Finnegans Wake* ("An Irish stew of verbiage by the author of *Ulysses* with unexpected beauty emerging now and then from the peculiar mixture"), with John Smith on guitar and Slick Jones on drums.

"Oh, how all throughout that blistering summer we hogged the letter 'O', rubbed it, feasted on it, tongued it and sucked it and kissed it and made it come, voluptuaries of assonance and the musky pleasures of *onomatopoeia* (and I shall say it again, nothing can stop me, *on-om-at-o-pee-a*!), sybarites of sensuous sounds. Oyez! Oyez! *Ophiomorphus* was enough to get you going, and, ah, how lazily, loveably, you licked and sucked on *obelisk*!

"Remember? Your fingers brushed against my *occiput,* making me tingle; together, like crazed animals, we fell on *oral* and *orangery,* orating shamelessly. *Obesity* was a plump strumpet with gigantic breasts, *orb* was smooth and exciting. *Oho*! you chortled, catching me up to my old tricks with *odalisque;* when I had finished I nuzzled your *omphalus. Organ-grinder* made us giggle; *orgiastic* and *orgasm* and *orifice* caused us to *oscillate* alarmingly, leaving us *oscitant* as if from too much *opium.* Ah, the strange uses to which we put *olive oil*! Ooooh! Who could forget how you slipped your slender fingers over the stop-cock of *oxygen,* making us both roar. How *onanism* made us shiver with forbidden delights, so that we both tried rubbing ourselves with the *onomasticon. Osmosis* (I must be frank) drove us both to strange and unnatural practices, until at last, sated with the *ordinary*, we turned to *obscurity, obfuscation* and *obscurantism.* Our lusts dulled by repetition and variety, we turned, ultimately, to the pricks of *onopordon* (a composite genus of 20 species including the Scottish thistle). Farewell the unspeakable pleasures of *ouretic* and *outlandish, outsoar* and *oxfordian;* forgive my *oxyphonia.* In the end, as lovers always must, we returned to the mainland. We came back — you must remember this! — fatigued and pale, both of us suffering from *oxyuris, ozaena* and *ophthalmophobia,* keeping my *orchitis* from our friends, huddled against the funnel of the MacBrayne's steamer and making periodic checks with the *ozonometer* as the vessel steamed towards Oban."

"If you say so."

"If I say so! I not only say so, I also say that it is time to put the past behind us and concentrate on getting the interview with Nietzsche's moustache. My Nietzsche entry in Professor Krzcecebit's philosophical dictionary will win me considerable prestige at the Institute, you know. Not to mention among the neighbourhood at large. Several important periodicals contacted me before we left. Even the *Penge Gazette* rang me up. They wanted scoops, can you believe! Scoops! Of course I told them that philosophy is not about money. I even turned down a lucrative deal with Gillette. They wanted to sponsor me."

"I can't believe what I'm hearing. You know we need to move to a better part of town. And now you're telling me you've been throwing money down the drain. What do you think we are — millionaires?"

"Shut up!"

Bulb scowled and pursed her lips like Mussolini. "Don't you tell me to shut up, Claude Factotum Bodrum! I've worked my fingers to the bone so that you could explore doubt, universals, intelligible information, the dialectic, the certainty of existence, the argument for objective reality, immaterialism and the repetition of resembling events! And what have I got at the end of the day? A washing machine with a leak which hasn't been fixed for over a year! Two missing tiles which should have been replaced last September! Not to mention the state of the front garden. Where's the wedding ring you promised me? Where are the children we were going to have? All I ever hear from you is Plato this and Plato that! I don't think you really care about me at all! What do you care about my interests? What do you care about the canvases of Henri Edmond Cross (1856-1910), who only adopted the pointillist technique in 1891 and went on to use it with increasing freedom in his later years?"

"Shut up! I thought I heard something. Listen!"

Bulb fell silent. Grudgingly, she realised he was right. There was a low murmuring, like water running among rocks. Then the murmuring metamorphosed into a strange hum.

"Ask me a question, any question," a curious, hollow-sounding voice boomed at them, from somewhere deep in the tangled undergrowth.

Bodrum yelped with pleasure. "It's Nietzsche's moustache! It knows I'm here!" And it was bilingual, too — what a relief! He had been a little anxious on that score; his German was shakier than he cared to admit, and he was still at the stage of *Can you tell my Grandmother where the nearest bookbinders is, please; she urgently wishes to repair her Aristotle.*

His pulse beat maniacally. But now that the moment had come his mind was blocked by clutter. Idiotic questions tickled him with a feather duster. *Why are bananas yellow? Why do bees hum? Should salt be excluded in the diet of a sufferer from warty lupus?*

Fighting for control of himself, Bodrum gasped out his first question. "The British say knee and a sneeze: *knee-chah!* The Americans say *knees-itch.* As someone closer than anyone to the great philosopher, how do you pronounce his name?"

Silence.

Then the low murmuring, followed by the strange hum. At last the hollow-sounding voice boomed out (though to be honest he didn't quite catch the last six words), *The name Nietzsche is pronounced: Nietzsche.* Then it cackled with laughter, and faded away into the distance.

"My second question ..." Bodrum began. But the moustache did not seem to be in a conversational mood that night, and none of the other questions he put in swift succession to the undergrowth provoked a response. He began to feel melancholy welling up inside him again, the kind which, if not dealt with at once, soon results in anxiety of mind, suspicion, aggravation, restless thoughts, paleness, meagreness, neglect of business, perturbation, a bitter fire, a pernicious curiosity, vertigo, plague and madness. He groped around for his fondue pot. He began to wish he had started with one of the vital epistemological conundrums rather than his warm-up question.

Now they were both out of sorts — and out of digestive biscuits too, they realised. Bodrum blamed Bulb, Bulb blamed Bodrum and next the tent collapsed, tipping the bacon omelette on to the ground. Slapping each other with cold omelette made them feel sexy, and after they had sated their lusts (it seemed ages since they'd practised pompoir), Bodrum went off to forage for gruyère, which he grated into a half-filled pot of dry white wine, adding four whipped egg yolks, five tablespoons of cream and a pinch of grated nutmeg, stirring the mixture over their little stove until it began to bubble and Nietzsche's moustache slowly filled up with the mouth-watering scents of Fondue de Berne.

5: *Next day*

Next day. They walked on and came across Leonard, a bronzed, handsome, muscular young disciple of Lyotard. He wore a leotard, kept a leopard and lived in a tree house which reminded Bulb of *The Swiss Family Robinson.*

"Howdy!" he said, switching off the video of *Castaway* and inviting them in for a beer (which, as Bodrum had guessed from the moment he'd heard Leonard's accent, turned out to be canned, yellowish gold and fizzy, with a pitiful alcohol content).

It came as an unpleasant shock to Bodrum when Bulb said, "It's over, man" and told him she was staying on with Leonard in his tree house. Here, she said, she could say goodbye to *Angst* and begin to live a simpler, more interesting life, carving from old brown crusts exquisite miniatures of antelopes and giraffes, and little Eiffel Towers and elongated witch-doctor face masks which the tourists would buy, while Leonard spent his mornings in vapid gesturing and his afternoons writing a monograph on wind.

"How can you do this to me?" sobbed Bodrum.

"I'm a character in an Ellis Sharp story," Bulb retorted, eyes flashing. "I can do anything I want to." She added, menacingly: *"Anything.* Watch."

To Bodrum's dismay she swelled to twice her usual size, briskly translated Thucydides' *Peloponnesian War* into the kind of Gaelic they would understand in Stornoway, plucked a guitar from her black lacy bra and sang, dazzlingly, "A Frog He Went A-courting", in the version sung by Mrs Tom Rice at Big Laurel, N.C., August 16th 1916, only weeks after Lenin completed his pamphlet *Imperialism, The Highest Stage of Capitalism,* a work distilled from 739 pages of notes culled from 148 books and 232 articles and written (as Lenin explained) with an eye to the Czar's censor, using "Aesopian language", and which was not intended (as snivelling, sniggering liberal humanists sometimes imply) as an original work of theory but as a political tract which deliberately avoided a plunge into such enticing deep waters as the vexed problem of the decline of the rate of profit (say) or (say) the problem of the realisation of surplus value, in order to relate economic theories of imperialism to contemporary life, demonstrating to workers that the concentration of capital leading to monopolies resulted in the Great War, which was an imperialist war and which, requiring as it did the co-operation of millions of workers, posed the alternative not of war or peace but of imperialist war or civil war against imperialism, Lenin being at this time far too busy to trace Bulb's delightful song back to 1580, when it was advertised and licensed for performance as "a most strange wedding of the frogge and the mouse", still less to the courtship between a Mr Frog and a Miss Mouse narrated in the 1549 Scottish broadside, "The Frog Cam To The Myl Dur", while Mrs Rice, undeterred by war, sang, as Bulb sang,

A frog he went a-courting and he did ride, a-ha,
A frog he went a-courting and he did ride
With a sword and pistol by his side, a-ha.
Steam stem a bum a tum, a ling dum a lar-er, ha,
Steam stem a bum a tum, a ling dum a lar-er,
Rig dum a bee-ly mat a ki-mo, ki-mo, ha.

Reverting to her usual size, Bulb slipped the guitar back inside her bra — a bra Bodrum would never again fumble with or slip off, a bra holding breasts as firm and perfect as those of Peg Entwistle, who posed nude, had a bit part in *Thirteen Women* and, a martyr to semiotics, jumped to her death from the last letter — the thirteenth — the most dreadful of all consonants — in the famous HOLLYWOODLAND sign on Tinsel Town hillside — and said, as if explaining everything there was to explain, "Time is short, my strength is limited, the office is a horror, the apartment is noisy, and if a pleasant, straightforward life is not possible..."

Was she pregnant, he wondered? Eclampsia, involving fits, strange convulsions, outbursts of song, the concealment of musical instruments within undergarments and generally unacceptable behaviour, is a common condition in pregnant women, he reflected. The exact cause of eclampsia (he knew) is not known, but it had something to do with disordered body chemistry and natural poisons not got rid of in the ordinary and by no means uninteresting ways by which women rid themselves of waste products. But Bodrum didn't have the heart to introduce this new complication into their relationship (and besides, he had never heard of a sufferer hiding anything other than castanets, gongs, triangles, cymbals, xylophones and jingling johnnies). Or was it Leonard's Akai Video Recorder, programmable by remote control with on-screen prompts, digital auto-tracking and child lock and matching Tatung 51cm FST TV with black quartz screen, remote control and on-screen display? Much better (he decided) to ignore pregnancy or television and stick instead to reason and a frank admission of possible shortcomings in himself.

"Be honest with me, Bulb! It's because I'm taciturn, isn't it? It's because I'm reserved, incommunicative, curt, gruff, laconic, monosyllabic, withdrawn, tight-lipped, standoffish, morose, unclubbable, stiff and unforthcoming, eh? I can't help it. That's how I am. Even as a child I never finished my sentences. I used to leave them on the side of my plate. My parents didn't care. I never liked company, I'm a go-it-alone-type, a grumble-guts who talks to nobody, and prefers to stay at home with all the house lights turned up bright, reading Nietzsche. But let me tell you something! *I ain't no quitter!* Skew-whiff things can be straightened out. One day you'll be taken bad and you'll wish this had never been. You think you'll be happy with Leonard but what happens when the two of you get cardiovascular disease simultaneously? My advice to you, sister, is: pack it in. Things will be different between us from now, I swear. A foutre for the world and worldlings base! A pox on't! I'll play the orator as well as Nestor! Listen to this!

> There was a young lady named Bright
> Who could travel much faster than light
> She went off one day in a relative way
> And came back the previous night.

Not bad, eh? And listen to this. *Question:* What is it that you have that everyone else uses more than you do? *Answer.* Your name! Not bad, eh? Listen to this. *Question:* What can speak every language in the world? *Answer:* An echo! Not bad, eh? I'll give up being moody and introverted and become loud and amusing. How about this for starters. *I say, I say, I say. What did the first spirochaete say to the second spirochaete?"*

"Screw you," Bulb retorted, slamming the intricately woven hair door in his face.

For weeks afterwards, like one lost in a thorny wood he wandered, sore, sorrowful, a little delirious, feeling spasms (and occasionally weekends) of shallow grief, all alone among the densest and darkest tufts of the moustache. Day after day he fried in his own grease, squatting amongst axioms until he felt a touch of cramp in his legs, dreaming of fruitful vine, fuming, flummoxed and floppy, everything foozly and funereal. Some days, like the naughty boy who ran away to Scotland, he just stood in his shoes and wondered. Perhaps he should have been more forceful with Bulb. Perhaps he should have smacked her gently across the buttocks with a Jesuit's ferula, or smothered her cleavage in lukewarm custard, or mesmerised her with an account of Bismarck's 1863 dream about a whip which grew, and grew, and grew...

Too late, now. But then again perhaps she had never been right for him. Had he been Berkeley at the famous dinner, eloquently putting forward his scheme for a college in Bermuda, would she have been among those who sprang to their feet, crying, "Let us set out with him immediately!"? He rather doubted it.

Whatever else might happen, there was something he didn't doubt. A wild boar might burst from the undergrowth, a strange humming saucer-shaped craft might hover in a sinister fashion above him, a hundred-and-one unexpected events might occur amid Nietzsche's twilight tufts, but whatever his reactions (engaging the boar in mortal combat, deflecting the UFO beam with a non-stick frying pan, lashing out with both fists) he was confident the boar would not topple like an empty box, the UFO would not crumble into papery shreds, the all-encompassing gloom would not blend into the winter's morning darkness of his Basildon bedroom, nothing he wrestled with would turn into hot blankets, no phantoms would metamorphose into white cotton sheets, no bedroom carpet would soften his fall from cliffs, this was not one of those risible narratives where everything is a dream and where you dodge horrors by skipping deftly back into daily life, into the comforting familiar world of slippers and coffee percolators and newspapers and lollipop men and shoe shops and familiar smiling faces reading the regular bulletins or standing in front of that familiar comforting map charting the progress of that cold front coming in over the Atlantic with occasional rain though east of the Pennines staying mostly dry with temperatures not too bad at about eight or nine degrees with cloud thickening but generally bright with some sunshine and just an odd shower and becoming mild in spite of all that wind, a world where you could put your feet up and enjoy what the commentators called "the feel-good factor", mixing yourself a Frisco Sour, say, or a Morning Glory, say, or a Tijuana Sunrise, say, and relax to *The Best of Nanci Griffith,* say, or Mozart's Piano Concerto No. 21 in C Major, K. 467, say, and blot out those end-of-the-news things, those remote troublesome situations, the situation regarding the economy, say, or the unemployment figures, say, or homelessness, say, or starvation in Africa, say, or the situation in Angola, say, or the situation in East Timor, say, or the situation in Bosnia, say, or El Salvador, say, or the situation in South Africa, say, or in Rwanda, say, or in the L.A.P.D., say, and (drink up! cheers!) forget you were ever in an anxiety-laden dream where a little water makes a sea, a small puff of wind a tempest, a grain of sulphur a flame like Etna or a small spark in the bowels a lightning over all the chamber — the consequence, almost certainly, of eating beans, cabbage or onions, or of manifold internal stimuli such as the position of the sleeper, the bedding, water dripping into the loft, a car alarm going off, the tolling of bells, cannon shots, sirens, no. No way. And knowing this made him melancholy once again.

Nietzsche's moustache had quite lost its sparkle. Bodrum felt much as the Epicurean pope Leo Decimus must have felt when, pondering the meaning of life and contemplating the question of the soul's immortality, he at last spurned the weighty rhetoric of the tracts of Faventinus, the complex philosophical proofs and illuminations of Soto, Canas, Thomas, Persius, Dandinus, Colerus and Zanchius, even Tolet's Sixty Reasons and Lessius's Twenty-Two Arguments, to conclude, along with Cornelius Gallus, *Et redit in nihilum, quodfuit ante nihii.* It began of nothing and in nothing it ends.

6: *How did Bodrum survive?*

How did Bodrum survive? Adversity brought out the best in him. He ate pellets of compressed *Robinson Crusoe* and sucked the juice from an old copy of *An Outcast of the Islands.*

Hallucinations cannot be denied. A jocular and exuberant crowd of thick flesh-coloured protuberances which made him think of haemorrhoids obstructed the bare hallway where the tenants kept their perambulators! The hallway filled with water, flushing away the haemorrhoids and letting in the whale from *Pinocchio,* which was wearing an opera cloak and carrying a stick. The whale prodded him in the ribs and demanded answers to four questions:

i) Who did the hot hailstones fall on which, at Moses' intercession, remained suspended in the air when they were about to fall on the Egyptians?

ii) How can you get into a locked graveyard at night?

iii) Disjuncts can be divided into two main classes: style disjuncts and attitudinal disjuncts. If attitudinal disjuncts comment on the content of a communication, what do style disjuncts convey?

iv) Is so-called consciousness a more or less fantastic commentary on an unknown and perhaps unknowable but felt text?

Before Bodrum could even think of answering, the whale bellowed, "Oh dear! Oh dear! I shall be too late!" and swam off. The water drained away, leaving him stranded in Nietzsche's moustache once again.

In the end he probably owed his life to the protein in *The Old Curiosity Shop.* Chewing each mouthful twenty-nine times before he swallowed gave him just enough energy to go on until help came. Until that time he occupied his days shouting wilder and wilder questions at the massed trunks.

The moustache seemed to be tormenting him deliberately. *Welche Farbe hat der Vogel?* it would ask (stupid question — everyone knew what colour bats were) or mutter, *Wie traurig dieser Abend* (as if he didn't know how sad the evening was!). The closest he came to what he was after was when the moustache woke him up in the middle of the night, bellowing *Ernst ist das Leben, heiter ist die Kunst,* which as Maisie explained meant something along the lines of: *life's dreadful, art's a gag*, adding unhelpfully: *Wittgenstein.*

Bodrum had a horrible feeling that if he hadn't met Maisie he wouldn't have expired but would instead have ended up with Bulb and Leonard in the Avenue of Grotesques. He told Maisie everything — about the hold-ups, the *Penge Gazette,* Leonard's lager, the whole caboodle. It was Maisie who rescued him from the Vale of Whispers, explaining that it was full of headlice and weasels who liked nothing more than to fool the unwary traveller with their mimicry. "Even the answer to your first question was almost certainly bogus. No one has ever known the moustache to communicate — which isn't to say the woods aren't full of half-starved sexually repressed wretches having technicolour visions and building temples where they bite on crisp dandruff wafers, sip cups of sweat and experience Hairy Communion."

"I see," said Bodrum, miserably.

He reached into his pocket and pulled out a fistful of fluff (most of it an intriguing shade of Italian Pink), a scrap of tweed, a lump of ore, a pair of tweezers, an old bus ticket which read *London Regional Transport NOT TRANS-FERABLE,* Ariadne's thread, a yellow plastic button stamped *Made in Aleppo,* an egg box containing half a dozen theses on the philosophy of history, two crumpled photographs (one of the Johnson Wax Research Laboratory Tower at Racine, the other of the giant elliptical galaxy NGC 5128 in the constellation Centaurus) and a copy of a 1911 letter signed by Thomas Hardy and others calling on all nations to desist from the use of aerial vessels in war.

"Bother!" (Wrong pocket.)

Reaching into his other pocket, Bodrum brought out the draft of his dictionary entry and gave it to Maisie to read.

Friedrich Wilhelm Nietzsche (1844-1900)

Friedrich Wilhelm Nietzsche came from a long line of German butchers. He was born on October 15th, the exact day fifty-five years later that, less than one year before Nietzsche's death, Frankie Baker shot Allen Britt dead in St Louis, Missouri, inspiring the song "Frankie and Johnny", which has appeared in various forms sung by The Leighton Brothers, Mississippi John Hurt, Leadbelly, Jimmie Rodgers, Darby and Tarlton, Charlie Poole, Gene Autry, Johnny Cash, Elvis Presley and Bob Dylan; he died on August 25th, the day Olivia Newton-John made her debut in the American country charts with "Let Me Be There" (the pedal steel guitar on the record which helped win acceptance with country DJs was added after Olivia had recorded her vocal parts).

None of Nietzsche's ancestors were Polish noblemen. King Friedrich Wilhelm IV of Prussia, after whom Nietzsche was named, later went mad, as did Nietzsche's father, as did his favourite poet Friedrich Holderlin, as did Nietzsche himself, in January 1889, just five years after the birth of Huddy Ledbetter, whose best known songs include "Pick A Bale O'Cotton", "Rock Island Line" and "Goodnight Irene".

Nietzsche's moustache is without parallel in the history of Western philosophy. Records of his early life reveal that Plato's *Symposium* was Nietzsche's *Lieblingsdichtung*, that he suffered from myopia and migraine and that he was horrified by the sight of flimsily clad women. In 1867 he fell off a horse. Painful vomiting made him miserable for ten years. Only Paul Gast could read his handwriting. Nietzsche had a sister, Elisabeth, whom he called "a vengeful anti-Semitic goose" and a "llama", after the latter animal's habit of squirting saliva and half-digested food. Hitler was her friend. Bernhard, her husband, poisoned himself. Elisabeth became Queen of Nueva Germania, in northern Paraguay, just beyond the confluence of the Aguaraya-umi and Aguaraya-guazu.

Nietzsche was fond of deliberations, aphorisms and dithyrambic forms, and wrote twenty volumes of books and notes, including fragments, unfinished essays and outlines for projected but unwritten works. For the last eleven years of his life he remained inert.

In *Ecce Homo* Nietzsche wrote, "I am no man, I am dynamite", alluding to the discovery that a porous silicate of hardened algae absorbed nitro-glycerine and allowed it to be packed into bombs and transported, making it at last possible to assassinate Czar Alexander II, a substance named "dynamite" by its inventor, Dr Alfred Nobel, who at sixty wrote, "I am totally sick and tired of the explosive substance field", and whose invention of a percussion cap to replace the quickmatch fuse also proved of real value to contemporary terrorists, a man who, when asked to describe himself at the age of fifty-four, wrote *Important events in his life: none*, and who subscribed to the *Times Literary Supplement*, who was interested in avant-garde literature and whose conversation, "spiced as it was with sudden sallies of wit and outbursts of ideas", his assistant Ragnar Sohlman fondly remembered: *You had to stay on your toes to follow the wild sallies of his unexpected turns of thought and startling paradoxes. He would soar like a wind-driven swallow from one subject to another though at times his whims bordered on the absurd.*

In 1938 Frankie Baker, a shoeshine parlour proprietress in Portland, sued Republic Pictures for $200,000 damages, when the song "Frankie and Johnny" was used in a film, testifying that the song referred to a murder she had committed in Nietzsche's lifetime.

An Interview with Nietzsche's Moustache

Bodrum twitched half a dozen times; fingered his hair; laughed nervously. "It's not finished yet," he explained hurriedly, observing the expression on Maisie's face. "I know what you're going to say. There needs to be more about Alexander II. There's not enough about Nobel or C & W singers born in the month Nietzsche went mad. Fair comment. I'd be the first to admit it may need a bit of a polish here and there. And the stuff about the pedal steel guitar perhaps ought to go into a footnote. But overall... what do you think?"

Maisie grimaced. Before Bodrum could protest she skilfully folded the sheet into an eight-winged dart and sent it flying. When last seen it was heading towards Paris.

"Use this instead," she commanded, pulling out a sheet from under her see-through blouse.

GET SOAP AND SOMETHING SHARP!

Beware the roots and the aporias of Nietzsche's baroque moustache and his critique of reason! Nietzsche's assertion that the self is a fiction, that different forces engage in a perpetual struggle for domination and that only relativism is valid is hairy obscurantism! How to understand Nietzsche's moustache? Get soap and something sharp! Peel away the impostor's disguise! Nietzsche's ideal was the rapacious bourgeois freed from inhibition and stripped of pretences! Expose him for what he was — a South German, from one of the most technically backward parts of Europe. Expose a variant of Romantic anti-capitalism — an intellectual product of the period after German reunification in 1871 when Junkerdom and industrial capitalism fused in a peculiarly complacent, authoritarian and materialistic mould. The mystical doctrine of the eternal return of all things is a static, pessimistic, despairing version of the great

truth that the problem which history presents
to humanity recur and recur. Nietzsche's
writings reflect the violence and despair of
the final imperialistic phase of capitalism!
Wake up! Aestheticism anaesthetises! Metropolitan Police and middle class managerial
moustaches stink! Bring barbers and hot water!
Nietzsche had not the slightest interest in
changes in methods of production! He seems
never to have noticed a machine in his whole
life. Yes, Nietzsche saw through and exposed
with unmatched vigour of bitter raillery the
shoddy, unhistorical, impoverished philosophy
of nineteenth-century liberalism. But let's
face it, folks: most people's lives are still
shaped by their lack of access to productive
resources and the need to sell their labour
power in order to live! So join SARTLIN today
and SAY NO to NIETZSCHE and NATO!

"Hmm," muttered Bodrum. He was still cross about that dart. "I am not sure that Professor Krzcecebit..." His voice flickered. SARTLIN? The word seemed vaguely familiar. "Perhaps I could ask you — " he began, then paused, feeling an unexpected coastal gust blow over him. Next the GROUND seemed to DROP AWAY in front of them.

7: "Jump!" cried Maisie

"Jump!" cried Maisie. Before he knew what was happening Bodrum felt her hand close upon his arm and drag him into space. A SHOWER of GINGERY HAIRS exploded around them, and Bodrum caught a glimpse of Nietzsche's face. The philosopher's eyes were closed, as if asleep or deep in serious thought. The legendary nose loomed above them, familiar as the Matterhorn. Then the light faded and they were plunging through darkness, Maisie a grey blur beside him.

Next thing, before you could say, "Mary Poppins!", they

were crashing among bushes, big billowing bushes with branches and twigs which tore at their clothes, stripped them garment by garment, then hurled them nude among strange soft bushes thick with lacquered leaves which playfully tossed them to and fro, lower and lower, until at last they plopped gently into a pale, warm forest clearing, where, throbbing and mildly concussed, they lay on a mattress of soft leafmould until dawn, when Bodrum woke to find Maisie smiling at his erection.

"Are you familiar with Gauguin's famous painting *Annah the Javanese?*" she asked.

Bodrum shook his head.

"Pity. I once had a boyfriend who told me I was identical to Gauguin's model. She was of mixed race and so am I. My father came from Java and my mother was born in Montreux and taken to Penge when she was three. He said every contour of my firm, brown, desirable body was the very image of Gauguin's Annah and that if he ever became a postmodernist writer he simply wouldn't waste his time or the reader's writing pages about rounded breasts and taut nipples and so on. He'd simply refer the reader to Gauguin, with savings all round."

"Savings?"

"On electricity (assuming one was using a computer). On forests (less words equals less pages equals less paper). And on imagination (why tire the reader after a hard day's work?)."

"And did he become a postmodernist writer?"

Maisie screeched with laughter. "Of course not, silly. He became a hairdresser. Last I heard he was living in Theydon Bois."

"You've been there, have you?"

"Oh for God's sake, don't be silly. I finished with Gerald *centuries* ago."

"SSSSSSH!"

"What is it?"

"God is dead, remember? *Don't upset Nietzsche.* He might

hear you. We don't want a scene. He'd be quite capable of causing an earthquake. Germans can be quite prickly people."

"You're forgetting something. We're not in Nietzsche's moustache any more. We're somewhere else."

"Shiver my timbers! I'd completely forgotten. I think I'm still a little concussed."

"*And* you've lost your erection. Pity. I was just feeling in the mood. Want me to fix it for you?"

"Wouldn't mind. I'm feeling a little frisky myself. It's the stress of all I've been through, I guess."

"Okay, okay, professor. Cut the psychoanalysis."

Ffffffffffffffingers of hers approached and

ffffffffffffffifteenth-letter-of-the-alphabet!

Again, again!

Afterwards Bodrum said: "Maisie."

"Mmmm."

"Can I ask you something?"

"Mmmm."

"You sound like a girl who's been around, seen a few things in her time. What I want to know is this. If we aren't in Nietzsche's moustache, *where are we*? And how did we get here?"

"How did we get here? Easy: through the Time Vortex. But this is not the time to talk of the Aleph detector, supersymmetry, the nine dimensions of space, the top-quark, rotating black holes, Carl Sagan's *Contact*, wormholes, cosmic string, quantum antigravity, exotic quantum states or Hawking's ludicrous chronology protection hypothesis. What I will say is this: *negative pressure implies negative gravity*. Nothing so far discovered in Einstein's general theory of relativity forbids travel into the past. But let me ask you something. What does the light tell you?"

Bodrum frowned. "Nothing. But then there isn't any light. Well, hardly any. It's dark. Like nightfall."

"Precisely. Whereas in Nietzsche's moustache there was a constant coppery light, was there not?"

"Now you mention it, there was, yes."

"Okay. Let me tell you what I think. *I don't think we're in a moustache anymore.*"

"We aren't?"

"No."

"Then what the hell *are* we in?"

"Something richer, deeper, denser. Something more profound. I personally think we are in a beard."

Bodrum said: "I don't understand."

"Don't bother trying. Later we'll go exploring, find ourselves some clothes and get something to eat. In the meantime try and get some sleep. We'll need all the strength we've got."

"You're talking of the challenges that lie ahead? Of adversity, danger and self-reliance?"

"Yes."

Bodrum groaned. He felt twinges of claustrophobia. "The hair — or? The hair — or?" he wildly whispered, Kierkegaard flitting in and out of his mind like a frantic bat.

He was beginning to rue the day his class teacher had advised him to take up a career in epiphenomenalism.

8: *They moved forward slowly*

They moved forward slowly through the dark, tangled undergrowth, alert for snakes. What a day it had been (or what a night!). They had feasted on a crop of new potatoes and wild carrots, carved wooden swords out of a sheet of dandruff and constructed pantaloons from scraps of wool and fluff. Resting from their endeavours, they sipped at rust-dark blobs of beer which hung in trembling clusters from the fever trees. Afterwards, woozy and grinning, Maisie made herself a fetching deerstalker hat out of toothbrush bristles, dyeing and criss-crossing the bristles after the colour and pattern of the clan Morag. While she was busy with her new headwear Bodrum, who was also a little drunk, peeled away scraps of bark and quickly put together a superb scale model of the *Titanic*. After she had admired his funnels they stripped off their pantaloons and engaged in two frenzied bouts of intercourse.

The night seemed to dilute — or was it simply their eyes, adjusting to the pitch? Maisie was a grey wisp gliding beside him. She stumbled on a stray crumb and brushed against his ribs. "Woops," she whispered, trying to keep up his spirits by furnishing him with information, adding confidentially that whereas Storax may be mixed with an equal amount of olive oil and rubbed into the scalp to destroy nits and lice, Copaiba is used as a disinfectant in cases of diseases of the bladder, kidneys, or in gonorrhoea, and gives the breath a very disagreeable odour, that a scup is a kind of porgy, that in October 1924, after almost a year's work, Mayakovsky completed his poem "Vladimir Ilyich Lenin", and that *Annah the Javanese* was the first important painting in Western culture to show female pubic hair.

Bodrum said nothing.

He thought about Gerald, and felt a flash of anger. How the name "Gerald" disgusted and upset him! If he was Prime Minister he would introduce LEGISLATION making it COMPULSORY for the penultimate letter in "Gerald" to be replaced by an "r", in honour of the great poet, manly Hopkins.

He would also see to it that all statues of Queen Victoria and Earl Haig were torn down and replaced by statues of Hopkins and strategic thinker Sverdlov.

"It's Gauguin's time in Peru that really interests me," he replied at last, a little wearily. But, disappointingly, Maisie knew nothing of Gauguin's life in the years 1849-55. The conversation fizzled and went out, and they wandered glumly on in the gloom.

Bodrum felt his sense of time ebbing away. He began to yearn for the demented cries of a cockerel or the soft stupid cooing of doves. His mind wandered over Waterloo Bridge, swam three times around Vivien Leigh, then sat down at the railings, basking in chimes, until moved on by a rude and aggressive constable.

Dead hairs crackled around them like fallen twigs in winter.

A light flashed ahead of them, making them start. They moved slowly towards it, wooden swords at the ready. Then Bodrum laughed a brittle nervous laugh. "It's alright," he said. "It's only a silver hair blowing gently in the wind, luminous under the shining moon."

"Do you realise what this means?" asked Maisie, who (Bodrum reflected) was beginning more and more to resemble Sherlock Holmes.

Wearily, Bodrum shook his head.

"We are talking early middle age," said Maisie. "We are talking of the first silvery-grey streaks. That's my theory, what's yours?"

"I don't do theories, only interviews."

"Sorry. I was forgetting."

"I don't mean to be rude. Your theory sounds reasonable. But Maisie, let me ask you a question. Who are you? It wasn't an accident, was it, you bumping into me in Nietzsche's moustache like that?"

Maisie grinned. "Hell, no. Of course I had no idea it would be *you* I'd find but I won't pretend I wasn't there for a purpose. I work for SARTLIN. See, here's my badge."

"The Socialist Association for the Rescue of Those Lost in Nietzsche! Of course! I knew I'd heard of SARTLIN. An Alpine guide told me about the work of you people. I don't think he approved. He was an Hegelian, needless to say. But naturally I didn't pay much attention to what he said because at that time I never thought for a moment I'd end up getting lost."

"People don't. One moment the way ahead seems bright and clear. Next moment the fog comes down and you end up blundering around utterly exhausted. You've no idea of the numbers who end up in the Avenue of Grotesques. We only manage to rescue a tiny percentage. It isn't easy getting here, I'm afraid — even with help from Marx, Lenin and the others achieving the maximum flow of cerebral energy is quite a struggle, and after lift-off there are all the problems of irregularities in the sub-stratum not to mention attendant associations, latent revisionism, deviation and problems occurring on the fringe of a partially relaxed attention. People simply don't appreciate the risks once you start tampering with time and bourgeois ideology. J. W. Dunne wasn't joking when he warned, *Taking the train to Dover instead of the express to Southampton may lead to being decapitated by Russian politicians instead of being clubbed by a New York policeman.* Half the time we end up miles from Nietzsche. If I told you of the number of times I've crash-landed into Dutch clergymen's sideburns you'd never believe me. The Association does its best but ours is only a small organisation."

"So where are we going?"

Maisie frowned. "Out of here, I hope. But don't ask me where here is. There are some things the Time Vortex leaves you to find out for yourself. All we can do is press on until we get to a cliff."

"Then what?"

"Then we take a leap into the quotidian, of course. Do you know those marvellous lines from Sharp's 'Sunday Morning in July'? *Fervour propels them, defies the heavy gravity of things-as-they-are, gives them wings as (hurrah!) they make it, make that dreamlike, dizzying, fantastic, necessary, luminous leap.* All members of SARTLIN are at all times required to wear earrings engraved with those words."

"Sharp?" he muttered, puzzled. The name seemed to ring a remote, tinny bell. Wasn't that the name Bulb had mentioned just before her fit? Not that her trick of doubling her size had fooled him for a moment. There was an obvious rational explanation, namely the effects on a concealed pregnancy of a mirage of the type described in the Appendix to the Report of the Royal Geographical Society's bathymetrical survey of Loch Ness, 1903-1904.

"A writer. Forget it. There isn't time to explain I can see daylight ahead. Look!"

Bodrum saw that she was right. A milky light glowed in the distance, casting spoke-like shadows across the forest's pale floor.

Hand-in-hand they hurried towards it.

9: *"Jibbooms and bobstays!'*

"Jibbooms and bobstays! I am *so* excited. I am so fucking excited."

Bodrum didn't doubt it; Maisie's whole body was shaking, like someone suffering from tropical fever who requires a large dose of calomel, followed by salts, followed by 30 grains of quinine sulphate daily and possibly even pamaquin (the British equivalent of the German plasmoquin), which has been proven to be efficacious in cases of benign tertian malaria resistant to quinine but which does not prevent relapses in subtertian infections.

He wriggled forwards on his principle organ cf digestion and peered over the edge of the cliff.

Beneath them, on the plain, was a large wooden desk. On the desk was a manuscript. On the mountains beyond lay shelves bearing hundreds of books. The books were stacked in untidy piles, and many had sheets of paper protruding from them.

"I once spent a month inside Tennyson's beard. It was awful. All the bastard did was write sycophantic letters to Queen Victoria. I dreamed one day I might land inside the facial hair of William Morris. But never *this.*"

She jabbed an excited finger at the manuscript. "Read it," she breathlessly whispered.

Just as the period of crisis occurred later on the Continent than in England, so did the period of prosperity. The original process always takes place in England; it is the demiurge of the bourgeois cosmos.

Frowning, Bodrum glanced further down the page.

While this general prosperity lasts, enabling the productive forces of bourgeois society to develop to the full extent possible within the bourgeois system, there can be no question of a real revolution.

"So?" he said, blankly.

"Don't you see? Don't you recognise it? It's Marx. *The Class Struggles in France: 1848 to 1850.* One of Marx's first great concrete analyses of contemporary capitalism and class struggle! To think that you and I are inside Karl Marx's beard! I'm so happy I think I've wet myself."

"Hmm," said Bodrum. He added, "What's happening?"

But Maisie didn't know either. The ground beneath them trembled then abruptly moved, throwing them off balance. They crashed against each other and fell into some undergrowth. The forest suddenly rang to a series of cacophonous noises — a garden gate clicking shut, a door creaking open, stairs being mounted, the Niagara-like thunderous laughter of a woman. There was the rattle of curtains being pulled to and day changed to night, then to a grey twilight. A sudden jolt sent Maisie and Bodrum smashing through hedges and a small shrubbery. Stunned, they clung to each other, hearing more laughter, and vast, echoing, distorted words. Again the forest was shaken by tumultuous squalls, again they were thrown this way and that, bouncing from bush to bush.

Bodrum thought, "This is no joke."

An immense grinding noise filled the universe. Bodrum stared at Maisie and Maisie stared over his shoulder, frowning, as if into the eye of an adversary, as if to penetrate a hidden intention and guess the aim and force of the thrust. Dazed, Maisie gasped, "Don't ask... This has never happened to me before." Bodrum, tightlipped, clung to a stout, pillar-box-sized hair. It was no use. Another shudder ripped through the beard and Bodrum and Maisie found themselves flying over the treetops, crashing down into a region of marshland.

An Interview with Nietzsche's Moustache

"Strange," said Maisie. "I've never been anywhere like this before." They were in a coppice of light brown hair. The texture was completely different to that of Marx's beard. There was a pungent salty smell which reminded Bodrum of the coast east of Hunstanton, the only west-facing resort in East Anglia.

"Good grief!" Bodrum STARED in AMAZEMENT. An aerostat, was it? A blancmange-coloured zeppelin? Neither. It really *was* a tongue, a massive, pinkish-red saliva-shiny tongue which swooped across the sky and plunged into the marshland.

The moaning was louder than ever. The marsh erupted with earthquakes, and once again Bodrum and Maisie were thrown every which way, causing bruises on Maisie's thigh and forearm which on the following Tuesday, Susan, her archivist lover, told her (soaping them gently) were very reminiscent of old maps of Schwarzburg-Rudolstadt, Schwarzburg-Sondershausen and Schwyz.

The tongue rose gracefully and floated away into space. Within moments a cigar-shaped spacecraft loomed into view, a solitary port-hole in its purple nose-cone. With a soft squelch it buried itself nose first into the salt flats. Then, as if trying to free itself from the quagmire, it began to pump up and down like a primitive piston. It was something formidable and swift, like the sudden smashing of a vial of wrath. The entire marsh seemed to explode with an overpowering concussion and a rush of great waters. Bodrum fancied himself whirled a great distance through the air. Everything disappeared — even, for a moment, his power of thinking, so that he began to gabble (had he been reading "The Aleppo Button"?), "Gah shlooh lye bopdoosh" and "Zsomber, Zingg, Zero!" and "Sodaine shakings! Sodaine flashes! Sodaine noises!" and "Mainspring!" and "Yeah, go on" and "A mixt and dubious Animall!" and "You know, I went up in a balloon in Paris!" and "Marienbad is unbelievably beautiful!" and "A lumber room of unreason!" and "The Locusts! The Plaza! The Room!" and "The problem is urgent, yes" and "I just got here, Harry!" and "My heart was hot within me!" and "I must eat my dinner" and "The junk heap of the shoulder pads worn for one day on the Princeton freshman football field!" and "The only eiderdown in the place was still in a cupboard!" and "Outside the bright gardens had a haunted look!", until Maisie slapped his face, twisting his arm until she'd forced a footnote out of him.

He breathed in gasps. *Kenneth Koch, Malcolm Lowry, John Donne, Franz Kafka, Patrick Lane, Sir Thomas Browne, Anton Chekhov, Franz Kafka, Weldon Kees, The Book of Common Prayer, William Shakespeare, F. Scott Fitzgerald, Celeste Albaret and Raymond Chandler*, he ejaculated sullenly. For the most part Bodrum kept his eyes shut tight, as if suspecting his sight might be destroyed in the immense flurry of the elements. They tumbled over and over, Bodrum gasping, "Two gone!" and "I must eat my dinner!" until Maisie shut him up with another slap.

The storm seemed to go on long enough for a viewing of *Key Largo* followed by a hot bath and drinks. Maisie's wristwatch, however, indicated at best a Tom and Jerry short and a hurried can of 7-Up.

The fronds of palms stood still against the sky. Not a branch stirred. A pungent dampness; the grass heavy and white with dew; a bitter-sweet fragrance over everything. How lush the scent of mushroom and wild strawberry! Somewhere a blackbird was singing; somewhere a humming bird sucked nectar; butterflies with blazing wings fluttered here and there in the sunlit clearings. Stupefied, Maisie and Bodrum realised what had happened. Bodrum seemed about to say something, but Maisie frowned and pressed a finger to his lips.

Helene Demuth stood up, spilling the intruders into space and time. Holding each other tightly, Bodrum and Maisie felt themselves twisting and turning in a strange misty nothingness. As they began to be sucked away by the Time Vortex they saw beneath them the room beginning to shrink.

Demuth wiped her crotch with the Doctor's rather dirty

handkerchief, and pulled on her grey skirt. Bodrum felt a sudden stab of pain in his throat and stomach; a faint whirring noise filled his ears, something pushed down hard on his chest. It felt like being inside a 747 just before take-off; a rising, racing whine drilled through his head, things began to vibrate, something powerful and irresistible began to drag him out of that place, drawing him steadily upward, upward...

As they accelerated away, back to their own time, Bodrum pulled Maisie towards him. The glow of the time-field made her shine like someone on television advertising a beach holiday; holding her tightly, feeling her heart fluttering like a panicky sparrow caught in netting, he kissed her gently on her empurpled, radiant cheek. "You and me, babe," he started to say, but it sounded infantile and so he stopped. He caught a glimpse of a white three-storey house, a house on a steep hill overlooking the harbour in Weymouth, where he worked late into the night, correcting the proofs of his hoax *Philosophical Review* article, "An Interview with Nietzsche's Moustache", and completing his treatise on referential indeterminacy, listening to old Crosby, Stills, Nash and Young albums, while in the bay the white hydrofoil came and went and the twins, Conundrum and Zarathustra, slept peacefully in their bunk beds, and the whitewashed circle in the bare basement glowed and began to throb, signalling Maisie's return from another adventure-packed voyage into the tangled heart and treacherous terrain of mid-Victorian facial hair.

A happy ending! He had grown middle-aged and cynical and had lost his faith in such things, but now, forgetful of everything except himself and Maisie, feeling a little dizzy, a little intoxicated, ignorant of her bi-sexuality and her intimacy with jealous, freckled Susan, and pulled round and round by invisible forces, he could feel himself swept helplessly towards it.

"Maisie," he whispered, but Maisie, eyes closed, was limp and oblivious and letting herself go with the flow.

Steam stem a bum a tum, a ling dum a lar-er, ha, Steam stem a bum a tum, a ling dum a lar-er, Rig dum a bee-ly mat a ki-mo, ki-mo, ha!, he felt like singing (but didn't).

Bodrum, twisting and turning, glanced away. Somewhere a dark thunderstorm was brewing; a lightning flash drenched him. Risking an attack of vertigo, he looked down.

Beneath them the rumpled bed was reducing itself to the dimensions of a matchbox.

"Men!" Bodrum distinctly heard Demuth say, in a grey, faraway, shrinking voice. "All the same. Only interested in one thing."

Growing smaller and smaller, and starting to hum the chorus from Shostakovich's Second Symphony, she went back to her housework.

A MAZE, A MUSE, A MULE

1

Picture it. Wheeeeeeeeeeeeeeeee! Yaaaa-whooooooooooooo! Elated, excited, exuberant, jubilant, chuckling, stupendous Marx and Engels emerge from No. 20, hop, skip, fly down Great Windmill Street, past the muffin man, yaaaa-whoooooooooooo!

Turn cartwheels. Cartwheel from one end to the other. Back again. Wheeeeeeeeeeeeeeeee! Yaaaa-whooooooooooooo! Beards flapping, turn cartwheels to Shaftesbury Avenue, back to Brewer Street, to Shaftesbury Avenue again! Wheeeeeeeeeeeeeeeee!

There is nothing that can compare to shooting speed. There is nothing that can compare to sex. There is nothing that can compare to piña coladas for breakfast, screwdrivers for lunch, and Southern Comfort through the night. There is nothing that can compare to getting on stage for the first time and singing into a microphone and the people dancing and the lights a-blazing and the band going BOOM! BOOM! BOOM! There is nothing that can compare to being given the task of writing a Manifesto to publicise the doctrines of the Communist League!

Picture it. *An endless maze of connections and interactions, in which nothing remains what, where and as it was, but everything moves, changes, comes into being and passes away.* Wheeeeeeeeeeeeeeeee! Yaaaa-whooooooooooooo! A Hendrix number thumped through the half-light. Friedrich had some old material he could use. He was in El Quijote, drinking tequila. He was trying to put Marx's stuff and his stuff together when Janis happened by. She was attracted to tall slender men with beards. "Buy y'uh drink." It wasn't a question. She slammed down on to the next stool.

"Wizzit?"

"This, my dear young woman, is a preliminary draft of a comprehensive theoretical and practical programme, incorporating the fundamental principles of Communism, of the

193

Communist League, formerly the League of the Just."

"You silver-tongued devil, you!" Glances round. "Hey, bartender!"

Engels could see at once that Janis Joplin was one of those young women who are suffering because of the relative disappearance of a generally accepted systematic metaphysics that bears on daily life.

"Y'ain't s'old y'self." What's that? Friedrich daydreaming again. Thinking of how J, the tenth letter and seventh consonant, is a comparatively recent addition to the English alphabet. Thinking of how, between JAB and JUZAIL, it yields JACKANAPES and JAIL and JAKES and JANUS and JAUNT and JAZZ and JOINT and JUXTAPOSE. Thinking of the cartwheels. The expression on the muffin man's face. The tanned, limping muleteer herding his half dozen surly charges towards them along Brewer Street. Of how, ankle deep in mule dung, Marx called a halt.

Engels liked it in El Quijote. It was dark in there. He liked the rotating bar stools that didn't squeak, the booths with red leather seating. He liked the dark picture of the mulette; the sprigs of mulewort tucked behind the carved mulga. The low light coming from thickly shaded lamps. When you are a hundred years old you are grateful for any darkness. The wrinkles smoothed away, the blotches and scarlet pinpricks. You met interesting people there (Mohammedans, Muggletonians, mugwumps, mulattos) in the night, in the darkness.

"Mules. The family... Shoooooooooosh! *A mule is the offspring of a mare by a male ass; a variety of canary; a hybrid; a machine for cotton spinning.*"

"An end to the exploitation of mule spinners! Abolition of the family!" Had Friedrich said that? Or was it a whisper mouthed by a glass? Blue-grey as her eyes.

"The family... Shoooooooooosh!" Staring in at the melting cubes, the slosh of vodka and juice. That hollow, recessed word, *reality*. Lord! The drab, drabber years. The calcined days. The moths. The broth of boredom, the wastes. Quarrels and lonely nights, dreadful mornings, heavy, heavy weeks, meaningless empty months. Deathly, deathly washed-out afternoons.

Mnemosyne! Tales of a zapped-out life. Started, rank amateur, at the Half-Way House in Beaumont, the Purple Onion in Houston. The time she cut a tape, a commercial for a bank in Nacogdoches. Set to — sheeeet! — set to the music of Guthrie's "This Land is Your Land". Summer 1962, to the U of T, joined a trio, the Waller Creek Boys (!), sang pure clean ballads in a clear Jean Ritchie voice. Sang C & W in a Rosie Maddox voice. You know, who had a big hit with "Sing a Little Song of Heartache". Split to San Francisco, sang at the Coffee and Confusion on Upper Grant Avenue, sang at The Coffee Gallery. In those days sang alone, using her autoharp. Overweight, with straggly brown hair, rough, acned skin. "Searchin'" her favourite song, split to NYC. Apartment on the Lower East Side, sang folksy blues at Slug's. Hussled here and there, a spell in Port Arthur, hit San Francisco again on 4 June 1966. Hung out with The Grateful Dead.

Barmen, Friedrich said, and J.J. roused herself, erupted from the bed of her vodka orange.

Bartender! Same again. Twice! A rich hoarse liquored tender voice.

Ach, families! Friedrich whispered. Iron-barred brick-walled Christianity! Cotton spinning! Lace factories! When all he wanted to do was write poetry. Papa sent him to Bremen. To get — horrible notion! — *business experience.* Read there — devastating! — Strauss's *Life of Jesus.* Met — mind-blowing! — Moses Hess.

"I dig Hesse too."

Then off to Manchester, to work for Papa. Returning to Germany, stopped off in Paris, met the fellow who edited the *Rheinische Zeitung,* name of Marx, at the Cafe de la Regence, 28 August 1844. "Our complete agreement in all theoretical fields became obvious!"

The night went on. Into a car, down the main drag, a decayed hotel. They got wired. It wasn't what Friedrich had wanted. Didn't even know until too late. Slipped it into his Bloody Mary. Next they were smoking grass, she was peeling away his shirt, his socks. Nude. A jittery picture on the wall, Mexico, hats. Laughing his head off, hysterical, wh-eeeeeeeeeeeeeeeee! Yaaaa-whoooooooooooo! She went there later, he never knew this, early '68, an abortion. His?

What's this? Forcing over his legs a pair of silver-white pants. And matching jacket. As worn at the Monterey festival.

What's this?

"What's that?" Her voice crackling like that of the head attendant at the Hotel Cosmopolitan.

What's this? Stripping off the pants, slipping on the fishnet stockings, short pink skirt, gold mesh vest, rhinestone jacket.

Hideous!

Not finished yet.

Dangling a bell from his waist, forcing on cheap gold shoes. Shimmery peacock's tail down the back of his neck, boa feathers, purple and green, in his hair. Not finished yet. Blue beads round his neck, gold bracelets on his wrists. Not finished yet. Gets out her jar of rouge, dabs a blotch on each cheek. Yaaaa-whoooooooooooo!

"What's that?"

"Just something I'm writing. With Marx."

She snatched the papers. A sheet fluttered to the floor.

"Hey! Gimme back."

"*Man must face up to the real conditions of life and to his social relationships.* Man, are you a sociologist or something?"

"Gimme!"

"Friedrich, you should take a look at yourself in the mirror. Honey, you look out of this world."

Engels hiccupped. "Marx," he began, realising for the first time the immense effort required to utter that name, as if something was sucking at his vocal cords, making him gasp for breath, a strange immense centrifugal force, the rooms of the wall (no, wrong, the walls of the room) being slowly twisted in an anti-clockwise direction. "Given the task of writing a Manifesto to publicise the doctrines of the Communist League!" he concluded, in a rush, grinning, a surge of good feeling flooding through his veins. He inhaled, blew out a Zanzibar-shaped swirl of smoke.

"Your style, Friedrich. It's sort of slow. You need to unwind, man. Let it rip."

She went over to the record player and put on the Mississippi Sheiks. They were singing — he was hearing it for the first time in his life — "Sitting On Top Of The World".

Janis was right. He dipped his quill in the inkpot and began writing, fast. "Play it again, J.J."

She played it again.

He looked up, grinning. "How about this. *Man is at last compelled to face with sober senses his real conditions of life!*"

Janis made a face. *"With sober senses*! Man, you need a Gingersnap. Here, gimme that." She sloshed some vodka and ginger wine in a jug, squirted in three bursts of soda, fired a jet over Engels, zapped the door, poured out the drinks. She took a biro to his scrawl, balanced some insertions on leaning spidery stems. Handed it back.

"All that is solid melts into air! All that is holy is profaned! Keep on rocking, man! That's more like it, man."

Engels nodded. "I like it, I like it." He finished towelling his hair and began tapping his foot to the Mississippi Sheiks. *All that is solid melts into air.* A little derivative, perhaps (that bastard Shakespeare had got there first) and yet... Profoundly true! Everything was dissolving, the walls, the dry old clock on the wall, the night sky... What an endless maze of connections and interactions, in which nothing remains what, where and as it was, but everything moves, changes, comes into being and passes away! It reminded him of the old days, jumping into a van at 3am, heading for the coast, Leonard Cohen's "So Long, Marianne" drowning the noise of the engine, a warm capsule hurled through the night, the salt sea, shingle, embraces. The waves! Their phosphorescence, their crunching, slapping, sucking... Night, dawn, the fire of the sun. A flick of gold. Youth! And middle age. And the clock limp, yes, limping off along the valley of the Arve, past the spot where Shelley was bitten by a squirrel, where you overtake the clock (which has stopped) and hurry on along the zig-zag road that leads up the mountainside, between the pines, to the hotel overlooking the great glacier, where you sit on the terrace, drinking chocolate, contemplating the orange tree, the cocoa-nut, the palm, the mango, the treefern, the banana, after which you enquire from the harsh Swiss waitress the whereabouts of the urinal, down the corridor, second on the left after the reproduction of Max Ernst's *First visible Poem, no. 5,* a cool tiled blissful place smelling of peaches and moist vaginas, with a glass roof reminiscent of the Watts gallery outside Guildford, causing you to hum through the cloud of steam Martinu's jaunty *Half-time,* until it is time to descend the mountain and return to the rented room where you would very much like to complete your article on hyphens in *Through the Looking-Glass,* were it not for the couple in Room 212, having a row about the theme of building sites in Antonioni's *oeuvre,* and the youth in 214 playing "Mr Tambourine Man" at full blast, and the noise — bababadalgharaghtakamminnarronnkonnbronntonnerronnt uonnthunntrovarrhounawnskawntoohoohoordenenthurnuk! — of thunder, which turned out simply to be Simon, a Joycean, growling as he chased down the corridor after a black jittery swarm of false apostrophes escaped from slipshod newspaper references to *Finnegans Wake,* not to mention the drunk across the corridor howling "Sitting On Top Of The World" and thumping on the wall with a volume (two and three) of *Capital* in each hand. THUMP! THUMP! THUMP! *Keep on rocking* would have to go, of course (Marx would never stand for *that*). But the other bit... that was good, very good.

"Fetch me an autographed photograph of a septuagenarian pontiff! Or a light-sensitive plastic portrait of Jesus from the gift shop at the Abbey, Fort Augustus! Or the flag of the United States of America! I wish to defecate!"

"Shit, man, what's *defecate* mean?"

"It means *all that is holy is profaned*! It means a shameless voiding of the bowels upon all that is false and loathsome! It means commodity fetishism in action! What is it that's sitting — shitting! — on top of the world? Capitalism!"

"I'll make some coffee. Sounds like you could use a cup."

"That would be swell." Engels picked up his quill pen, had another go. "Hey, listen to this. *All that is solid melts into air, all that is holy is profaned, and man is at last compelled to face with sober senses, his real conditions of life, and his relations with his kind.*"

"Can't hear a word. The coffee grinder."

"I said I'm very pleased with it. I'll mail it off to Marx in the morning. I think he'll like it. I'll send him some grass too. I'll tell him it's a joint production."

"Black or white?"

"Dialectical. No sugar."

Suddenly Engels felt tired. He put the draft of *The Communist Manifesto* down. That was enough for one night. There was a grey round the edges of things, the dawn. He had that bleak middle-of-the-night, washed-out "Visions of Johanna" feeling. He downed a tumbler of Red Mountain bourbon. "Come here, little girl!" he chuckled. "Take that bra off!"

Janis grinned, obeyed.

Scowled.

"What the fuck?"

"I wanna try it on! All that is holy is profaned! All the years I was a choirboy I had this craving to put on a bra, slip in a couple of pears and parade about the room, stark naked! Now, thanks to you, my dream has come true!"

She had to help him with the hooks. Engels walked to and fro, admiring himself in the mirror. While Friedrich contemplated his shapely buttocks and jutting artificial breasts and pondered questions of gender, sexuality, ideology, modes of production and events at Elberfeld, Janis put on Leroy Carr singing "When The Sun Goes Down", followed by Johnnie Temple singing "Lead Pencil Blues".

Between the sheets she was holding *Little Big Man*, then put it down, picked up *The Sensuous Woman*.

"Come to bed, you red pervert!"

"At once, my chubby little songstress."

Wheeeeeeeeeeeeeeeee! Yaaaa-whoooooooooooo!

*

Islington, Tottenham, Bayswater. Minnipuka, Ophir, Snakes-breath. Forget. *Picture an endless maze of connections...*

Restless, agitated, screwing, riding the express across Canada, the dull plains, the far-off farms, Janis unable to sleep a wink, peeking through the blind, moaning, "Ah, the desolate idiocy of rural life!", the General scribbling something down on an empty pack of cigarettes, the others singing, or drinking, or sleeping, or reading penny dreadfuls and dime novels and shilling shockers (the morose Englishman, for example, deep in a purple paperback entitled *A Maze of Death*), all the while the wheels going clickety-click clickety-click clickety-click, hitting the bottle, slugs of Southern Comfort, carton of orange and jug of vodka, tequila, beers, J.J. reading his horoscope ("Destiny puts your name on a smart door"), reading her own ("The love planet moves into your marriage chart and passion is back"), clickety-click clickety-click clickety-click, riding riding riding the Festival Express in the Year of the Kozmic Blues, sketching a song, writing a chapter, Saskatchewan plains sliding by, Janis crooning "Long Gone Lonesome Blues", Friedrich at a table by the window, writing *The history of these Unions is a long series of defeats of the working-men, interrupted by a few isolated victories*, writing the Labour Movements chapter of *The Condition of the Working Class in England*, then pulling her to their compartment, pushing her on to the narrow bunk bed, causing her to revise her belief that Scorpios fuck best, shifting some beers, then getting dressed again, returns to the window seat, dips the quill pen in the inkpot, writes *and requested Mr Sharp to turn his inventive mind to the construction of an automatic mule,* a marshalling yard slipping past, oil tanks, clouds of dust, billowing...

Inertia: that's what they're fighting. *Working Men!* Capitalism is like a ball and chain! You got to get it while you can! Try, just a little bit harder! Set — Wheeeeeeeeeeeeeeeee! Yaaaa-whooooooooooooo! — the avalanche in motion!

Motion. That's what they have in common, revolutionaries and rock stars. True internationalists. Movement, transitions, connections. *Uninterrupted disturbance of all social relations, everlasting uncertainty and agitation distinguish the bourgeois epoch from all earlier ones.* Another — Wheeeeeeeeeeeeeeeeee! — of Janis's contributions. So to speak. Marx pieced it all together, of course; gave it a final polish.

At Calgary she split. Kissed Friedrich on the cheek outside the Capitol Theater. "Goodbye for now," she whispered. "I have to go and change into Janis Joplin. She's upstairs in a box!"

Engels headed for Remington's, drank eight beers, wrote on a napkin, *This primitive, naive, but intrinsically correct conception of the world is that of ancient Greek philosophy, and was first clearly formulated by Heraclitus: everything is and also is not, for everything is in flux, is constantly changing, constantly coming into being and passing away.* Just then Seth Parsons from Wisconsin passed by, inadvertently knocked the table, caused the glass to topple, the napkin of a sudden sodden, darkly golden, the words melting into puffy blue billowings, provoking Seth (who was unaware that at that precise moment, plummeting through the grey sky over Omaha, his cousin Bob's parachute was failing to open) to draw a slurred analogy with Patrick

Heron's *Manganese in Deep Violet: January 1967* until, seconds later, he was knocked over by a pair of panicky ostriches which had burst in from the adjacent field, where an over-the-limit driver, Charles, 23, from Seattle, whose mother Diane, in Nebraska, was dying, had split open the fence.

"Garbage," growled Pete, the bartender, who happened to have a postcard of Wols's *Composition* in his pocket. "Who?" said Engels. "Wols," retorted Pete.

"The pseudonym of Alfred Otto Wolfgang Schulze (1913-1951)," explained Seth, sitting up and rubbing his head energetically. Since January, wondering if Wols had been tormented, as he Seth Parsons was tormented, by the origins of everything human in a grotesque, farcical, rotating nebulous mass, not to mention the worrying possibility of a repeat of the shattering explosion which occurred in the upper reaches of the River Podkamennaya Tunguska on the last day of June 1908, and perplexed by the brevity of the painter's life (suicide? car smash? hideous illness?), he had been intending to read a biography of Wols. This intention had been frustrated, however, both by his failure to locate a biography of Wols in any of the seventeen bookstores he'd visited in Arkansas, and by his work on the three books he was writing, for different publishers, about Coleridge, plagiarism, the four basic types of reader.

The four basic types? *Buy you another.*

1. Sponges, who absorb all they read, and return it nearly in the same state, only a little dirtied.

2. Sand-glasses, who retain nothing, and are content to get through a book for the sake of getting through the time.

3. Strain-bags, who retain merely the dregs of what they read.

4. Mogul diamonds, who profit by what they read, and enable others to profit by it also.

His conclusion, triumphantly built on layers of questionnaires and taped interviews, was that though 84% believed themselves to belong to category 4, only 2% truly did, with over 65% unwittingly belonging to category 3. It was in Arkansas that he had got into a fight with a Trotskyish airliner pilot, a man who had read Sharp's "Da-Da Vogt", and who had taken great exception to the word "profit" in category 4.

Just then someone played Joplin's "Piece of My Heart" on the jukebox. Claws raked Engels's heart. He slammed his fist down on the table. "Every moment every organic being assimilates matter supplied from without and gets rid of other matter! Every moment some cells of the body die and others are being born! Every organic being is always itself, and yet something other than itself! Pete, make that four more beers!"

"I insist," insisted Seth, his face flickering with bands of blue, pulling out a blue, pulsing snakeskin wallet. The light from the patrol car, in which sobbing Charles, flushed with liquor and shaken by the presence of gigantic birds, was speaking seamlessly of his poor Mom, and of the polyps, and of Tuesday, a pert, pretty, brown-eyed blonde, fantastic in the sack, who had done him wrong and run off to San Francisco with a bearded anarchist in a black T-shirt.

Engels, disturbed at being forced to the margins of the narrative by these maddeningly superficial secondary figures, decided to make use of a telekinetic trick he had acquired from *Dr Who and the Brain of Morbius*. Seconds later Seth, Pete, Charles and a large silver-white police patrol car with a block-headed uniformed brute behind the wheel were whisked away, making gurgling noises. With a grunt of relief Engels found himself alone again, back at El Quijote. He looked at the clock (a quarter to six). By eleven he had drunk five brandy sours and written all twenty-one pages of *The Bakunists at Work*.

"Ooooo-eeeeee!" Janis again.

She adjusted her glasses, stared down at his lap. "Wizzit?"

"This manuscript? A review of the uprising in Spain in the summer of 1873. An account of ignominious actions of the Bakunist anarchists in an ignominious insurrection. An exposé of their intrigues, villainies and empty phrases. An acid test of how they put into practice their ultra-revolutionary phrases on anarchy and autonomy, on the abolition of all authority, especially that of the State, and on the immediate and complete emancipation of the workers! Read it, J.J. Hear the militant phrases of docile men! Witness the confusion, complete inactivity and total ineptitude of anarchism in action! See the enemies of authority becoming members of the Committee of Public Safety! Gasp with amazement as they re-establish the pass system! See how the anarchists wasted time in empty debates and paper resolutions. *Recognise how, in the end, when it came to action, the ultra-revolutionary cries of the Bakunists gave way to evasion, uprisings doomed to defeat in advance, or adherence to a bourgeois party which not only subjected the workers to the most shameful political exploitation but even rewarded them with blows!"*

"Lemme see."

Janis was dazzled by the clarity and power of Friedrich's prose. It was after reading *The Bakunists At Work* that she wrote "Mercedes Benz". The next day J.J., Engels and Full-Tilt Boogie headed for Honolulu.

*

Engels and Janis Joplin dozed, knowing nothing of Sharp's "Martina" or of the activities taking place in Markarian 1, a galaxy in the constellation Pisces, a constellation which features two fish tied by their tails, the knot marked by (alpha) Piscium, a double star 98 light years away from readers of "A Maze, A Muse, A Mule", who will require a 75mm telescope and a high magnification to observe them, the constellation sometimes identified with Venus and Cupid, who transformed themselves into fish and swam away from the attack of the monster Typhon.

"The spectroscope confirmed the existence in cosmic space of incandescent masses of gas in various stages of condensation," Engels explained to the stewardess pouring the drinks. How was he to know that the invention of the radio telescope would result in the discovery of water 200 million light years away, contained in clouds rotating at thousands of miles an hour around the centre of Markarian 1? The stewardess projected an understanding smile, asked Engels what he'd like to drink. Suddenly a powerful and invisible force pressed him back into the first draft of "A Maze, A Muse, A Mule". Here, cosmic matter had not yet entered. Engels was gazing down at the flashing blue ocean below, reflecting on the great merit of the Hegelian system.

"A gin and tonic, please. Oh, and one of those tasty muffins I saw you with earlier."

"Sorry, sir, the muffins are all gone. The other passengers ate them in the second draft."

"Ah, too bad." He reverted to Hegelianism. Its value lay in representing things — the world — *reality* — as a *process*, as something in constant motion, change, transformation, development. Human history was no longer a wild whirl of senseless deeds but a process of evolution. It meant things could change. It meant things could be different.

A screen was opened up. Headsets were being distributed. Shirley MacLaine and a mule? What is this shit? The inflight movie, sir. Very popular with business travellers. *Two Mules for Sister Sara*, sir.

Mules? Mule... Something... a dim memory.

Next, the bearded, frowning face of the Nixon supporter Clint Eastwood appeared on the screen. *What a crap film*, thought Engels. He'd seen it before, years ago. Bourgeois individualist violence and mealy-mouthed eroticism dressed up as anti-imperialist struggle, doubly nauseating and hypocritical in so far as it was an *American* production. "Hey!" he shouted, to no one in particular. "Stop the projection! Remove this garbage from the screen! Replace it with *The Battle of Algiers*. At once, do you hear! Or *October*. Or show *Bad Timing*. Blast out Club Class with *Céline and Julie Go Boating*. I demand *The Wages of Fear*! I'd settle for

The Go-Between. I'm a reasonable theorist. I'm even prepared to make do with *Dr Zhivago.* What else does the history of ideas prove, other than that intellectual production changes its character in proportion as material production is changed?"

No one said a word. It was *Carnival of Souls* all over again. Sounds muted, murmurings, jittery watery shadows dancing across ceilings. Maybe he was dead; maybe that's why everyone was ignoring him. Even Janis.

It had to end. There was no future in the relationship. She was a star with a speck of blood on her pants. She spent too long at Nobody's and the Terminal Bar. She never made a recording of The Internationale. She was a puffy, mottled junkie and he was too lined and old. Far too old. He smelled of ash and the salt sea. Comes a time when you have to leave all this and concentrate on *The Wages System* and *On Marx's "Capital"* and *Letters on Historical Materialism 1890-94.* She took the name of the silvery-white smooth and iridescent product of many bivalved molluscs. She started to miss out her vowels, not realising it was the consonants she needed to worry about. She was a honky-tonk woman who fused fantasy with reality to establish the Fantality Corporation but who didn't see what would happen if the "n" fell away. She saw *8½*, which opened in Paris the same month as Visconti's *The Leopard* (starring Alain Delon) and *Strip-Tease* (starring Krista Nico) — and died.

And died. Call it Sunday morning, coming down. To the lobby of the Landmark Hotel. October 4th 1970. The five dollar bill. The pack of cigarettes. Ash. Friedrich's death. Friedrich was cremated. The ashes scattered in the sea off Beachy Head. They burned her body, too. The remains scattered from the air along the coastline of Marin County.

Myra Friedman remembered encountering Joplin near the end. The star was alone in a dingy dressing room. She was sitting on a soiled red chair, reading a book. *As she walked into the corridor, 1 lingered for a second and glanced into her bag to see what she'd been reading. It turned out to be some*

A Maze, A Muse, A Mule

philosophy anthology. Be more precise, Myra! Be more precise. Where facts are lacking, speculation thrives. Just the other day I found what I had long been looking for, in a second hand bookshop near King's Cross station. *Engels: Selected Writings.* A 1967 Pelican Original, seven shillings and sixpence. And on the yellowing flyleaf, beneath the inscription *N. Y. C. 1969*, circled by an ancient coffee stain, two faded, grey, identical, intoxicating meat hook initials.

2

Everyone knows of that long afternoon at the Smolny when Kamenev, Riazanov were all for capitulation and a joint all-Socialist government crammed with cowards and conciliators, and of how Lenin stood firm, and of how, later, while representatives of the *Bund* and the Mensheviks frothed and gesticulated and whinged, he stood quietly, waiting his turn, humming "Me and Bobby McGee", until at last the moment came and, stepping forwards and gripping the edge of the reading stand, he uttered a line not even Trakl or Vallejo or Yeats or Dylan has bettered, ringing and resonant, sweetly melodious yet powerfully charged: "We shall now proceed to construct the Socialist order!"

The whole world now knows of those earlier, obscurer years and of my brief friendship with Lenin at the University of Kazan. My struggle to end his enthusiasm for Dire Straits was intense, exhausting but in the end successful. I blasted him with Mahler and Leonard Cohen, assisted by regular shots of the Cowboy Junkies. What is altogether less well known is Lenin's passion for Nico.

In 1897, in exile in eastern Siberia, Lenin began writing a long ode, of which only the opening three lines survive:

In Shushu, at the feet of the Sayan Mountains,
I first heard Nico,
Nico and the Velvet Underground.

The reference, of course, is to that legendary Andy Warhol production *The Velvet Underground and Nico* (note Lenin's characteristic inversion of the title).

What happened was this. On February 10th, 1897, the Tsarist government sentenced Lenin to a three-year term of exile in Siberia, under police surveillance. He was sent to Shushenskoye, a rural backwater on the River Shusha, bordered by forest and mountains. On the train to Krasnoyarsk he met the young revolutionary Krutovsky. The countryside glistened with a strong, two-fold brilliance reminiscent of descriptions in Turgenev. Wild, overgrown orchards pressed against the flanks of isolated cottages, where, on the side of a shallow ravine, had Lenin not been napping at the time (exhausted by a five-hour stint refreshing himself on absolute and relative surplus value, different formulae for the rate of surplus value, the transformation of the value of labour power into wages, the transformation of surplus value into capital and the general law of capitalist accumulation), he might have seen, close by some wattle fencing, a bee garden, above which projected sharp-tipped stalks of dark green hemp, giving way, in time, as everything does, to other things; of other rusty or cloudy or green hues, in this instance passing away in a matter of a mere minute, unfolding punctually on the sixty-first second a facade of plausible forests, fabulous country estates, a deserted terrace, ivy-shrouded stables, a veranda, woods, a porch, a quaint rotting summer house, a sunlit tennis court framing two creamy immaculate cretinous aristocratic figures patting a furry blur to and fro, deservedly erased by graves, then a plot of reddish dusty earth, which in turn gave way to a vast green lawn bearing a single white garden bench and a circular iron table.

Krutovsky pulled down the window and leaned out, staring with narrowed eyes at the featureless white narrative void ahead of the dirty buffing-puffing tank engine where what appeared to be a gigantic black dragonfly zoomed on ahead, scattering soot. Borrowing a telescope from a passing admirer of Amedee Pichot's prose translation (2 vols., Paris, 1820) of Thomas Moore's *Lalla Rookh: an Oriental Romance* (London, 1817), he scanned the extraordinary insect. It was, he realised with a shock, some sort of aerial device — presumably an aerostat of advanced design. As a materialist, Krutovsky's perceptions were admirably sound. However, not even a firm grasp of *Materialism and Empirio-Criticism* (1908) would have enabled him to recognise the tail rotor drive shaft, swashplate assembly and engine cowling of a Huey helicopter with T53-L-11 gas turbine engine capable of developing eleven hundred horsepower while weighing only five hundred pounds.

Through an open hatch a strange figure wearing an Edgar Allan Poe mask and a white NO M11 LINK ROAD T-shirt was emptying two sacks of soot.

No, not soot. Words. One sack was labelled "TRACK", the other "TURGENEV". When the contents of the "TRACK" sack hit the ground they instantaneously formed sleepers and rail lines, fortunately conforming to the idiosyncratic Russian gauge, enabling both train and story to continue at a reasonable if, at times, wheezing pace.

"TURGENEV" provided the surrounding landscape. A light scattering of language produced a rich crop of oak forests, buckwheat and clover and ripening rye. Spirals of gnats glittered in the shade, birds sang peacefully, women with long rakes wandered in the fields.

Lenin woke. Krutovsky, pale and sweating slightly, began to point at the aerostat, only to realise that it had vanished. Strange.

They were passing more gorgeous expanses of Turgenev, where larks (if the translation was reliable) poured silver beads of resonant song and fluttered under a clear sky. Scattered dwellings glowed in the sunshine.

"Do you know, Krutovsky, that it is one of the curses of a mind with a turn like mine that I must look at everything with reference to my own special subject. The bourgeoisie look at landscapes like these and are impressed by their beauty. They always fill me with a certain horror. I look at them and think of *the idiocy of rural life*. I think of the sheer backwardness of Russia. The proletariat alone can be the *vanguard fighter* for political liberty and for democratic institutions!" Krutovsky nodded absently.

At Shushenskoye Lenin lodged at the house of Apollon Zyrianov. Here, like Sherlock Holmes in "The Copper Beeches", he would sit for half an hour on end, with knitted brows, and an abstracted air, crying impatiently, "Data! data! data!"

As the weeks passed Lenin grew bored with his modest record collection (which consisted of an LP of Tchaikovsky's songs, Mozart's Piano Concerto No. 21 in C Major, K. 467, Couperin's *Suites for Harpsichord,* Glenn Gould's recording of Haydn's six last piano sonatas and Faure's *Requiem*). In the long hot summer of that year he slipped away to the record store in Minusinsk. A disappointment. A meagre stock. *Deep Purple in Rock* did not sound like his cup of tea. Neither did That Petrol Emotion's *Manic Pop Thrill*. In the end it was a toss-up between Al Stewart's *Past, Present and Future* or *The Velvet Underground and Nico*. The Velvets won. He walked back through the forest, thinking that almost anything was better than having to sit through that bloody Mozart again. Listening to Louis Firbank singing "Sunday Morning", Lenin's spirits sank at the sugary concoction, reviving only a little with the lively "I'm Waiting for the Man". And then it happened. That voice! The opening lines of "Femme Fatale"! And more to come... Amid the dross and Firbank the haunting intensity of "All Tomorrow's Parties" and "I'll Be Your Mirror". Electrifying! If anything kept him going through that long dreary summer of mosquitoes and stifling heat it was Nico's deep, dark, drawling voice. His muse. Her influence unmistakeable in such lines of his as:

That is why the merging
Of the democratic activities of the working-class

A Maze, A Muse, A Mule

With the democratic aspirations of other classes and groups
Would weaken the democratic movement,
Would make it less determined,
Less consistent,
More likely to compromise.

On his next trip to Minusinsk Lenin could not believe his
astonishing good luck! Nico had just released her first solo
album! With songs by Tim Hardin, Bob Dylan, Jackson
Browne, John Cale!

How he hurried back to his room, with what care did his
trembling hands cradle the fragile album! Desolating song
produced by a needle pressing against vinyl at thirty-three-
and-a-third revolutions per minute! Exquisite thought! Let
the petty bourgeois conciliators while away their time with
Judy Collins or Carole King! Nico was something else:
something hard and strange and uncompromising, something altogether different from the usual syrup-slop of catchy
melody and bland, honeyed lyric.

Months later the music papers arrived. Lenin gazed in
stupefaction at the descriptions of Nico's album in *New
Musical Express* ("Joan Baez-like") and *Melody Maker* ("in
the mould of Marianne Faithfull"). About as accurate as
calling Marx "Bakunin-like" or "in the mould of Samuel
Bailey"! Lenin practically wore out *Chelsea Girl*. Zyrianov
remembered "the awful drone" which used to come from
Lenin's room, and how the great revolutionary would
emerge, tired but twinkly-eyed, and cry, *"Magnificent!* Nico
is *the Social-Democrat of song!"*

Certainly anyone who takes the trouble to read *The Tasks
of the Russian Democrats* (1897) will find unmistakeable
echoes of Nico's uncompromising attitude to rhythm and
lyric structure:

Many and most
Diverse strata
Of the Russian people

Are opposed to the omnipotent,
Irresponsible, corrupt, savage, ignorant
And parasitic
Russian bureaucracy.

One evening in May 1898 Lenin returned to his room to find himself confronted by a tall, bad-tempered woman who subjected him to her bleak gaze and barked, "You've grown awfully fat!" It was his future mother-in-law, the religious bore Elizaveta Vasilyevna. Behind her lurked Krupskaya. Neither of these formidable women liked Nico, complaining bitterly that her singing was "excruciating", "just too awful for words" and "negative". Nico was silenced. Nico slipped from Lenin's life. Lenin gave up listening to records and set to work writing his 535-page study, *The Development of Capitalism in Russia.*

The release of *The Marble Index* in January 1905, coinciding with the abortive upheavals of that year, was, as historians have now proved beyond doubt, a complete coincidence. When Nico remarked that the album's stark melodies "are from my Russian soul" she knew nothing of the Putilov strike or "Bloody Sunday" or the activities of the Petersburg Soviet of Workers' Deputies. And when she sang *the game comes to a start* how could she know of the chord struck in Lenin's heart, or of how he crooned this line, month after month through that long and bloody year? And when it was all over, how could she know how her third solo album, *Desertshore*, would sustain the great revolutionary in the bleak, hopeless years that followed. 1907-1910, in particular.

Then, in 1911, tragedy. Lenin came home one day to find that his complete Nico collection had been inadvertently destroyed. Krupskaya showed him the fragments. It was, she explained, the result of electrostatic vibrations from a passing meteorite. Lenin was unperturbed. 1911 seemed like the turning point. A general strike of students! The workers going on the offensive! Street demonstrations and protests! The launch of *Pravda*! The Bolsheviks becoming a mass revolutionary party! And then, on August 1st, 1914, Russia went to war.

Engrossed in pamphlets, oppressed by imperialist war, Lenin had more or less forgotten Nico until that unforgettable time she appeared on *The Merv Griffin Show*. Lenin watched it on the little monochrome TV in his Zurich lodgings. *The Merv Griffin Show* went out live to millions (there was even a rumour it was the Czarina's favourite TV programme). Nico was magnificent. Mournfully, accompanying herself on her legendary harmonium, she intoned one of her opaque, dirge-like songs. It ended, leaving her staring blankly at the studio audience.

Merv stepped forwards, a synthetic smile on his face (he'd been expecting a cheerful ballad designed to boost the morale of the fighting men at the front).

"Nico, where do you come from?"

Silence.

The synthetic smile twitching slightly at each end.

"What exactly was the song about, Nico?"

Silence. Titters in the audience. Merv's bogus smile growing vaster all the time.

"Well, do you have anything to tell us, Nico, anything at all?"

Silence. Oh God. Pandemonium. Premature fadeout. Run some commercials! Never in the whole history of the programme... Who hired that fucking cow to come on the show in the first place?

Lenin wrote that, after Rosa Luxemburg's Junius pamphlet, it was the most devastating critique of the barbarism of imperialism he had encountered. Hearing of the new album, Lenin sent Krupskaya out to the local record shops but she returned, her bonnet soaked, to report that *The End...* was unobtainable. The entire consignment had been torpedoed off the Cork coast.

And then, on March 8th 1917, in Petersburg —

*

They met, just once, in Redwood country. It was during the civil war. Weldon, the Redwood Mouse, fixed it up. He wasn't just an entertainer in a rodent outfit on stilts, he was also a long-time Party member. High cheekbones, an interest in cycling, an inability to compromise — Weldon knew right from the start Lenin and Nico had a lot in common.

"I used to adore Martov. But now he means nothing to me. I'm through with him. Now I think only of your writings. I think about them all the time," Nico whispered. "Their clarity, their starkness. Like gleaming granite in a dark, stormy night." (*Has she been reading MacDiarmid?* he wondered.) "You are my muse!"

"And you mine," Lenin retorted, gallantly. He mentioned the old days, that time in exile in Siberia he'd first heard *The Velvet Underground and Nico*. "That cover! A yellow banana on a white background. Stunning!"

"What most people don't realise," said Weldon (who couldn't help overhearing), "is that the very same banana used on this cover was put by Andy in the Factory's deep freeze and guarded in sub-zero conditions for a quarter of a century, then defrosted and given to Leonard Cohen for use on the cover of *I'm Your Man*."

"Is that a fact?" asked Gerald, a hanger-on with bureaucratic tendencies.

"In postmodernist fiction *everything's* a fact," Weldon retorted. "It's like the moon. It's like doubting its cheddar gorges. See?"

"Yes," muttered Gerald, who didn't, hadn't and wouldn't, and who was subsequently abducted by aliens while out hill-walking in the Urals, subjected to a number of hideous medical experiments and returned to earth in a semi-lobotomised state as a character in a naturalistic first novel praised as *a haunting parable of modern life by a writer of extraordinary imagination and power* but which sold badly and was remaindered, causing Gerald to die of dehydration.

"Did you know," said Nico in her slow drawl, "that *The Velvet Underground and Nico* never got higher than 171 in the album charts? The record company actually withdrew it from sale."

Lenin shook his head. "Capitalism! Incredible, sometimes, are the anarchic lunacies of the market."

"But it eventually went gold, of course," Nico smiled. "Just like *The State and Revolution*," she added, tactfully.

Afterwards, when asked what he liked about Nico, Lenin replied: "Her complete lack of pretension. Very refreshing!" She, for her part, admired his "austerity" and "clear thinking".

Before departing they had a little celebration. Nico sang "Femme Fatale", Lenin wrote down on pieces of card the names Clio, Euterpe, Thalia, Melpomene, Terpischore, Erato, Polyhymnia, Uranmia and Calliope, and Weldon drank too much Budweiser and fell off his stilts, fracturing six ribs and causing $400 damage to the mouse suit. Then they all went their separate ways: Lenin to Moscow, Weldon to the local Bolshevik fracture clinic, Gerald to his fateful encounter with extra-terrestrials, and Nico to Manchester.

*

Why Manchester? Because of Engels. Because she said she felt closer to him there than anywhere in the whole wide world. When Nico saw how the Revolution had failed she said she wanted to go back to the beginning. To understand.

The incredible thing was that Nico had once met Engels! She realised this only years afterwards. It was at Monterey, June 1967. She remembered being introduced to this fat, spotty little singer named Janis Joplin, who in those days was a *nobody*. Joplin had an interesting fellow German in tow, Friedrich. But Friedrich seemed to be tripping: he kept rushing off across the grass, shouting he was in pursuit of *the laws of motion of cataclysm*! He looked like someone who'd be interested in Blake and Coleridge. If things had been different they would probably have been lovers. But Friedrich only had eyes for Janis, and she herself was going with Brian Jones, and it was not to be.

When everything finally went wrong for her she headed for Manchester, clutching her copy of *The Condition of the Working Class in England.* Engels was dead by then, of course, along with Edie and Tim and Jim and Brian and Andy and Janis and all the others. *The Condition of the Working Class in England* was a book Nico could really empathise with — all that pain, all that suffering. The need for radical solutions. "I like cities best when they are burning and empty," she'd say.

Bleak Manchester. *This is the end...* She was living in a cul-de-sac in a southern suburb. A still crumbling nineteenth-century part of the city, where villas and merchants' houses decayed, split up into flats and bedsits, the paint peeling on the whitewashed walls, weeds sprouting in the choked roof-level gutters, gates hanging askew from broken hinges, rotting fenceposts soft as Aero bars.

In the early days she used to ride her ladies' bicycle to the other side of town, to stare at the house where Engels had lived. A wreck; a ruin. Derelict. Tiles gone, dark joists rotting in the rain that pattered unendingly from the daily grey miserable English sky. Garden a wilderness of nettles, fly-tipped rubbish, some blue, bulging plastic sacks. A rusty pram.

Then back to the Old Town in search of Ducie Bridge and Alien's Court and the coal-black Irk. In search of so much — the pauper burial ground, the railway station, the Work-house. St George's Road and Ancoats Street. Hulme and the far side of the Medlock. So much had altered; so much remained the same. Poverty with supermarkets, squalor with TV aerials, cracked pavements, dirty puddles, the same rows of desolate terraces. Cars everywhere, occupying the spaces where children once played, parked on footways, racing down the narrow streets, growling at red lights while pale blue poisons squirted from their dark anuses.

Loss of work. Bad food. Rags. Unclean interiors. Heaps of debris. *The filth and horrors...* A derelict life. Bad, bad years.

A Maze, A Muse, A Mule

Years of the curtains closed, watching TV. Years of grey skin and a diet of custard and wine and chocolate. The end. From which she began again. Emerged once more into the grey light, to make the music that consoled a desperate and then a dying Lenin ...

*

Kto kogo? Lenin would say. *Who will win?* Meaning: the final victory of socialism in one country is impossible.

Without another European revolution the workers' state in Russia was doomed. But in France the Communist Party was tainted with right-opportunism; in Italy, with ultra-leftism and the spinelessness of Serrati's centrist leadership. In Germany, in March 1921, the Party leadership tried to substitute the Party militants for the mass movement — with disastrous consequences. In Britain the movement was imbued with syndicalism and only in 1922 did the Communist Party set about transforming itself — too late for the great revolutionary moment of 1919. Even in Bulgaria the C.P. blew it, standing aside from the struggle when a reactionary military coup involving 20,000 Russian soldiers from Wrangel's White Army was launched against the newly elected Peasant Union government. And then the greatest defeat of all, that of the German revolution of 1923.

And in Russia? A workers' state with a bureaucratic twist to it. A proletariat atomized and exhausted. Peasant conservatism. Many of the best Party militants killed in the civil war. A shattered economy. NEPmen. Stalin. *The high tide is taking everything.* And Lenin getting iller and iller... No wonder he enjoyed listening to "You Forget To Answer" so much. No wonder he shut himself away for days, doing nothing but drink tea and listen, time and time again, to *The End...* and *Drama of Exile* and *Do or Die!* No wonder that the last time he met Trotsky he took his comrade by the arm and whispered, "The end of our elaborate plans... of everything that stands, the end..."

The end of Lenin. On 25 May 1922 Lenin suffered a stroke that led to partial paralysis. On 20 November he made his last public speech. On 13 December he suffered two major strokes. On 10 March 1923 a massive stroke paralysed half his body and deprived him of speech.

On 21 January 1924 he woke from a dream about the moon to find Nico standing at his bedside. She had retrieved his old black bicycle, the one stolen from him on the Rue Beaunier. "Come," she said. "We must go for a ride together." He was pleased to see her machine was the Prestwich one, a glaucous Raleigh with a wicker basket used for transporting groceries and methadone.

Methadone?

It was a fine, crisp sunlit Paris day. They pedalled gaily out of the Rue Marie-Rose and set off through the streets, heading for Fontainebleau.

Pebbles glittered on the pavement, weathercocks stood motionless on the houses. There was a brief, sharp, strange odour of aromatic vinegar which gave way to a soporific fragrance of hawthorn blossom. They passed grey apartments, grey squares, a fairy tale birch outlined starkly against a patch of pale sky. Outside the city, how white and powdery with snow the hedges! How darkly beautiful the ice in the silent ditches! Side by side they hissed down the empty country lane. A fresh cool breeze blowing over them, in the distance a watermill, half-hidden by willows, making a heavy thumping-thumping-thumping noise. Next, a dark shadow crawled over them, next a roaring of metal and skidding rubber slammed through the quiet morning, flipping them up into the cold air, so that, freed of the handlebars, they could stretch their arms, reaching out for each other in their moment of need.

A gorgeous morning! Hand in hand, still side by side, they flew on, the fields far below them now, a bourgeois quilt of fading yellows and greens, Nico's "Evening of Light" a far, dim chorus seeping across the hamlets, drowning the placid, fatuous hymns sung by the peasants in the toy churches,

Lenin humming along, Nico amusing him with anecdotes about Manchester, a blush-pink moon glowing in the south. He felt they could go on like this forever, had it not been for Krutovsky, swimming through the suddenly darkening air with a frightened expression on his colourless papery face, saying something absolutely incomprehensible about an aerostat and two empty sacks...

3

Lenin removed the polyencephalic cylinder from his head and placed it carefully on the familiar grey cradle. He felt tired and depressed. Remembering. Time for another spell of real time, of being an archivist/librarian again. Back on the ship. Just the six of them. The ship — *The Slight Hubbub of Conversations* — its engines and transmitter equipment damaged by fire, circling endlessly a dead star. With two thousand space tonnes of dehydrated astro-food still to eat. With years more in which to play these foolish poly-encephalic games when the psycho-sexual tensions and boredom threshold rose to DANGER.

As always, the chunky, bearded figure of Captain Pickdock was waiting for them in the relaxation room with a dish of tranquillisers. Pickdock and the ship's engineer always stayed behind, in case of black holes.

Cool clear melancholy music was playing. My mind's scrambled by Terra, Lenin thought. Then it came back to him. Nick Drake's *Pink Moon*.

"Phew!" Lenin said. "What a bummer. The best sections of the Party wiped out by civil war, capitalism returns as state capitalism and, to cap everything, I get poisoned by Stalin. A red one, please."

Pickdock gave him the tablet and a glass of tomato juice.

Nico came in next. She blew Lenin a kiss. "Still suffering from anxiety about hair loss, I see," she laughed. Lenin ran his fingers through his thick black hair and smiled. It was

219

true: in all the games, nine times out of ten he was bald. Once he'd even been configured as the inventor of a device which cured baldness by suspending the sufferer upside down in a cage while a machine slapped fresh cabbage leaves against the scalp. Though there was not a scrap of evidence the device worked he'd become a national celebrity and within months was the new leader of the British Labour Party.

Janis Joplin entered. She seemed unsteady on her feet. Evidently she was still in thrall to manufactured recall-datum implanted during fusion.

"You're quaking like a wet Nellie!" Nico cried, concerned.

"I'm okay. I just need a banana milkshake." Afterwards radio operator Joplin smiled. She fingered her silvery hair. She felt better now. Was pleased to be back. Any decade now she'd get the transmission equipment fixed and help would come.

The navigator, Engels, was last. Not for the first time his enormous beard had become trapped in the cubicle sliding door. A temporary malfunction. "Damn that door!" roared Engels. "I told Sharp to fix it before we got back."

Engineer Sharp was in charge of maintenance and growth. They didn't see much of him. He was a reclusive individual. He liked doors kept shut. He kept away from the main characters, inhabiting the vast regions of the ship outside the reality zone. Joplin said she'd heard he liked to go skinnydipping in the gutter margins. Sometimes he was more like a rumour than a reality. Nico smiled, recalling Lenin's theory that Sharp was actually a replicant. His interest in invention, postmodernism and mechanical jackdaws was certainly a little suspicious.

She remembered she hadn't seen Sharp since the time she'd found him asleep on a flyleaf. That must have been at least twenty years earlier.

"I'll speak with him," Nico said, pressing Engels gently back into his seat. It was better a woman dealt with such matters. Sharp could be prickly at times. She put on her raincoat, mounted her green Raleigh bicycle and pedalled briskly through Sports, Mountain Regions, Interiors For Weary Ex-Gunslingers, The Great Hall of Vitriolic Revolutionary Socialist Disagreements and Putney. In the Lukewarm Swamp of Liberalism the crocodiles snapped at her ankles, but she remembered they were toothless. At last she arrived at London In Decay Under The Tories, where, at a station situated in the basement, her bike was snatched from her by a thief.

She caught a Victoria line train to Oxford Street. En route she admired the design of the tiles (a William Morris pattern at Walthamstow; a black horse at Blackhorse Road; an ancient ferry at Tottenham Hale; seven trees at Seven Sisters; a pair of highwayman's pistols at Finsbury Park; a castle at Highbury and Islington; crowns at King's Cross; an arch at Euston). At Warren Street she felt impelled to get out and run her finger over the design. Twenty minutes later she was back on a southbound train. At Oxford Street she changed for the westbound Bakerloo line, which ran from Normal Homoencephalic Functioning through the P.K. Barrier and on to the end of the line where Postmodernist Playfulness was to be found.

Stand clear of the gap, the speakers boomed, as she emerged from the Victoria Line passenger tunnel. A silver train pulled in and she boarded it and sat down. "Please abandon your realist expectations," the train cautioned her.

"I'll try," Nico said. "What's your name?"

"Sylvia," said the train.

"That's a nice name."

"Why, thank you."

"And I love these poems along the walls."

"All my idea. Nothing to do with Sharp. He said it was vulgar."

"I couldn't disagree more."

"He didn't want the grey carpeting, either."

"He was wrong there, too."

"Well, can't stop," Sylvia said. "Mustn't keep the reader

waiting."

The train pulled out. Nico read the poems which ran above the windows. *Let Naomi rejoice with Pseudosphece, who is between a wasp and a hornet*, she read. Hmmmmm! On to Wilfred Owen's "The parable of the old man and the young". This was more like it... Lord Byron, Thomas Sheridan, Robert Burns, Thomas Hood, Walt Whitman, Ernest Jones. Then she changed to the seat opposite and read the ones which had been above her. Pope, Wordsworth, John Clare. Anon. Of these, the one she liked best was Thomas Sheridan's "A True and Faithful Inventory of the Goods Belonging to Dr. Swift".

Finished, she went through into the next carriage, where *The Dunciad Variorum* began. And a good thing too — the train was delayed by two suicides, signal failure, a security alert and a clean-up operation after yet another Conservative had exploded from a lethal build-up of internal gases and toxic hypocrisy. Finally, four hours and ten minutes later, she was there.

Remember to take all your luggage with you. Have a nice night.

"And you."

But Sylvia didn't answer. With a shrug, Nico headed off to find the escalators. The shrug left her at the foot of the deserted silver stairs and scuttled back to the Crater of Orthodox Narrative Spasms. Nico went through the automatic gate and walked briskly along a corridor of dancing mushrooms. Turning left at *The War Songs of the Allies*, she found herself muttering "marmoreal" and "marocain" and "marque" and "marquisette" and "marshalsea" and "martagon" and "martingale".

She looked for Engineer Sharp in the workshop but he wasn't there. A ginger cat with a Yorkshire accent advised her to try the badminton court.

"Is he in a good mood?" she asked.

"Miiaaow," retorted the cat, vanishing behind the afternoon matinee showing of *Jeopardy*.

Sharp didn't look up. Her footsteps clattered and echoed in the court. He was eating peanut butter sandwiches, feeding the crusts to a mule. The mule's tail wagged enthusiastically, like a dog's.

At last he acknowledged her presence. A crinkly smile. She was shocked by his appearance. He was different to how she remembered. Last time he'd seemed tall, young. Now he'd shrunk. He was wearing glasses and beginning to lose his hair. He looked tired. When you got up close there were tiny scarlet pinpricks. Burst blood vessels? Maybe he drank too much.

"Meet Muffin," Sharp said. "Muffin," he said to the mule, "this is Nico. The ship's pharmacist."

The mule gave a kind of whinny.

"Go on, stroke him. He won't bite."

Another strange whinny. Then the mule wandered off.

"I came about the capsule with the defective door. Engels trapped his beard in it again."

"Okay. I'll fix it."

Nico said reproachfully, "You said that last time."

"I've been busy. You people don't realise how time-consuming a commitment to postmodernist playfulness is. Apart from the maintenance and growth, there's things like having to change the ribbon on the printer, going shopping, the weeds in the garden, the window boxes to water, the hedge to cut, letters to write, checking that the new cactus isn't dying. Not to mention my commitment to the struggle against the M11 link road. It's alright for fictional characters like you. You just float about having a fun time, words on a page. I have to keep cycling over to Leytonstone. Why, only today I had to be at George Green, Wanstead, by 10am to join the WALK FOR THE EARTH crowd. Then it turned out that we were supposed to assemble in the little sunken park by the Green Man roundabout. Then it was announced that after speeches we'd be following the route of the link all the way to Hackney. I ended up walking as far as Claremont Road. After that I had to queue for a 58 bus. I didn't get back here to *The Slight Hubbub of Conversations* until one o'clock. I felt worn-out."

The mule gave a tortured laugh.

Nico looked across at it. "That's not *real*, is it?"

Sharp smiled ambiguously.

"It is, isn't it?" Nico continued. "That's why you keep away from the rest of us. You have a real live mule down here! Don't think I haven't read *Do Androids Dream of Electric Sheep?* It must be worth a fortune! Where on earth did you get it from?"

"It's not real. It's an artefact. Same as you. Same as me. Same as everything in this story. Any moment now it will all come to an end, on the word *budge*. You'll be left frozen in time and space. Don't think your pharmaceutical knowledge will help. It won't."

"You're lying! I'm calling security! I'm taking that mule back with me to show Captain Pickdock! I'm sure he'll want to know how an *engineer* has come into possession of a real live mule! If you ask me it's very suspicious. Nobody could afford a mule on an engineer's salary. Besides, it's in breach of quarantine regulations!"

Nico seized hold of the collar round the mule's neck. "Come on, Muffin. Let's take a ride on the Bakerloo line."

Docile, the mule allowed itself to be led towards the door. Sharp didn't seem bothered by the fact that she was taking it. Although a shrug was clearly what was called for, Sharp remained motionless, tightlipped. Drifts of Rimbaud slid softly through his mind, melted away. He sipped his mug of tea (milk, no sugar) and let things take their course.

Without warning Muffin halted, just as Nico had reached the doorway.

"Come on, boy. Nice mule. Come on, Muffin. Come with Nico."

The mule grunted; snorted; farted; attempted to retreat.

It occurred to Nico that perhaps the mule was artificial after all. The fart didn't fool her for a moment. Verisimilitude of that sort was one of the oldest tricks around. The foul stench curling around her nostrils was probably produced by a concealed Conservative Government Family Values cylinder. Sharp's mug of steaming tea was a disguised control panel. The handle of the mug was obviously the lever which operated the *stubborn* function. *Or am I paranoid?* she thought.

"God dammit, come this way!" Nico shouted, her temper flaring. She yanked hard on the collar and pulled with all her strength. But Muffin, as if wary of the normal homoencephalic functioning that lay at the other end of the Bakerloo line, as if suspicious of a group of people who fooled around with polyencephalic time and plunged themselves into a Terra of decaying capitalism, drug abuse and melancholy song, splayed out his tough, metallic legs, dug in his synthetic suction hooves, and refused to budge

FROM *TO WANSTONIA* (1996)

A RAG

Darkness, the sound of rain. An alarm goes off, stops. Darkness, rain bucketing down in the street, muffled noise of traffic, the sounds of someone getting out of bed. A grey glimmer where the heavy velveteen curtains don't meet at the top, a vague nude figure moving in the dark room. Outside the rain easing, a low soft hiss against the leaf-strewn footway, the street cleaners arriving in the dark street, scraps of shouts, the whirr-roar of the mechanised sweeper, the softer brushwork of the sweepers, rattle of a broken can, rags, old bones spilled from a split sack, dark figures gone by daylight.

It is early morning in London, in London, in London, and it begins, the story begins again, it picks up in the darkness where it left off, the rain still falling.

What story?

The story of the fall of rain, of the falling rain, of the rain crashing on the thin bathroom roof, of the rain tick-tocking in the dark leaky loft and tap-tapping on the ceilings and knock-knocking at the door and slivering down panes and blurring the shapes of things, the story of the mound of refuse and the yellowing cast-down cherry tree, the story of the sweepings of a street and the white puddles forming on a lawn, stories of the rain and the wind, old kettles, old bottles, rain soaking through your clothes, the story of rain beating down on a white cottage beside a river, of rain beating down on a grey cottage beside a brook, of rain on old stones and old bones and empty lawns, of rain blowing across empty fields, turbulent down brown dirty gutters, washing the blue-grey shining empty roads.

It is early morning in London. Cut to the rain sweeping across the deserted park; cut to the rain splashing down on the empty tennis court.

Cut to Bodkins reaching for *Halliwell's Film Guide* (and how Bodkins hates Halliwell, who never likes what he likes). The cover: flushed Marilyn in an ultramarine fifties bathing suit and ludicrous high heels, the fingers of her left hand splayed across the upper reaches of her thigh, a solitary little finger and perhaps the ghost of another peeking round the line of her right thigh, posed to display to best advantage the tight twin curves of her taut, bulging rump, her left breast obliterated by the letter L in FILM but recurring un-obliterated on the back cover, a breast which swerves out and up at a strange unreal ninety degree angle, her smile presumably intended to evoke a cheery *well-hi-there!* and *hey-you!* grin and maybe even a *boy-I-could-really-do-with-a-good-fuckin'-from-you-mister!* but which, when you look more closely, seems bleak and cheerless and posed as if what she was really thinking was *shit-I'm-freezing-in-this-dumbass-swimsuit* and/or *Christ-but-I-need-a-drink,* the wrinkles spreading upwards from her left elbow the wrinkles of the time when face and breasts begin to collapse, Halliwell not letting Bodkins' expectations down with his fatuous *Agreeable to look at for those who can stifle their irritation at the non-plot and non-characters*, with Steven H. Scheuer's *Movies on TV* ("Viewers may find the story baffling") almost in the same league.

Two nights earlier Bodkins dreams of the park, of the magic mysterious enticing park, of the crumbling boarded-up buildings by the park gate, of the pathway leading through a dense, luminous forest with an emerald interior crammed with trees reminiscent of the long-limbed ones in *Jurassic Park*, a forest he chooses to ignore as he hurries on, upward, to the meadow, now no longer like the one in either the movie or Maryon Park as it is today, a big, curving bowl of tree-lined grass, containing ghostly figures who involve him in startling, colourful and tightly plotted dream adventures worthy of an opium-fired collaboration between Wilkie Collins and Tolstoy, but which disintegrate into a collage of maddeningly vague fast-thawing scraps as Bodkins' hand punches through the fabric's bright colours, reaching out to silence the alarm. Silencing it, silencing it, and, amid the collapsing scenery, amid the elasticated, evaporating figures hearing again the rain sleeting down into the street, slapping against the pane, tick-tocking in the dark leaky loft and tap-tapping on the ceilings, knock-knocking at the door, a sour taste in your mouth, head aching, empty wine glass on the desk.

Hearing again the rain sleeting down into the street, slapping against the pane, tick-tocking in the dark leaky loft and tap-tapping on the ceilings, knock-knocking at the door, and it begins, the story begins again, it picks up in the darkness where it left off, the rain still falling, the story of the fall of rain, of rain on empty lawns and blowing across empty fields, turbulent down dirty gutters, washing the blue-grey shining empty roads, and all the while (cut to Bodkins in a crowded, smoky bar) a sweet, slow-slow mamba throbbing through the sun-baked emptiness of Tongue (cut to Tongue; cut to Bodkins happy as the grass was green), a vague nude figure moving in the dark room, (cut to a naked figure holding a telephone; cut to the rain sweeping across the deserted park; cut to the rain splashing down on the empty tennis court; cut to the slow-moving crowd on London Bridge), rain pouring down on the empty park and the deserted courts, heart-mysteries there, Martin Stephenson singing "Rain", luminous raindrops suspended from the netting, Leonard Cohen singing "Last Year's Man", green memories cooked to grey rags inside a spreading sabbath desolation, desolate as St Neots, wet as that black shiny childhood day his mother and father, waiting for a long connection, took him to see *Reach for the Sky*, the rain avalanching on the cinema roof, cold as that far seaside winter when her mother died, story upon story, enfolded in rain, sodden with it, and later, on West 10th, going to see *Five Easy Pieces*, going to see *Dead of Night,* going to see *Journey through the Past,* going to see *Don't Look Now*, the rain coming down on Glanville, the rain coming down on Chinatown, the rain coming down on Seattle, rags, tatters without catharsis and still continuing, yes, endlessly in the soft rain, still continuing as Bodmer Bodkins, rag picker and Engels specialist, shabby prestidigitator, amateur photographer, walks across London Bridge heading for the station, a train to Woolwich Dockyard, on his way to Maryon Park, *the magic park*, and as the trains come and go a sweet, pain-gorged slow-slow mamba still plays slow inside the slow, still falling rain.

It is early morning in London. Cut to the rain sweeping across the deserted park; cut to the rain splashing down on the empty tennis court; cut to the slow-moving crowd on London Bridge, every face coated in white paste; cut to Bodkins hurrying along a rainswept urban street, his head obscured by a large black umbrella; cut to young men and women with painted faces running across a wilderness of mud and shattered trees; cut to Bodkins staring at a screen; cut to Bodkins reading Cortázar; cut to Bodkins by a window, looking out at the rain; cut to the young men and women swarming over a yellow bulldozer; cut to Bodkins on the telephone; cut to Bodkins using the rewind button and then the still button; cut to Bodkins listening to *The Future*; cut to running men in yellow coats each bearing the label SECURITY; cut to Bodkins sat by a keyboard; cut to Bodkins at London Bridge station, watching his yellowish ghost in the glass frame of an advert cabinet (sunlit beach scene, woman reclining in blue one-piece bathing costume against an arc of deserted custard yellow sand) which reflects, palely, in the mirror of an adjacent scarlet weighing machine, and again, a misty backdrop of barely decipherable lines, in the big gold vanity mirror of the Italian woman standing by the gate to Platform 12, a frown on her face as she absently applies a rich ruby shade to her thin lips and stares upward at the blank departures board, her mind far from that day seventeen years earlier when she sat on a stool in the bar of the village near Valdagno and the man, ordering his second beer, casually asked her her name.

Rain pouring down on the dark empty park and the deserted courts, grey raindrops suspended from the netting, the rain easing, a low soft hiss against the leaf-strewn pathways, the street cleaners arriving in the dark adjacent streets, scraps of shouts, the whirr-roar of the mechanised sweeper, the softer brushwork of the sweepers, rattle of a broken can, rags, old bones spilled from a split sack, dark figures gone by daylight.

Caro Antonioni... Cut to a train pulling out of London Bridge station; cut to an old man lying in a narrow bed; cut to rain slivering down a pane; cut to Bodkins, motionless by a keyboard; cut to a blank screen. Darkness, the sound of rain. An alarm goes off, stops. Darkness. Nothing happens; no one gets out of bed; there is no one there. Sound of a bulldozer tearing up a tree by the roots; sound of something smashing through a brick wall. Cut to rain pouring down on a waste of shattered trees, mud, caterpillar tracks. Cut to a blank screen, two thin white lines framing a black rectangle, the lines ruptured in the lower right corner by the words BLOW-UP.DOC. Long shot of Bodmer Bodkins standing on a patch of bare grass by two tennis courts; close-up of his face, a nervous half-smile; long shot of a man fading away leaving a rectangle of grass, the green disfigured by darker blotches of weed.

Cut to Bodkins in a phone booth; cut to Bodkins sitting on the floor, telephone in hand, frowning. The lack, the lack of information, the difficulty of getting through to British Rail, phone 071-928-5100 for services to East Anglia, Essex, Southern England, North East, East and South London, beep-beep-beep-beep-beep, beep-beep-beep, forever engaged until, finally, after several days of trying, you get through and learn that on weekday mornings there are four trains an hour from London Bridge, one departing at seven minutes past the hour arriving at Woolwich Dockyard at twenty-five minutes past the hour, one at twenty-one minutes past arriving at thirty-nine minutes past, one at thirty-seven minutes past arriving at fifty-five minutes past and one at fifty-one minutes past arriving at nine minutes past, and then, days later, when you get there, you find that the electronic departures board has a malfunction, that the timetables don't identify the platforms so that, ticket in hand, you walk briskly to and fro across the crowded concourse, you wander from platform to platform, no BR staff anywhere, no one able to answer your question, up and down stone corridors, the electronic departure signboards frozen on every platform, no one you ask knowing where the train to Woolwich Dockyard goes from, until, in the end, in desperation, you go to the ticket office and join the long queue at information/reservations and, later, learn that the train you want is leaving Platform Four at 9.51, and you hurry off, and wait, and wait, and at 9.58 it pulls in and you board and you're on your way, seeing the far aerial on the hilltop, seeing the wastes of south-east London, seeing the grotesque monolith capped by a winking pyramid, pulling in to Deptford, glancing at your *London A-Z*, trying to locate the church where Marlowe's dead body was taken, failing to spot it, the train moving on, arriving at Charlton, your pulse beginning to quicken, wondering if (as the map seems to indicate) the line goes high over the park with a view of the courts, but no, Bodkins is plunged into darkness, into a tunnel and a deep cutting where whirled greenery and dark branches race across the grey sky, and a high grey wall encloses you as the train slows, and I flick back the door lock and step down onto the deserted platform.

Woolwich D-D-D-D-D-Dockyard, d-d-d-d-d-dereliction, d-d-d-d-d-d-decay, drear as d-d-d-d-d-death, dismal, d-d-d-d-d-deadly, dying, dying and out across a f-f-f-f-f-footbridge, down steps, nervy and a little anxious, a prickling sense of unease, along a short boarded-up corridor, out into the fresh air, desolation, an empty street, the narrow footway lined with wooden bollards, turn right for the royal dockyard, the great brick chimney still there, dark and stained with age, the chimney you glimpse as Thomas reaches the strange blue building on the corner and steers the Silver Cloud right, cruising alongside a new housing estate, the buildings at once familiar to Bodkins as he hurries along cheerless Woolwich Church Street, a confetti litter of broken glass on the pavement, the traffic on the dual carriageway racing by at speed, but the blue building's not there, you pictured it probably-no-longer-blue but it's not there at all, it's gone, obliterated by the developers, and there's roadworks at the entrance to Cleveley Close, as you turn sharp left, guessing that this is the little quiet street in the film, the place with the antique shop on the corner, and there ahead of you, yes, *the magic park*, the familiar-from-fifty-viewings park entrance, the environs changed, everything else around here different, everything else wiped from existence at some time during these past twenty-seven years but the park entrance the same, and he walks towards it, stepping in through the open gateway, Colour by Metrocolor and a cold October breeze, pulse thudding, camera loaded and ready, the leaves rustling, still there the four big trees bifurcating the circle of asphalt, still there (and how pleased he is about those trees) (how Bodkins never tires of that sinister, magical shot, Thomas's casual stroll into the mysterious park, the four trees waiting like sentinels, the breeze rustling a foregrounded branch, the sense of someone looking down on Thomas), the queer-looking plump dressed-in-black park-keeper stabbing at litter with his pointed stick, pigeons gathered on the open grass beyond the courts, and Bodkins moving along the path, seeing no one, dense foliage on every side, yellow and amber leaves in thick drifts everywhere, comes to the point where the pathway splits, and following Thomas turns to mount the familiar stepped pathway to the low rise and the opening, mounting with beating heart, camera loaded and at the ready, emerging into the sinister meadow, the picket fence completely gone (not quite: a final half-fallen section of eleven sticks and two posts still there), and the two trees still there, the meadow narrower than you imagined but also longer, the grass not mown and kempt as in the film but thick and wild, and Bodkins loiters by the trees and starts — clack, clack — to take photographs, unnerved by the absence of people, the strange concealing wildness of this park, and now Bodkins knows better, Bodkins, who always used to think it was implausible, a murder in an English park, a body lying there all day under a bushy tree, not noticed by anyone, now he knows better, nothing more plausible than an assassination in this lonely place, hedged in on all sides by dense concealing foliage, concealing branches, flickering leaves, the director never returning to the park, a fragment of his gone life, blasted by a stroke in 1985, born 1912, fifty-four when *Blow-Up* was released, a middle aged man's film, yet present in the furrowed grasses, the pale sky, the hooded ominous deathly casual nothingness, the absences, the director now an old man, speechless, living in Rome perhaps, Ferrara, Verona, don't know, resting in an armchair, perhaps in bed, perhaps at that very moment as you walk to the end of the meadow and back again, trying to work out where the tree was, the tree with the corpse behind it, the tree gone, and another one at the far end a neat sawn stump and a third tree gone down at the foot of the stepped path, a bigger stump with a curious grey-white fungoid growth of overlapping circles spreading across the huddled circle of the long years, twenty-seven years gone like yesterday, gone with the tides of turning time, gone with the draining rain, gone with those bleeding blue lines on that scrap of paper shot down a foaming gutter and lost amidst a low soft hiss against the fouled kerbs and the leaf-strewn pathways, the street cleaners arriving in the nearby streets, shouts and laughter, the whirr-roar of the mechanised sweeper, the softer brushwork of the sweepers, rattle of a broken can, rags, old bones spilled from a split sack, dark figures gone by daylight.

It is early morning in London, in London, in London, and it begins, the story begins again, it picks up in the darkness where it left off, the rain still falling.

What story?

The story of how the trees were cut down at Cambridge Park. The story of Bodkins walking through a waste of mud and shattered branches, taking photographs. The story of the rag-and-bone shop, the absent woman, the records of Hawaiian music. The story of the M11 link road. The story of

111 minutes coming to an end. The story of Bodkins leaving the park, catching the train back to London Bridge. The story of Bodkins' disappearance (long shot of Bodmer Bodkins standing on a patch of bare grass by two tennis courts; close-up of his face, a nervous half-smile; long shot of a man fading away before your eyes, of a rectangle of grass, the green disfigured by darker blotches of weed). The story, say, by the suicide, Pavese. The story of how Clelia, sorrowful and sour, waits to see her treacherous lover for the long last time at the drear station, not seeing him, not seeing him hiding behind the kiosk like a louse, and so the train departs, departs with Clelia at a window, and a sweet, pain-gorged slow-slow mamba plays slow, slow, slow as rain going drip-drip-drip might go, goes, from gutters or inside a damp-smelling loft of cobwebs and darkness.

Darkness, the sound of rain. Extinguished in this night, the blue, the red gold, as Bodkins' hand punches through the fabric's bright colours, the obscurities, the heart-mysteries, a hand with slender fingers reaching out to silence the alarm, terminating a dream, a dream where a low, embedded voice slyly whispers of old iron, old bones, old rags, a dream where rain drifts across a desolate park and malicious gusts whisper obscurely *Dein roter Mund besiegelte des Freundes Umnachtung*, or maddeningly *Denkt die nahe Stille Vergessenes, erloschene Engel*, until terminated abruptly by a hand reaching out. Silenced, the scenery collapsing, the elasticated, evaporating figures fast vanishing, hearing again the rain sleeting down into the street, slapping against the pane, tick-tocking in the dark leaky loft and tap-tapping on the ceilings, knock-knocking at the door, a sour taste in your mouth, head aching, empty wine glass on the desk.

It begins again, the rain sleeting down into the street, slapping against the pane, tick-tocking in the dark leaky loft and tap-tapping on the ceilings, knock-knocking at the door, and it begins, the story begins again, it picks up in the darkness where it left off, rain pouring down on the dark empty park and the deserted courts, grey raindrops suspended from the netting, the rain easing, long shot of Bodmer Bodkins standing on a patch of bare grass by two tennis courts, close-up of his face, a nervous half-smile, long shot of a man fading away leaving a rectangle of grass, the green disfigured by darker blotches of weed, a low soft hiss against the leaf-strewn pathways, the street cleaners arriving in the dark adjacent streets, leaving you in the end at the end where you began, amid darkness and the sound of rain.

THE HENRY JAMES SEMINAR AT MY LAI

Questions have been raised about the Henry James seminar at My Lai. The criticism has even been levelled that the seminar lacked the well-formedness outcome which is the desirable consequence of any organisation seeking improvements in product quality and enhanced customer satisfaction. The company has therefore invited the application of recently developed knowledge elicitation techniques in order that any negative entrenched attitudes or beliefs among team participants may be reframed to a more positive orientation. Through the application of rapport development and the erasure of communication inflexibility high quality information can be elicited enabling team members to become aware of negative cross-functional impacts which may be introducing elements of dysfunction within the parameters of the organization's target of reduced operating costs, increased productivity and improved product.

Gentlemen, ladies, colleagues, let me begin with some of the core values embedded in the company's program which do not simply contribute to the perceptual empowerment of team members but which also permit the enabling of a functional evaluation of negative attitudes in relation to the outcome of the Henry James seminar at My Lai. Core value one: *good decision making requires accurate information.* Core value two: *the intention of all behaviour is positive.*

Common sense? Precisely. I ask you all therefore to remember these core values when contextualising modes of pacification and quality control procedures involved in a strategic environment. What we are scrutinising here is the question of client and customer satisfaction within a problematic rural development situation relating to New Life hamlets, specifically the alleged lack of a well-formedness outcome in relation to the Henry James seminar at My Lai (4), Quang Ngai Province, Republic of Vietnam, 16 March 1968.

Contextualisation will also be assisted by conceptualising

the seminar's physical space parameters. These were: the width of one football field (American); the length of three football fields (American). However, allowances must be made for thick foliage, bamboo trees, banana trees and other vegetation.

What are the facts?

The seminar lasted four hours.

A keynote speech proposing that Henry James's fiction yokes the European sense of the objective limits of life with an American sense of its limitless conceivable possibilities was prematurely terminated by tracer fire and exploding grenades and rockets along the perimeters of the group. The seminar then broke up into smaller discussion groups, with the emphasis on narrative technique and James as a novelist of manners.

Some problems were experienced almost from the word go. For example, a seminar participant was seen running with a copy of *The Notebooks of Henry James* when he was killed with a round from an M-79 grenade launcher. It seems likely that this was an honest mistake, the cover bearing a remarkable similarity to *The Ghostly Rental*.

Before being judgmental about what eventuated it is necessary to recall core value one: *good decision making requires accurate information. As* Captain Medina explained, any sporadic shootings which occurred after lunch on the date in question were not in his line of vision.

Other episodes have been well documented. Infantrymen Bergthold and Maples entered a hut and discovered a copy of *The Jolly Corner*, around which were grouped three children, a woman with a flesh wound in her side and an old man who had been shot in both legs. Bergthold aimed his .45 pistol and blew the top of the old man's head off (an instinctive reaction to doppelgänger fiction, he later explained). Almost at once an elderly woman came staggering down a path. She was still gripping the copy of *The Golden Bowl* which she had been reading when someone shot her with an M-79 grenade. The grenade had torn into her stomach but had failed to explode. Though in considerable pain she insisted on paying tribute to the astonishing inventiveness of the baroque imagery in the final chapters.

Two middle-aged farmers were brought out holding a sheet of notes on *Watch and Word*, Henry James's little known first novel. Infantryman Boyce said their conclusion that *Watch and Word* ended in "melodrama" made him "kinda mad". He stabbed one with his bayonet, killed him. The second one he shot in the neck and threw down a well, dropping an M-26 grenade after him.

"Literary criticism can be a powerful thing," agreed infantryman Roschevitz as he shot three seminar participants in the head with an M-16 "for not having anything new to say about the first paragraph of *The Ambassadors*".

"It can cut both ways," added infantryman Simpson, with a hearty chuckle. He fired at a woman with a baby from a distance of about 25 metres. Her right hand was almost completely severed from the wrist, obliging her to drop her selection of James's criticism. Instead of saying whether or not she agreed with James that Swinburne's *Essays and Studies* all too frequently lapse into flagrant levity and perversity of taste, she ran off. Someone yelled to kill her *and* the baby. This was no sooner done than Hutson and Wright came across a middle-aged woman climbing out of a tunnel. She started to quote James's remark that the perusal of a story by an author who knows what he is talking about "is one of the most elevating experiences within the reach of human mind" when they machine-gunned her. As Wright indignantly explained, this was more to do with James's low estimation of *Our Mutual Friend* than anything *personal*.

8am. Medina radioed that fifteen seminar participants had been removed from ongoing discussions.

8.30am. Medina reported that 84 seminar participants had been silenced. As he explained later, not a single one of them could say where Henry James had been on the day of the great London unemployment riots in 1886; the single word "Bournemouth" would have ensured prompt medical aid, evacuation and a three-semester Nixon scholarship coupon, redeemable at West Lawrence College of Bible Studies.

From a mud and clay building emerged a mature student. He started to say something about James's surprisingly haphazard use of parentheses and of square brackets in the manuscript of *The Notebooks* when infantryman Crosley shot him just below the left elbow, severing his arm. At this a woman wearing a white shirt and carrying a baby came out. Defiantly shouting, "Foreign words and phrases are sometimes underlined in the manuscript of *The Notebooks of Henry James* — and sometimes not!", she managed to drag the man back inside. Hutson and Wright went after her with a machine gun and put an end to her pedantry.

In a rice paddy at the far northwest corner of the seminar a young girl aged eleven or twelve lay, shot in the chest. "What I remember most about *The Wings of the Dove,*" she whispered, "isn't the plot or the characters but the wonderful delicacy with which so fragile a web of human entanglement has been constructed." Leonard Gonzalez tried to give the girl some water. When he walked away he heard a shot and saw that one of his colleagues had asserted the superior merits of *The Ambassadors.*

In a clearing a group of fifteen seminar participants were gathered — seven women, three teenage girls and five children (who the week before had been allowed to sit up late to watch Marion Brando in *The Nightcomers*). One of these children, which was being held by its mother, precociously asserted that *The Pupil* would make an even better movie, a comment that was altogether too much for someone! A bullet zapped its way across the clearing and blew out the back of the child's skull. "Personally," said one of the teenage girls, "I think the spookiest of any of James's supernatural tales is *Owen Wingrave.*" It is not clear whether this exasperated Hutto, Torres or Roschevitz, but soon everyone was firing into the fourteen seminar participants who remained alive.

Precocity was quite a problem that day. Another seminar group consisted entirely of children aged about seven years.

They ran forward with hands outstretched, proudly holding identical paperback copies of *The Tragic Muse*. "One of James's underlying themes is connecting the story of public and political life with the story of art," the group leader explained. Further discussion was muted by a sustained spray of automatic fire.

In another clearing an even larger group of seminar participants had been gathered together. Lieutenant Galley came along. Galley had always agreed with Ford Madox Ford that *The Spoils of Poynton* is James's greatest novel. When he heard someone whisper that *The Golden Bowl* was a symphonic *tour de force* he flushed. Galley didn't know French but he guessed it was a compliment. If there was one thing Galley couldn't stand it was James's late style. Galley got Meadlo to help him and together they sprayed the seminar group until Galley was sure he had curtailed all possible future discussion of suspense and emotional excitement in Chapter XXXVI of that difficult text.

The troops pushed on through the seminar discussion area. Meadlo arrived with Grzesik and found Galley with ten other members of the platoon. They had rounded up some forty to fifty James enthusiasts, including babies (who were drooling with pleasure as they fondled brightly jacketed paperback copies of *The Awkward Age*). The seminar leader seemed to be a Buddhist monk in white robes with a goatee beard. The monk was shaking his head and waving a copy of *The Portrait of a Lady*. Just then a child aged about two crawled away from its mother, gurgling what sounded very much like "Emerson" (almost certainly alluding to James's 1887 review of James Elliot Cabot's *Memoir of Ralph Waldo Emerson*).

Galley picked the child up, threw it down and shot it.

Various negative entrenched attitudes or beliefs have emerged in connection with this action (mostly, it must be said, from personnel displaying a wilful disregard for the company's target of reduced operating costs, increased productivity and improved product). But as Galley himself explained afterwards, "On babies everyone's really hung up.

The little innocent babies! But babies grow up. If your son is forced into a Henry James seminar and totally paralysed by the lack of narrative pace in *The Golden Bowl* you'll cry at me, 'Why didn't you kill those babies that day?'"

The monk with his copy of *The Portrait of a Lady* wasn't making any sense. Galley had had it up to here with these participants. "Load your machine gun and shoot these people," Galley ordered.

The entire seminar group was shredded by M-16s. There was one final cry of *It is astonishing how one's wayside is strewn with ENDS after one has reached middle life!* — then silence.

The 2nd Platoon was particularly hard on seminar participants who were exploring the art-life problem in *Roderick Hudson.* One woman had a rifle barrel forced up her vagina and the trigger was pulled. One girl aged about seventeen was taken into a hut and raped by Hutto, Hutson and a third soldier (apparently she'd described the characterisation of Mary Garland as "weak"). When they were finished the girl's face was shot off. Several troops stood and watched, remarking on the timeless truth of James's observation that there are occasions when just to watch something can provide "an education of the taste, an enlargement of one's knowledge". Another young woman said *Roderick Hudson* had a serenity of tone markedly superior to James's other representations of Americans in Italy. For this she was sodomized by three platoon members, then raped by eight more, by which time others had heard of what was going on and came along to join in. When they were done they cut out her tongue, then mutilated her vagina with a bayonet. Regrettably some personnel with negative entrenched attitudes have commented adversely on such episodes, failing to contextualise them within cross-functional team methodology while at the same time overlooking core value two: *the intention of all behaviour is positive.* Additionally, there are many extenuating circumstances. Many of the girls and women who were forcibly buggered provoked their attackers by wearing silky black pajamas. Even senior officers, understandably, were unable to restrain themselves. As for Captain Kotouc, F-2 intelligence officer, it was perfectly reasonable that he should be acquitted of assaulting and maiming a seminar member by cutting off the little finger of his right hand. Kotouc explained that the fellow was thumbing through *Washington Square* at speed, a look of insolence on his jaundiced face, offensively oblivious to the comic brilliance which informs every page.

I repeat, the criticism has been levelled that the seminar lacked the well-formedness outcome which is the desirable consequence of any organisation seeking improvements in product quality and enhanced customer satisfaction. In all some five hundred seminar participants died, and many others were injured, and this, in so far as it affected customer satisfaction targets, must be a matter for some regret. Additionally, while incurring no extra costs, the seminar discussion area was, undeniably, left in a state of disarray. It is important, however, to identify modelling processes in the complex world of experience and relate them to the company's overall goals. In evaluating procedures adopted on 16 March 1968 negative or obsolete belief systems may require re-framing or pattern-interruption in the context of the broader goal of American values and lifestyle programs.

It must be emphasized that the seminar outcome enjoyed senior management approval. Senior management had, and continues to have, every confidence in personnel who made interventions at the seminar. Benchmarking continues to be done into the successful marketing techniques involved in obtaining positive changes in employee satisfaction in relation to the seminar outcome. General Westmoreland himself sent a cable: CONGRATULATIONS ON THE OPERATION FOR TASK FORCE BARKER TO OFFICERS AND MEN OF C-1-2 FOR OUTSTANDING CRITICAL ACTION. The Pacific edition of *Stars and Stripes* ran a story headlined US TROOPS PUT REDS STRAIGHT ON COMPETING ABSOLUTISMS IN 'THE BOSTONIANS', CONFUTE 128. The *New York Times* ran a wire item about the mission's success. What's more, the prestigious *Henry James Review* carried a two thousand word report entitled, "A New Approach to Henry James: Theme of Morality and the Self Undergoes Vigorous Interrogation in Quang Ngai Province Seminar".

Sadly, time is running out. There will be no opportunity for questions, nor is there any space left to discuss the seminar's contributions towards an improved understanding of *The Beast in the Jungle, The American* or *The Liar*. But the company is confident that Henry James himself would not have condemned any communications difficulties which may be conceded to have occurred at My Lai. "LIFE" he once wrote (with rare emphasis) "is less criminal, less obnoxious, less objectionable, less crude, more *bon enfant,* more mixed and casual," than the ridiculous concoctions of modern fiction — had he been reading Sharp, one wonders? — "and even in its most offensive manifestations, more *pardonable."*

And there you have it. Americans abroad mean well, but are liable, on occasion, to blunder. As Henry James knew, all too often they are deceived by wily foreigners. Medina, for example, was widely regarded as a warm-hearted man. Everyone testified to the warmth of his personality. Character witnesses for Medina included such fine soldiers as Brigadier General Lipscomb, Colonel Luper, Colonel Blackledge, Major Calhoun and *Washington Square* specialist Captain Kotouc. The company is confident that Medina was as committed to its overall goals and to the bringing of well-being, peace, comfort, confidence and success as anyone. Let no one forget what that other Henry — Henry Ford — once said. *Excellence in action means thinking laterally, progressing strategically and succeeding impressively.*

What conclusions can be drawn from all this? Point of view, as James himself well understood, is all important. It is all too easy to make snap judgments from the comfort of an armchair many years later. For the man on the ground, up to his neck in a confused situation and faced by possibly hostile Jamesians babbling of symbolic imagery and transcendent humanism, things are not so simple. As Captain Medina explained, how can you be sure that the fellow next to you is seeing the same as you? Has the other soldier turned his head away at the crucial moment, was his view blocked? What if the safety catch is off and a seminar member is several metres ahead of you or several metres behind, holding a copy of *The Princess Casamassima* in a suspicious or provocative manner?

In short, why is there all this fuss about the Henry James seminar at My Lai and so little about what happened during the Hawthorne seminar over at My Khe (4)? Why dig up the past when there are much livelier, more interesting things happening today, like the ongoing Iris Murdoch seminar in East Timor?

The thing to do, as all responsible and successful business people know, is to concentrate on the task in hand. Stronger institutional links between industry, finance and government must be forged to overcome tendencies towards short-termism. Investment in human resources is the precondition of competitiveness. Above all else, the thing to remember is that in any successful organisation seeking to improve work activities and enhance employee satisfaction within a framework of total quality control and increased productivity, strong feelings are best avoided.

PAPER HEART (A STORY IN THREE ALBUMS)

Planet Waves
"Who are you? Where you been? Where you going?" Headlights against the sky, headlights coming over the hill, down the road, screech of brakes. "What you doin' here?" The hard-eyed frowning cop's questions that empty road night in Norfolk. What, where, who? *What's happening?* The Headquarters boys putting the pressure on. Who? The name's Hawkins. He wasn't doing anything, not that winter. Walking along the verge, no streetlights or cityglow, twenty-six years old, same as Keats, and the Van Gogh incandescent stars sparkly-shimmering, iced-up inside. Afterwards recalled as one of the bleakest of bleak winters. Mister Hawkins was living at The Patch, rat-sized hole under the front door, on the dole, sense of emptiness, of going no place & nowhere, crapping unremarkable dull brown crap while the rain beat down always & always on the murky skylight, ancient hissing boiler and rooms with old striped wallpaper, grey bed of the Polaroid fun and the quick Bianco screw, big old multi-tenanted house on the Norwich road, the death of the heart and the rotting stables out the back where the lidless dustbins dribbled soggy girly magazines & dragon-mouth Heinz cans. Huge padlock hung inside the iron staple, green mould covered the wood of the fence and of the gates, a dark wide entrance hall, communal stairs from the last century & a cold breeze blowing as from a cellar. From the hall he got up the stairs, sloven, swaying, worn lino, scraps of brown dark threadbare carpet, cut off from everything, like being stuck inside a crumby little town in the nineteenth century dead heart of a plain in Russia, dread defunctive days where the colour all drained to the steel of the sea and the mud of the cliffs, the rain beating down down down on the skylight, overwhelming him, the waves breaking on the empty winter shingle, the crumbling cliffs with the half houses, split homes, wallpaper exposed to the rain & gulls, the gull mobs screeching in the blank sky, empty sea, & the songs matched everything, sense of nostalgia, winter, snow

flurries across the cliffs, *ennuyé,* sparks of rage, hatred, fashed by a gash & anxious to be out of all this, desperate, the rancour, the grey bitter bed and that sobbing sour day, wizened months, bricked-up, the boredom piled on boredom, and desperate to be going, to be going, to be gone.

Desire

Lo and behold! 747 high over the Prairies, high over the Rockies, crawling over the planet to another world. To the library, the high tower. The papers. O bright and breezy day! O hot spicy rapturous season of Carnival and Masks! Flax and fire. Oooooooooh! Sweet beginnings. Pulling over at night, the airport across the sound. Navigation lights gliding in the sky, rising, dropping. 747s, coming and going. Coming. On tenterhooks, Mister Hawkins and Mrs Mozart! Staring at each other wildly, her widow's nails digging into his arm. Kindling eyes, the blood's lava. Flax, fire, growing fond, fonder, fondling, growing... The pulse a blaze, dark eyes darting light. Firstkiss. Moist gorgeous filtrum. Clasping grasping clenching pulling and pooling and suck. In ferment! Astray! Wild sweet attunement, each kiss a heart-quake. Bare feet hurrying bedward, covers that won't turn back fast enough. Lo, in flames in a crack, behold flax fork flesh and forefinger and all the burning tongues. Fleshly meddle, on to the forfended place, ferret and firk! Impaled by motes, speared by fire, rolling among blizzards of gold. One flesh. Broken words and burning tongues, days of gold in an iron age. Stark white fritillary basking on a black stone outside München, broken glass at the Strand Palace Hotel! Cream pastries in St. Anton, reckless scented morning in Seattle! Frisky lambs in Derwentwater pastures, burning snow on the slopes of Wenatchee! Sweet morning in Tongue! A hot liaison under the huge cotton sheets, fiery dust amidst Ottawa's drifts and ice, and the sparkling stars their nuptial torches. Splashing in the pool at the Chateau Laurier! Raspberry smear on the carpet attracting the granite blonde chambermaid's harsh comment in Zell! The moons rolled on.

Frenzied agonizing rush! Hot whirling motel-hotel season of nimble tongue and castanets, blazing eye and tingling nose, skilled finger and burning marshland delta. Trembling Mister Hawkins thrice plunging the scooped squirming electric widow. Stirred, stirring, sweetness, lapping lips and fingerstrokes, gash wet & pupils hot & dark, arrowhead mouthed, go gentle, gentle, lingering-out, quivering, tenderness-frenzy, speech rapid & vehement, plough and die, clasp and buckle, buck and flood, shudder, discharges stupendous, meltings, sticky angels, earthless, plummeting. Then again. So quite new a thing. Bodies, a body. What it does, its hows, spine and bone and the trembling, the slow stroking, the thrill. Clouds of marsh fragrance, rolling. Swelling organ, seas of flame. Come and go, go and come, here, there and — Taking flight, hopping landscapes, crossing borders, time zones, continents. Over dunes of sand and snow, covering a lot of territory that year. Haste and glare and glitter. Mister Hawkins at the opera. Goggled Mister Hawkins on skis, twenty-eight, zig-zagging the dazzling blanks. Mister Hawkins on Wreck Beach. Mister Hawkins depositing a fertile soft & chocolate coloured trail. Mrs Mozart hoisting her skirt and pissing on leafmould in the grounds of Cawdor Castle. Mister Hawkins freshening up at the Oregon Memory Motel, watching a TV evangelist. Bare-assed Mister Hawkins & the electric widow rocking among the ancient ferns. Mister Hawkins and the widow with Johann in Bent's basement. Delighted eyes, Mister Hawkins hand-in-hand with Mrs Mozart by the spangled summer lake & happy so happy. Oh chymic treasure! Oh wine-sharp and honey-still warp of tideless joyous morning, oh golden juiced Cantata afternoons. Rocking with the widow among the pines, yes! Look at it loom there, Thing that she... Pumped-up, quivering. Trumpets out of a blue morning, floorfucks, fernfucks, miraculous basement afternoons, bedsheet slimed with grey, and next day's dry, coin sized blotches. Rustlings, murmurings, sucking, licking, high voltage sweats and spurts, rejoin rejoice separate and rejoin,

separate, spent, nightblur of slippingawayfatigue, jam on
cock, honey on crotch and breasts, cushioned by warm
thudding ribs, tumbling to voluptuous slumbers, the big
voluptuous slumber as a dying might be, should be.

Hard Rain

Torpor, lassitude. Blossoms fallen, sap gone. Moon still
bright, revels long ended. Gone, wallop. Passed away,
thrown away. Cut and dried. Phantoms and dust, echoes.
Put it down in the end, all of it, eh? What's over, over. A
September chill in the air, the mountains and the seas
between. Narrow England again. Fizzles in Finchley, then
off. North past the cooling towers, mind cascading, low raggy
middle-grey clouds scud the white sky, trainload of
metallically smart salesmen & the track muttering *no home
to go to, no home to go to, no home to go to.* Singular
vicissitudes, oh yes. Mister Hawkins, older now, lost in the
backwash, throbbing heart and a blurred drugged look to
him, a thoughts-against-thoughts thoughts-elsewhere
expression, rueful, dressed in an old Oxfam overccat crossing
the bridge on the retreat from Moscow, to the far platform
and out, yellow-tinted ancient walls. Cold and getting colder,
September ending, walk on greyheart across the black
footbridge beside the line, river below high & fast, city
background of strange smoky phosphorescent half world.
Sorely tried and sadly changed. Motley's the only wear.
Disowned, so to speak. Forsaken and forlorn. All amort.
Absence inconspicuous, nobody can tell what he — A new
place to dwell. Living in obscurity, on very small means.
Leading a sort of soundless, inert life. An out-of-the-way
street; the flat dilapidated. Domestic desolation in a little
room. To end in languor. Empty skies, scumbled greys,
drizzle. The grey signal flag. Fall's bleak beginning. Mister
Hawkins enters the lit house, climbs up the narrow winding
stairs, slips a coin in the meter. Lassitude, torpor. All day in
the rocker. The ticking in the walls, the sapless cinders. Eyes
resolutely cast down, fingers twining and untwining

themselves restlessly in lap. The clenched fist. Day and night. Not one minute in an hour, no. When his throbbing heart; when he did not — No, not one minute. Immured in a little room. Dawdling discordant Sundays, travesties of blemished time. Tea-cup with a crack in it. And how would you describe Mister Hawkins? What sort of mood did he seem to be in? Condition of atrophied coma, alas. Cumbered by coils; wrung out; selfstrung. Arachnoid, buried above ground. Alone in the snivelling hours. The voice barely audible, a thin, stretched, barbed whisper. Quis-quae-quae croak. With slower and slower articulation. Speech failing. A wintery summary. Old, cold, grey. Pallid. Smell of parboiled cauliflower and greasy bacon, dead cigarettes, cold ashtrays, sinkfull of greasy plates and smeared tarnished cutlery beneath the pale shallow silent scum. Mute nights, darkled defunctive days. The no-colour void. Mornings of deep, desolating emptiness. Mornings when all the heartstrings like wild horses pull... Not even in Utah, no. Cold laughter, dead laughter. The sound of distant barking heard from Maryon Park. The reckoning. Life's strange principle lying deep and the yellow leaf everywhere. By a guttering candle, gutted, clawed, taken aback, lying aback & broken, half-sodden, washed by stale and detritus, tipped in Time's gutter, turns, gets onto his knees, falls back. The sediment. The inner weight. The unknown thing. The impulse to... No continuance. His old desire to — Preparing to leave all this; preparing to leave... Going out, once or twice, nowhere really. Scuffed suede shoes. Takes a walk, yes. Down the old familiar street. Hotel neon flashing blue, crimson, blue. Chocolate the colour of shit, from an automatic machine. Bread tasteless, biscuits of sand. Cigarettes, flat warm beer. The afternoons of the dying year steadily shortening. Then back up the narrow winding stairs. A fool whose bells have ceased to ring at all. Fingers beating the wall in time to an old tune. Into sleeping bag. Stone age, age of iron and scrap. Stretched out, on his stomach, dead to the world. Frail, frailer. Mumbles as he turns. Face buried in the pillow. Dead face nightly appearing. Cramped in every limb. Barely a breath. Buried in the broken mine. Drowned, bloated on the black lake's rubbish-littered bed. Smashed and swallowed by an avalanche. Sweating in a bed-roll. Delving the dead days. Delving with stone fingers the black depths, the unending silence. Ice blocks. Eyes that have stared too long stare at the wedge of light at the end of an unwarmed room. Speared by a slash of soupy light, in a moment dissolved. The residue. The no-colour void. Become a ghost, a meagre transparency. Mausoleum mornings, graveyard afternoons. The verdigris. Dead up-ended stiff-leg robin on the pale verge, saplings broken. *Elle vous suit par tout.* Days brimming with deadness and darks. Hands plunged in cloudy water, up to the wrist. Dullness and cold glasses, dreary evenings, congealed beerfroth. Scatter all away, dead nights washing away, down, down the drain. Called it dead winter of plucked cabbage stalks, dead monuments and toad-dark carpets, ubiquitous mist. Those selfsame months of the sculful Pole's hit symphony. Hawkins, his discomposure bleakly evident, composes nothing, else unsent letters, abandoned stanzas, lists, rolls in a sleeping roll on a kitchen floor, a mouse patters over his heart and he wakes shrieking. Numbness, pins and needles. Hangovers. Bubbles of bitterness. Notices a strange shape — una extraña forma — his shirt's all torn and filthy — y sucia mi camisa — and, and, and. And so on and so on and so on. *Ah riedi ancora qual eri allora* and all that jive. By what ravaged, by what blanched? The punishing wind's frost fingers making him shiver enclosed though he was by layers of blackness. Steam rising from pockmarked lugubrious urinals. Scourged by the sting and rip of petty, poisoned minutes, impossible to think, concentrate. Bolted; captived; speaks to dead walls. Time so slow, you'd think it had stopped for bad & all, tepid November, perilous dead December, barren January, bitter torpid February. A long and snake-like life. The long year linked with heavy day on day. The black empty nest in the dead ash filling with grey snow. The bathroom down the stairs, subterranean dull green walls, shitting pellets, dark cartridges, in an ill humour. Up and down Bootham, past the Auden plaque. Up and down, down and up. Down, down, down. Down and desperate. Desperate, getting out of the city in a hired car alone, crashing the gears, through dale and doleful valley. Empty rainswept hillside carpark. Moor barren, seeing the farm faraway in the cup of the bleak vale. A high, desolate place where the mountains came crashing down and crumbled at his feet. Wrinkles, the first grey hairs. The blur and crumble of great hearts failing. A day spent walking among ruins. His need naked, his mind spinning dizzy into rages of space, wanting to be gone. Back to the city to face the musty corridors of a crooked year, the indictment, the gradual disremembering. Mister Hawkins watching his step; circumscribed Mister Hawkins on the dole, dealing in morsels again. His Münchenpain and madness and all the dahlias in the sooty garden undulating in Munchpainwaves, raw sienna ribbed and shivering. Poor drudge engulfed in sleet, shivering in the drifts of his need. Madly blind. Bereft. Sans everything. Briars, brambles. In a dark obscure wood perplexed. The sear, the yellow leaf. Heart-stopping shots nearby, and the burrs, the burrs. Everything grey, shrunk and shrivelled. As turns the needle — Bearings lost and bleakness unrelenting until — Until the coming back. Back to Hellfire Corner and the long crawl through the chattering mud. The impulse ... No continuance. Butterflies. Then the impulse again. Doggedly pulling back the covers, then pulling them stiffly forward again. No continuance. Then motion, motions. Definite circumgyratory movements! Then total collapse. Utter fatigue. A trail of cartoon zeds swimming from nose to ceiling. Then close-up of eyes opening. Heavy eyes. Baggy eyes. Eyes dying. Dead marble. Stone. Stone eyelids lowered, voice like gravel. The long grass growing above his burnt out brain. A ruin. Fractured, fragmented, broken. Cold-pinched. In a pretty pickle. Picking up the pieces, pooling stagnant resources, pulling his selves together. Cigarette, flaring match. Trickle of smoke. Speechless. In thought, deeper. Thinking, stupidly, to come through the waste, the hazard... Barren fabulation. Paralysed by poetry, the pelting rain. Killer words, late Beethoven. Melancholy and whisky, Bach and solitude, empty house, derelict factory that Sunday, Balmacaan ruin, margarine, eggs, fist-fucking phantoms, *Hamlet,* Kees. String Quartet No. 13 played beside a whale carcase rotting on a rainy beach. Call him pitiful, helpless. Old leather-back turtle, in torment. Forget-me-nots brittle in an old book. Obliterated mornings, obliterated nights. The motes showering Mister Hawkins slumped drunk, soft interminable tread of the long gone, odd specks and flakes in the wall mirror. The first mysterious lines of age turning a human face into an old, wretched, used-up thing, a child's puzzled eyes staring out of the ruin. Out there, through the blear pane, time accelerating. Yellow fields, sparkly starlings, children pouring brightly out of school. This is how the story ended, is it, in dribs & drabs? Dazed, done in mentally and the money running out. Considerations pinching his heart, lack of breath, Mister Hawkins getting fat and sluggish. Thinks: how quiet everything is. This could go on forever. This is what it is to die. Rain, days, liquor, a dripping tap; the store laid away for a monotonous future being eaten away. Another beer, another slug. And another. Remembering the dead rat below the clear water at the very edge of the loch. Thwarted by language, class and money. Born in a Yorkshire mist, dying in one. Remembering, disremembering, having come this far, twenty-nine. No! in drizzle. Call it between-times. Call it coming slowly back to what's imminent and real. Lukewarm radiators, tired animals, crooked neighbours, the finny people slow-circling in bowls and tanks, erasers, foliage leaking laughter, the sad and quiet weddings, name tags, milk, gunsights, complete strangers, digits, guitars and sugared almonds. Apples, melons. Flowers and herbs. Coping with what vanishes and never returns. Bodies, names, empires, gone in a puff of smoke. Rushing, pointlessly, after the melting drifts. Exhausted, coming back. To life. To start afresh! A forward course for Mr What's-your-name. Face growing eager, yes. Brightening into a smile. More. Feverish eagerness, breathless interest. Sunny side up on the sun-sun-sunny side o' the street. Kiki Dee and Elton John and "True Love", Terry Evans singing "That's The Way Love Turned Out For Me". The good things that make it all so — Children's laughter. Roses, daisies, sun dried tomatoes. Mixed herbs and Chablis and Aberdeen Angus. Cigarettes and sex, beers and fondling. How's things? Dripping lips; trickles, splashes. Luscious clusters. Okay, I guess. So-so. "At five? I'd love to. Pretty well. And you?" Putting your finger on it. Putting it in, putting it down in the end, all of it. Yes. Back again. Pause, rest for a while. Not, perhaps, time wasted. *Listen to me.* Shaping at that table between his hands, the story. Setting it down, an incomplete thing. Dreams, too. The inmates. A globe of glass, cracked. From the first capital to the last period. Literary concupiscence! Monosyllabic invention! Sheets of sorrow. In his old lunes again. Turning a distich. In paper-durance bound. One sustained frenzied agonizing rush. Lines, circles, scenes, letters and characters. Words on words. The anaesthesia of them. The mist; the scorching; a little drop of ink and the tap-drip of desolate weeping. Soliloquies. Useless, helpless reiteration, elegies on brambles. Get a grip on your selves. The lines all running together. Paper heart where the lines are smudged, where the ink's bled. Yellowed, brittle. Zoo now I hope — Writing steadily on, pausing only to sit while his fingers rested. *The glow and the shadow, every scrap of memory, every remembered speech, every letter...* To hold a farthing candle to the sun. A world of words! Cigarette scarring slowly into the edge of the rented table. Halts; half remembers. Crammed with observation, perishing fast. Burnt out by time and liquor. Down at zero. Then starts again. In fits and starts, in mangled forms, the visible lines. Fettered hand and foot by a little strip of inked ribbon. Motley-minded; getting more and more enmeshed, like a roach in a web. Memory's crupper. Rags and dust, rigmarole. As the torrent widens... Tumult of recollections pressing upon his mind, frowns. Journeys through the bygone time. Shadows of shadows. Then remembers the cigarette, raises it to rub uselessly at the new scorch before — Open brackets: Ah, the pleasures of frottage. Perpend; close brackets. Seated placidly in shirt sleeves. Applying his mind. Keeping the atrocious reader in suspense. Reaching the end, at last, almost. To have done. Waste and idle papers. The words all fallen from his cracked lips, disfiguring the page's whiteness. Disclosures over. Past mastered, perhaps. Then raising his eyes, staring for a long time at the chipped cup, the steaming bowl. Go ltel bok, go. Sipping the tea. Taking the bread, taking the spoon, beginning to eat.

Eating a little, three or four spoonfuls. Without appetite, head aching less now. Hearing the clock for the first time, its ticking filling the room. Raising his head, looking at the window. The York mists, the mists on the mountain hung. Dull aquarium glow, morning again. New morning! Tiptoeing to the door, quietly opening it a little. Going out. Stumbling, falling on grass, springing up. Chipper. Jaunty gait, cheery whistling. Passing through the passing day, the crucible, the petty dust. Not even in Utah, no. Cracked and smashed, dust. Gone, almost. The faintest of faint shadows, the merest echoes of echoes, fading, ebbing, almost gone. The lines running in the rain. The lines blown, smudged. A kind of sigh; things indecipherable. Eyes down, raised; alert for eyes of grey. Learning in which direction to turn, to turn and turn again. Congratulations! Have a nice day! And old paper heart goes on, goes on. To search. To search again for salmon singing in the street. Learning to walk once more. Pitter-patter, pitter-patter, old paper heart. Water in a gutter, burbling. Goes on. Then gone, almost. Almost gone. Gone.

FROM *DRIVING MY BABY BACK HOME*
(1999)

Classic

Jethro, sharing his creamy chocolate truffle bar with Janet, his new girlfriend, confided that the greatest sensual pleasure he knew, after sex and chocolate, was reading a good book while defecating.

Janet wrinkled her pretty, snub nose. What kind of book?

Preferably a full-bodied fiction excreted from the putrefying innards of a culture on the turn, he replied. To wit: a modernist tome.

Jethro was slightly strange, she felt, but intriguingly so. On the wall above his bed was a large framed photograph of Paul Bern and a poster of Jonathan Swift.

Jethro was two metres tall, handsome and rugged. He had inchworms tattooed on both buttocks. Janet was somewhat smaller, with no tattoos. Jethro's most precious possession was a signed first edition of *Gravity's Rainbow*.

That night they went to see *Titanic* and she thought no more about what Jethro had told her. At the end she wept salt tears as the drowned ones gathered around the great stairway, applauding the endurance of love. Back at Jethro's apartment they discussed the movie over several glasses of fine Chablis, then went to bed. Here they made fiery, satisfying love.

In the morning Jethro brought her a mug of tea in bed. The side of the mug bore a portrait of William Faulkner. Excitedly he began to tell her about *Barton Fink*.

For breakfast Jethro ate his usual bucket of cereal. This comprised a base of bite-size shredded wheat and Grape Nuts, mixed with sesame seeds, pumpkin seeds, sliced apricots, sliced figs, dried coconut and sliced apple, topped with a layer of oat and bran flakes and chopped organic walnuts, drenched in a litre of organic soya milk.

Janet said she'd just have toast and honey. After his second bucket Jethro announced that it was time for his morning crap. I may be gone some time, he quipped, alluding to an explorer of whom Janet had never heard.

Upstairs in the bright, attractive bathroom overlooking the

beach Jethro lowered himself on to the lime green lavatory seat. In his left hand he held a copy of *Under the Volcano*, in his right two squares of luxury soft toilet tissue. Folding the tissue, he reached between his legs and began to knead his anus. Simultaneously he began reading the introduction to Malcolm Lowry's masterpiece. It told him that the novel was one of a number of works about the breakdown of values in the twentieth century.

Janet peeked in. I'm off to work now. I'll be back around six. Love you.

Love you, Jethro replied.

Frowning, he got on with the serious business of the day.

*

During the first chapter of *Under the Volcano* Jethro passed no stools at all. This did not perturb Jethro in the slightest. He had always been something of a late starter, in defecation as in life. As he immersed himself in Lowry's fictional Mexico he continued gently massaging his anus. The pleasure was minor but nevertheless indubitably there.

Lowry's introductory characters, M. Laruelle and Dr Vigil, finished their conversation, and M. Laruelle climbed the embankment. *How continually, how startlingly, the landscape changed!* Jethro read. M. Laruelle wandered on. He entered the little cantina. Sr. Bustamente gave him the book of Elizabethan plays. M. Laruelle unfolded the sheet of paper and read the Consul's unposted letter. He set fire to the letter, the wheel went backwards, Yvonne entered the Bella Vista bar.

The Consul and Yvonne went outside.

From a nearby hotel *belated revellers like half-dazed wasps out of a hidden nest issued every few moments*, Jethro read. His brow furrowed slightly. He had once had to deal with a wasps' nest. He knew what Lowry was getting at but he wasn't entirely sure *half-dazed* was apt. The motion of wasps outdoors involves confident cruising beelines, swoopings and sudden horizontal zig-zags. When wasps emerge from a nest they drift out laterally, get their bearings, then shoot off. They do not appear dazed. Why should they be? Going in and out of a nest for a wasp is like going in and out of a house for a human.

As Yvonne and the Consul moved on past the front of Cortez Palace there was a slight pop and a solitary ball-bearing shot out, hitting the placid lake with a soft splash. Jethro grinned. His first turd of the book! He always remembered these moments. The quick sudden chipolata as Mr Deasy laughed with rich delight, putting back his savingsbox. The strange jets of pale malodorous jelly as the heel of the slipperless foot in its sloppy anklet rubbed against the pile of old magazines on the sofa. The slim soft pale brown stool a good two metres in length which emerged as the men worked from sunup to sundown while parties of horsemen rode up and the architect in his formal coat and his Paris hat and his expression of grim and embittered amazement lurked about the environs of the scene. The curious rectangular turd which squeezed itself out as Neville explained that he needed someone whose mind falls like a chopper on a block. The strangely ornate, twisted, almost *Gothic* stool that came out slowly as the young man's expression became something vivid and concrete — a beautiful personal presence, diffusing the sense of a function.

It was like the first lyrical droplet of a spring shower. Yvonne and the Consul walked on through the streets of Quauhnahuac and at last reached the house. The Consul sat on the broken green rocker facing Yvonne. The telephone rang and he went to answer it. Yvonne went to the bathroom. The Consul slipped out of the house. Then, just as half a dozen marbles suddenly showered down, he collapsed face down on the Calle Nicaragua.

The marbles made quite a commotion in the lake. Waves rocked to and fro against the steep china walls. Jethro paused briefly to stare down between his thighs. Seven. Each one almost perfectly round. This sort always made him think of Barnes Wallis, the inventor.

Jethro gave just a short flush (in order to benefit the environment) and returned to his classic. The Consul was helped to his feet. He returned to the house. Yvonne lay on the bed. The Consul began to caress her, but couldn't get an erection. He fell asleep in the chair. Hugh returned to the house. He and Yvonne went out for a walk. They hired horses. They came to the headland and stood gazing back the way they'd come. The Consul woke up and went into the garden. He encountered his neighbour Mr Quincey, a walnut grower. Walnuts! Strange coincidence... Two more turds had dropped into the lake, bigger than their predecessors, gnarled and glistening, their skin texture wrinkled and glossy, the spitting image of a pair of sleek easy-on-the-eye supermarket walnuts.

Hugh and Yvonne had returned. So too had Janet. She was downstairs, calling his name. Jethro, are you there? Hi, honey! I'm home.

He managed to reach the end of Chapter Five before she located him.

*

Honey, are you back in here *again!* Anyone would think you had a problem! Some people might think you spent ALL DAY in the bathroom.

But I have done. Today, I mean. Look! I read all the way to page one hundred and fifty.

Jethro was reading the Plume paperback, the April 1971 printing, which reproduces the text of the first American edition.

Good God, Jethro, you are *strange*. Now you hurry up and be on down soon. I'll fix us some food.

I'm not coming out of here until I've finished the book.

And how long will that take?

At a rough guess, another twenty-four hours or so.

You are going to sit there for another twenty-four hours!

That's right. So I'd appreciate it if you could bring me my supper in here. And a beer. I need a beer.

You're sick!

Janet slammed the door behind her. She left him there, undisturbed, for another hour. Bliss! During that time he read the whole of Chapter Six and deposited a real steamer into the bowl. *The road turned a little corner in the distance and vanished*, he read, just as Janet came into the room with a tray.

*

Although his main focus was on what was occurring in Laruelle's house Jethro enjoyed Janet's food and apologies. The beer was cold and refreshing. The baked veal chops garnished with fresh parsley, the rice-stuffed sole, the corn fritters and the hazelnut lattice pie all held the promise of pungent future faeces. He patted his anus gently with a wad of fresh tissue as Janet said she was sorry for her attitude. She'd just never known anyone like him before. It took some getting used to, that was all. Did he need anything else?

Nothing apart from a box of peanut butter sandwiches and two flasks of coffee to get him through the night. Oh, and would she mind turning the light on?

Black or white?

Brown.

*

Honey, we have a problem.

Janet said, entering the bathroom, still wearing her yellow kimono. An hour and a half had passed since he'd asked her to switch the bathroom light on. During that time he'd accompanied the Consul to the fairground and on into the Terminal Cantina El Bosque, then hopped on the bus, a 1918 Chevrolet, which *jerked forward with a noise like startled poultry*. The simile suddenly reminded him slightly of one in an Ian McEwan story: *They scattered before him like fright-ened fowl.* A mild coincidence, presumably. The bus went on as far as the dying Indian. The policeman pushed Hugh back on to the bus and the Consul restrained him.

Had she been enthusiastic for Joseph Conrad, Henry James or Vladimir Nabokov, she might have found this situation repugnant. But Janet, a Yeats scholar, had been schooled on Gogol and Burroughs. There wasn't much she couldn't handle.

Honey, I need to be where you are, she said coyly.

You can be. But not for another twenty-four hours at the very least. I don't care if you pee in the tub. I'm broad-minded.

It's not just a pee I need.

In that case I'm sorry. You'll just have to tell yourself you don't need to go until later.

I'll try. With a wicked grin Janet slipped off her kimono. Underneath she was naked. She walked towards him. You're going to have to *distract* me, she grinned.

Even though he was giving his all to the text, she managed to raise some interest on his part.

She clambered aboard and did the fitting herself. Resting her hands lightly on his shoulders she stared past him at the stiff tall cactus in the pot on the green cistern. The way things had turned out excited her no end. Fragments of Yeats flashed in her mind as she gently rode her way to the climax. Her pleasure she vocalised as a sequence of low involuntary whisperings in which Jethro was sure he heard the word *excrement*. He gave a quick brief grunt, which was followed by a substantial splash in the shadowed waters beneath them. A few watery pearls appeared as if by magic across her stomach.

Smiling, she ran from the room.

Some things just won't wait. She ran outside on to the patio and squatted, releasing a glistening, curling, circling, flawlessly sculpted art object that might almost have been patterned by a Pict. The neighbourhood voyeur, Jack

Reading, was so excited he dropped his night scope and suffered a major stroke.

She wasn't sure whether to tell Jethro what she'd done or just feign surprise and attribute the mess to Barbour, the notoriously incontinent dog which belonged to the old man next door, a retired paranoid named Jackson Nix.

Wiping herself on a sheet of kitchen towel, she went upstairs to bed.

*

The coffee kept Jethro going through the long night. He went with the others to the Arena Tomalin. Yvonne relived her past. Hugh wrestled with the bull. They went to a bar and had a row. The Consul ran off. Yvonne and High went to look for him. At one point Jethro must have dozed off. He woke to the words *Yvonne knew where she was now* and a firm, solid pleasurable ooze which dangled almost as far as the lake before it snapped off and slid into the cool depths, hitting the bed of the lake with such force that it left a broad smear as big as an important footnote in the smooth, curving depths of that shimmering subterranean world.

This was the beginning of the end. The rain fell heavily. The horse ran towards Yvonne and struck her. The Consul, in the Farolito, entered the whore's room. *The Consul's eyes focused a calendar behind the bed.* The ooze had started again, was pushing forwards, sending firm pulses of pleasure which matched the throb of Lowry's exquisite prose. *His versatile companion*, Jethro read, giving a grunt of pleasure, feeling the stick of rock snap, the big splash, the refreshing spray slapping his tattoos.

The Consul was asked his name. Someone shouted: Trotsky. The Chief of Rostrums pushed the Consul towards the door. The Consul lashed out. The Chief fired. Jethro felt a sudden tumultuous final slither and rush and knew that his bowels were finally emptied. A stench rose up between his thighs. *Somebody threw a dead turd down the ravine,* he misread and looked again, seeing his mistake.

The bathroom was filled with yellow light. Outside birds chattered and sang. He looked at his wristwatch. Just after six. He realised he hadn't touched the peanut butter sandwiches. Hungrily he began to wolf them down. Moments later Janet came in, yawning.

The perfume needs changing in here, she said, returning moments later with the pine-scented odour-eater.

I finished the book, said Jethro.

Was it good?

Terrific. But it didn't make me want to read anything else by Lowry. Anyway, honey. I've finished here. It's all yours.

This time Jethro used full flush.

Janet sat down. Mmm, the seat is deliciously warm, she said appreciatively.

*

Over breakfast Jethro said he was very tired.

I'm going to call in sick.

Good idea, said Janet. You rest. Then tonight we could go and see *Deep Impact*. I've always wanted to see that film.

Before you leave, honey, there's one thing I want to ask.

Shoot.

Janet, will you marry me?

If you promise me that you'll stop spending all that time in the bathroom, the answer's: yes.

I promise. It was just a phase, I guess. Besides, I'm finished with modernism and toilet seats. I've read all I ever wanted to read. It's time to move on from the mixed pleasures of the text and defecation. From now on I'm embracing post-modernism! Although I have never read *Wittgenstein's Mistress* or *Da Vinci's Bicycle* or *The Public Burning* or *To Wanstonia*, I feel that they might well be my cup of tea!

Jethro stood up and whooped.

From now on I'm only going to read slim paperbacks of experimental fiction while going down flumes. I want to be swept off my feet! Hurled down dark pipes, not knowing where I'm going! Be splattered with spray when I least expect it! Be shot out into mysterious glittering surfaces and plunged into strange depths to crawl along white tiles while tiny whirling worlds boil around me.

He sat down again.

I mean this. Seriously, Janet. I'm through with all that other crap.

ELEPHANTS

The wind blows hard from the east. In this world of sharp contrasts you cannot see a foot ahead; it's all turns and twists. Big rocks and boulders are clustered around, coated with luxuriant green moss and ferns. The mountains are covered with grey grass and flowers rise over the trees like smoke.

Sweating, trouserless, Vladimir Ilyich Lenin crouches by the mopane tree, eyed by a dwarf mongoose bearing a curious resemblance to Rodzianko...

To be caught out in Africa wearing nothing but a shirt is tremendously inconvenient! Most especially so after a successful — relatively! — socialist revolution.

The ground is broken in short ridges of hills coming down close to the forest. Soon you are out of the hollow, out of the reeds, out of the forest. On the plain impala fly past, kicking out their legs, activating the scent glands on their fetlocks. Helmeted guineafowl scratch in the dust at dawn. Hippos wallow in the filth, keeping pleasantly moist. How Engels would have liked it here! He would have made a special study of the baboons. The worrying thing is one simply does not know what has happened to one's trousers! One suspects the Social Revolutionaries. Or British intelligence. That oaf Reilly.

Nothing but a crumpled white shirt. The hot sun beating down on one's buttocks, one's leathery genitals. And so many animals with horns. Impala rams. Buffalo bulls. Rhinos. And birds with sharp, slashing beaks: green-backed herons, woodpeckers, cormorants, grey-headed gulls.

What was it Marx said? About the proposition that man cannot live without buying trousers. About the proposition that a man cannot enrich himself without buying trousers. That the purchase of trousers is a condition of enrichment in the same way as the circulation of the blood or the process of breathing.

Stuff and nonsense! For as Marx observed, in themselves neither the circulation of my blood nor my breathing make me any richer...

Help! Elephants!

Elephants mud-bathing at a pan. Drowsy and calm. But any moment now they will lumber to their feet and come chasing after you, hooting malevolently, squirting you with dirty water!

Over there is an elephant bull using a termite mound as a step while stretching for the branch of an Acacia albida tree. A branch which he will use to give you a thrashing!

Elephants at water. Watching. Refreshing themselves before the pursuit of Vladimir Ilyich Lenin.

An angry elephant bull, ears outstretched. A real brute. Those eyes, those fierce reactionary wrinkles. The spitting image of Kornilov.

A herd of elephants tramping along at dawn! Thunder, thunder, thunder. How the ground trembles!

Now the herd is crashing towards you! You begin to run, aware of your horribly vulnerable penis going flip-flop-flip! Run, run, as fast as you can, darting in among the bushes, the ground shuddering as if during an earthquake, a maniacal trumpeting and hooting rending the hot syrupy African air, a forest of wrinkled grey trunks swinging wildly, pounding legs, eruptions of dust, pillars of boiling muck, a choking spreading nightmarish haze of noise and your amplified booming pulse.

A haze which fades, a noise which fades, opening out into a strange white silence, a silent whiteness, an Arctic desolation, a vast stretched wilderness containing nothing but a rather grotesque representation of solid, overcoated Marx, standing solemnly on a white gigantic china dinner plate, the plate balanced carefully upon the spines of four motionless elephants, wrinkly rumps pressed together as each in turn stares mirthlessly north, south, east and west.

Aaaaaaaaaaaaaaaaaaaaaaaaaaaaaaaaaaaaaaaaaaaaagh!

THUMP!

The sheet tangled around his ankles, his nightshirt wrapped around his waist, Vladimir Ilyich Lenin wakes to find that some entity — some malicious narrator — has resorted to one of the dustiest tricks in the tale-teller's treasure chest. Preposterous and ridiculously implausible dreams of being trouserless in Africa terminated by a sudden fall out of bed!

"Ilyich."

Krupskaya leaning over him, anxious, attentive. A slight scowl as she takes in his throbbing inguinal regions.

Lenin shakes an angry fist at the ceiling (believing that if a whimsical postmodernist is anywhere, the creature is likely to be at ceiling level looking down rather than at floor level looking up). A playful nip in the ankles from a semi-materialised Yorkshire terrier quickly corrects the error. The terrier rushes between Krupskaya's legs, springs on to a chair, takes on the form of a miniature elephant, meta-morphoses into the Cheshire cat, then melts away into thin air, leaving behind a grin-shaped mark on the west-facing Kremlin wall which was probably there in 1905.

"Dog?" Krupskaya mutters, puzzled, aware only of a brief brown blur and entirely oblivious of the brief circus display at her rear.

Lenin rocks with laughter, waves the matter away. Wild, grinning whiskery semi-materialised creatures, echoes and empurpled whisperings from *Hydriotaphia* along the cold stone Kremlin corridors, small bare rooms where spirals of sunlit dust twist feverishly against a cage of shadows — bosh and nonsense! Away with them! Away with green triangular faces and amorphous soft sacks hoisted on stilts and provided with two scarlet five-pronged forks! There are more pressing matters to attend to. To urinate, to wash, to shave. To put on one's trousers! To consider electrification, surplus grain appropriation, dialectics, eclecticism, factional pro-nouncements and syndicalist and anarchist deviation in the Party. To consider (strange what a burden the affair has turned into!) the competition to design a monument in honour of Karl Marx.

Wearisome Comrade Mikhailovsky, with his itch to be

awarded the first prize. Having to sit at one's desk humouring the fellow. Staring absently at the potted palm, the large photograph of Marx, the bronze statuette, the scissors, the paper knives, the cigarette lighter. Hoping that the telephone will ring.

"Comrade Mikhailovsky! How nice to see you!" Karl Marx Supported By Four Elephants. Can the fellow be serious? Is this some sort of joke?

Evidently not. Comrade Mikhailovsky flourishes his sketches.

Apparently he is one of the nation's leading sculptors. And a good Bolshevik.

But this is grotesque! Marx addressing the masses from the backs of four elephants! One arm raised in a profound gesture, holding some papers. Evidently completely unaware of the quadrupeds beneath his feet.

Bizarre creatures, elephants. Dream creatures. A species more at home in *Alice in Wonderland* than the real world. "But the elephants, comrade... I don't quite see..." And now Mikhailovsky is off again, jabbing his finger at yet more sketches. The phone rings. Bliss.

"What's that you say? Hills like white elephants? Who is this please?" Wrong number!

"Comrade Lenin, I insist on first prize. Who else can possibly portray the grandeur of Marx. His greatness. Standing head and shoulders above we ordinary mortals. Towering above us. With the grandeur and nobility of the mighty elephant itself. We need four for balance, of course. A firm foundation is absolutely necessary. Marx himself would have understood the necessary link — ha! ha! — between base and superstructure. And four elephants of course gives us twenty sturdy supports. Yes, twenty! You look puzzled, Comrade Lenin. You are thinking that if four elephants each have four legs that gives us sixteen supports. But — tee hee! — you are forgetting the trunks! Easily done, Comrade. Easily done!"

The telephone again.

"Yes?"

Stalin.

Another complaint about Trotsky.

Says that Trotsky has been going around telling people that he keeps dreaming of Stalin in the body of an elephant. When asked why, Trotsky replies, "Vous me trompez!"

Very good!

Stalin, of course, doesn't understand a thing. Yes, yes, I'll speak to Lev about it.

"Elephants?"

Mikhailovsky begins to stammer. "There are other possibilities..." He reaches into his case, pulls out more sketches.

Karl Marx Supported By Four Lions. "The tails, you see, also give us a total of twenty supports!"

Karl Marx Supported By Four Kangaroos!

"Symbolising a leap into the future, Comrade Lenin. Marx, as you see, supports himself by placing his boot in the animal's pouch, while holding on with one arm to the neck..."

"Yes, yes. Most imaginative, I'm sure. I will certainly speak to Comrade Lunacharsky. Of course the final decision rests with the jury."

"But a word from you, Comrade Lenin. Concerning a fellow Party member. First prize, you understand, to someone of my — ".

"Yes, yes. Well, goodbye Comrade."

Rid of the fellow at last!

The phone rings.

"Have I heard the story of the elephant which foretold the birth of the Buddha? Of course I haven't! Who is this, please?"

The line goes dead.

Exasperated, Lenin rushes from the room. Outside, in the hallway, he finds himself skirting a slough of high dry reeds. Beyond, on the opposite bank, is dense forest, and above, the steep face of a canyon. Ahead, at the end of the reeds, the banks narrow and the branches of the big trees almost cover the stream.

Lenin crosses the stream on a log and then another log. The second log stirs, then rises abruptly from the water. Recognising the elephant's bulk, Lenin goes soaring through space.

Crash! Back on the floor by one's bed. A trick! A dream within a dream! A wearisome sleight of hand by a narrator with worn cuffs and patches on his elbows.

Lenin wags a reproving finger at the floor (believing that if a whimsical postmodernist is anywhere, the creature is likely to be at floor level looking up rather than at ceiling level looking down). A playful nip in the neck from a semi-materialised parrot quickly corrects the error. The parrot flashes over Krupskaya's head, perches on the telephone, briefly takes on the form of a frog, then with a mild squawk springs through the half-open window, out into Red Square.

"A budgerigar?" Krupskaya muses, puzzled, aware only of a brief, coloured blur, oblivious of the frog, which at that moment is hopping away towards the Cathedral, pursued by a pair of panting futurists.

Lenin rocks with laughter, waves the matter away.

"Hurry," Krupskaya mutters. "Comrade Mikhailovsky is coming to see you at nine with his designs for the monument to Marx."

"Just as long as he gets the hair right. The hair must be lifelike. Lots of detail. Not slabs. I am sick of what they keep doing to Marx's head. Turning it into a gross, ugly thing. With a beard like a petrified dishcloth."

The phone rings.

Lenin nods at Krupskaya.

"You answer it."

ULYSSES

1 Briskly, stout James Connolly came up Sackville Street, leading a band of militants in which an anger and a theory lay mixed. The countermand having been countermanded.

2 — You, comrade, what city sent for him? — Dublin, Jim.— Very good. Well? — There was a rebellion. — Very good. What was it all about?

3 Ineffable postmodernity of the risible: displaced, nationalist and imperialist, cast through an Irish I.

4 Mr Vladimir Ilyich read with disgust the article in *Berner Tagwacht* entitled "Their Song is Over" and signed with the initials K.R.

5 At the Four Courts on King's Inn Quay Mr Edward Daly instructed his men to open fire on a passing company of Lancers riding soberly from the harbour at the North Wall to Phoenix Park.

6 Joseph Mary Plunkett, first, took tea in the GPO commissary and, the others having left the room, was examined by the doctor who had, less than a month before, carried out throat surgery for glandular tuberculosis.

7 ARMED REPUBLICAN GANGS SEIZE BUILDINGS, 30 DEAD **Army Moves In To Prevent Bloodbath** On Lower Abbey Street shells fell, exploded, at first just trickles of smoke, then finally pillars of flame pouring from the collapsing interior of the *Irish Times*'s reserve print shop.

8 Mailbags, desks, ledgers, office supplies. Books! Tables, chairs, pads of postal blanks. Correspondence files and old Post Office records. More books and blanks. All pushed against the casements. Bullet stoppers. The entire interior torn apart and restructured. Hardly a thing left in its original place apart from a scaffold near the front. A Volunteer named Daly fixing a telephone line to the roof.

9 The upper floors, what about them, O'Rahilly quizzed.

— Up there, that stairway, the Henry Street side. Have we cleared everyone out up there?

10 Giggling nervously, the girls descended the wide staircase from the telegraph office.

11 A detonation intense, heard by all, artillery, a nine-pounder, bombarding.

12 Jaysus, isn't that a lovely bike, would ye look at the bloody eejits throwing it away and them other eejits pushing them rolls of newsprint across Lower Abbey Street, anyone would think there was a giant needing to wipe his arse and now look if them eejits isn't trying to blow up the pillar.

13 The poles at opposite corners of the noble old building now held the two new flags of Ireland which waved proudly in a crisp breeze. Beneath them could be seen the brave figure of Patrick Pearse. In a stirring voice he read out the eloquent proclamation of Irish independence in the name of God and of the dead generations. We place the cause of the Irish Republic under the protection of the Most High God, quoth he, whose blessing we invoke upon our arms. A mighty cheer rang out from the assembled multitude.

14 Deshil Abbey Eamus.

15 (The top of O'Connell Street, down which comes an astonishing vehicle with a hooded, armoured body gashed by thin slits and small holes from which protrude phallus after phallus.)

16 Preparatory to anything else Mr Connolly hurried from group to group bucking them up generally and urging them to get a move on. Afterwards it was said that simply by going up to them he accelerated his men. Speedily and with renewed enthusiasm they carried bags of sand and pushed the furniture around. Eagerly were reserves despatched to the forces holding Jacob's biscuit factory and Gilbey's distillery.

17 What were the failings of James Connolly's politics? Numerous. The failure to recognise the need for an openly socialist political group. An opportunist alignment with nationalist politics. Substituting armed citizens for the organised power of workers. Syndicalist tendencies. Pessimism about the revolutionary potential of workers. Naïve illusions about German social democracy. A desire for insurrection irrespective of objective circumstances. The

belief that in December you can plan a revolution to take place on a fixed date some four months later. A lack of international working-class solidarity as evidenced by his attacks on British workers who fled to Ireland to avoid being conscripted.

Why then did Mr Vladimir Ilyich read with disgust the article in *Berner Tagwacht* entitled "Their Song is Over" and signed with the initials K.R.?

Because of its monstrously doctrinaire and pedantic assessment of the Easter Rising as a putsch by an urban petty bourgeois movement without mass support. Because the term *putsch* in its scientific sense may be employed only when the attempt at insurrection has revealed nothing but a circle of conspirators who arouse no sympathy among the masses. Because the Rising involved a revolutionary outburst by a section of the petty bourgeoisie with all its prejudices but nevertheless involving a section of the workers. Because it was the misfortune of the Irish that they rose prematurely, before the European revolt of the proletariat had had time to mature. Because it is only in premature, individual, sporadic and therefore unsuccessful revolutionary movements that the masses gain experience, acquire knowledge, gather strength, and get to know their real leaders, and in this way prepare for the general onslaught.

Does the Easter Rising prove or disprove Laird's theory of tympoptanomania?

It proves it. In 1909 a resident of Dublin, a Mrs Nora Barnacle Joyce, gave vent to what an impartial witness with excellent hearing described as fat dirty spluttering farts, an arse full of farts, big fat fellows, long windy ones, quick little merry cracks and a lot of tiny little naughty forties ending in a long gush. Within just seven years the city was shaken by these noises magnified and repeated on an epic scale — hardly a coincidence. What form did Ireland take subsequently? A grocers' republic. Was there one low point in particular?

There were many. Metafictionists may wish to consider the treatment meted out to Brian O'Nolan. But unquestionably outstanding was the visit in May 1945 of the wily opportunist Eamon De Valera to the residence of the German ambassador to Dublin to pay his condolences and express his deep regrets upon the death of Herr Hitler.

18 No Jim said when asked to express his thoughts on the rising no thinking only of that bloody book of his which they turned into a film no this can't be right no one of Kirk Douglas's least successful independent productions this heavily dubbed Italian epic emphasizes dialogue over thrills I mean what the fuck is this Kirk does his best but gets mired in a slow retelling Kirk? would that be James Tiberius whose heroes include Garth of Izar and who has a quick mind and a great sense of humour I mean this must be something else let's try Halliwell that's better a facile and ludicrous reduction that's more like it a cheaply produced film being sold at exorbitant prices based on an unmanageably prolix novel etcetera etcetera what I want to know is why when you are writing about 1904 over a period of however many fucking years how can you ignore the events of April 1916 afterwards I mean how can you also you ask any academic what's special about 1922 of course they'll say that's when that classic book was published they won't say that's when the Special Powers Act was brought in no the fact is ha ha if a man is determined to have a rising nothing will stop him Fitzgerald looking out of a loophole in the narrative at the delete key then turning to look back at the flags flying from the roof of the Post Office and outside it Pearse and saying this is worth being wiped out for O'Nolan just four at this time and the sky lurid in Inchicore you could hear the thud and sludge of shells and once O'Nolan saw an aerostat over the house a Brit machine where's it going? to hell I hope came the reply and in less than three years 25 January 1919 to be precise a huge strike starting in Belfast the shipyards and the engineering works shut down and the gasworks the electric power station the trams stopped too

even the graveyard workers in February the Brits sending in the troops to restore power fully armed infantry wearing shrapnel helmets armed with machine guns a Sinn Fein Bolshevik plot they called it no says Jim no I never write articles a lie that was and him saying once that his political opinions were those of a socialistic artist and then drawing us down into those big books of his all flux and ontological uncertainty and his discourse going mad as a weaver and I thought no this isn't socialistic no it's not no nor the rising neither the red flag beneath the green and the winners in the end the Irish bourgeoisie and without a revolutionary party and a coherent, principled revolutionary ideology there's no socialism no future no there isn't no

TYMPOPTANOMANIA

1

A spectre is haunting Ventnor — the spectre of Marx. All the brochures, books, guides, booklets and leaflets have entered into an alliance to exorcize this spectre.

Take a look at *The Official Isle of Wight Guide*, *Holiday News*, *Island Visitor*, *Welcome to Ventnor* and *Ventnor Town Trails*. Nothing. No mention of Karl Marx at all. You would never believe that Marx once lived in Ventnor.

But it is not simply the bourgeoisie who seek to airbrush away Marx's connection with Ventnor. The Stalinists of the U.S.S.R. were no better. Take a look at *Karl Marx and Frederick Engels: Selected Correspondence*, published in Moscow in 1965 in the Progress Publishers Izal Miserabilist Series. It contains not a single one of the letters Marx wrote from Ventnor!

The academics of the British liberal establishment are no better. *Karl Marx: His Life and Environment* has gone through four editions over four decades. The dustjacket informs the reader that the distinguished author "is a Fellow of All Souls College, Oxford, and President of the British Academy". And what does this chump have to say about Marx and Ventnor? Absolutely nothing at all! Worse, this buffoon actually LIES, in order to delete the link with Ventnor. In 1882, the book informs the reader, Marx went to Paris, where he stayed for a time with his eldest daughter, Jenny Longuet. "Not long after his return to London, news came of her sudden death."

This is, quite simply, fiction.

Marx was not in London when he learned the terrible news of poor Jenny's death.

Where was he? Answer: on the Isle of Wight. Whereabouts on the Isle of Wight?

Just so.

2

It was Laird who alerted me to the curious importance of the Isle of Wight in understanding Karl Marx's life and writings. It was also typical of my old friend that, having ignited my interest in this matter, he himself grew suddenly bored with it. The last communication I had from him before his disappearance was an unsigned postcard showing an aerial view of Ventnor. On the back, in his familiar scrawl, was a single sentence.

The history of all existing society is the history of tympoptanomania.

3

Laird had a puckered face and a slight kink in his intelligence. Most people have a skeleton in the cupboard. Laird had a sheepskull, which he had found on the shores of Loch Morar.

"Marx," he once remarked to me (I have quite forgotten where), "once remarked somewhere that all the great events and characters of world history occur the first time as tragedy, the second time as farce. He forgot to add: especially in connection with the Isle of Wight!"

I do, however, remember the slight froth on Laird's lips and a portrait of the Emperor Napoleon III on the wall, next to which was a mirror in which I caught a glimpse of myself. My face seemed gathered into small interesting folds. There was also a frown of perplexity, of the sort commonly found on the faces of those who engaged Laird in conversation. That frown was, I am certain, much the same as the frown which deepened on my face as I thumbed through my precious dictionaries. *Tymp, tympanic, tympanitis, tympany, type.* But no *tympoptanomania.* This was another of Laird's tricks. As Laird knew well, I am not the sort of person to give up on a strange word.

4

On 10 October 1917, Vladimir Ilyich Lenin arrived at the meeting of the Central Committee of the Bolshevik Party wearing a wig and spectacles and minus his beard, and proposed that the time was now ripe for armed insurrection. Simultaneously, on the Isle of Wight, what a thick volume published by the Oxford University Press describes as "renovations in 1917" also involved the gravediggers of the bourgeoisie.

In Petrograd they stormed the Winter Palace.

In Newport, armed with sickles, spades and chisels, they filed in an orderly fashion into the old churchyard and began tidying it up. They also added the inscription "The Friend of Keats" to the gravestone of the former clerk to the County Court, John Hamilton Reynolds (d. 1852).

5

In 1969, Bob Dylan performed on stage live at the Isle of Wight. In 1970: Tiny Tim.

On 7 May 1882, in search of fine weather, Marx arrived at the Hotel de Russie, Monte Carlo, where he stayed until 3 June. "I encountered splendid weather," he wrote. On 30 October 1882, in search of finer weather, Marx went to a boarding house in Ventnor. The weather changed. December bought days of "raw cold, alternating with dirty mild dampness".

Laird, for his part, reported that Ventnor was "very windy".

6

On 12 January 1883 Karl Marx left Ventnor for the last time and returned to 41 Maitland Park Road, London NWS, to die (tragedy). On 12 April 1885 Eleanor Marx wrote that

Edward Aveling and his penis had "gone off for a few days to Ventnor" (farce).

7

Seeing what's going on is difficult (Laird wrote on his first postcard). All the windows are misted up. A patch of blue sky is rimmed by fog. The ghostly structure of nearby buildings is barely visible. The outline of the tall white pillar in the distance, dedicated to the drowned and the lost, is erased by crusts of salt. Dark indeterminate figures on the shore have the substance of wandering phantoms. The frail, inflating craft begins to emit a low whine. The whine changes tune. The noise of an accelerating engine rises to a powerful screech. Next, a huge shuddering, as of a massive, eminent Victorian male experiencing a thunderous orgasm. Then a violent rushing, a terrific gale, a sensation of powerful gusts. Abruptly, without warning, the world lurches sideways and begins to shift from the horizontal. The motion sucks at your stomach. You feel yourself trapped. Everything seems to be slipping out of control. Befuddled V. D. Nabokov must have felt like this! But now the hovercraft is leaving Southsea beach and heading out across the Solent. I think of what Marx wrote on a barge in Holland! Cheers, Laird.

8

That strange pattern in world history which is refracted every which way through the strange medium of the Isle of Wight is underscored by the astonishing events of 1848 (wrote Laird, later).

On 19 March 1848 news reached Paris that the Emperor had been forced to grant the demands of revolutionaries in Vienna. Next day came news of revolution in Berlin. The German Legion, formed by the German Democratic Assoc-

284

iation and other émigré groups in France, held exercises on the Champ de Mars and marched out of Paris on 1 April. That very same day, at about half past twelve in the afternoon, while the sky was clear and the air perfectly calm, a girl employed in trampling clothes in a tub on the common at the foot of St Boniface Down heard a loud and sharp report overhead, succeeded by a gust of wind of extraordinary vehemence, and of only a few moments' duration. The violence of the wind was such that the woman, who at the time was holding a blanket, found herself having to let go for fear of being carried away. Sheets, socks and three pairs of trousers were scattered across the common for a distance of some three hundred metres. A number of curtains and smaller items were carried upwards to an immense height, so as to be almost lost to the eye, gradually disappearing from sight in the direction of France. Some nearby sheep were later observed running about in a state of panic, afterwards cowering together in evident terror.

9

On his second postcard from the Isle, Laird wrote: A Ship of Fools can perhaps be allowed to drift before the wind for a good while; but it will still drift to its doom precisely because the fools refuse to believe it is possible. This doom is the approaching revolution. (Marx)

10

Figures in postmodernist fiction spurn the dictates of petty bourgeois naturalism! Laird decided to move back in time and take a different route to the Isle of Wight. Doing sixty in a customised red Ford Fiesta, he headed east on the A27. Soon after the Bedhampton plaque to Keats he slowed down for the A3 intersection and afterwards took the M275 to the ferry terminal, where an official wearing a cap like Lenin's ushered him into Lane Seventeen. As the ro-ro left Portsmouth Harbour a recorded message warned passengers that four short blasts of the ship's horn would signify an emergency.

The *Helene Demuth* passed out of the narrow harbour entrance, throbbing like the hero of a novel by David Herbert Lawrence. Ahead, the island appeared long and low, its green slopes fuzzed with mist. Another short announcement, this time from the captain. The name of the ship would change during the crossing; there was no cause for alarm.

As it turned sharply to starboard the *Finnegan's* wake formed a turbulent, spreading "V". Laird stared down at the water, seeing a squiggle of rainbow coloured oil like an "S" and a misplaced apostrophe which much resembled a dark, cruising gull. It made him think of gull-sharpers. Then his attention was drawn back to the "V", inside which a subsidiary wake was boiling exactly like the water in the jacuzzi at Leyton Leisure Lagoon. The grey mainland seemed to be still attached to the vessel by this intricate, thinning seam of bubbles, just as the souls of space-travelling dreamers are connected to their earthly bodies by a thin shimmering elasticated umbilical-style cord in the degenerate, bogus, occult fiction of Dennis Wheatley, for example *The Ka of Gifford Hillary*.

Laird noticed a vessel in trouble. Bobbing amid the milky froth below was the tiny *Nietzsche Studies*. Its engine appeared to have failed. Tiny figures ran animatedly to and fro, gesticulating. Laird, who had always been impressed by the sound common sense of the captain of the *California* turned away irritably.

Up ahead lay the island. It seemed to float in the air like the one in **TRAVELS INTO SEVERAL Remote NATIONS of the WORLD** In FOUR PARTS By *LEMUEL GULLIVER*, Firft a SURGEON, and then a CAPTAIN of feveral SHIPS.

Nearing Ryde, Laird was able to make out on the distant skyline the monument to Czar Alexander I.

11

The pattern in world history which was shaping itself in Laird's mind found astonishing confirmation in Ventnor's *South Wight Chronicle*, which replicated the famous Marx/Gladstone controversy.

Every schoolgirl knows that on 7 March 1872 the Berlin *Concordia* accused Marx of fabricating a quotation from Gladstone's Budget Speech of 16 April 1863 in his book *Das Kapital,* proof correction of which was completed at 2am on 16 August 1867 at 1 Maitland Park Road, London NW3.

Marx replied in the *Volkstaat* of 1 June 1872, citing the *Times'*s report of Gladstone's speech published on 17 April 1863.

Marx's anonymous critic replied in the *Concordia* of 4 July and 11 July 1872, continuing to accuse Marx of falsification.

Marx replied in the *Volkstaat* of 7 August 1872, citing in addition to the *Times* the reports of Gladstone's speech given in the *Morning Star* and *Morning Advertiser* of 17 April 1863.

Marx's critic did not reply.

The matter appeared to be at an end.

Then, some eleven years later, on 29 November 1893, eight months after Marx's death, there appeared in the *Times* a letter from Sedley Taylor (1834-1920), author of the long forgotten *Profit Sharing between Capital and Labour* (1884) and Fellow of Trinity College, Cambridge, repeating the claim that Marx had misquoted Gladstone. Taylor revealed that Marx's anonymous critic had been Professor Lujo Brentano (1844-1931), then of the University of Breslau.

Eleanor Marx wrote to the *Times,* which declined to print her letter.

She subsequently defended her father in the journal *To-day* (February 1884), denying that Marx had "lyingly inserted" a bogus sentence not uttered by Gladstone.

Sedley Taylor replied in *To-day* (March 1884), saying that that aspect of the controversy was "of very subordinate importance" compared to the question of whether or not Marx had deliberately perverted Gladstone's meaning.

In the same issue Eleanor Marx replied: "Marx has not suppressed anything worth quoting, neither has he 'lyingly' added anything. But he has restored, rescued from oblivion, a particular sentence of Mr Gladstone's speeches, a sentence which had indubitably been pronounced, but which somehow or other had found its way — out of *Hansard*."

Taylor made no reply.

Unlike the Ventnor Taylor.

Page seven of the *South Wight Chronicle* of 17 October 1996 reads as follows: ONE-MAN TRIBUTE SHOW TO PINK FLOYD. *The one-man show will be a first for Ventnor, nothing like this has been done here before.*

But that is not what we are looking at. Our eyes scan, as did Laird's, the letters column. And there it is. From tragedy to farce. The most uncanny replication of the Marx/Gladstone controversy it is possible to imagine!

In reply to the untrue letter published in the "Chronicle" last Thursday from Mr Richard Cutler (for which I await an apology), may I put the record straight, wrote a man named Taylor.

After the record-straightening the *Chronicle*'s editor added a note of explanation to the effect that when Cutler gave his letter to the newspaper on the previous Tuesday morning, pushing it, as requested, through the letter box of Raffles Restaurant, 29 High Street, Ventnor, between 9am and 7pm Monday-Saturday, he had not received a reply from Taylor, but that on Wednesday morning Cutler informed the *Chronicle* that he had now received a reply, but by this time the pages of the *Chronicle* were complete and had gone to print, therefore the letter could not be removed, since the *Chronicle* pages have to be completed by Tuesday evening, after which Taylor also contacted the *Chronicle*, on Wednesday, after Cutler had telephoned Taylor, who was told the same as Cutler, that it was too late to do anything about it, and that a reply would have to wait for the following week's issue.

The coincidence was impressive.

I saw *exactly* what Laird was getting at.

12

"Hi there!"

Laird turned and saw that it was the dead American singer Karen Carpenter. She gets everywhere, he thought, crossly. With a velvet smile and a bucketful of perfect white teeth, she began crooning "Ticket to Ryde". Her soulful eyes didn't fool him for a moment. He lit a cigarette and prodded her hip. With a low pop she vanished.

On the ferry, apart from dipping into Morgan Philips Price's masterly *Dispatches from the Revolution*, he had planned to begin reading *Il trashetto per Gabriola*, but the book lay unopened at his side. Now the draft of the story changes tense and Laird holds the handrail firmly in one hand. In the other he keeps a firm grip on his precious copy of *Capital*, Volume One. In rough seas it expands, keeping you afloat. In hard winters it can feed a family of six. Submerged, it contains enough oxygen and life-giving nutrients to keep you alive until rescue comes. On the greyest of English days it can take you far back into the past, or up, up, and away, through the murk, through the damp toxic drifts, into immense sparkling expanses. Now it is a powered capsule, plunging on across the wastes and darks, towards that luminous gorgeous unimaginable socialist future.

The *Victor Serge* surged towards Fishbourne Harbour. A recorded announcement instructed car passengers to descend to the vehicle decks. Laird felt a little queasy, which he attributed to a strange homesickness for his planet, Titan.

13

Left (that's good) out of the ferry terminal, through Ryde (where Marx stayed at 11 Nelson Street in July 1874, making a tour of the island by boat to Ventnor, Sandown, Cowes and Newport), past the pink wax museum at Brading, and on through the dreary urban wastes of Sandown and Shanklin.

Beyond Shanklin a few mild hairpin bends, then down a hill into Ventnor. The first thing you see is a thriving palm on a roundabout and a large stone three-decker house, one of those big solid structures at which the Victorians excelled. Then the one-way system sends you down to shore level and The Gaiety, a gaudy amusement arcade, prop. A. Brila.

Laird tracked down the house of the landlord, a rapacious bourgeois who demanded a £25 breakages deposit. Sullenly, Laird handed it over, collected the keys and went off to his flat overlooking the esplanade. The description of this dark, claustrophobic, depressing apartment with its windowless bathroom, stains on the ceiling and poky kitchen, will wither here.

14

Marx wrote several letters from Ventnor, giving his address as 1 St Boniface Gardens.

Laird scowled at his street map of *Ventnor and environs*.

No such road listed! Has the name been changed? Has the road been built on? The man in the tourist office thinks it may have been obliterated. He points at the map. The tennis courts on St Boniface Road look like a possible location. You could always try the museum.

A gorgeous sunlit afternoon. Laird walks briskly along Pier Street (which once led to, now gone). He arrives outside The Ventnor Heritage Museum at 16.29, in time to witness a wrinkled hand flick the OPEN card in the glass door to

CLOSED.

Laird raps on the pane. In the murk beyond dim figures move along the stands. They pointedly ignore him.

The streets as hot and deserted as those in *High Noon*. Long shadows crawl across empty side streets and up cool deserted alleys. Laird sets off along Grove Road, in the direction of the industrial estate and the old railway station. It's a very steep road.

In the end, he found the house. It's at the end of St Boniface Road. The first house you meet when you drive down into Ventnor. By the palm.

15

You want to know my favourite word in *Capital*? I'll tell you, said Laird. It was a word Marx wrote in English: *understrapper*. The capitalist and his *understrappers*. When I first encountered it I assumed it was a coinage. But it's not.

This is a word we must revive, comrades! The inferior agents of capital. Members of Parliament, each with an alimentary canal dilated beyond belief. Trade union leaders, all biological prodigies with thirty-three false vertebrae. Enough to make anyone lose all control of that important voluntary muscle supplied by the haemorrhoidal branch of the fourth sacral nerve.

16

Someone had attached a blue plaque to the east-facing wall of the house, recording Marx's occupation. Home-made, not official; a painted wooden disc, not dignified metal. Laird snapped it with his Praktika, then went back to the palm to record the front of the house. As he fiddled with his focus the large blue front door opened and a figure stepped out.

"I'm interested in Marx," explained Laird, slightly embarrassed to be caught out photographing a stranger's front door.

And then he realised who it was.

"But I thought you were..."

"A lot of people make that mistake. But don't stand out there catching your death. Come in, come in!"

17

Marx led Laird up to his sitting room on the first floor.

"Sorry about the mess. All these books, y'know. Coffee? Or something stronger?"

"Something alcoholic would be just the ticket."

"I know the feeling. It's Ventnor, isn't it? This place would drive anyone to drink. I'm only here for my health. The fine weather. Anything to get away from all those traffic fumes in London."

Marx went into the kitchen and returned with a bottle of Jack Daniel's. "I'm afraid I finished the Talisker yesterday." He poured a couple of generous tumblers.

"Now I suppose, young man, you've come to talk to me about my book. The fact is, I put it aside in order to concentrate on some short stories."

"Short stories!"

"Don't sound so surprised. Once, when I was very much younger than I am today, I contemplated a career as a writer of fictions. But then, somehow, I became involved in demolishing other people's!"

No, I can't believe Marx talked like that. All I have to go on is what Laird told me. I'm afraid I pestered him with trivia. What did Marx look like? What was he wearing? What CDs did he have? What soaps did he watch?

Laird said Marx had an immense forehead and mottled, hairy hands. His face at first just ghostly turned a Wighter shade of pale. But after a drink his complexion seemed unusually dark. What else? Twinkly eyes, surrounded by lines of laughter. Bushy eyebrows, glittering black eyes. Oh,

292

and his favourite group was Echo and the Bunnymen.

That surprised me.

Marx didn't watch any soaps. That didn't surprise me. But he watched a lot of videos, and was full of praise for *Falling Down* and *Indecent Proposal* (apart from the endings, which were crap).

In the dark, cluttered room Laird made out the silhouette of an exercise bicycle, a *Collected Poems of Malcolm Lowry* (Marx had underlined Lowry's famous Isle of Wight poem, "Crossing the Bar"), somebody's *On Literature and Art*, a book of stories including "Da-Da Vogt", two science-fiction novels — *Excession* and *The Cassini Division* — a world atlas, a guide to the planets, a work of literary criticism entitled *Crackpot Texts,* a biography of Virginia Woolf, a copy of *Crash* and a volume of essays on Jean-Luc Godard.

Marx had a number of cuttings pinned to the wall. The *Independent on Sunday* ran a large photograph of Marx in his younger days, alongside the headline **Was He Right All Along?** *The Financial Times* gave a rave review to *The Communist Manifesto*, remarking "Marx and Engels described a world economy more like that of 1998 than 1848." A *Financial Times* editorial called Marx "a shrewd, subtle analyst of capitalist society".

"Everything has changed — and nothing! Victoria's Britain gave us bread adulterated with alum, soap, pearl-ashes, chalk and Derbyshire stone-dust. Elizabeth II's gives us farmed salmon drenched in organophosphate, invermectin, azamethipos and cypermethrin. Capitalist fish farming discharges toxic waste into Scottish lochs! Incidences of paralytic shellfish-poisoning are on the increase! And the body which is supposed to regulate the industry, but which nakedly serves the interests of capital, is laughably called the Scottish Environment Protection Agency, set up, appropriately, on All Fools' Day, 1996. So don't let anyone fucking tell me that Marxism is out of date!"

Marx calmed down and looked at his watch. "Is that the time? I'm afraid I must fly. But it's been interesting meeting you. Let me give you a little souvenir of our time together."

Marx thrust a CD at Laird and saw him to the door. "Track six!" he shouted.

Walking back downhill into Ventnor, Laird examined the album *Evergreen*.

Laird wasn't sure about this. He was more of a Metallica fan.

18

The curious, cryptic message written on my friend's final card seems to indicate a certain disillusionment, a cynicism and fatigue which sometimes afflicts disappointed theorists.

Shortly before I received that postcard Laird mailed me *Evergreen*, along with an unfinished manuscript setting out his theory that the Isle of Wight is an heterotopia which exists at a momentous angle to history. He proved this by multiplying the attraction of water to matter, increased and decreased according to the square of the distance, and subtracting this from Heidegger's contention that an elephant in the Indian jungle "is" just as much as some chemical process at work on Mars.

Furthermore (asserted Laird), when D. H. Lawrence wrote in *The Trespasser*, a novel set on the Isle of Wight, *I should have nothing but mortification*, what he actually meant to write was *metafiction*.

"Call me a Ventnortriloquist, if you must," he concluded.

19

It was only two years later, having read everything Marx wrote, that I was forced to recognise that, although Laird was deranged (I cannot really believe he has gone back to Titan), there may be nevertheless be a grain of truth in his ravings.

294

Consider this.

On 5 May 1818, Karl Marx was born.

On 5 May 1826, just as Maria Eugenia Ignancia Augustina was born, the town of Granada was shaken by an earthquake.

In 1969, Bob Dylan performed on the Isle of Wight and sang "Blowing in the Wind".

On 25 March 1853, Karl Marx wrote of Maria Eugenia Ignancia Augustina, who by now was the wife of Napoleon III, that she was given to "uncontrolled *farts*. One calls it tympoptanomania. Her *'detonations fortes'* made even the beribboned Decembraillards blush. *Ce n'est qu'un petit bruit, un murmure, un rien; mais enfin, vous savez que les Français ont le nez au plus petit vent.*"

20

In one of his last telephone calls, Laird told me that Marx had quoted something from Edmund Wilson's famous book about a railway journey through Europe. Wilson complained that *Marx's writings tend to lack formal development; we find it hard to get hold of a beginning or an end.* Laird said that Marx downed his third tumbler, became flushed, and shouted: "This is a cause for celebration, comrade! Let the ruling classes tremble at an ontological perspectivism! Readers have nothing to lose but their cognitive complacency! World-builders of all cut-ups, mutate!"

21

I sit in the deserted bar of the *Eighteenth Brumaire*, drinking Glenfiddich from my hip flask and listening to track six of *Evergreen* on my Sony Walkman.

Marx was right. It's a wonderful song.

It was only after he disappeared that it occurred to me that

Laird, maddeningly, had said nothing at all about the short stories which Marx said he was writing. I knew then that I had no alternative but to go to Ventnor and ask Marx himself.

I estimate that I shall be there in less than two hours.

22

Marx wasn't there.

The neighbours said he'd gone away for good and wasn't ever coming back. They pointed to a note which Marx had left pinned to the front door.

The note said:

The writers of fiction have only *interred* Marx, in various naturalistic and pseudo-psychological ways; the point is to *collage* him.